Lockwood & Co.

BOOK THREE

The Hollow Boy

Lockwood & Co.

BOOK THREE

The Hollow Boy

JONATHAN STROUD

 • HYPERION

LOS ANGELES   NEW YORK

First Edition, September 2015

Printed in the United States of America

1 3 5 7 9 10 8 6 4 2

FAC-020093-15166

Library of Congress Cataloging in Publication Control Number: 2015015076

ISBN 978-1-4847-0968-9

Reinforced binding

Visit www.DisneyBooks.com

For Rosie and Francesca, with love

Contents

I

Lavender Lodge

Chapter 1

I think it was only at the very end of the Lavender Lodge job, when we were fighting for our lives in that unholy guesthouse, that I glimpsed Lockwood & Co. working together perfectly for the first time. It was just the briefest flash, but every detail remains etched into my memory: those moments of sweet precision when we truly acted as a team.

Yes, every detail. Anthony Lockwood, coat aflame, arms flapping madly as he staggered backward toward the open window. George Cubbins, dangling from the ladder one-handed, like an oversized, windblown pear. And me—Lucy Carlyle—bruised, bloody, and covered in cobwebs, sprinting, jumping, rolling desperately to avoid the ghostly coils. . . .

Sure, I know none of that *sounds* so great. And to be fair, we could have done without George's squeaking. But this was the thing about Lockwood & Co.: we made the most of unpromising situations and turned them to our advantage.

Want to know how? I'll show you.

Six hours earlier. There we were, on the doorstep, ringing the bell. It was a dreary, storm-soaked November afternoon, with the shadows deepening and the rooftops of old Whitechapel showing sharp and black against the clouds. Rain spotted our coats and glistened on the blades of our rapiers. The clocks had just struck four.

"Everyone ready?" Lockwood asked. "Remember, we ask them some questions, we keep careful psychic watch. If we get any clues to the murder room or the location of the bodies, we don't let on. We just say good-bye politely, and head off to fetch the police."

"That's fine," I said. George, busily adjusting his work belt, nodded.

"*It's a useless plan!*" The hoarse whisper came from somewhere close behind my ear. "*I say stab them first, ask questions later! That's your only sensible option.*"

I nudged my backpack with an elbow. "Shut up."

"*I thought you wanted my advice!*"

"Your job is to keep a lookout, not distract us with stupid theories. Now, hush."

We waited on the step. The Lavender Lodge boardinghouse was a narrow, terraced building of three floors. Like most of this part of London's East End, it had a weary, ground-down air. Soot crusted the stucco exterior, thin curtains dangled at the windows. No lights showed in the upper stories, but the hall light was on, and there was

was a yellowed VACANCIES sign propped behind the panel of cracked glass in the center of the door.

Lockwood squinted through the glass, shielding his eyes with his gloved hand. "Well, *somebody's* at home," he said. "I can see two people standing at the far end of the hall."

He pressed the buzzer again. It was an ugly sound, a razor to the ear. He rapped the knocker, too. No one came.

"Hope they put their skates on," George said. "I don't want to worry you or anything, but there's something white creeping toward us up the street."

He was right. Far off in the dusk, a pale form could just be seen. It drifted slowly above the sidewalk in the shadows of the houses, coming in our direction.

Lockwood shrugged; he didn't even bother looking. "Oh, it's probably just a shirt flapping on someone's line. It's still early. Won't be anything nasty yet."

George and I glanced at each other. It was that time of year when the days were scarcely lighter than the nights, and the dead began walking during the darkest afternoons. On the way over from the Tube, in fact, we'd seen a Shade on Whitechapel High Road, a faint twist of darkness standing brokenly in the gutter, being spun and buffeted by the tailwinds of the last cars hurrying home. So nasty things were out already—as Lockwood well knew.

"Since when has a flapping shirt had a head and spindly legs attached?" George asked. He removed his glasses, rubbed them dry, and returned them to his nose. "Lucy, *you* tell him. He never listens to me."

"Yes, come on, Lockwood," I said. "We can't just stand here all night. If we're not careful, we'll get picked off by that ghost."

Lockwood smiled. "We won't. Our friends in the hall *have* to answer us. Not to do so would be an admission of guilt. Any second now they'll come to the door, and we'll be invited inside. Trust me. There's no need to worry."

And the point about Lockwood was that you believed him, even when he said far-fetched stuff like that. Right then he was waiting quite casually on the step, one hand resting on his sword hilt, as crisply dressed as ever in his long coat and slim dark suit. His dark hair flopped forward over his brow. The light from the hallway shone on his lean, pale face, and sparkled in his dark eyes as he grinned across at me. He was a picture of poise and unconcern. It's how I want to remember him, the way he was that night: with horrors up ahead and horrors at our back, and Lockwood standing in between them, calm and unafraid.

George and I weren't *quite* so stylish in comparison, but we looked all business nonetheless. Dark clothes, dark boots; George had even tucked his shirt in. All three of us carried backpacks and heavy leather duffel bags—old, worn, and spotted with ectoplasm burns.

An onlooker, recognizing us as psychic investigation agents, would have assumed that the bags were filled with the equipment of our trade: salt-bombs, lavender, iron filings, silver Seals and chains. This was in fact quite true, but I also carried a skull in a jar, so we weren't entirely predictable.

We waited. The wind blew in dirty gusts between the houses. Iron spirit-wards swung on ropes high above us, clicking and clattering like witches' teeth. The white shape flitted stealthily toward us down the street. I zipped up my parka, and edged closer to the wall.

"*Yep, it's a Phantasm approaching,*" the voice from my backpack said, in whispers only I could hear. "*It's seen you, and it's hungry. Personally, I reckon it's got its eye on George.*"

"Lockwood," I began. "We *really* have to move."

But Lockwood was already stepping back from the door. "No need," he said. "What did I tell you? Here they are."

Shadows rose behind the glass. Chains rattled, the door swung wide.

A man and a woman stood there.

They were probably murderers, but we didn't want to startle them. We put on our best smiles.

The Lavender Lodge guesthouse had come to our attention two weeks earlier. The local police in Whitechapel had been investigating the cases of several people—some salesmen, but mostly laborers working on the nearby London docks—who'd gone missing in the area. It had been noticed a number of these men had been staying at an obscure boardinghouse—Lavender Lodge, on Cannon Lane, Whitechapel—shortly before they disappeared. The police had visited; they'd spoken to the proprietors, a Mr. and Mrs. Evans, and even searched the premises. They'd found nothing.

But they were adults. They couldn't see into the past. They couldn't detect the psychic residue of crimes that might have been committed there. For that, they needed an agency to help out. It so happened that Lockwood & Co. had been doing a lot of work in the East End, our success with the so-called Shrieking Ghost of Spitalfields having made us popular in the district. We agreed to pay Mr. and Mrs. Evans a little call.

And here we were.

Given the suspicions about them, I'd half expected the owners of Lavender Lodge to look pretty sinister, but that wasn't the case at all. If they resembled anything, it was a pair of elderly owls roosting on a branch. They were short, roundish, and gray-haired, with soft, blank, sleepy faces blinking at us behind large spectacles. Their clothes were heavy and somehow old-fashioned. They pressed close to each other, filling the doorway. Beyond them I could see a grimy, tasseled ceiling light, and dingy wallpaper. The rest was hidden.

"Mr. and Mrs. Evans?" Lockwood gave a slight bow. "Hello. Anthony Lockwood, of Lockwood and Co. I rang you earlier. These are my associates, Lucy Carlyle and George Cubbins."

They gazed at us. For a moment, as if we were conscious that the fate of five people had reached a tipping point, no one spoke.

"What's it regarding, please?" I don't know how old the man was—when I see someone older than thirty, time sort of concertinas for me—but he was definitely closer to coffin than crib. He had wisps of hair oiled back across his scalp, and nets of wrinkles stapled around his eyes. He blinked at us, all absentminded and benign.

"As I said on the phone, we wanted to talk with you about one of your past residents, a Mr. Benton," Lockwood said. "Part of an official Missing Persons inquiry. Perhaps we could come in?"

"It'll be dark soon," the woman said.

"Oh, it won't take long." Lockwood used his best smile. I

contributed a reassuring grin. George was too busy staring at the white shape drifting up the street to do anything other than look nervous.

Mr. Evans nodded; he stepped slowly back and to the side. "Yes, of course, but best to do it quickly," he said. "It's late. Not long before *they'll* be coming out."

He was far too old to see the Phantasm, now crossing the road toward us. We didn't like to mention it either. We just smiled and nodded, and (as swiftly as we decently could without pushing) followed Mrs. Evans into the house. Mr. Evans let us go past, then shut the door softly, blocking out the night, the ghost, and the rain.

They took us down a long hallway into the public lounge, where a fire flickered in a tiled grate. The decor was the usual: cream woodchip wallpaper, worn brown carpet, ranks of decorated plates, and prints in ugly golden frames. A few armchairs were scattered about, angular and comfortless, and there was a radio, a liquor cabinet, and a small TV. A big wooden hutch on the back wall carried cups, glasses, sauce bottles, and other breakfast things; and two sets of folding chairs and plastic-topped tables confirmed that this single room was where guests ate as well as socialized.

Right now we were the only ones there.

We put our bags down. George wiped the rain off his glasses again; Lockwood ran a hand through damp hair. Mr. and Mrs. Evans stood facing us in the center of the room. Close up, their owl-like qualities had intensified. They were stoop-necked, round-shouldered, he in a shapeless cardigan, she in a dark woolen dress.

They remained standing close together: elderly, but not, I thought, under all their heavy clothes, particularly frail.

They did not offer us seats; clearly they hoped for a short conversation.

"Benson, you said his name was?" Mr. Evans asked.

"Benton."

"He stayed here recently," I said. "Three weeks ago. You confirmed that on the phone. He's one of several missing people who—"

"Yes, yes. We've talked to the police about him. But I can show you the guest book, if you like." Humming gently, the old man went to the hutch. His wife remained motionless, watching us. He returned with the book, opened it, and handed it to Lockwood. "You can see his name there."

"Thank you." While Lockwood made a show of studying the pages, I did the real work. I listened to the house. It was quiet, psychically speaking. I detected nothing. Okay, there was a muffled voice coming from my backpack on the floor, but that didn't count.

"Now's your chance!" it whispered. *"Kill them both, and it's job done!"*

I gave the pack a subtle kick with the heel of my boot, and the voice fell silent.

"Can you remember much about Mr. Benton?" In the firelight, George's doughy face and sandy hair gleamed palely; the swell of his stomach pressed tight against his sweater. He hitched up his belt, subtly checking the gauge on his thermometer. "Or any of your missing residents, for that matter? Chat with them much at all?"

"Not really," the old man said. "What about you, Nora?"

Mrs. Evans had nicotine-yellow hair—thin up top, and fixed in position like a helmet. Like her husband's, her skin was wrinkled, though *her* lines radiated from the corners of her mouth, as if you might draw her lips tight like the top of a string bag. "No," she said. "But it's not surprising. Few of our guests stay long."

"We cater to the trade," Mr. Evans added. "Salesmen, you know. Always moving on."

There was a silence. The room was heavy with the scent of lavender, which keeps unwanted Visitors away. Fresh bunches sat in silver tankards on the mantelpiece and windows. There were other defenses, too: ornamental house-guards, made of twisted iron and shaped like flowers, animals, and birds.

It was a safe room, almost ostentatiously so.

"Anyone staying here now?" I asked.

"Not at present."

"How many guest rooms do you have?"

"Six. Four on the second floor, two at the top."

"And which of them do *you* sleep in?"

"What a lot of questions," Mr. Evans said, "from such a very young lady. I am of the generation that remembers when children *were* children. Not psychic investigation agents with swords and an over-inquisitive manner. We sleep on the ground floor, in a room behind the kitchen. Now—I think we have told the police all this. I am not entirely sure why you are here."

"We'll be going soon," Lockwood said. "If we could just have a look at the room Mr. Benton stayed in, we'll be on our way."

How still they were suddenly, like gravestones rising in the center of the lounge. Over by the hutch, George ran his finger down the side of the ketchup bottle. It had a thin layer of dust upon it.

"I'm afraid that's impossible," Mr. Evans said. "The room is made up for new guests. We don't want it disturbed. All trace of Mr. Benton—and the other residents—will be long gone. Now . . . I must ask you to leave."

He moved toward Lockwood. Despite the carpet slippers, the cardigan on the rounded shoulders, there was decisiveness in the action, an impression of suddenly flexing strength.

Lockwood had many pockets in his coat. Some contained weapons and lock-picking wires; one, to my certain knowledge, had an emergency store of tea bags. From another he took a small plastic card. "This is a warrant," he said. "It empowers Lockwood and Co., as DEPRAC-appointed investigation agents, to search any premises that may be implicated in a serious crime or haunting. If you wish to check, call Scotland Yard. Inspector Montagu Barnes would be happy to talk to you."

"Crime?" The old man shrank back, biting his lip. "Haunting?"

Lockwood's smile was wolf-like. "As I said, we just wish to take a look upstairs."

"There's nothing supernatural here," Mrs. Evans said, scowling. "Look around. See the defenses."

Her husband patted her arm. "It's all right, Nora. They're agents. It's our duty to help them. Mr. Benton, if I recall, stayed in Room Two, on the top floor. Straight up the stairs, two flights and you're there. You won't miss it."

"Thanks." Lockwood picked up his duffel bag.

"Why not leave your things?" Mr. Evans suggested. "The stairs are narrow, and it's a long way up."

We just looked at him. George and I shrugged our bags onto our backs.

"Well, take your time up there," Mr. Evans said.

There was no light on upstairs. From the semidarkness of the stairwell, filing after the others, I looked back through the door at the little couple. Mr. and Mrs. Evans stood in the middle of the lounge, pressed side by side, ruby-red and flickering in the firelight. They were watching us as we climbed, their heads tilted at identical angles, their spectacles four circles of reflected flame.

"What do you think?" George whispered from above.

Lockwood had paused and was inspecting a heavy fire door halfway up the flight. It was bolted open, flush against the wall. "I don't know *how*, but they're guilty. Guilty as sin."

George nodded. "Did you see the ketchup? No one's had breakfast here in a *long* time."

"They must know it's all over for them," I said as we went on. "If something bad happened to their guests up here, we're going to sense it. They know what Talents we have. What do they expect us to do when we find out?"

Lockwood's reply was interrupted by a stealthy tread on the stair behind. Looking back, we caught a glimpse of Mr. Evans's gleaming face, his hair disarranged, eyes wild and staring. He reached for the fire door, began swinging it shut . . .

In a flash Lockwood's rapier was in his hand. He sprang back down, coat flying—

The fire door slammed, slicing off the light from downstairs. The rapier cracked against wood.

As we stood in the dark, we heard bolts being forced into place. Then we heard our captor laughing through the door.

"Mr. Evans," Lockwood said, "open this now."

The old man's voice was muffled, but distinct. "You should've left when you had the chance! Look around all you like. Make yourselves at home! The ghost will have found you by midnight. I'll sweep up what's left in the morning."

After that it was just the *clump, clump, clump* of carpet slippers fading downstairs.

"*Brilliant,*" said the voice from my backpack. "*Outwitted by a senior citizen. Outstanding. What a team.*"

I didn't tell it to shut up this time. It kind of had a point.

Chapter 2

Hold it. I suppose I should stop before things start getting messy, and tell you exactly who I am. My name is Lucy Carlyle. I make my living destroying the risen spirits of the restless dead. I can throw a salt-bomb fifty yards from a standing start, and hold off three Specters with a broken rapier (as I did one time in Berkeley Square). I'm good with crowbars, magnesium flares, and candles. I walk alone into haunted rooms. I see ghosts, when I choose to look for them, and hear their voices, too. I'm just under five feet six inches tall, have hair the color of a walnut coffin, and wear size seven ectoplasm-proof boots.

There. Now we're properly introduced.

So I stood with Lockwood and George on the second-floor landing of the boardinghouse. All of a sudden it was very cold. All of a sudden I could *hear* things.

"Don't suppose there's any point trying to break down the door," George said.

"No point at all. . . ." Lockwood's voice had that far-off, absent quality it gets when he's using his Sight. Sight, Listening, and Touch: they're the main kinds of psychic Talent. Lockwood has the sharpest eyes of us, and I'm the best at Listening and Touch. George is an all-arounder. He's mediocre at all three.

I had my finger on the light switch on the wall beside me, but I didn't flick it on. Darkness stokes the psychic senses. Fear keeps your Talent keen.

We listened. We looked.

"I don't see anything yet," Lockwood said finally. "Lucy?"

"I'm getting voices. Whispered voices." It sounded like a crowd of people, all speaking over one another with the utmost urgency, yet so faint it was impossible to understand a thing.

"What does your friend in the jar say?"

"It's not my friend." I prodded the backpack. "Skull?"

"There's ghosts up here. Lots of them. So . . . now do you accept that you should've stabbed the old codger when you had the chance? If you'd listened to me, you wouldn't be in this mess, would you?"

"We're *not* in a mess!" I snapped. "And, by the way, we can't just stab a suspect! I keep telling you this! We didn't even know they were guilty then!"

Lockwood cleared his throat meaningfully. Sometimes I forgot that the others couldn't hear the ghost's half of the conversation.

"Sorry," I said. "He's just being annoying, as usual. Says there's lots of ghosts."

The luminous display on George's thermometer flashed briefly in the dark. "Temp update," he said. "It's dropped eight degrees since the foot of the stairs."

"Yes. That fire door acts as a barrier." The pencil beam of Lockwood's flashlight speared downward and picked out the ridged gray surface of the door. "Look, it's got iron bands on it. That keeps our nice little old couple safe in their living quarters on the ground floor. But anyone who rents a room up here falls victim to something lurking in the dark. . . ."

He turned the flashlight beam wide and circled it slowly around us. We were standing just below a shabby landing—neat enough, but cheaply furnished with purple curtains and an old cream carpet. Several numbered plywood doors gleamed dully in the shadows. A few dog-eared magazines lay in a pile on an ugly bureau, near where a further flight of stairs led to the top floor. It was supernaturally cold, and there was ghost-fog stirring. Faint wreaths of pale green mist were rising from the carpet and winding slowly around our ankles. The flashlight began to flicker, as if its (fresh) battery were failing and would soon wink out altogether. A feeling of unquantifiable dread deepened in us. I shivered. Something wicked was very close.

Lockwood adjusted his gloves. His face glowed in the flashlight beam, his dark eyes shone. As always, peril suited him. "All right," he said softly. "Listen to me. We keep calm, we take care of whatever's up here, then we find a way to tackle Evans. George, rig up an iron circle here. Lucy, see what else the skull has to say. I'll check out the nearest room."

With that he lifted his rapier, pushed open a door, and disappeared inside, long coat swirling behind him.

We got to work. George took out a lantern and set it on low; by its light, he busied himself with the iron chains, creating a decent circle in the center of the carpet. I opened my backpack and—with some difficulty—took out a large, faintly luminous glass jar. Its top was secured by a complex plastic seal and, inside it, floating in green liquid, was a leering face. And I don't mean *nicely* leering. This was more the kind you get behind bars in a high-security prison. It was the face of a ghost—a Phantasm or Specter—tied to the skull that rested in the jar. It was godless and disreputable and had no known name.

I glared at it. "Are you going to be sensible now?"

The toothless lips grinned awfully. *"I'm always sensible! What do you want to know?"*

"What are we dealing with up here?"

"A cluster of spirits. They're restless and unhappy and . . . Hold on, I'm getting something else—" The face contorted suddenly. *"Ooh, that's bad. That's real bad. If I were you, Lucy, I'd find a window and jump out. So what if you break both legs in several places? It's better than staying in here."*

"Why? What have you found?"

"Another entity. Can't tell what it is yet. But it's strong and hun-gry, and . . ." The bulging eyes looked sidelong at me. *"No, sorry, there's a limit to what I can sense, imprisoned in this cruel jar. Now, if you let me out, on the other hand . . ."*

I snorted. "That's not going to happen, as well you know."

"But I'm an invaluable member of the team!"

"Says who? You spend most of the time cheering when we nearly die."

The rubbery lips screwed tight in outrage. *"I hardly ever do that now! Things have changed between us. You know that's true!"*

Well, it was sort of right. Things *had* changed between us and the skull. When it had first begun talking to me, some months before, we'd viewed it with suspicion, irritation, and distaste. However, as the weeks passed and we'd gotten to know it properly, we'd learned to really despise it, too.

George had long ago stolen the ghost-jar from a rival agency, but it was only when I'd accidently twisted a lever in the lid that I realized that the spirit trapped there could actually speak to me. At first it was simply hostile; gradually, however, perhaps out of boredom or a desire for companionship, it had begun offering help in supernatural matters. Sometimes this was useful, but the ghost was untrustworthy. It had no morals worth speaking of, and more vices than you would think possible for a disembodied head floating in a jar. Its evil nature affected me more than the others, for I was the one who actually talked to it, who had to put up with the gleeful voice echoing in my mind.

I tapped the glass, making the face squint in surprise. "Concentrate on this powerful spirit. I want you to locate its Source—find where it's hidden." With that, I stood up. George had finished the circle around me. A moment later Lockwood emerged onto the landing and joined us both inside the chains.

He was as calm and composed as ever. "Well, that was horrible."

"What was?"

"The decor in that bedroom. Lilac, green, and what I can only describe as a kind of bilious off-yellow. None of the colors went at all."

"So there's no ghost there?"

"Ah, there *is*, as it happens. I've fixed it in position with salt and iron, so it's safe enough for now. Go and look, if you like. I'll replenish supplies here."

George and I took our flashlights but didn't switch them on. We didn't need to. We were in a paltry little bedroom. It had a single bed, a narrow dresser, and a tiny window, black and studded with rain. All this was illuminated by a horizontal orb of other-light that hung above the bed, merging into the pillows and bedsheets. In its center reclined the ghost of a man in striped pajamas. He lay on his back, as if asleep, his limbs hovering slightly above the sheets. He had a small mustache and rumpled hair. His eyes were closed; his toothless mouth sagged against a stubble-dusted chin.

Cold air streamed from the apparition. Twin circles of salt and iron-filings, emptied by Lockwood from the canisters on his belt, encircled the bed. Whenever the pulsing aura drew too close, the particles of salt ignited, spitting out green fire.

"Whatever they charge for a room in this place," George said, "it's way too much."

We withdrew to the landing.

Lockwood had refilled his canisters and was reattaching them to his belt. "See him, did you?"

"Yes," I said. "Think that's one of the missing men?"

"Definitely. The question is, what killed him?"

"The skull says there's a powerful spirit here. Says it's a bad one."

"That'll be on the prowl at midnight. Well, we can't wait till then. Let's see if we can hunt it down."

We checked the next bedroom, and the bathroom next to that.

Both were clear. But when I opened the fourth door, I found *two* ghosts within. One man lay on the single bed, much as the Visitor had in the other room, only curled on his side, with one arm bent beneath his head. He was older, thickset, with sandy hair cut very short, and dark blue pajamas. His eyes were open, staring into nothing. Close by—so close that their auras of other-light nearly touched—stood another man. He wore pajama bottoms and a white T-shirt. He looked as if he had just gotten out of bed, clothes rumpled, straggle-bearded, long black hair all tangled. I could see the carpet showing through his feet. He gazed up at the ceiling as if in mortal fear.

"There are two death-glows," Lockwood said. "One's much brighter than the other. Different dates, different incidents. Something killed both these men while they were sleeping."

"I'm just glad neither of them slept naked," George said. "Particularly that hairy one. Let's pen them in. They look passive, but you never know. Got your iron, Lucy?"

I didn't answer him. Spectral cold was beating upon me, and with it came echoes of emotion: of loneliness and fright and sorrow, as experienced by the lost men in these rooms. I opened myself up to it. Out of the past I heard the sound of breathing—the steady breathing of a person heavily asleep. Then came a slithering—a soft, wet flapping noise, like a landed eel.

Out of the corner of my eye, I saw something on the ceiling.

It beckoned to me, pale and boneless.

I jerked my head around, but there was nothing there.

"You all right, Lucy?" Lockwood and George were at my side. Over by the bed, the ghost of the bearded man stared upward. He was looking at the same spot on the ceiling where my eyes had rested a moment before.

"I saw something. Up there. Like a hand reaching down. Only it wasn't a hand."

"Well, what do you think it was?"

I gave a shiver of disgust. "I don't know."

We penned in the two ghosts and checked the final bedroom on the floor. It had no dead occupants, which made a nice change. Then we considered the final flight of stairs. Greasy filaments of ghost-fog were pouring down it, cascading like water in a weir, and the beams of our flashlights seemed to warp and twist as they probed the darkness.

"Yup, that's where the action is," Lockwood said. "Come on."

We gathered what remained of our stuff. From the depths of the ghost-jar, the grotesque face watched us keenly. *"You're not going to leave me behind, are you? I'm hoping for a ringside seat when you perish horribly."*

"Yeah, yeah," I said. "Have you located the Source of all this?"

"Somewhere above. But you knew that already, didn't you?"

I slung the jar unceremoniously into my backpack and hurried after the others. They were halfway up the stairs.

"Didn't much like the way Evans said he'd come back to sweep us up in the morning," George whispered as we neared the final landing. "It sort of implied there wouldn't be much of us remaining. But I suppose he's exaggerating."

Lockwood shook his head. "Not necessarily. Some spirits suck so much energy out of their victims, the bodies go all dry and papery, like empty shells. That might explain why the police couldn't find

flowed toward us, white arms reaching. Ectoplasm fizzed against the barrier of chains.

Up the ladder we went, first Lockwood, then George, then me. Lockwood reached the hatch. He shoved it hard. A band of blackness opened, expanding slowly like the edges of a paper fan. A smattering of dust fell down.

Was it me, or had the assembled ghosts below us suddenly grown quiet? Their whispering stilled. They watched us with blank eyes.

Lockwood pushed again. With a single crash, the hatch fell back on its hinge. Now there was a hole, a black slot gaping like a mouth. Chill air poured down from it.

This was where it stemmed from, the horror of the house. This was where we'd find the cause. We didn't hesitate. We scrambled up and, one after the other, were swallowed by the dark.

Chapter 3

It was *cold*, that was the first thing.

It was also pitch-black. A hazy column of other-light drifted up through the attic hatch from the ghosts below and lit our three pale faces; otherwise we could see nothing.

And there was something with us, close and all around. We felt the pressure of its presence, hovering over us in the dark. The force of it made it hard to breathe, hard to move; it was like we were suddenly crouching in deep water, with the awful weight of it crushing down. . . .

Lockwood was the first to fight back. I heard rustling as he reached into his bag and drew out his lantern. He flicked the switch and turned the dial; a soft warm radiance swelled from it and showed us where we were.

An attic: a cavernous space, broad at its base, and rising into darkness beneath the eaves of a steeply pitched roof. There were old brick gables at either end, one with chimneys built in, and one pierced by a single tall but narrow window. Great crossbeams spanned the shadows high above us, supporting the weight of the roof.

A few broken tea chests lay in one corner. Otherwise the room was empty. There was nothing there.

Or *almost* nothing. Cobwebs hung like hammocks between the rafters, thick and gray and heavy, like ceiling drapes in an Arabian bazaar. Where the rooflines hit the floor, they were piled in drifts, plugging the corners, softening the edges of the abandoned room. Threads of webbing dangled from the crossbeams, twitching in the little air currents our activities had stirred.

Some of the webs glittered with frost. Our breath made bitter clouds.

We got stiffly to our feet. There's a well-known fact about spiders, a curious thing. They're attracted to places of psychic disturbance; to longstanding Sources, where invisible, unknowable powers have loitered and grown strong. An unnatural congregation of spiders is a sure sign of a potent and ancient haunting, and their cobwebs are a dead giveaway. To be fair, I hadn't seen any in the guest rooms of Lavender Lodge, but then, Mrs. Evans was probably pretty handy with her duster.

It was a different matter in the attic, though.

We gathered what remained of our equipment. In our haste to climb the ladder George had left his bags below, and between us we'd used up our chains and most of the salt and iron. Luckily, Lockwood still had his bag containing our vital silver Seals, and we each had our magnesium flares tucked safely in our belts. Oh, and we still had the ghost-jar too, for what it was worth. I dumped it beside the open attic hatch. The face had grown faint, the plasm dark and cold.

"*You oughtn't to be up here. . . .*" it whispered. "*Even I'm nervous, and I'm already dead.*"

I used my rapier to cut away a few dangling cobwebs near my face. "Like we've got a choice. You see anything, let me know."

Lockwood went over to the window, which was almost as tall as he was. He rubbed a circle in the filthy glass, brushing off a thin crusting of ice. "We're overlooking the street," he said. "I can see ghost-lamps far below. Okay. The Source *must* be here somewhere. We can all feel it. Go cautiously, and let's get this done."

The search began. We moved like climbers laboring at altitude: it was slow, painful, painstaking. All around us the dreadful psychic weight bore down.

There were recent handprints by the hatch, perhaps where the police had made their cursory inspection. Otherwise, no one had been in the attic for years. In places, the floor had been roughly boarded, and Lockwood pointed out the thick layers of dust lying over everything. We noticed certain swirls and curling patterns traced faintly into that dust, as if it had been stirred by curious motions of the air, but no footprints at all.

George poked in the corners with his rapier, winding cobwebs around his blade.

I stood in the middle, listening.

Beyond the freezing rafters, beyond the cobwebs, the wind howled around the roof. Rain lashed against tiles; I could hear it running down the pitch and drumming onto the window. The fabric of the building trembled.

Inside, however, it was quiet. I could no longer hear the whispering of the ghosts in the rooms below.

No sounds, no apparitions, not even any ghost-fog.

Just vicious cold.

We gathered at last in the center of the attic. I was grimy, tense, and shivering; Lockwood, pale and irritable. George was trying to get a mass of sticky cobwebs off his rapier, rubbing the blade against the edge of his boot.

"What do you think?" Lockwood said. "I've no idea where it can be. Any thoughts?"

George raised a hand. "Yes. I'm hungry. We should eat."

I blinked at him. "How can you possibly think about eating now?"

"Very easily. Mortal fear gives me an appetite."

Lockwood grinned. "Then it's a pity you haven't any sandwiches. You left them in your bag, back down with the ghosts."

"I know. I was thinking of sharing Lucy's."

This made me roll my eyes. Mid-roll, my eyes stopped dead.

"Lucy?" Lockwood was always first to notice when anything was wrong.

I took a moment before replying. "Is it me," I said slowly, "or is there something lying on that beam?"

It was the crossbeam almost directly overhead. Cobwebs hung down from it, merging with the shadows of the eaves. Above was a funny patch of darkness that might have been part of the beam, or part of an object resting directly on it. You couldn't really see it from below, except for something poking out on one side that might have been hair.

We regarded it in silence.

"Ladder, George," Lockwood said.

George went to get the ladder, pulling it upward through the hatch. "Those guys are still down there," he reported. "Just standing around the chains. Looks like they're waiting for something."

We set the ladder against the beam.

"You want my advice?" In its jar, the ghost had stirred. *"The worst thing you can do is go up and look. Just chuck a magnesium flare and run away."*

I reported this to Lockwood. He shook his head. "If it's the Source," he said, "we *have* to seal it. One of us has to climb up. How about you, George? Seeing as how you went for the broom closet just now."

George's face generally expresses as much emotion as a bowl of custard. It didn't display overwhelming delight now.

"Unless you want me to?" Lockwood said.

"No, no . . . that's fine. Hand me a net, then."

At the heart of every haunting is a Source—an object or place to which that particular ghostly phenomenon is tethered. If you snuff this out—for instance, by covering it with a Seal, such as a silver chain net—you seal up the supernatural power. So George took his net, ready-folded in its plastic case, and started up the ladder. Lockwood and I waited below.

The ladder jerked and trembled as George climbed.

"Don't say I didn't warn you," the skull in the ghost-jar said.

George climbed out of the lantern light, drew close to the shaded beam. I took my sword from my belt. Lockwood hefted his in his hand. We met each other's eyes.

"Yes, if anything's going to happen," Lockwood murmured, "I'd say it's likely to happen just about—"

Shimmering white tentacles erupted from the beam. They were glassy and featureless, with stubby tips. They uncoiled with ferocious speed—some aiming high for George; some striking low at Lockwood and me.

"Just about now, really," Lockwood said.

Down swung the tentacles. We scattered, Lockwood diving toward the window, me toward the hatch. High above, George jerked away, dropping the chain net, losing his balance. The ladder toppled back. It wedged against the angle of the roof behind, knocking George's feet clear, leaving him dangling by two hands from the topmost rung.

A tendril flopped against the floorboards next to me, merged with them, went through. It was made of ectoplasmic matter. Unless you wanted to die, you had to prevent it touching your bare skin. I gave a frantic jump sideways, tripped, and dropped my sword.

Worse than dropped it—it vanished through the open hatch to fall among the ghosts below.

High above, things weren't much better. Letting go of the ladder with one hand, George tore a magnesium flare from his belt and lobbed it at the coils. It missed them completely, erupted against the roof in a brilliant explosion, and sent a cascade of white-hot burning salt and iron down on Lockwood, setting his clothes aflame.

That's how it went with us, sometimes. One thing just led to another.

"*Oh, good start!*" In the ghost-jar, the face had visibly perked up; it grinned cheerily at me as I bounded past, dodging the lunges from the nearest tentacle. "*So you're setting each other on fire, now? That's a new one! What will you think of next?*"

Above me more tendrils of ghostly matter were emerging from the crossbeam and the rafters of the roof. Their nub-like heads protruded like baby ferns, blind and bone-white, before whipping outward across the breadth of the attic space. On the other side of the room, Lockwood had dropped his rapier. He staggered backward toward the window, the front of his clothes feathered with darting silver flames, his head craned back to avoid the heat.

"Water!" he called. "Anyone got some water?"

"Me!" I ducked under a glowing tentacle and reached inside my bag. Even as I found my plastic bottle, I was shouting a request of my own: "And *I* need a sword!"

There was a rush of air through the attic, unnatural in its strength. Behind Lockwood, the window slammed open with a crash of breaking glass. Rain gusted through, bringing with it the howling of the storm. Lockwood was only two steps, maybe three, from the dreadful drop to the street below.

"*Water*, Lucy!"

"George! Your *sword!*"

George heard. He understood. He gave a frantic wriggle in mid-air and just about avoided the blind thrust of another coil. His rapier was at his belt, glittering as he swung. He reached down, ripped the sword clear.

I jumped over a slashing frond of plasm, spun around with the water bottle, and hurled it across to Lockwood.

George threw his rapier to me.

Watch this now. Sword and bottle, sailing through the air, twin trajectories, twin journeys, arcing beautifully through the mass of swirling tendrils toward Lockwood and me. Lockwood held out his hand. I held out mine.

Remember I said there was that moment of sweet precision, when we jelled perfectly as a team?

Yeah, well, this wasn't it.

The rapier shot past, missing me by miles. It skidded halfway across the floor.

The bottle struck Lockwood right in the center of his forehead, knocking him out the window.

There was a moment's pause.

"*Is he dead?*" the skull's voice said. "*Yay! Oh. No, he's hanging on to the shutters. Shame. Still, this is definitely the funniest thing I've ever seen. You three really are incompetence on a stick.*"

Frantically dancing clear of the nearest tentacles, I tried to get a view of Lockwood. To my relief, the skull was right. Lockwood was hanging out over the drop, his body a rigid diagonal, clinging to the broken shutters. The wind howled around him, tugging his hair across his long, lean face, seeking to pluck him away into the November night. Happily, it was also buffeting his burning coat. The silver flames were dwindling. They began to die.

Which was what we were *all* in danger of doing. Any second now.

George's sword was only yards away, but it might as well have been in Edinburgh. Ghostly coils swirled around it like anemones waving in a shallow sea.

"You can get it!" George called. "Do a cool somersault over them or something!"

"*You* do one! This is your fault! Why can't you ever throw things accurately?"

"Coming from you! You chucked that bottle like a girl!"

"I *am* a girl. And I put Lockwood's fire out for him, didn't I?"

Well, that was sort of true. Over at the window, our leader was hauling himself back inside. His face was green, his coat gently smoking. He had a neat red circle on his forehead where the bottle had struck. He wasn't exactly tossing thanks my way.

A particularly long and silver tentacle had homed in on me; it was steadily pushing me back toward the hatch, among cobwebs large as laundry.

"*Faster, Lucy!*" That was the skull in the jar. "*It's right behind you!*"

"How about a little help here?" I gasped as a tendril brushed my arm. I could feel the stinging cold right through the fabric of the coat.

"*Me?*" The hollow eyes in the face became hoops of surprise. "*A 'dirty old pile of bones,' as you call me? What could I do?*"

"Some advice! Evil wisdom! Anything!"

"*It's a Changer—you need something strong. Not a flare—you'll just set fire to something. Probably yourself. Use silver to drive it back. Then you can get the sword.*"

"I don't *have* any silver." We had plenty of silver Seals in the bag, but that was near Lockwood, on the other side of the room.

"*What about that stupid necklace you always wear? What's that made of?*"

Oh. Of course. The one Lockwood had given me that summer.

It was silver. Silver burns ghostly substances. All ghosts hate it, even powerful Changers that manifest as ectoplasmic coils. Not the strongest weapon I'd ever used, but it just might do.

Squatting back against the angled roof, I put my hands behind my neck and undid the clasp. When I brought my fingers around, cobwebs hung from them in greasy clumps. I held the necklace tight, and whirled it around and around my fist. The end made contact with the nearest tendril. Plasm burned; the tentacle snapped upward and away. Other coils flinched back, sensing the silver's nearness. For the first time, I cleared a safe space around me. I stood up, supporting myself against the rafter behind.

As my fingers touched the wood, I was hit by a sudden wave of emotion. Not *my* emotion—this feeling came from all about me. It seeped out of the fabric of the attic, out of the wood and slates, and the nails that held them there. It seeped out of the flailing coils of the ghost itself. It was a vile sensation—a sickly, shifting mix of loneliness and resentment, speared with cold, hard rage. The strength of it beat against my temples as I looked across the room.

A terrible thing had happened here, a terrible injustice. And from that act of violence came the energy that drove the vengeful spirit. I imagined its silent coils slipping through the floor toward the poor lodgers sleeping in the rooms below. . . .

"Lucy!" My mind cleared. It was Lockwood. He had stepped away from the window. He'd picked up his sword. One-handed, he slashed a complicated pattern through the air, shearing through the nearest tentacles. They burst like bubbles, scattering iridescent pearls of plasm. Even with his coat all charred and crispy, even with that red circle on his forehead, he had reasserted himself. His face was pale in the spectral light as he smiled across the attic at me. "Lucy," he called, "we need to finish this."

"It's angry!" I gasped, ducking under a grasping coil. "I got a connection with the ghost! It's angry about something!"

"You don't say?" High above, George raised his knees to avoid the thrashing tentacles. "Your sensitivity is amazing, Luce. How I wish I had your Talent."

"Yes, that isn't the most surprising insight you've ever given us." Lockwood bent over his bag. "I'll get a Seal. Meanwhile, you might just want to rescue George. . . ."

"Anytime you like," George said. "No hurry." His position was looking precarious. He still dangled by one hand, and the fingers of that hand were slipping fast.

Spinning my necklace, I leaped between the coils, feeling them dart aside. I snatched up the rapier as I passed by, skidded under the ladder, and wrenched it bodily forward, dragging its length below George just as his grip gave way.

He fell—and landed on the middle rungs like a scruffy sack of coal. The ladder bowed; I heard it crack. Well, that was better than him breaking his neck. He'd have made *such* an annoying ghost.

A moment later he'd skittered down the ladder like a fireman down a pole. I tossed him his rapier.

"What's up there?"

"Dead person. Angry dead person. That's all you need to know." Pausing only to adjust his spectacles, he leaped past to attack the coils.

Across the room, Lockwood had brought something out of the

bag. "Lucy—I'm going to throw it! Climb up and get ready to catch!" He drew back his hand, then darted aside as a swiping tentacle narrowly missed his face. A flick of the rapier; the coil was gone. "Here it is!" he called. "It's coming now."

Lockwood, of course, *could* throw. I was already moving up the ladder. A small square object came spiraling straight up and over the central beam; down it came, landing right in my hand. Not even a fumble. Close by, George was slashing with his rapier, watching my back, carving coils asunder. I reached the top of the ladder, where it touched the beam.

And the Source *was* there.

After so many years, it lay with surprising neatness on its secret perch. The cobwebs that fused it to the wood had smoothed out the contours of the bones and buried them under a soft gray shroud. You could see the remains of old-style clothes—a tweed suit, two brown shoes tilted at an angle—and the bone ridges around the dust-filled sockets of the eyes. Strands of dark matter—was it hair or matted cobwebs?—ran like water over the lip of the beam. How had it happened? Had he purposefully climbed up there, or been tucked away (more likely) by a murderer's careful hand? Now was not the time to worry either way. The dead man's fury pounded in my mind; below me, in the weaving lantern light, Lockwood and George did battle with the coils.

In those days the Sunrise Corporation provided silver chain nets in plastic boxes, for ease of use. I cracked the lid open, took out the folded net. I let it slip outward until it had fully unfurled between my fingers, thin and loose like an uncooked pastry case, like a shimmering skin of stars.

Silver snuffs out Sources. I flicked it up and over the beam, over the bones and cobwebs, as calmly and casually as a chambermaid making a bed.

The net sank down; the fury winked out of my mind. All at once there was a hole there, an echoing silence. The coils froze; a second later they had faded from the attic like mist from a mountaintop: one moment there, the next gone.

How big the attic seemed without the Changer in it. We stopped dead, right where we were: me sinking down against the ladder, Lockwood and George leaning against the rafters, weary, silent, rapiers gently smoking.

Smoke twisted from one side of Lockwood's overcoat. His nose had a residue of silver ash on it. My jacket had burned where the plasm touched it. My hair was a nest of cobwebs. George had contrived to tear the seat of his trousers on a nail or something.

We were a total mess. We'd been up all night. We smelled of ectoplasm, salt, and fear. We looked at one another, and grinned.

Then we began laughing.

Down by the hatch, in its green glass prison, the ghostly face looked on in sour disapproval. "Oh, you're pleased with that fiasco, are you? Typical! I'm ashamed even to be faintly associated with Lockwood & Co. You three really are hopeless."

But that was just it. We weren't hopeless. We were good. We were the best.

And we never fully realized it until it was too late.

II

Whitechapel Nights

Chapter 4

BED & BREAKFAST—AND MURDER!

HORRIFIC SECRETS OF WHITECHAPEL GUESTHOUSE

BODIES FOUND IN PIT BENEATH GARDEN SHED

Authorities in East London acted yesterday to seal off Lavender Lodge, a guesthouse in Cannon Lane, Whitechapel, after the discovery of human remains on the property. The owners, Mr. Herbert Evans (72) and his wife, Nora (70), have been arrested and charged with murder and robbery, and with failure to disclose a dangerous haunting. A powerful Visitor, located in the attic of the house, has been destroyed.

It is believed that over the last ten years many lodgers may have died of ghost-touch while staying at the Lodge. Mr. and Mrs. Evans then disposed of the corpses in a fruit cellar hidden in the back garden. Police have recovered a large number of watches, jewelry, and other personal effects that were taken from the victims.

The decisive investigation was carried out by the Lockwood & Co. agency, led by Mr. Anthony Lockwood. "Records show that a previous owner of Lavender Lodge vanished in mysterious circumstances more than thirty years ago," he says. "We think that the mummified body in the attic belonged to him. It was his angry spirit that stalked the house, killing guests as they slept. Mr. and Mrs. Evans took advantage of this for their own personal gain."

After subduing the ghost, the agents were forced to break a window and climb down a drainpipe to escape the Lodge, before finally confronting the geriatric duo in their kitchen. "Old Evans proved quite handy with a carving knife," Mr. Lockwood says, "and his wife came at us with a skewer. So we knocked them on the heads with a broom. It was a ticklish moment, but we're happy to have survived unscathed."

"And that's it," Lockwood said disgustedly. He lowered the newspaper and sat back into his armchair. "That's all the *Times* gives us for our trouble. There's more about the scuffle in the kitchen than there is about the Changer. Doesn't exactly focus on the important stuff, does it?"

"It's the 'unscathed' bit that *I* object to," George said. "That old cow gave me a right old whack. See this horrible red blob?"

I glanced up at him. "I thought your nose always looked like that."

"No, here, on my forehead. This bruise."

Lockwood gave an unsympathetic grunt. "Yes, dreadful. What really bothers me is that we only made page seven. No one's going to notice that. The massive Chelsea outbreak is dominating the news again. All *our* stuff's getting lost."

It was late morning, two days after the Lavender Lodge affair, and we were stretched out in the library of our house in Portland Row, trying to relax. Outside the window a gale was blowing. Portland Row seemed formed of liquid. Trees flexed; rain pattered on the panes. Inside, it was warm; we had the heating on full-blast.

George was slumped on the sofa beside a giant pile of crumpled ironing, sweat pants akimbo, reading a comic. "It *is* a shame they don't talk more about the actual case," he said. "The way the Changer created its own little cluster of other ghosts was fascinating. It's how the Problem spreads, some say—strong Visitors causing violent deaths, which lead to secondary hauntings. I would have *loved* to study it in more detail."

That was how George always was, once the panic of a case died down. He was *curious* about it: he wanted to understand *why* and *how* it happened. Me, it was the emotional impact of each adventure that I couldn't quite shake off.

"I just felt sorry for all those poor ghost-touched men," I said. I was sitting cross-legged on the floor below the sofa. Officially, I was sorting the mail; *unofficially*, I'd been having a gentle doze, having been up till three on a Lurker case the night before. "I could feel their sadness," I went on. "And even that Changer . . . yes, it was terrifying, but it was unhappy, too. I could feel its pain. And if I'd had more time to try to connect with it properly—"

"It would have killed you stone dead." From the depths of his chair Lockwood gave me a look. "Your Talent's amazing, Luce, but the only ghost you should communicate with is the skull, because it's locked up in its jar. . . . And to be honest, I'm not even sure *that's* safe."

"Oh, the skull's okay," I said. "It helped me with my Lurker case last night. Gave me a fix on the Source, so I could dig it up. We were quite close to Chelsea, where we were. What about you two? Either of you hear the sirens?"

Lockwood nodded. "Another three people killed. DEPRAC is completely clueless, as usual. They were evacuating a couple of streets, I think."

"Way more than that," George said. "The outbreak stretches a good square mile along the King's Road. More ghosts every night, in greater concentration than ever before, and no one knows why." He adjusted his glasses. "It's weird. Until recently, Chelsea was pretty quiet, everything peaceful—then, all at once, things go into haunting overdrive. It's like an infection spreading. But here's what I want to know—how do you actually fire ghosts up? How do you infect the dead?"

There was no answer to this, and I didn't try to provide one. Lockwood just groaned; he'd been chasing a Specter through Hackney marshes until the early hours and was in no mood for George's ponderings. "All *I* care about," he said, "is how Chelsea's hogging our publicity. You do know that Kipps's team is working on it? He's on page one today, giving some stupid quote or other. Page one! That's where we should be! *We* need to take part in something big like that. I should speak to Barnes, maybe, see if he wants us to help out. Trouble is, we're already so overworked. . . ."

Yes, we were. . . . It was November, as I've mentioned, at the beginning of what would become known as the "Black Winter," the deadliest period yet in the history of the Problem. The epidemic of hauntings that had beset the nation for more than fifty years had reached new levels of intensity, and the terrifying outbreak in the district of Chelsea was just the tip of the iceberg. All psychic investigation agencies were stretched to the breaking point. Lockwood & Co. was no exception. "Overworked" didn't really cover it.

We lived, the three of us, in a four-story property in Portland Row, London, which was the headquarters of our agency. Lockwood himself owned the house. It had once belonged to his parents, and their collection of oriental wards and ghost-chasers still lined the walls of many rooms. Lockwood had converted the basement into an office, with desks, iron stores, and a rapier practice room. At the rear, a reinforced glass door led out into the garden, complete with a little lawn and apple trees, where we'd sometimes lounge in summer. On the upper floors were bedrooms; the ground floor contained the kitchen, the library, and the living room, where Lockwood interviewed our clients. It was here that we spent most time.

For several months, though, time had been in extremely short supply. This was partly due to our own success. In July our investigation at Kensal Green Cemetery had ended with the so-called "Battle in the Graveyard," featuring a fight between agents and a group of violent black-marketeers. Along with our encounter with the horrific Rat-Ghost of Hampstead, it had aroused a lot of interest in the press, and this interest continued during the trial of the chief marketeer, a man named Julius Winkman. Lockwood, George, and I had all testified against him; by the time Winkman was sent down for a stiff stretch in Wandsworth Prison, it was the middle of September, and our period of free publicity had lasted nearly two months. During this time, our phone had seldom stopped ringing.

It was true that most wealthy clients preferred to stick with the large agencies, which had swankier equipment and bigger reputations. Most of *our* business came from poorer districts like Whitechapel, where clients didn't pay so well. But jobs were jobs, and Lockwood didn't like to turn any of them down. This meant that free evenings were few and far between.

"Anything going on tonight, George?" Lockwood said suddenly. He'd thrown a weary arm over his face, and I'd assumed he was asleep. "Please say no."

George said nothing, just raised three fingers.

"*Three?*" Lockwood uttered a long and hollow groan. "What are they?"

"Woman in a veil on Nelson Street, Whitechapel; a haunted apartment in a housing project, and a Shade spotted behind some public restrooms. The usual glamorous stuff."

"We'll have to split up again," Lockwood said. "Dibs on the veiled woman."

George grunted. "Dibs on the Shade."

"What?" My head jerked up. The dibs rule was second only to the biscuit rule in terms of importance. It always held firm. "So I get the housing project? Brilliant. I bet the elevators will be out, and everything."

"You're fit enough to manage a few stairs, Luce," Lockwood murmured.

"What if it's twenty-one floors? What if there's a Raw-bones at the top, and I'm too out of breath to deal with it? Wait, what if the elevator *is* working, but the ghost's hidden inside? You remember what happened to that girl from the Sebright Agency when she got stuck in that haunted elevator at Canary Wharf? They only found her shoes!"

"Stop burbling," Lockwood said. "You're tired. We all are. You know it'll be fine."

We all subsided again. I leaned my head back against the sofa cushions. Rivulets of water laced the library window like veins of blood.

Okay, not *really* like veins of blood. I was tired . . . like Lockwood said.

Lockwood . . . Through half-closed eyes, I watched him now, trapping him tight between my lashes. I looked at his long legs, loosely crossed over the side of the chair; at the bare feet, at the slim contours of his body half-concealed beneath the rumpled shirt. His face was mostly covered by his arm, but you could see the line of his jaw and the expressive lips, relaxed and slightly parted. His dark hair spilled softly over the white sleeve.

How did he manage to look like that after five hours' sleep, lying curled and crumpled in the chair? Being half-dressed never did *me* any favors; with George, it practically came with a health warning. Yet Lockwood managed to carry it off perfectly. It was pleasantly warm in the room. My eyelashes squeezed a little tighter. I put my hand to my silver necklace, turning it slowly between my fingers. . . .

"We need a new agent," Lockwood said.

I opened my eyes wide. Behind me, I heard George put his comic down. "What?"

"We need another operative. Another working agent to back us up. Don't we? We shouldn't have to keep separating all the time."

"We worked together at Lavender Lodge," I said.

"That was a one-off." Lockwood moved his arm, and pushed the hair out of his face. "Hardly ever happens now. Anyway, look around. We're not really coping, are we?"

George yawned. "What makes you say that?" He gave an almighty stretch and knocked over the pile of ironing, which collapsed on my head. Like a giant amoeba undulating purposefully across a petri dish, a pair of George's briefs flopped slowly past my nose.

"Case in point," Lockwood said as I shook myself free. "One of you should have sorted all that. But you haven't had time."

"Or *you* could always iron them, of course," George said.

"Me? I'm even busier than you."

This was the way it always went now. We were working so hard at night, we had no energy for doing stuff during the day. So we no longer got around to inessential things, such as keeping the place tidy or sorting the laundry. All of 35 Portland Row was suffering. The kitchen looked like a salt-bomb had gone off in it. Even the skull in the jar, no stranger to vile surroundings, had made indignant comments about the environment we lived in.

"If we had another agent," Lockwood said, "we could properly take turns. One of us could rest at home each night and do odd jobs during the day. I've been considering this for a while. It's the only answer, I think."

George and I were silent. The idea of a new colleague didn't much appeal to me. In fact, it gave me a twisty sort of feeling in my belly. Overstretched as we definitely were, I *liked* the way we operated. As we had at Lavender Lodge, we backed each other up when necessary, and we got things done.

"Are you sure?" I said at last. "Where would they sleep?"

"Not on the floor," George said. "They'd probably get some disease."

"Well, they're not sharing the attic with me."

"They wouldn't have to *sleep* here, you idiots," Lockwood growled. "Since when has living under the same roof been a requirement for the job? They could turn up for work in the morning, like ninety-nine percent of other people do."

"Maybe it's not a full agent that we need," I suggested. "Maybe we just need an assistant. Someone to tidy up after us. In all the important stuff, surely, we're doing fine."

"I agree with Lucy." George returned to his comic. "We've got a good setup here. We shouldn't mess it up."

"Well, I'll think about it," Lockwood said.

The truth was, of course, that Lockwood was far too busy to think about it at all, and so nothing was ever likely to happen. Which suited me just fine. I'd been at the company eighteen months so far. Yes, we were overworked; yes, we lived in partial squalor. Yes, we risked our lives almost every night. Yet I was very happy.

Why? Three reasons: my colleagues, my new self-knowledge, and because of an opened door.

Of all the agencies in London, Lockwood & Co. was unique. Not just because it was the smallest (total number of agents: three), but because it was owned and run by someone who was *himself* young. Other agencies employed hundreds of child operatives—they had to, of course, because only children could detect ghosts—but these companies were firmly controlled by adults who never got closer to a haunted house than shouting distance across the street. Lockwood, however, was a leader who fought ghosts himself—his skills with the rapier were second to none—and I knew I was lucky to work at his side. Lucky in a *lot* of ways. Not only was he independent, but he was an inspiring companion, managing to be both coolly unflappable and recklessly audacious at the same time. And his air of mystery only added to his allure.

Lockwood seldom spoke of his emotions, desires, or the influences that drove him, and in the first year of living at Portland Row, I had learned almost nothing about his past. His absent parents were an enigma, even though their possessions hung on every wall. How he'd come to own the house, with enough money to start his own agency, I likewise didn't have a clue. To begin with, this didn't much matter. Secrets followed Lockwood about like the flapping of his coat, and it was nice to be close enough to feel them brush against me, too.

So Lockwood's proximity made me happy. George, it had to be said, had been more of an acquired taste, being scruffy, acerbic, and renowned around London for his casual approach to the application of soap. But he was also intellectually honest, had boundless curiosity, and was a brilliant researcher whose insights kept us all alive. Plus—and this is the crucial point—he was ferociously loyal to his friends, who happened to be Lockwood and me.

And it was precisely because we *were* friends, because we trusted one another, that we were each free to explore the things closest to our hearts. George could happily research the causes of the Problem. Lockwood could steadily build the reputation of the firm. Me? Before arriving at Portland Row, I'd been ignorant—even uneasy—about my ability to hear the voices of the dead and (sometimes) communicate with them. But Lockwood & Co. gave me the opportunity to explore my psychic Talents at my own pace, and uncover what I could do. After the pleasure I got from my companions, this new self-perception was the second reason why I was so content that grim November morning as the rain poured down outside.

And the third? Well, for some months I'd been growing frustrated by Lockwood's ultimate remoteness. All three of us certainly benefited from our shared experiences and mutual trust, but as time went by the mysteries that surrounded him had begun to weigh heavily on me. This had been symbolized by his refusal to tell us anything about a particular room on the first floor of the house, a room we had never been allowed to enter. I'd had a lot of theories about this strange, shut door, but it was clear to me it had something to do with his past—and probably with the fate of his missing parents. The secret of the room had steadily become an invisible block between us, keeping us apart, and I'd despaired of ever understanding it—or ever understanding him.

Until one summer's day, when Lockwood had unexpectedly relented. Without preamble he'd taken George and me up to the landing, opened the forbidden door, and shown us a little of the truth.

And do you know what? It turned out I'd been wrong.

It wasn't his parents' room at all.

It was his sister's.

His sister, Jessica Lockwood, who had died there six years before.

Chapter 5

To protect our clients' sanity, and my own peace and quiet, the skull in the ghost-jar ordinarily resided in a remote corner of our basement office, concealed beneath a tea cozy. Occasionally it was brought up to the living room and the lever in its lid opened, so that it could communicate eerie secrets of the dead—or exchange childish insults with me, whichever it felt like doing. It so happened that it was sitting on the sideboard late that afternoon, when I came in to gather equipment for the evening.

As arranged earlier, we were splitting forces. George had already departed for the Whitechapel public restrooms in search of the reported Shade. Lockwood was readying himself for his expedition in search of the veiled woman. My visit had been canceled; I'd just been gearing up for the block of apartments when I'd had a call from my client, postponing the visit due to illness. That meant I had a swift choice: stay at home and sort the laundry or accompany

Lockwood instead. You can guess which one I picked.

I gathered my rapier from where I'd chucked it the night before, and also a few scattered salt-bombs that had been dumped beside the sofa. As I made for the door, a hoarse voice spoke from the shadows. "*Lucy! Lucy . . .*"

"What now?" With the onset of evening, dim flecks were swirling in the glass. The hunched mass of the battered skull faded from view. The flecks congealed to form a malicious face, glowing green and soft in the darkness.

"*Going out?*" the ghost said agreeably. "*I'll come along.*"

"No, you won't. You're staying here."

"*Oh, do a skull a favor. I'll get bored.*"

"So dematerialize. Rotate. Turn inside out. Stick around and enjoy the view. Do whatever it is ghosts do. I'm sure you can find ways to amuse yourself." I turned to go.

"*Enjoy the view? In this hellhole?*" The face swiveled in the jar, the tip of its nose dragging against the inside of the glass. "*I've been in mortuaries with better standards of housekeeping. I wish I didn't have to see the squalor I'm surrounded by.*"

I paused with my hand on the door. "I could help you with that. I could bury you in a hole and solve your problem altogether."

Not that I was truly likely to do this. Of all the Visitors we'd encountered—of all the Visitors *anyone* had encountered in recent times—the skull was the only one capable of true communication. Other ghosts could moan, knock, and utter snippets of coherent sound; and agents such as me, who were skilled at psychic Listening, were able to detect them. But that was a long way from the skull's ability to engage in proper sustained conversation. It was a Type

Three Visitor, and very rare—which was why, despite great provocation, we hadn't thrown it in the trash.

The ghost snorted. *"Burying requires digging, and digging requires work. And that's plainly something none of you is capable of. Let me guess . . . I bet it's Whitechapel again tonight? Those dark streets . . . those winding alleys . . . Take me! You need a companion."*

"Yep," I said. "And I'm going with Lockwood." In fact, I had to hurry. I could hear him putting his coat on in the hall.

"Aha . . . Are you? Oh, I see. Better leave you to it, then."

"Right. Good." I paused. "Meaning what?"

"Nothing, nothing." The evil eyes winked at me. *"I'm no third wheel."*

"I don't know what you're talking about. We're going on a case."

"Of course you are. It's a perfect contrivance. Quick, better run upstairs and change."

"Lucy—got to go!" That was Lockwood in the hall.

"Coming!" I shouted. "I don't *need* to change," I growled at the skull. "These are my work clothes."

"They don't have to be." The face regarded me critically. *"Let's take a look at you. Leggings, T-shirt, raggedy old skirt, moth-eaten sweater. . . . Like a cross between a demented sailor and a bag lady. How does that make you look pretty? Who's going to notice you if you go out like that?"*

"Who says I want to look pretty for anybody?" I roared. "I'm an agent! I've got a job to do! And if you can't talk sense . . ." I scuttled over to the sideboard and grabbed the tea cozy.

"Ooh, have I hit a nerve?" The ghost grinned. *"I have! How fascin—"*

Regrettably, the rest was lost. I'd turned the lever, jammed the cozy over the jar, and stalked out of the room.

Lockwood stood waiting in the hall, immaculate, inquiring. "Everything okay, Luce? Skull giving you trouble?"

"Nothing I can't handle." I smoothed back my hair, blew out flushed cheeks, gave him a carefree smile. "Shall we go?"

No ordinary taxis were licensed in London after Curfew, but a small fleet of Night Cabs operated from well-protected night stations, catering mainly to agents and DEPRAC officials whose business took them out after dark. These cars—shaped like conventional black cabs, but painted white—were driven by a hardy breed of often bald middle-aged men, taciturn, unsmiling, and efficient. According to Lockwood, most of them were ex-convicts, let out of prison early in return for taking on this dangerous and unsociable task. They wore a lot of iron jewelry and drove very fast.

The nearest Night Cab station was at Baker Street, not far from the Tube. Our driver, Jake, was one we'd had before. Silver earrings swung wildly at his neck as he pulled out of the underground garage and accelerated eastward along Marylebone Road.

Lockwood stretched out on the seat and grinned across at me. He seemed more relaxed now that we were out on a case; his weariness of the morning had fallen away.

By contrast I still felt flustered after my conversation with the skull. "So," I said in a businesslike voice, "what's this Visitor we're after? A domestic job?"

He nodded. "Yes, an apparition spotted in an upstairs room. Our client is a Mrs. Peters. Her two young boys saw a sinister veiled lady, dressed in black, seemingly imprinted within the glass of the bedroom window."

"Ooh. Are the kids okay?"

"Just barely. They were driven to hysterics. One's still heavily sedated. . . . Well, I expect we'll soon see this lady for ourselves." Lockwood stared out at the deserted sidewalks, the grid of empty streets stretching away.

The driver looked over his shoulder. "Seems quiet tonight, Mr. Lockwood. But it isn't. You're lucky to get me. I'm the only cab left in the station."

"Why's that, Jake?"

"It's that outbreak in Chelsea. There's a big push on to try to quash it. DEPRAC's calling up agents left, right, and center. They've commandeered a lot of taxis to stand by."

Lockwood frowned. "So which agencies are they using?"

"Oh, you know. Just the major ones. Fittes and Rotwell."

"Right."

"Plus Tendy, Atkins and Armstrong, Tamworth, Grimble, Staines, Mellingcamp, and Bunchurch. Some others, too, but I forget the names."

Lockwood's snort sounded like a moped backfiring. "*Bunchurch?* *They're* not a major agency. They've only got ten people, and eight of them are useless."

"Not my place to say, Mr. Lockwood. Do you want lavender piped through the air conditioner? New car this, got it as an extra."

"No, thanks." Lockwood breathed in deeply through his nose. "Lucy and I *do* have a few defenses of our own, even if we're not from a 'major agency.' We feel safe enough."

After that he fell silent, but the force of his annoyance filled the cab. He sat staring out of the window, tapping his fingers on his knee. From the shadows of the backseat I watched the intermittent glow from the streetlamps running down the contours of his cheeks, picking out the curve of his mouth and his dark, impatient eyes. I knew why he was angry: he wanted his company to be spoken of as one of the great ones in the capital. Ambition burned fiercely in him—ambition to make a difference against the Problem.

And I understood the reason for that fire too.

Of course I did. I'd known it ever since that day in the summer, when he'd opened the door on the landing and led George and me inside.

"My sister," Lockwood had said. "This is her room. As you can probably see, it's where she died. Think I'll close the door now, if you don't mind."

He did so. The little wedge of sunlight from the landing snapped shut around us like a trap. Iron panels lining the interior of the door clicked together softly, cutting us off from all normality.

Neither George nor I said anything. It was all we could do to stand upright. We clung to each other. Waves of psychic energy broke against our senses like a storm tide. There was a roaring in my ears.

I shook my head clear, forced myself to open my eyes.

A blackout curtain hugged the window opposite. White slivers from the summer afternoon showed around its edges; otherwise there was no light anywhere.

No *natural* light.

Yet a radiance—thin as water, silvery as moonlight—occupied the room. Even *I* could sense it, and I'm useless when it comes to deathglows. I usually have to take Lockwood's word for it that they're there at all. But not this time. A bed stood in the center of the room: a twin bed, arranged with the headboard flush against the right-hand wall. The legs and frame had been painted white or cream, and there was a pale bedspread draped over the bare mattress, so that the whole thing hung in the dimness like a cloud in a black sky. Superimposed on top of the bed was something else: a roughly oval, egg-shaped glow, tall as a person, blank and bright and coldly shimmering. It was a light without a source—there was nothing at its center—and I couldn't truly *see* it. Only, when I looked away, it flared into prominence at the corner of my vision, like one of those spots you see after you've looked too closely at the sun.

It was from this faint oval smudge that the psychic energy poured, strong and unceasing. No wonder the strips of iron had been bolted to the door; no wonder the walls of the room shone bright with silver wards. No wonder the ceiling was thick with silver mobiles that stirred now in the breeze caused by the closing door. Their tinkling was softly melodic, like far-off children's laughter.

"Her name was Jessica," Lockwood said. He moved past us, and I saw that he had taken the dark glasses out of his pocket—the ones he used to protect himself from the brightest spectral glows. He put them on. "She was six years older than me," he said. "And fifteen when it happened to her—right here."

He spoke like it was the most normal thing in the world to be standing with us in the dark, revealing the existence of a long-dead sister, with her death-glow hovering before us, and the psychic after-shock of the event battering our senses. Now he approached the bed; being careful to keep his hand clear of the oval light, he pulled back the bedspread, revealing the mattress below. Halfway along it was a broad, blackened, gaping wound where the surface of the fabric had been burned as if by acid.

I stared at it. No, not acid. I knew ectoplasm burns when I saw them.

I realized I was gripping George's arm even harder than before.

"I'm not hurting you, am I, George?" I said.

"No more than previously."

"Good." I didn't let go.

"I was only nine," Lockwood said. "It was a long time back. Ancient history, if you like. But I figure I owe it to you both to show you. You do *live* in this house, after all."

I forced myself to speak. "So," I said. "Jessica."

"Yes."

"Your sister?"

"Yes."

"What happened to her?"

He flicked the bedspread back into position again, tucked the end neatly against the headboard. "Ghost-touched."

"A ghost? From where?"

"From a pot." His voice was carefully toneless. The dark glasses that protected his eyes also hid them very successfully. It was impossible to read his expression. "You know my parents' stuff?" he went on. "All the tribal ghost-catchers on the walls downstairs? They were researchers. They studied the folklore of the supernatural in other cultures. Most of what they collected is junk: ceremonial head-dresses, that sort of thing. But it turned out that some pieces *did* do what was claimed. There was a pot. I think it came from Indonesia someplace. They say my sister was sorting through a crate; she got the pot out and—and she dropped it. When it shattered, a ghost came out. Killed her."

"Lockwood . . . I'm so sorry. . . ."

"Yes, well, it's ancient history. A long time ago."

It was difficult to focus on anything but Lockwood's words, on them and on the ferocity of the spectral light. But I could see that the room contained an armoire and two dressers, and there were boxes and tea chests lying about too, mostly stacked against the walls, sometimes as many as three or four high. Resting on top of everything were dozens of vases and jam jars holding bouquets of dried lavender. The room was filled with its sweet, astringent odor. This was so different from the normal smells in our house (particularly on the landing, George's bedroom being just opposite) that it only added to the feeling of unreality.

I shook my head again. A sister. Lockwood had had a *sister*. She'd died right here.

"What happened to the ghost?" George said. His voice was indistinct.

"It was disposed of." Lockwood crossed to the window and pulled the blackout curtains back. Daylight stabbed me; for a moment my eyes recoiled. When I could look again, the room was brightly lit. I could no longer see the glow above the bed, and the sense of psychic assault had been subtly muted. I could still feel its presence, though, and hear the faint crackling in my ears.

The room had once been a pleasant blue, the wallpaper decorated with a child's pattern of diagonally arranged balloons. There were posters of lions, giraffes, and horses stuck to a bulletin board, and old animal stickers slapped randomly all over the headboard of the bed. Yellowing glow-in-the-dark stars dotted the ceiling. But that wasn't what drew the eye. On the right-hand wall two great vertical gouges had torn straight through the paper and into the plaster beneath. They were rapier slashes. In one place the cut had gone as deep as the brick.

Lockwood stood quietly by the window, staring out at the blank wall of the house next door. Some dried lavender seeds had dropped onto the sill from the vases that sat there. He brushed them with a finger into his cupped hand.

Something like hysteria was building in my chest. I wanted to cry, to laugh uncontrollably, to shout at Lockwood. . . .

Instead I said quietly, "So what was she like?"

"Oh . . . that's hard to say. She was my sister. I liked her, obviously. I can find you a picture sometime. There'll be one in the drawers here somewhere. It's where I put all her things. I suppose I should sort through it all one day, but there's always so much to do. . . ." He leaned back against the window, silhouetted against the light, pushing the seeds slowly around his palm. "She was tall, dark-haired, strong-willed, I guess. There's once or twice I've seen you out of the corner of my eye, Luce, and I almost thought . . . But you're nothing like her really. She was a gentle person. Very kind."

"Okay, you *are* hurting my arm now, Lucy," George said.

"Sorry." I pried my hand free.

"My mistake," Lockwood said. "It came out wrong. What I was trying to say was—"

"It's all right," I said. "I shouldn't have asked you about her in the first place. . . . It must be difficult to talk about this. We understand. We won't ask you anything more."

"So, this pot," George said, "tell me about it. How *did* it keep the ghost trapped? Pottery on its own wouldn't have done the job. There must've been some kind of iron lining—or silver, I suppose. Or did they have some other technique, which— ow!" I'd kicked him. "What was *that* for?"

"For not shutting up."

He blinked at me over his spectacles. "Why? It's interesting."

"We're talking about his sister! Not the bloody pot!"

George jerked a thumb at Lockwood. "He says it's ancient history."

"Yes, but he's clearly lying. Look at this place! Look at this room and what's in it! This is *so* right now."

"Yes, but he's let us in, Luce. He wants to talk about it. I say that includes the pot."

"Oh, come on! This isn't one of your stupid experiments, George. This is his family. Don't you have any empathy at all?"

"I've got more empathy than you! For a start I can see the bleeding obvious, which is that Lockwood *wants* us to discuss it. After years of emotional constipation, he's ready to share things with us—"

"Maybe he does, but he's also completely brittle and hypersensitive, so if—"

"Hey, I'm still standing here," Lockwood said. "I didn't go out, or anything." Silence fell; George and I broke off and looked at him. "And the truth is," he went on, "you're *both* right. I *do* want to talk about it—as George says. But I also don't find it very easy, so Lucy's spot-on too." He sighed. "Yes, George, I believe the pot had a layer of iron on the inside. But it cracked, okay? And maybe that's enough for now."

"Lockwood," I said. I looked toward the bed. "One thing. Does she—?"

"No."

"She's never—?"

"No."

"But the glow—"

"She's never come back." Lockwood tipped the lavender seeds into one of the vases on the sill and wiped his long, slim hands. "In the early days, you know, I almost hoped she would. I'd come up here, when I was in the house, thinking I might see her standing at the window. I'd wait a long time, looking into the light, expecting to see her shape, or hear her voice. . . ." He smiled at me ruefully. "But there was never anything."

He glanced over at the bed, his eyes still penned in behind the blank black glasses. "Anyway, that was early on. It wasn't healthy, my just hanging out in here. And after a while, when I'd had rather more experience with death-glows and what goes with them, I began to dread her return as well as want it. I couldn't bear to think how she might appear to me. So then I stopped coming in here much, and I set up the lavender to . . . to discourage surprises."

"Iron would be stronger," George said. He was like that, George; cutting, in his bespectacled way, to the nub of the issue quicker than everyone else. "I don't see any iron here—apart from on the door."

I looked at Lockwood; his shoulders had gone tight, and for a moment I wondered whether he was going to get angry. "You're right, of course," he said. "But that's too much like dealing with an ordinary Visitor—and she's *not* that, George, she's *not* ordinary. She's my sister. Even if she does come back, I couldn't use iron on her."

Neither of us said anything.

"The funny thing is, she *loved* the smell of lavender," Lockwood said, in a lighter voice. "You know that scrubby bush of it around the side of the house, out by the trash bins? When I was a kid she used to sit with me and make lavender garlands for our hair."

I looked at the vases with their plumes of faded purple. So they *were* a defense—but a welcome, too.

"Anyway, lavender's good stuff," George said. "Flo Bones swears by it."

"Flo just swears in general," I said.

We all laughed, but it wasn't really a room for laughter. Nor for tears, oddly, or for anger, or for any emotion other than a sort of solemnity. It was a place of absence; we were in the presence of something that had left. It was like coming to a valley where someone had once shouted, loud and joyously, and the echo of that shout had resounded between the hills and lasted a long time. But now it had vanished, and you stood on the same spot, and it was not the same.

We didn't go back to the room. It was a private place, and George and I left it alone. After that first seismic revelation, Lockwood didn't bring up the subject of his sister again, nor did he hunt out the photograph he had promised. He rarely mentioned his parents, either, though he did let slip that they had left him 35 Portland Row in their wills. So—somehow, somewhere—they had died, too. But they and Jessica stayed in shadow, and the questions hovering around the silent bedroom largely remained.

I tried not to let it worry me, and instead be satisfied with what I had learned. Certainly I felt closer to Lockwood now. My knowledge of his past was a privilege. It made me feel warm and special at times like this, speeding with him in the back of the taxi through the London dark. Who knew—perhaps one night, when we were working alone together, he might open up and tell me more?

The cab braked suddenly; both Lockwood and I jerked forward in our seats. In front of us, moving figures filled the street.

The driver cursed. "Sorry, Mr. Lockwood. Way's blocked. There are agents everywhere."

"Not a problem." Lockwood was already reaching for the door. "This is exactly what I want." Before I could react, almost before the car had stopped, he was out and halfway across the road.

Chapter 6

Our route to Whitechapel had taken us via the center of the city. We were in Trafalgar Square. As I got out of the taxi, I saw that a crowd had gathered below Nelson's Column, lit by the sputtering white light of many ghost-lamps. They were ordinary citizens, a rare sight after dark. Some carried signs; others were taking turns to make speeches from a makeshift platform. I could not hear what was being said. A ring of police and DEPRAC officers surrounded them at some distance; farther out still, and spilling out into the street, stood a large mass of psychic investigation agents, presumably there to protect the assembly. They wore the brightly colored jackets that most agencies use. Silver Fittes ones; the burgundy splendors of the Rotwell agency; the canary yellow of Tamworth; Grimble's green pea-soupers: all these and many more were present and correct. A DEPRAC tea van had parked on one side and was doling out hot drinks; and many other cars and taxis waited close by.

Lockwood made a beeline straight across the square. I hurried after him.

I don't know what the collective noun for a group of psychic investigation agents is, but it ought to be a *posture* or a *preen*. Knots of operatives stood in color-coded groups, eyeing their hated rivals, talking loudly and uttering barks of raucous laughter. The smallest agents—kids of seven or eight—stood drinking tea and making faces at one another. Older ones swaggered to and fro, exchanging insulting gestures under the noses of their supervisors, who pretended not to notice. Chests swelled, swords glinted in the lamp-light. The air crackled with condescension and hostility.

Lockwood and I passed through the throng to where a familiar figure stood, gloomily regarding the scene. As usual, Inspector Montagu Barnes wore a rumpled trench coat, an indifferent suit, and a bowler hat of dark brown suede. Unusually, he was holding a Styrofoam cup of steaming orange soup. He had a weathered, lived-in face, and a graying mustache the approximate size and length of a dead hamster. Barnes worked for DEPRAC, the Department of Psychic Research and Control—the government bureau that monitored the activities of agencies and, on occasions such as this, commandeered them for the common good. He wouldn't have won any prizes for grace or geniality, but he was shrewd and efficient, and not noticeably corrupt. That didn't mean he enjoyed our company.

Beside him stood a smallish man resplendently decked out in the plush livery of the Fittes Agency. His boots shone, his skintight trousers gleamed. An expensive rapier swung from a jeweled belt strap at his side; his silver jacket was soft as tiger's pelt, and perfectly matched by exquisite kidskin gloves. All very swish; impressive, even. Unfortunately, the body within the uniform belonged to Quill Kipps, so the overall effect was like watching a plague rat lick a bowl of caviar. Yes, the classy element was there, but it wasn't what you focused on.

Kipps was red-haired, scrawny, and pathetically self-satisfied. For a variety of reasons, possibly connected to the fact that we often said this to his face, he had long disliked us here at Lockwood & Co. As a team leader for Fittes's London Division, and one of the youngest adult supervisors in that agency, he had regularly worked with Barnes at DEPRAC; in fact, he was reading to him from a three-ring binder as we approached.

". . . forty-eight Type One sightings last night in the Chelsea containment zone," he said. "And, if you take the reports as gospel, a possible *seventeen* Type Twos. That's a staggering concentration."

"And how many deaths so far?" Barnes asked.

"Eight, including the three tramps. As before, the Sensitives report dangerous emanations, but the origin is not yet clear."

"Okay, once this demonstration is over, we'll head down to Chelsea. I'll want the agents split across the four sectors with the Sensitives organized into supporting bands that— Oh, *gawd*." Barnes had noticed our arrival. "Hold on a minute, Kipps."

"Evening, Inspector." Lockwood wore his widest smile. "Kipps."

"*They* aren't on the list, are they?" Kipps said. "Want me to run them off?"

Barnes shook his head; he took a sip of soup. "Lockwood, Miss Carlyle . . . To what do I owe the pleasure?"

Since he spoke with all the joy of a man giving a speech at his mother's funeral, "pleasure" was evidently a relative thing for Barnes. It wasn't that he *hated* us—we'd helped him out too often for that—but sometimes mild irritation went a long way.

"Just passing by," Lockwood said. "Thought we'd say hello. Looks like you have quite the gathering here. Most of the agencies in London are represented." His smile broadened. "Just wondering if you'd forgotten our invitations."

Barnes regarded us. The steam from his cup curled around his mustache fronds like mist in a Chinese bamboo forest. He took another sip. "No."

"Good soup, is it?" Lockwood asked, after a pause. "What sort?"

"Tomato." Barnes gazed into his cup. "Why? What's wrong with it? Not quality enough for you?"

"No, it looks very nice. . . . Particularly the bit on the end of your mustache. May I ask why DEPRAC hasn't included Lockwood and Co. in the whole Chelsea operation? If this outbreak's so dreadful, surely you could do with our assistance?"

"Don't think so." Barnes glared across at the crowd gathered beneath the Column. "It may be a national crisis, but we're not *that* desperate. Look around you. We've got plenty of talent here. Quality agents."

I looked. Some of the operatives standing close were familiar to me, kids with reputations. Others, less so. At the base of the steps, a group of pale girls in mustard jackets had been marshaled by an immensely fat man. By his dangling jowls, rolling belly, and self-importantly clenched buttocks, I recognized Mr. Adam Bunchurch, proprietor of that undistinguished agency.

Lockwood frowned. "I see the *quantity.* Quality, not so much." He leaned in, spoke softly. "Bunchurch? I mean, *come on.*"

Barnes stirred his soup with a plastic spoon. "I don't deny your talents, Mr. Lockwood. If nothing else, those pearly teeth of yours could light our way in the darkest alleys. But how many of you *are* there in your company? Still three? Exactly. And one of those is George Cubbins. Skilled as you and Miss Carlyle undoubtedly are, three more agents simply won't make any difference." He tapped his spoon on the edge of the cup and handed it to Kipps. "This Chelsea case is huge," he said. "It covers a massive area. Shades, Specters, Wraiths, and Lurkers—more and more of 'em appearing, and no sign of the central cause. Hundreds of buildings are under surveillance, whole streets being evacuated. . . . The public aren't happy about it—that's why they're holding this protest here tonight. We need numbers for this, and people who'll do what they're told. Sorry, but that's two excellent reasons to leave you out." He took a decisive sip of soup and cursed. "Ow! Hot!"

"Better blow on it for him, Kipps." Lockwood's expression had darkened as Barnes spoke; he turned away. "Well, have a good evening, Inspector. Give us a call when things get difficult."

We set off back toward the taxi.

"Lockwood! Wait!"

It was Kipps, stalking after us, the binder under his arm.

"Can I help you?" Lockwood spoke coolly, his hands shoved deep in his pockets.

"I'm not coming to crow," Kipps said, "though heaven knows

I could. I'm coming with advice—for Lucy, mainly, since I know *you're* unlikely to listen to sense."

"I don't need advice from you," I said.

Kipps grinned. "Oh, but you do. Listen, you're missing out. There're weird things going on in Chelsea. More Visitors than I've ever seen before. More *different* kinds, all close together—and dangerous, too, like they've been stirred up by something. Three nights running, my team's covered the same lane behind the King's Road. First two nights: nothing. Third night, a Raw-bones came out of the dark; nearly got Kate Godwin and Ned Shaw. A Raw-bones! From nowhere! Barnes doesn't have a clue why. No one does."

Lockwood shrugged. "I've offered to help. My offer's been rejected."

Kipps ran fingers through his close-cropped hair. "Of course it has. Because you're nobodies. What are you doing tonight? Some small, pathetic case, I'm sure."

"It's a ghost bringing terror to ordinary people," Lockwood said. "Is that pathetic? I don't think so."

Kipps nodded. "Okay, sure, but if you want to work on the important stuff, you need to be part of a *real* agency. Either of you could easily find a proper job at Fittes. In fact, Lucy's got an open invitation to join my team. I've told her that before."

I stared him down. "Yes, and you've heard my answer."

"Well, that's your choice," Kipps said. "But I say, scrub up, swallow your pride, and get stuck in. Otherwise, you're wasting your time." With a nod at me, he stalked away.

"Bloody nerve," Lockwood said. "He's talking nonsense, as usual." Even so, he said little in the taxi, and it was left to me to give renewed directions to 6, Nelson Street, Whitechapel, and our appointment with the veiled ghost.

It was a terraced house in a narrow lane. Our client, Mrs. Peters, had been watching out for us: the door swung open before I could knock. She was a young, nervous-looking woman, made prematurely gray by anxiety. She wore a thick shawl over her head and shoulders and clutched a large wooden crucifix in gloved hands.

"Is it there?" she whispered. "Is it up there?"

"How can we tell?" I said. "We haven't gone in yet."

"From the street!" she hissed. "They say you can see it there!"

Neither Lockwood nor I had thought to look at the window from outside. We stepped backward off the sidewalk and into the deserted street, craning our necks up at the two windows on the upper floor. The one above the door was lit; tiles indicated that it was a bathroom. The other window had no light within it, nor (unlike the other windows) did its glass reflect the glare from the streetlight two doors down. It was a dull, black space. And in it, very difficult to see, was the outline of a woman. It was as if she were standing right up against the window with her back to the street. You could see a dark dress and strands of long black hair.

Lockwood and I returned to the door. I cleared my throat. "Yes, it's up there."

"Nothing to worry about," Lockwood said, as we shuffled past Mrs. Peters into the narrow hall. He flashed her his fifty-percent smile, the reassuring one. "We'll go up and see."

Our client gave a whimper. "You understand why I can't sleep easy, Mr. Lockwood?" she said. "You understand now, don't you?"

Her eyes were frightened moons; she hovered close behind him, keeping the crucifix raised like a mask before her face. Its top almost went up Lockwood's nose when he turned around.

"Mrs. Peters," he said, gently pushing it down, "there's one thing you could do for us. Very important."

"Yes?"

"Could you pop into the kitchen and put the kettle on? Think you could do that?"

"Certainly. Yes, yes, I think I can."

"Great. Two teas would be marvelous, when you get a moment. Don't bring them up. We'll come down for them when we're finished, and I bet they'll still be hot."

Another smile, a squeeze of the arm. Then he was following me up the narrow staircase, our bags bumping against the wall.

There was no landing to speak of, more of an extended top step. Three doors: one for the bathroom, one for the back bedroom—and one for the bedroom at the front of the house. About fifty heavy iron nails had been hammered into this door; they were hung with chains and hanks of lavender. The wood itself was scarcely visible.

"Hmm, I wonder which one it is," I murmured.

"She's certainly not taking any chances," Lockwood agreed. "Oh, lovely—she's a hymn singer, too. Might've guessed."

Downstairs we'd heard the door close and footsteps in the kitchen, followed by a sudden snatch of shakily warbled song.

"Not sure *that* does any good," I said. I was checking my belt, loosening my rapier. "Or the crucifix. It's pointless if it's not iron or silver."

Lockwood had taken a thin chain out of his pack and was

looping it at the ready across one arm. He stood so close that he brushed against me. "Gives comfort, though. Half the things my parents brought back are the same. You know the bone-and-peacock-feather tambourine in the library? Balinese spirit-ward. Not an ounce of iron or silver on it. . . . Right, are we ready?"

I smiled at him. There was a horror behind that door. I would see it in seconds. Yet my heart sang in my breast, to be standing beside Lockwood in that house. All was as it should be in the world.

"Sure," I said. "I'm looking forward to that nice hot tea."

I closed my eyes and counted to six, to get my eyes ready for the transition from light to dark. Then I opened the door and stepped through.

Beyond the barrier of nails the air was cold, skin-bitingly so. It was as if someone had left a freezer door wide open. As Lockwood closed the door behind us, darkness swallowed us like we'd been immersed in ink. It wasn't just that the ceiling light was off—it was a more profound blackness. No light came in from the street outside.

But there had been no curtains at the window; it had been a bare piece of glass.

Something was blocking it, preventing light from coming through.

Away in that cold, cold inky dark, a person was weeping—a horrible sound, desolate yet wheedling, as of one spiritually bereft. The noise echoed oddly, as if we were in a vast and empty space.

"Lockwood," I whispered, "are you still there?"

I felt a friendly prod. "Right beside you. Chilly! Should have put my gloves on."

"I hear crying."

"She's at the window. In the pane. You see her?"

"No."

"You don't see her clawing hands?"

"No! Well, don't *describe* them to me. . . ."

"It's a good thing I don't have any imagination, or I'd be having nightmares tonight. She's wearing a lacy gray gown, and a sort of ragged veil over her face. Some kind of letter in one hand, spotted with something dark. Don't know what *that's* about—might be blood or tears. She's clutching it to her chest with her long, shriveled fingers. . . . Listen, I'm laying out the chains. Best thing we can do is smash the window. Smash it and burn it in the furnaces. . . ." His voice was calm; I heard the hasty clink of iron.

"Lockwood, wait." Standing blind, with air blistering my face, I composed myself—opened my ears and mind to deeper things. The crying sound receded just a little; in among it I heard a whisper, a tiny out-breath. . . .

"*Safe* . . ."

"What is?" I asked. "What's safe?"

"Lucy," Lockwood said, "you're not seeing what I'm seeing. You shouldn't be talking to this thing. It's bad." More chinking at my elbow; I could sense him moving forward. The whispers cut out, resumed, cut out again.

"Put the chains away," I snapped. "I can't hear."

"*Safe, sa-afe* . . ."

"Lucy—

"*Quiet.*"

"*I kept it safe.*"

"Where did you do that?" I said. "Where?"

"*There.*" As I turned to look, my Sight cleared. I caught the outline of the window in the corner of my eyes—and within it, darkness superimposed on darkness, a long-haired shape, hunch-shouldered, bent arms raised above the head as if caught in the midst of some frenzied dance or rite. The fingers were grotesquely long; they seemed to spear toward me across the room. I cried out. At my side I could feel Lockwood jumping forward, swinging his sword out and upward. The fingers broke, became separate beams of black light, scattered as if by a prism. Screaming filled my ears. Then the noise splintered like shattered glass. It fell away into silence.

My eardrums flexed; pressure left the room. Light filled it. It was only the pale pink streetlight from out on Nelson Road, but it cast everything into three soft, grainy dimensions. How small it was; not a vast echoing chamber at all. Just an ordinary room with a kids' bunk bed and chairs, and a dark armoire at my back. Warm air sucked in from the landing, caressing my ankles as it came under the door. Lockwood stood in front of me, rapier out, iron chain trailing through the broken window. Lights shone in the houses opposite. Broken glass jutted from the frame like teeth.

He spun around, staring, breathing hard. His disheveled hair hung dark and loose over one eye. "Are you all right?"

"Of course." I was looking at the armoire. "Why wouldn't I be?"

"She was attacking you, Lucy. You didn't see her face when her veil blew back."

"No, no," I said, "it was okay. She was just showing me where."

"Where what?"

"I don't know. I can't think. Shut up."

I waved him to one side, walked to the armoire. It was a big one, and old, too—the wood so dark it was almost black. It had decorative tracing on it, scuffed with ancient use. The door was stiff when I pulled it open. Inside hung children's clothes, overlaid with white moth-strips. I stared at them, scowling, then flicked them aside. The base of the interior was a single piece of wood. Its level seemed a full foot higher than the bottom of the armoire when viewed from outside. I took my penknife from my belt.

Lockwood was hovering uncertainly at my shoulder. "Luce . . ."

"It was showing me where it hid something," I muttered, "and I think—yes!"

Jamming the knife in a crack at the back did the trick. When I twisted, the panel came up. It took quite a bit of fiddling with angles, and chucking half the clothes out onto the floor, but I got the piece clear. I put away my knife and got my penlight out.

"There you are," I said. "See?"

Inside the cavity, bundled up: a dusty, folded piece of paper, fixed with a wax seal. Dark spots stained it. Tears or blood.

"She was showing me," I said again. "You didn't need to worry."

Lockwood nodded, his face still doubtful. He was studying me closely. "Maybe . . ." All at once he broke into a smile. "And better still, that tea will still be warm. I wonder if she's got biscuits, too."

Happiness filled me. My instinct had been right. Those few seconds had been all I needed to connect with the ghost and understand its purpose. Yes, Lockwood saw appearances, but I could see beyond that. I could uncover hidden things. He held the door open for me; I grinned at him, squeezed his arm. When we went out onto the staircase, we could hear the frail voice of Mrs. Peters, still singing in the kitchen.

Chapter 7

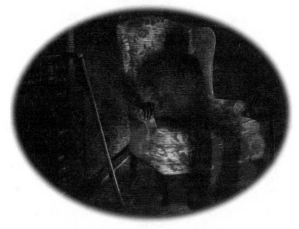

It turned out that the paper I'd found was the ghost's confession—or at least, it was the confession of someone named Arabella Crowley, written in 1837, a date that roughly matched the Specter's clothes. It seemed she'd smothered her husband in his sleep and gotten away with it. Her guilty conscience had kept her spirit from its rest; now that the document had been found and her crime revealed, the ghost was unlikely to return.

That was *my* interpretation, anyway. Lockwood took no chances. The following morning he had the fragments of windowpane incinerated in Clerkenwell Furnaces, and he encouraged Mrs. Peters to have the armoire broken up as well. Slightly to my annoyance, he repeated his orders to me not to try communicating with Visitors that weren't safely constrained. Of course I understood *why* he was cautious—his sister's fate loomed heavily over him—but to my mind, he overstated the risks. I was increasingly confident that my Talent could bypass such anxieties.

Over the next few days, new cases continued to come in thick and fast for Lockwood & Co. Lockwood, George, and I continued tackling them separately.

This led to problems. For a start, our hectic schedule meant that we had little time to research any job in advance, an omission that was always dangerous. One night Lockwood was nearly ghost-touched at a church near Old Street. He had cornered a Phantasm beside the altar and almost missed a second one creeping up from behind. If he had read up on the history of the church beforehand, he would have known it was haunted by murdered twins.

Fatigue was an issue, too. George was ambushed by a Lurker he hadn't spotted near Whitechapel Lock, and he only escaped by jumping headfirst into the canal. I fell asleep during a stakeout in a bakery and totally missed a charred ghost emerging from the oven. The sudden smell of roasted meat woke me just as it was reaching for my face with blackened fingers, much to the amusement of the whispering skull—which had been watching from its jar but hadn't said anything.

Our narrow escapes bothered Lockwood, who saw it as yet further proof that we were undermanned and overworked. No doubt he was right, but I was more interested in the freedom that my solitary expeditions gave me. I was waiting to make a proper psychic connection with a ghost—and it wasn't long before I got precisely that opportunity.

My appointment was with a family in apartment number 21 (South Block), Bermuda Court, Whitechapel. It was the housing project case, the one I'd been stuck with because of the dibs rule. It had been postponed twice due to client illness, and I nearly couldn't take it on the third time, either, because I'd already booked train tickets to go back home to see my family. I hadn't set eyes on my mother or sisters since coming to London eighteen months before. Though I viewed the trip with mixed feelings, Lockwood had given me a week off, and I wasn't going to rearrange *that* for a job that involved climbing lots of stairs.

I agreed to pop in the night before I left. Lockwood and George were busy with other cases, so I took the skull along. It provided company, of a disagreeable, unsavory sort. If nothing else, its jabbering helped keep the silences at bay.

Bermuda Court proved to be one of those big concrete housing projects they'd built after World War II. It had four blocks of apartments arranged around a grassy yard, each with external stairs and walkways running around the sides. The walkways acted as protection against the weather but also cast the doors and windows of the flats into perpetual shadow. The surface of the concrete was rough and ugly, dark with rain.

As I'd predicted, the elevators were out. Apartment 21 was only on the fifth floor, but I was out of breath when I arrived. My backpack, weighed down by a certain jar, was killing me.

The light was almost gone. I took a rasping breath and rang the bell.

"*Man, you're unfit,*" the skull said in my ear.

"Shut up. I'm in good shape."

"*You're wheezing like an asthmatic sloth. It would help to lose a little weight. Like that bit on your hips Lockwood's always going on about.*"

"What? He doesn't—"

But at that moment the clients answered the door.

There was a mother, gaunt and graying; a large, silent, slope-shouldered father; and three small kids, all under six, living together in a unit with five rooms and a narrow hall. Until recently there'd been a sixth person, too: the kids' grandfather. But he'd died.

Slightly to my surprise, the family didn't usher me into the living room, which is where such awkward conversations usually take place. Instead, they led me into a tiny kitchen at the end of the hall. Everyone crowded in; I was pushed so tight against the stove, I twice turned a dial with my bottom while I heard their story.

The mother apologized for the uncomfortable surroundings. They *did* have a living room, she said, but no one went in it after dark. Why? Because the grandfather's ghost was there. The children had seen him, every night since he'd died, still sitting in his favorite chair. What did he do? Nothing, just sat there. And beforehand, when he was alive? Mostly sat in that same chair, while he wasted away from the sickness he'd refused to get treated. He'd been skin and bones at the end. So light and papery, you'd think a draft would have carried him away.

Did they know why he'd returned? No. Could they guess what he wanted? No. And what had he been like, when alive? At *that* there was a lot of shuffling of feet. The uncomfortable silence told me much. He was a difficult man, the father said, not generous with his money. He was tight and grasping, the mother added. Would have sold us to the devil, if the devil offered cash. Sad to say, but it was true: they were glad he was gone.

But he *wasn't* gone, of course. Or, if he had left, he'd now come back.

They made me tea, and I drank it standing under the single bright light of the kitchen, with the children's eyes, as wide and green as those of cats, staring up at me. At last I set the cup down in the sink, and there was a sort of collective sighing that the moment had now come. With that they showed me to the living room. I stepped through onto the worn carpet and closed the door behind me.

It was a rectangular room, not large, centered on an electric fireplace. A metal guard ran around the hearth to keep the kids away. I did not switch on the light. A wide window looked out over the grassy wasteland behind the estate. There were lights on in the other units, and an old neon streetlight—left over from the times when ordinary people went out at night—on the path below. Its glow gave shape to my surroundings.

The furniture was of the kind that had been fashionable a couple of decades back. Hard, high-backed chairs with jutting armrests and spindly wooden legs; a low, stiff-sided sofa; side tables; a plain glass cabinet set in a corner. A deep-pile rug had been arranged before the fire. Nothing quite matched. I saw kids' games stacked in another corner and sensed they'd tried to tidy up for me.

It was chilly in the room—but not *ghost*-chilly. Not yet. I checked the thermometer on my belt. Fifty-three degrees. I listened but caught only a noise like distant static. I carried my bag over to the sofa below the window and set it quietly on the floor.

The jar, when I pulled it out, was glowing its palest green. The face rotated slowly, eyes glinting in the plasm.

"*Cramped little hovel,*" the voice whispered. "*Won't fit many ghosts in here.*"

My fingers floated over the lever in the jar's lid that would cut off communication. "If you've nothing useful to say . . ."

"*Oh, I'm not knocking it. Hell of a lot tidier than your place, that's for sure.*"

"They say this is where it happens."

"*And they're right. Someone died in here. The air's stained with it.*"

"You sense anything else, you let me know." I set the jar down on a side table.

Then I turned to face the high-backed chair opposite.

I already knew it was the one. You could guess from its domineering position, the way it sat closest to the TV in the corner, closest to the fireplace; all the other seats were less conveniently situated. Then there was the walking stick propped against the wall in the shadows beyond; the little side table marked with mug rings. The chair itself was decorated with some god-awful flowery pattern. The fabric had been worn white on the armrests, and repaired with leather patches near the ends. There was a dirty bald mark halfway up the back, too. The sponge of the seat cushion had been compressed thin with long usage; it was almost as if someone sat there still.

I knew what I *should* do. Agency practice was clear. I should get out the chains, or, failing that, a sensible amount of filings, and carefully encircle the chair. I should set up lavender crosses as a secondary barrier, and place myself at a safe distance from the likely manifesting point. George would certainly have done all that. Even

Lockwood, always more cavalier, would have whipped up a chain circle in double-quick time.

I did none of those things. I went as far as loosening the strap of my rapier and opening my bag, so that my tools were near at hand. Then I sat back on the sofa in the orange-pink darkness, crossed my ankles, and waited.

I wanted to test my Talent.

"*Naughty,*" the skull said in my mind. "*Does Lockwood know you're doing this?*"

I didn't reply; after a few more gibes, the ghost fell silent. Beyond the door came muffled noises—kids being told to shush, clinks of crockery; sounds of an evening meal being made. A smell of toast permeated the air. The family was *so* close by. In theory I was endangering them by not putting out defenses. The *Fittes Manual* was very clear on this. DEPRAC rules expressly forbade contact without adequate protection. In their eyes, I was committing a crime.

Outside the window the night grew black. The clients ate their meal; the children were ushered into one of the bedrooms. Toilets flushed. At the sink, someone was doing the washing up. I sat quietly in the dark, waiting for the show.

And it began.

Slowly, insensibly, a malign atmosphere began to invade the room. I heard the change in the quality of my breathing; I was taking quicker, shorter gulps of air. The hairs on my arms prickled with disquiet. Doubt rose in me; also anxiety and a strong feeling of self-loathing. I took some gum, chewed steadily, made the usual adjustments to counteract the malaise and creeping fear. The temperature dropped; the reading on my belt thermometer showed fifty degrees, then forty-eight. The quality of the light altered; the neon glow became fuzzier, as if struggling through molasses.

"Something's coming," the skull said.

I chewed and waited. I watched the empty armchair.

At nine forty-six precisely (I checked my watch), it was empty no longer. A faint outline became visible in the center of the chair. It was very weak, and scuffed and smudged in the middle, like a pencil drawing poorly erased. You could see what it was, though: the shrunken figure of an old man, sitting there. He exactly fitted the contours of the worn sponge seat; the outline of the head rested precisely over the grubby bald spot on the back. The apparition remained transparent, and I could still see every detail of the appalling flowery pattern of the cushions behind, but steadily its features grew more certain. It was a very small, shriveled man, bald except for a few long white hairs straggling behind his ears. I guessed he had once been fat, round-faced even; now the flesh on his cheeks had fallen in, leaving the skin hanging empty. His limbs, too, had wasted away; the fabric of his sleeves and trousers hung horribly flat. One bony hand lay cupped amid the folds and looseness of his old man's lap. The other curled at the end of the armrest like a spider.

He'd been a wicked thing, that was for sure. Everything about him projected a discomforting malice. The eyes glittered like black marbles; they were staring fixedly at me, and there was the faintest of smiles on the thin lips. My every instinct told me to defend myself: bring out the rapier, lob a salt-bomb or a canister of iron—do *something* to get the presence away from me. But it didn't move, and neither did I. We sat in our seats and stared at each other across the thick fur rug and the gulf that separates the living from the dead.

I had my hands folded in my lap. I cleared my throat. "Well," I said finally, "what is it that you want?"

No sound, no reply. The shape sat there, eyes shining in the dark.

Over on the side table, the skull in the jar remained silent and shrouded too; only the faintest green haze behind the glass showed that it was present, watching.

Without the protection of iron chains, the full chill of the apparition tore into me. The temperature at my belt was down to forty-four degrees; it would be colder still near the chair. But the *degree* of cold isn't really the point; it's where it comes from. Ghost chill is a fierce, dry cold; you can feel it sucking the life and energy from your bones. I bore it. I didn't move at all, but just stared at the old man.

"If you have a purpose," I said, "you might as well tell it to me."

Just the silence and the glittering of the eyes, like starlight in the dark.

No real surprise. It wasn't a Type Three, scarcely even a Type Two; it couldn't speak, couldn't communicate in any obvious way.

Even so . . .

"No one else is going to listen," I said. "Better take this chance while you can."

I opened my mind, tried to empty it of sensation, see if I detected anything new. Even an echoing mess of emotion, like I'd gotten from the Changer at Lavender Lodge, might be enough to set me on the right track. . . .

From the chair came a scratchy rustling of fabric, a *pick-pick-pick*ing sound, like cloth being teased and pulled by the tip of someone's nail. I heard shallow breathing, a person muttering under their breath. My skin crawled. I couldn't take my eyes off the smiling apparition in the chair. The sounds came again—muffled, but very close.

"Is that it?" I asked. "Is that what you're telling me?"

A crash in the corner—I sprang up in fright, scrabbling for my rapier. The ghost was gone. The chair was empty; the squashed seat, the worn patch, everything exactly as before. Except for the walking stick, which had toppled over, cracking against the fireplace.

I checked the time—then rechecked it with something like alarm. *Ten twenty?* That was weird: according to the watch, the apparition had been present for more than half an hour, yet it had felt like scarcely a minute to me. . . .

"*Did you get it?*" The skull's voice jerked me back into action. The face in the jar had re-emerged, nostrils flaring smugly. "*Bet you didn't. I did. I know, and I'm not telling.*"

"What is it with you?" I said. "You're like a toddler. Yes, of course I got it."

I rose, crossed to the door, and switched on the light, ignoring shrill protests from the jar. The evil atmosphere had vanished from the room. Under the ceiling light, the outdated shabbiness of the furniture was revealed in all its muted oranges and browns. I looked at the stack of kids' games: Scrabble, Monopoly, and the Rotwell Agency's Ghost Hunter—that one where you have to remove the plastic bones and bits of ectoplasm without setting off the buzzer. Battered boxes, secondhand games. The house of an ordinary family without much cash.

He was a difficult man. Not generous with his money. . . .

I walked over to the chair.

"*You haven't a clue, have you?*" the ghost called. "*Tell you what: let me out of this jar, and I'll happily spill the beans. Come on, Lucy. Can't argue with that for a deal.*"

"Don't try to flutter your eyes at me. It doesn't work with empty sockets."

I bent beside the chair, inspecting the nearest armrest. The patch at the end was made of some kind of imitation leather, more plasticky than anything. It had been roughly sewn onto the original fabric, but in places the stitches had come undone, and one corner was curling up like the edge of a stale sandwich. I pushed at the edge experimentally, slipped my fingers underneath, and lifted it. There was a layer of foam stuffing, which came away easily. Then you could see the tightly wound wads of banknotes compressed into the space beneath.

I grinned at the skull over my shoulder. "Sorry. Looks like no deal for you today."

The face grimaced and vanished in a starburst of peeved plasm. "*That,*" its voice said, lingering, "*was just a lucky guess.*"

I took my vacation and went back north, to the town where I was born. I saw my mother, I saw my sisters; I stayed with them for a few days. It wasn't the easiest of homecomings. None of them had ever traveled more than thirty miles away in their lives, let alone gone to live in London. They looked askance at my clothes and shining rapier, frowned at the smallest changes to my accent. The scent and aura of the city hung around me. I spoke with an assurance they didn't recognize about places and people that meant nothing to them. For my part, I found them slow and hidebound by their fear.

Even in good weather, they went out only reluctantly; evenings saw them cowering by the fire. I grew impatient, and crosser still when they scarcely argued back. There was something in their sheeplike resignation that made me want to scream. What kind of life *was* it, to sit dumbly in the dark, in living fear of death? Better to go out and face it, head-on.

I left them a day earlier than planned. I had an itch to get back to London.

It was an early-morning train. I sat in a window seat, watching the tapestry flash by: the fields and woods, the spires of hidden villages, the chimney stacks and ghost-lamps of the ports and mining towns. Everywhere you looked, the Problem hung invisible over England. Brand-new cemeteries at crossroads and in wild, abandoned places; crematoria on the edges of cities; curfew bells in market squares. Superimposed upon it all, my face blurred in and out of view. I glimpsed the child I'd been when I first came down to London, and the operative I'd now become, a girl who spoke with ghosts. More than spoke: who understood their desires.

My encounter with the miser's ghost had changed everything for me. It had been that strange sensation I felt afterward, walking back through Whitechapel, with all my tools still on my back, and all those unused flares and canisters jangling in my belt. I hadn't needed any of them. I'd dealt with the Visitor without resorting to weapons or even defenses. No salt, no lavender; not an ounce of iron spilled. How many times, in any agent's career, had a successful investigation ended in quite so neat a way?

The old man in the chair had been unpleasant, and his ghost

still radiated that blackness of soul. Yet he had come back with a coherent purpose, a desire to make restitution—to reveal the hidden money to his heirs. My calm interrogation had given him the chance to do precisely that. If I'd blasted him in the usual way, that outcome would not have been possible. But I'd done it by giving my Talent free rein.

There were obvious dangers attached to my new approach, but great advantages, too; and as I gazed out through the window a new way of working began to open up in front of me.

The skull in the jar was still the exceptional case, the Type Three ghost with which full communication was possible. But I was coming to believe that there were other ways of bridging the gap between ordinary Visitors and the living.

My hunch relied on two things: that many ghosts had some objective in returning; and that, if you calmly sought to discover this, they would leave you alive long enough to find it out. The first part of the statement was uncontroversial—it had been accepted since the days of ghost-hunting pioneers Marissa Fittes and Tom Rotwell fifty years before. But the second part flew in the face of orthodox opinion. Every modern agency sought to *constrain* the ghost as a matter of first principles; when this was done, the Source could be found and destroyed, thus removing the ghost as well. It was universally assumed that the ghost would resent this process, and seek to prevent it. Since an angry ghost could quickly kill you, agents weren't inclined to mess about.

In some cases, weapons were certainly necessary. Could the terrible thing in the attic at Lavender Lodge ever truly have been reasoned with? Almost certainly not. But others—I thought of the sad Shades thronging in the boardinghouse, the veiled Specter in the bedroom window—were desperate for connection.

And I could provide that, however imperfectly.

What I needed was for Lockwood to let me experiment some more. He would be resistant—naturally so, because of what had happened to his sister—but I felt I would bring him around. At this thought, my mood lifted. The bulb of sadness that I'd been nurturing since visiting my mother shrank deep inside and was forgotten. I would talk to Lockwood and George about my ideas when I got home. I needed to share them with my friends.

Back in London, I asked the cab to stop by Arif's store at the end of Portland Row and bought a selection of iced buns. It was past eleven; Lockwood and George would be just about ready for a snack by now. I was back a day early. Since they wouldn't be expecting me, I could make my arrival an extra-nice surprise.

But there was a surprise waiting for *me* when I entered the house. It made me stop in amazement, keys held frozen in my hand. The hall had been vacuumed, the coat-rack tidied; the rapiers, umbrellas, and walking sticks arranged in size order in their pot. Even the crystal skull lantern on the key table had been dusted and polished so it shone.

I couldn't believe it. They'd actually done it. They'd tidied! They'd tidied up for me.

I put my bag down softly and tiptoed into the kitchen.

They were in the basement by the sounds of it, and they were in a *very* good mood. I could hear their bubbling laughter even from the kitchen. It made me smile to hear them. Perfect. The buns would go down well.

I didn't hurry. I made some tea, put the buns on our second-best plate (I couldn't find the best one), arranged them so Lockwood's favorites—the ones with almond icing that he rarely allowed himself—were on top, and set everything neatly on the tray.

I opened the door with a foot, nudged it wider with my hip, and pattered lightly down the iron stairs.

Happiness bloomed inside me. *This* was what it was all about. Portland Row was home. My real family was here.

I ducked through the arch into the office and stopped, still smiling. There they were, Lockwood and George, bent forward attentively on either side of my desk. They were laughing heartily.

Between them, sitting in my chair, was a shapely, dark-skinned girl.

She had black hair worn long at the shoulder, a pretty, roundish face, and a kind of dark blue pinafore dress with a nice white top underneath it. She looked very new and fresh and shiny, like someone had popped her out of a plastic case that morning. She sat straight-backed and elegant, and didn't seem particularly discomposed by having George and Lockwood draped so close. On the contrary, she was smiling too, and laughing a little bit. Mainly, though, she was listening to the boys laugh.

On the table were three mugs of tea and also our best plate, scattered with the remains of several almond buns.

I stood there, looking at the three of them, holding the tray.

The girl saw me first. "Hello." She said this in a mildly inquiring sort of way.

George's head jerked up; the fatuous grin on his face at once shrank into noncommittal blankness. Lockwood's smile tightened; he gave an odd little skip, a sort of sidling sidestep backward, then moved hastily toward me. "Lucy, *hello*. What a lovely surprise. You're back early! How was your trip? Nice weather, I hope?"

I stared at him.

"So . . ." he said. "Good journey? Oh—more buns? How lovely."

"There's a girl," I said. "A girl sitting in my chair."

"Oh, don't worry! That's only till the new desk arrives." He gave a light laugh. "Should be tomorrow, Wednesday at the very latest. Nothing to worry about. . . . We didn't expect you back so soon, you see."

"A new desk?"

"Yes, for Holly." He cleared his throat, smoothed back his hair. "Well now, where are my manners? This is a time for introductions! Holly, this is Lucy Carlyle, the *perfect* agent, whom you've heard *so* much about. And Lucy"—Lockwood gave me his biggest smile— "let me introduce you to Holly Munro. Our new assistant."

III

The Bloody Footprints

Chapter 8

It didn't help that Lockwood was entirely unapologetic when I cornered him in the office. Ms. Munro had left to catch the afternoon bus home. George, more than usually eager to stretch his legs, had accompanied her in case she got lost on the way to the stop, which was all of six doors down the street.

"What the hell happened?" I demanded. "I was only away three days!"

Lockwood was sorting through the papers on his desk. I noticed they had all been neatly paper-clipped, and organized with brightly colored labels. He didn't look up at me. "I thought you'd be happy. You're the one who suggested we get in a supporting member of staff, rather than a full-blown agent."

I stared at him, amazed. "So it was *my* idea to hire this girl? Please!"

"I told you we needed help. I told you we were going to find someone."

"Sure, and you waited until I was out of town to do it."

"Not at all! That's just a coincidence. Of course I didn't plan to get someone while you were away. The most I thought was that we could maybe arrange a few interviews, and I only had time to think of *that* because it's been so quiet these last few days." His eyes darted briefly up; he tried an appealing smile. "Obviously that's on account of you, Luce—we couldn't investigate new cases with you gone. Your contributions are just too vital."

"Oh, spare me. And she just jumped out of nowhere, did she?"

"Well, there's a funny story about that. I didn't even need to advertise. I bumped into a couple of Rotwell agents, and they gave me Holly's name. She'd been let go by their agency only last week. I got her in, and she seemed just the ticket, so . . ."

"So it's 'Holly' already," I said, interrupting him. "I seem to remember I was 'Ms. Carlyle' for months after I joined."

Lockwood had been more or less addressing his own neck so far. Now he finally looked me in the eye. "Well, that's because of you. I've become a bit less formal this past year. I'm just trying to help her settle in."

I nodded. "I saw that. If you and George had been settling her in any closer, you'd have snagged your noses on her earrings." A thought occurred to me. "Did you test her with the skull?"

"What?"

"Did you show her the skull? You know, like you did in *my* first interview? And all those other objects you made me assess? You gave me a really hard time."

Lockwood took a careful breath. He tapped long nervous fingers on the desktop. "Actually, we didn't. But the point is, she's not going to be a front-line operative, is she? She's an administrative assistant. Her job is simply to man the fort here. I asked her a few questions, of course I did, but she showed me her résumé, and that was enough."

"Really? It must have been a nice one."

"It was very presentable."

"So what can she do, then?"

"Well, she was at Rotwell for years, working pretty high up—for one of Steve Rotwell's deputies, I think—so she's clearly well qualified as a personal assistant. She has some psychic Talent, too. Not as much as us, obviously—but, in a pinch, in an emergency only, she could possibly help us in the field. Also, she seems to know a lot of important people, which might be useful to us one day." He cleared his throat and deposited himself back on his battered leather seat. The usual cloud of dust did not rise up. "All in all, Luce, I think we're very lucky to get her."

"She's cleaned your chair," I observed.

"You make it sound like that's bad. Yes, one of Holly's main roles will be to keep the place tidy and well organized. In fact, the first thing she did on Monday was roll up her sleeves, put on an apron, and do the whole housemaid bit. George and I couldn't believe our eyes." He caught my gaze and threw up his hands. "Well, isn't that good? One more chore off our list. And she even got us a nice new vacuum cleaner! You were always moaning about lugging that old one up to the attic."

"*What?* She's not been in my bedroom too?"

"Anyway"—Lockwood suddenly became interested in his desk

again; he reached out hurriedly for the topmost paper—"I'd better read this, I'm afraid. Some new DEPRAC regulations just came in. Important stuff. Needs a rapid response, and Holly wants me to get it to the mailbox by five . . ." He looked at me full-on then, serious-eyed and quiet. "I know it's all a bit sudden, Lucy, but you need to give it a chance. Holly's here to help us. You're the agent; she's the assistant. She'll do what we ask, and make life simpler for us. It'll work out well."

I took a deep breath. "Guess it'll have to." After all, we *did* need some help. Things *could* be made simpler. Still . . .

"Thanks, Lucy." Lockwood *really* smiled, then. The sudden warmth of its radiance made my misgivings seem mean and need-lessly hostile. "Trust me," he said. "It'll be fine. Soon you and Holly will be getting on like a house on fire."

It certainly didn't take our new admin long to make an impact. According to Lockwood, who seemed to know all her statistics, she was eighteen, but in raw competence and efficiency she seemed a good deal older. She arrived at Portland Row each day on the dot of nine thirty, letting herself in with a key. By the time we slouched down for breakfast an hour or so later, whatever debris had been left from the previous night's 3 a.m. post-work snacking had been spirited away. Our work belts hung from their hooks beside the iron stairs; our chains had been oiled, our bags restocked with appropriate levels of salt and iron filings. Our kitchen was spotless, the table set; a golden stack of hot buttered toast waited on the plate. Holly Munro herself was never present when we got there; before we arrived, she always diplomatically removed herself to the office below. She thus allowed us time to wake and compose ourselves, and also cleverly avoided the very real possibility of seeing George without his pants.

The very first day had set the tone. We'd had several difficult cases the night before, and were in fragile shape. Coughing, scratching, we made our sorry way to the office to find Ms. Munro dusting the suit of armor by Lockwood's desk. She was full of perk and polish; a bunny rabbit sitting in a chive bed could not have been more chipper. She bounded forward. "Good morning," she said. "Made you all some tea."

There were three cups on the tray, and the tea in each was different. One was a milky brown, just how I like it. One was strong and teak-colored, which is Lockwood's preferred taste, and the last (George's) had the strength and consistency of the wet earth you find in exhumed graves. In other words, they were perfect. We took them.

Holly Munro held a piece of paper neatly inscribed with a short list. "It's been a busy morning already. You've had five new requests so far."

Five! George groaned; I sighed. Lockwood ruffled his unkempt hair. "Go on, then," he said. "Tell us the worst."

Our assistant smiled, pushing a stray twist of hair back behind a shell-like ear. "It's really not too terrible. There's an interesting-sounding Visitor in Bethnal Green, something that seems to be half-buried in the sidewalk yet hobbles at great speed along the Roman Road, trailing a cloak of shadow."

"Following the ancient level of the street," George grunted. "Another legionary. We're getting more and more of those."

Ms. Munro nodded. "Then there's a strange hammering in a butcher's cellar; four orbs of yellow light revolving outside a house in Digwell; and two cobwebby ladies seen in Victoria Park, who dissolve as witnesses approach."

"Stone Knockers," I said. "Cold Maidens. And the lights are probably Wisps."

There was a glum silence. "That's the weekend taken care of," George said.

Lockwood nursed his tea dispiritedly. "The legionary's okay, but the others are pretty yawnsome. More annoying than dangerous. They're all Type Ones, scarcely even that, but they'll take a lot of time and effort to quell."

"Quite," Ms. Munro said brightly. "Which is why I declined them all. Except for the Bethnal Green legionary, which I've penciled in for Tuesday week."

We stared at her. "Declined them?" Lockwood said.

"Of course. You're taking on far too much; you have to save your energy for proper cases. The Stone Knocker can be subdued by hanging rosemary in the cellar, while the Wisps and Cold Maidens are outdoors, and so can be safely ignored. Don't worry about the clients. I'll send them typed instructions for dealing with their issues. Now, why don't you tell me about last night's cases while you drink your tea?"

We told her, and she sat there making notes to be recorded in our casebook. Then she typed up our invoices and went out to mail them, more or less while we were still sitting around in a daze. Afterward she took more calls, interrogated prospective clients over the phone, made arrangements for interviews, and scheduled a couple of evening visits. She did it all efficiently and well.

So well, in fact, that within days we found our diary becoming more manageable. As she'd promised, all the really small-time things—stuff that could be dealt with by ordinary people using salt, charms, and wards—were weeded out. Lockwood, George and I were suddenly able to have nights off, and work together on most cases again.

It was impressive, and I did my best to appreciate Holly Munro, really I did. There was much to appreciate. In so many ways it was hard to find fault with her at all.

Her manners and appearance were exemplary. She always sat up straight, with her neat little shoulders back, and a bright-as-a-button expression on her wide-eyed face. Her black hair was immaculate; there was never any grave-grit under the manicured nails of her small and pretty hands. She wore clothes well. Her skin looked as smooth and delectable as coffee-colored marble; it had the kind of flawlessness that made you acutely aware of all the fascinating blemishes you called your own. Come to think of it, *everything* about her had this effect. She was all smooth and clear and shiny, like a mirror; and like a mirror she reflected back your imperfections.

I was very polite to her, just as she was very polite to me. She was good at being polite, in much the same way as she was excellent at keeping the office floor swept and dusting the masks in the hallway. No doubt she also brushed her teeth well every night and cleaned behind her ears. We all have talents, and those were hers.

Our relationship consisted of lots of polite little encounters in which Holly's efficiency rubbed up against my way of doing things. Here's a fairly typical exchange:

H MUNRO (*sweetly, batting eyelashes*): Lucy, hi. Sorry to bother you, I know you're working hard.

ME (*looking up from my issue of* True Hauntings; *I'd been up until four the night before*): Hi, Holly.

H MUNRO: Just wondering. Would you like me to move your clothes from the drying line in the storeroom? I'm just tidying up in there.

ME (*smiling*): No, no, it's fine. I'll do it sometime.

H MUNRO (*beaming*): Okay. Only I've ordered a new set of shelves for that wall. It's coming today, and I wouldn't want the deliverymen to mess your stuff up. I could fold everything for you, if you like. It's no trouble.

ME: Don't worry. (*I was a big girl. I could fold my own pants.*) I'll do it later.

H MUNRO: Brilliant. The men are coming in about twenty minutes. Just so you know.

ME (*trilling laugh*): Oh, okay . . . I'll do it now, then.

H. M.: Thanks *so* much.

ME: No, no. Thank *you*.

All the while, Lockwood and George would be somewhere near at hand, smiling genially like two pipe-smoking dads watching their offspring playing happily in the garden. I could almost see them congratulating each other that their new employee was turning out so well.

And of course she would, in the end. I just needed to give her time.

One individual who didn't share this common view was the skull in the jar. Holly knew of its existence—she frequently had to dust around it—but not that it was a Type Three that could communicate with me. The skull didn't like her. Her arrival in the office each day was the cue for much elaborate rolling of eyes and puffing out of cheeks behind the silver-glass. On several occasions I caught the ghost making appalling faces directly behind her back, and then winking at me broadly as she turned around.

"What's with you?" I growled. It was late morning, and I was having a restorative bowl of cereal at my desk. "You're supposed to be a secret, remember? You know the rules: minimal manifestations, no rude faces, and absolutely *no* talking."

The ghost looked wounded. "*I wasn't talking, was I? Do you call this* talking? *Or this?*" It pulled a rapid series of grotesque expressions, each one worse than the last.

I shielded my eyes with my spoon hand. "Will you stop that? The milk's curdling in my cereal. You need to quit the tomfoolery when she's around, or I'll lock you up in the storeroom." I stabbed at the granola decisively. "Understand, skull: Holly Munro is one of the team, and you need to treat her with respect."

"*Like* you *do, you mean?*" The goggling face grinned at me. Today its two sets of fangs alternated from the top and bottom gums like the teeth of a zipper.

I took a mouthful. "I've got no problem with Holly."

"*Hark at you, Queen Fibber. I've told porkies in my time, but that shocks me something awful. You can't stand her.*"

I could feel my cheeks flushing; I collected myself. "Er, that's a slight exaggeration. She's too bossy, maybe, but—"

"*Bossy, nothing. I've seen the way you stare at her when she's not looking. Like you're trying to pin her bleeding to the wall with the power of your eyes.*"

"I *so* don't do that! You're talking complete nonsense, as usual." I returned primly to my breakfast, but the flavor had gone out of my granola. "What about you?" I said. "What's *your* problem with her?"

The ghost looked disgusted. "*She's got no time for me. Wants me gone.*"

"Well, don't we all?"

"*Ghosts aren't tidy enough for her. You see how she's neatened up that collection of relics downstairs? All those haunted trophies you've collected? Half of them tossed out, the others made safe, with new iron locks on the cases. . . . She likes everything under her thumb. Who knows, perhaps that includes A. Lockwood, Esquire. Which is maybe another reason you aren't so happy, eh?*" It gave me an evil sidelong grin.

"Absolute twaddle." And of course it was. Anything the skull said was false, by definition. It had often tried to stir up trouble in the house. I was fine with Holly. Really I was. So she was well-proportioned. So her hair was all glossy. So she looked as if her lips had never been the wrong side of a second doughnut in her life. What was any of that to me? I didn't care one bit. She wasn't perfect, by any means. Probably, for example, if I'd thought hard enough about it, I could have found something flawed about the width of her thighs. But I didn't need to. None of that was important. I was an agent. I had other things to do.

I left the room soon after. I wasn't that hungry anyway.

I went to the rapier room to practice a few moves on Esmeralda and let off a little steam. It wasn't long before our new assistant herself put her head around the arch.

"Hi, Lucy."

"Hey, Holly." I continued shuffling around the dummy, feinting with the rapier, sneakers sending up little clouds of chalk dust. My sweatshirt was pretty damp. I was timing myself, trying to keep going for ten minutes without stopping. It was good exercise as much as anything.

"Gosh, you *do* look warm," Holly Munro said. She wore her usual white shirt and pinafore dress and was just as unrumpled and sweat-free as when she'd shown up for work, hours before. "I've been calling around, talking to old Rotwell contacts. They've put me in touch with an exciting new client. *Not* from Whitechapel."

I stood back, wiping wet bangs out of my face. "Well?"

"Don't let me interrupt you. She's coming in tomorrow morning. Very urgent."

"Did she say what it's about?"

" 'A matter of life and death,' apparently. Something nasty in her house. But she's arriving at ten o'clock sharp."

"Okay." I steadied the dummy on its chain and resumed pacing around it, keeping my weight balanced on my toes.

"You'll be there?"

I made a series of small stabbing motions on either side of Esmeralda's battered old bonnet. "Well, where else am I going to be? I live here."

"Of course. I just thought maybe ten's a bit early for you."

"Not at all. I'm always up, aren't I?"

"Oh, I know. But not always dressed. It might put the lady off if you were sitting there in those big saggy old gray pj's of yours." She gave a little laugh.

"Don't worry, Holly," I said. "It's no problem. No problem at *all.*"

I thrust at Esmeralda and skewered her right through the middle of her neck. The dummy swerved away with the impact, twisting the rapier clean out of my hand. I stood there, hands falling to my sides, watching it swing.

"Ooh, glad *I'm* not a ghost," Holly Munro said. A tinkling laugh, a waft of perfume. She was gone.

Chapter 9

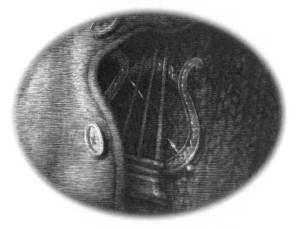

A t precisely ten o'clock the following morning, our client
arrived. She was a Miss Fiona Wintergarden, a tall, willowy,
somewhat desiccated lady in (I judged) her early fifties. Her
hair, cut short and sensibly, was approaching rain-cloud gray. She
wore a cream twinset and long black skirt, and a pair of small golden
spectacles on the crest of her angular nose. She sat perched on the
lip of the sofa with her knees tight together and thin hands folded
in her lap. Her spine was ramrod straight, her bony shoulders forced
back against the fabric of her cardigan like the stumps of dragon
wings. If she'd had a bust, it would certainly have been thrust forward; as it was, the effect was aggressively demure.

The employees of Lockwood & Co. positioned themselves
around her. Lockwood reclined in his usual chair. George took the
seat to the right of the coffee table, and I the one opposite. Our
newest member, Ms. Holly Munro, sat slightly back from the rest of

us, legs neatly crossed and with a notebook and pen held ready on her knee. She would take notes on the meeting. Eighteen months before, when I'd just joined the company, I'd had a similar role. But I'd never thought to sit so close behind Lockwood that I could lean forward and speak quietly in his ear or, by virtue of my proximity to the leader, tacitly become the second-most important person in the room.

There were thick slabs of carrot cake on the table, beside the obligatory tea. This, I thought, was a miscalculation on George's part. New company etiquette dictated that we couldn't eat cake unless our client did, and Miss Wintergarden didn't seem like a carrot cake type of person. And indeed she ignored the plate when it was offered to her and only sipped once at her cup before setting it aside.

The fire in the hearth leaped and sparked, casting angular red shadows along the side of our client's face. "It is good of you to see me at such short notice, Mr. Lockwood," she said. "I am at my wit's end and simply don't know what to do."

Lockwood gave an easy smile. "By choosing us, madam, you are already halfway to a solution. Thank you for selecting Lockwood and Co.—we know there are many alternatives out there."

"Indeed. I tried several others, but they are not taking on new customers at present," Miss Wintergarden said. "Regrettably, there seems to be an ongoing kerfuffle in Chelsea that is being given priority by all the major agencies, and I was forced to cast my eyes a little lower than I would otherwise have done. Still, I understand you are considered reasonably competent, and also cheap." She gazed at him over the rims of her spectacles.

Lockwood's smile had become a trifle stiff. "Er, we endeavor to give satisfaction as far as we are able. . . . May I ask the nature of your trouble?"

"I am being plagued by a supernatural phenomenon."

"Naturally. Which is?"

The lady's voice sank low; a thin wattle of loose skin, hanging beneath her jaw, wobbled briefly as she spoke. "Footprints. Bloody footprints."

George looked up. "Well, I'm sorry you're upset."

Miss Wintergarden blinked. "No. I mean they're *bloody*. Footprints made of blood."

"How fascinating." Lockwood sat forward in his chair. "This is in your house?"

"I fear so."

"Have you seen the prints yourself?"

"Certainly not!" She sounded almost offended. "They were first reported by the youngest members of my staff—the boot boy, the cook's lad, and others. None of the adults have witnessed them, but that hasn't stopped a ridiculous panic from spreading through the house. We have had *scenes*, Mr. Lockwood. Scenes and resignations! I was very put out by it. I mean, they're servants. Servants and children. I don't pay them to indulge in squealing hysterics."

She glared around, as if daring any of us to disagree. As I met her gaze, I took away the impression of a humorless, rather unintelligent person, for whom only prim correctness and snobbery kept the terrors of the world at bay. That's what I picked up from a quick look in her eyes, anyhow. No doubt she thought I was great.

Lockwood wore his gentle, placatory face, which he often used on Whitechapel housewives. "I entirely understand," he said. "Perhaps you had better tell us all about it from the beginning." He lifted his hand as if to pat her reassuringly on the knee, but then thought better of it.

"Very well," Miss Wintergarden said. "I live at Fifty-four Hanover Square in central London. My father, Sir Rhodes Wintergarden, bought the property sixty years ago. He was a financier; I expect you will have heard of him. As his only daughter, I inherited it on his death and have remained there ever since. In twenty-seven years, Mr. Lockwood, I have never once been troubled by ghosts. I do not have time for them! I do a great deal of work for charitable organizations, and host functions that are attended by many important people. The head of the Sunrise Corporation is a personal friend of mine! I cannot allow my house to gain a dubious reputation, which is why I have come here today."

None of us said anything, but there was a perceptible quickening of interest in the room. Hanover Square was an expensive location; if Miss Wintergarden was truly wealthy and well connected, success with this case might give Lockwood & Co. the very push it needed. Lockwood in particular seemed newly alert.

"Can you describe your home?" he asked.

"It is a Regency town house," our client said, "in one corner of the square. It has five stories—a basement level, containing the cellars and kitchens; the ground floor, which holds the reception rooms; an upper level with my personal chambers—a library, music room, and so forth; the third-floor bedrooms; and finally the attic level, where many of my staff—those who bother to remain!—have cots. The stories are connected by a curving staircase, a notable construction in mahogany and elm, designed by the architects Hobbes and Crutwell for the first owner of the house."

I shuffled in my chair. Lockwood's smile had faded, and George was staring longingly at the cake. We knew the signs; Miss Wintergarden, like so many of our clients, enjoyed the sound of her own voice. We would be here for a while.

"Yes, the staircase is easily the finest on the square," she continued, "with the most elegant and deep stairwell. When I was a child, my father tied my pet mouse to a handkerchief and launched it from the top. It parachuted down—"

"Excuse me, Miss Wintergarden." Holly Munro had glanced up from her notepad. "We need to hurry you a little. Mr. Lockwood is extremely busy, and we only have an hour scheduled for this meeting. Only *relevant* historical matters need be discussed here. Let's keep to the essentials, please." She gave a brisk smile, one that turned on and off as if a kid were fiddling with the switch, and bent her head to the pad.

There was a pause, during which Lockwood shifted around in his chair to stare at his assistant. We were all staring. George even had his mouth wide open, which made me relieved that he hadn't yet had any cake. "Er, yes," Lockwood said. "Well, I suppose we *do* need to muddle on. These footprints, Miss Wintergarden. Tell us about them."

The lady had been gazing contemplatively at Holly Munro. She pursed her lips. "I was about to do so, and my speaking of the staircase was entirely relevant, for it is there that the bloody footprints are found."

"Ah! Describe them."

"They are the marks of bare feet ascending the stairs. They are spattered about with blood. They appear sometime after midnight, last several hours, and fade before dawn."

"On which part of the staircase are they located?"

"They begin in the basement and stretch certainly as high as the third floor." The lady frowned. "Perhaps higher."

"What do you mean?"

"The prints apparently become less clear as they go up. Near the basement the full outline of the foot is visible, then the stains become smaller—it's just the toes and balls of the feet you see."

"Interesting," I said. "Someone going on tiptoe?"

"Or running," George suggested.

Miss Wintergarden gave a shrug, shoulder blades slicing against cardigan. "I am only reporting what the children said, and their accounts are incoherent. You would do better to look for yourselves."

"We shall," Lockwood said. "Are the prints found elsewhere in the building?"

"No."

"What surface do the stairs have?"

"Wooden boards."

"No carpet or rugs?"

"None."

He tapped his fingers together. "Do you know of a possible cause for this haunting? Some tragedy or crime of passion that occurred in the house?"

The lady bristled. She could not have been more shocked if Lockwood had sprung up, vaulted over the coffee table, and punched her in the nose. "Certainly not! To my knowledge, my home has never been the site of any violent or passionate incident whatsoever." She pushed out her meager chest defiantly.

"I can well believe it. . . ." Lockwood was silent for a moment, staring across at the dwindling fire. "Miss Wintergarden, when you phoned yesterday you said this was a matter of life and death. The prints you describe are certainly disturbing, but I don't think they can be the whole story. Is there something you're not telling us?"

The cast of the woman's face changed. Her haughtiness diminished; she looked both tired and wary. "Yes, there has been an . . . accident. You must understand that it was not my fault. The prints had never been a problem, no matter *what* the servants said." She shook her head. "I acted entirely correctly. It was not my fault."

"Hold on. So the footprints have been appearing for some time, then?" I said.

"Oh yes, for years." She glared at me. Her voice carried a defensive ring. "Do not think I have been neglecting my duty, young madam! The prints, and their accompanying phenomena, have always been faint and insubstantial. And they came so very rarely. No one was ever harmed by them. Aside from the warblings of a few servants, no one even noticed they were there. In recent weeks, however, they began to be reported more frequently. Finally"—she looked away from us—"it was a nightly occurrence. So I hired three night-watch children to keep an eye on things."

We glanced at one another. Night-watch kids have Talent, but they're not as strong or sensitive as agents. And they aren't half as well armed, either.

"You didn't think of mentioning this to DEPRAC?" Holly Munro asked.

"The phenomena amounted to almost nothing!" Miss Wintergarden cried. "I did not see the need to bring in agents at that stage." She plucked at the fabric of her pullover as if it were sticking to her shoulder. "There are major hauntings all over London! You cannot trouble the authorities over every Wisp or Glimmer, and I have a reputation to keep up. I certainly did not want dirty DEPRAC boots tramping around my house."

Lockwood gazed at her. "So what happened?"

She tapped a small white fist irritably against her lap; her agitation remained, but she was mastering it once more. "Well, I ask you, what did I employ the watch-children *for*? It was their job to ensure that things did not get out of hand. I gave them the simple task of observing the stairs, of understanding the nature of the apparition. I was sleeping in the house. Many of the servants had left, but there were still some staff upstairs. It was important we were safe . . ." Her voice trailed away.

"Yes," Lockwood said drily. "Your safety was of course paramount. Go on."

"After the first night—this is three days ago, Mr. Lockwood—the children reported to me while I took my breakfast. They had waited in the basement, watching the stairs. At some point after midnight, they saw the footprints appear—just as I have described them to you. The prints formed, one after the other, curling up the staircase, as if someone were slowly climbing. As they went, the pace of the prints grew faster. The children followed, but only for a short distance—to my vexation, when they reached the ground floor, they stopped and did not go on. I ask you, what good was that?"

"Did they say why they hung back?" Lockwood asked.

"They said the visitation was moving too fast. Also that they were scared." The lady glared around at us. "Scared! This was their job!"

"How old *were* these children, please?" I asked.

Miss Wintergarden's mouth twisted. "I should think nine or ten. I have no experience with the species. Well, I made no secret of my wishes that they should watch more closely the next night, and to be fair to them, they did. The following morning they came before me, white and trembling, and said that they had climbed halfway between the second and third floors before being unable to continue. A sensation of appalling terror had gripped them, they said, which grew worse the higher they got; they felt as if something were waiting for them around the bend in the staircase. There were three children, don't forget, and all with those iron sticks they wave about. It seemed a poor excuse to me.

"I requested they watch again the third night. One girl refused point-blank—I paid her off and sent her packing—but the other two thought they might try. You must understand that the footprints had never caused us any actual trouble. I did not for a moment dream that—"

She broke off, reaching toward the table. Her gaunt hand hovered above the carrot cake, then veered away to pick up her cup of tea.

"It wasn't my fault," she said.

Lockwood was regarding her closely. "What wasn't your fault, Miss Wintergarden?"

She closed her eyes. "I sleep in a bedroom on the third floor. Yesterday morning I woke early, before any of my servants were about. I came out of my room and saw a watch-stick lying on the landing. It was wedged right through the balusters, its end hanging out over the stairwell. I called, but heard nothing. So I went over to the banister, and then I saw . . ." She took a shaky sip of tea. "I saw . . ."

George spoke feelingly to no one but himself. "I can sense this is going to make me need some cake."

"I saw one of the night-watch children above me, huddled on the staircase, between the third and attic floors. She had her back to the wall, and her knees drawn up, and she was rocking to and fro. When I spoke to her, she did not answer. I could not see the other—it was a boy, I do not know his name—but I noticed that the girl's watch-stick was there on the stairs next to her, and that made me suddenly look down." She took a short, sharp breath, as if reliving the moment of shock. "I have told you about the stairwell—how it stretches from the attic level to the basement. And he was down there, lying in shadow on the basement floor. He had fallen, and he was dead."

There was a long silence in the room. The veneer of superiority Miss Wintergarden had attempted to maintain throughout the interview hung from her at an angle, skewed, flapping, and distasteful, like a highly wrought gate blown off its hinges in a gale.

Still she clung to it. "It was their job," she said. "I paid them for the risk."

Lockwood had gone very still. His eyes glinted. "I hope you paid them well. Was he ghost-touched?"

"No."

"Why had he fallen?"

"I don't know."

"Where had he fallen from?"

A bony shrug. "I don't know that, either."

"Miss Wintergarden, surely the other child could—"

"She could say nothing, Mr. Lockwood. Nothing at all."

"And why is that?"

"*Because she had lost her mind!*" The words came out almost as a shriek; we all jerked back. The woman rocked forward, arms rigid, white hands clasped in her lap. "She has lost her mind. She says nothing. She scarcely sleeps. She goggles at the empty air, as if it would itself attack her. She is at present in a secure unit in a psychiatric hospital in north London, being tended to by DEPRAC doctors. It is a post-traumatic catatonic state, they say. The outlook is not favorable."

"Miss Wintergarden." Holly Munro spoke in a brittle voice. "Those children should *not* have been used. It was very wrong of you. You should have called in an agency."

There were two red points in the lady's cheeks. I thought she was going to erupt with fury, but she said only, "I am doing so now."

"From the outset."

"Young lady, I do not intend—"

George stood decisively. "I was right, you know. After that story, we all need to revive ourselves. We need energy, we need nourishment. This is definitely a carrot cake moment. No—please, Miss Wintergarden, I insist." He scooped up the cake and, like a croupier dealing cards, tipped a slice onto her plate. "There. It'll make us all feel better." Four others were doled out in the blink of an eye. Lockwood and I took ours. I offered a plate to Holly.

She held up a perfectly manicured hand. "No thanks, Lucy. You tuck in. I'm good."

Of course she was. I sat back heavily with my plate.

The story of the night-watch kids had cast a pall over us. We ate, each after our own fashion. Our client, pale-faced, nibbled a corner of her slice with the fastidious motions of a field mouse. I gulped mine down like an antisocial seabird. Lockwood sat in silence, frowning into the fire. Accounts of deaths at the hand of ghosts always weighed on him.

George, unusually, had been slow to begin his cake. Something about our visitor had caught his attention. He gazed at a silvery object pinned to her pullover. It was just visible beneath her cardigan.

"That's a nice brooch you have there, Miss Wintergarden," he said.

She glanced down. "Thank you." Her words were scarcely audible.

"It's a harp symbol, isn't it?"

"A lyre, an ancient Greek harp, yes."

"Does it represent something? I'm sure I've seen it before."

"It's the symbol of the Orpheus Society, a club in London. I do charitable work for them. . . ." She brushed cake crumbs off her fingers. "Now—Mr. Lockwood, how do you wish to proceed?"

"With extreme care." Lockwood roused himself; his face was serious, unsmiling. "We shall accept the case, of course, Miss Wintergarden—but the stakes are high, and I will not take unnecessary risks. I assume the house will be left empty for us this evening? You and the servants will be elsewhere?"

"Most of them have given notice! Yes, you will have a free hand."

"Very well. Now, one final question. Earlier on, you mentioned certain 'accompanying phenomena' that had been noticed alongside the bloody footprints. What were they?"

Miss Wintergarden frowned; the lines in the center of her brow corrugated. Going into detail was a matter of distaste for her. "I hardly remember. The footprints were the focus of the haunting."

"It's not just visual things that count," I said. "Did the night-watch hear anything? Feel anything odd, perhaps?"

"There were sensations of panic, as I have told you; I think it was also very cold. Maybe one girl reported movement in the air—a feeling of something passing her."

There was nothing here that we couldn't have predicted. It told us little. Lockwood nodded. "I see."

"Oh, and one child reported two rushing forms."

We stared at her. "What?" I said. "When were you going to mention this?"

"I had forgotten. One of the night-watch said it; the boy, I think. It was a garbled account. I was unsure whether to take it seriously."

"In my experience, Miss Wintergarden," Lockwood said, "one should always take the accounts of dead night-watch children very seriously indeed. What did the boy see?"

Her lips pursed thin. "Two cloudy figures: one large, one small. According to him they raced, one after the other, up the stairs. Following the line of footprints. The big shape had its hand out-stretched, as if to seize the smaller. The little shape—"

"Was running," I finished. "Running for its life."

"Don't think it worked out for them, whoever it was." George said. "Call me intuitive"—he pushed his glasses up his nose—"but I'd hazard a guess they didn't make it."

Chapter 10

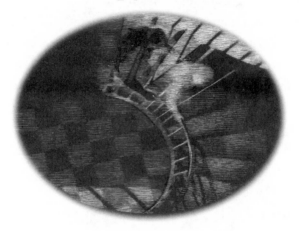

"She's an utterly awful woman," Lockwood agreed. "Callous and ignorant and hysterical all at once. But she's given us a good and dangerous case here, Luce, and we mustn't mess it up."

I smiled happily across at him. "Suits me."

We were standing under the elm trees in the gardens of Hanover Square, looking toward Miss Wintergarden's house. Number 54 was a dark, thin shard, wedged like a rotten tooth between other, indistinguishable terraced town houses on the shadowy side of the square. How elegant they should have been, with their painted facades and columned porticoes framing their neat black doors. But the recent storms had left dark stains on the stuccoed fronts, and the sidewalks and porticoes were a scattered waste of splintered twigs. No lights were on. The effect was of drabness and decay.

It hadn't rained since the morning, but patches of standing

water studded the grass, dull as fallen coins, reflecting the gunmetal sky. A strong wind was blowing, and the naked branches of the trees did the thing all naked branches do in winter with the daylight slowly failing. They rasped and rustled like giant papery hands being rubbed together. The world was heavy with unease.

The house waited for us on the other side of the street.

"Reminds me of Berkeley Square," I said. "That was dangerous, too. Probably worse. I broke my rapier, and George nearly cut your head off, but we still came out of it well."

I'd come out of it particularly well; it was one of my favorite cases. Perhaps this one would be even better. I felt optimistic about it, even cheerful. George was on his way, but he'd been working in the library and hadn't yet arrived. Holly Munro was back at Portland Row, doing neat things with paper clips. For the moment it was just Lockwood and me.

He pulled his collar up against the wind. "Berkeley Square was in summer. Nice short night to get through. This one may be a long haul. It's only three, and I'm hungry already." He nudged his bag with the toe of his boot. "Tell you what, though, Holly's sandwiches look fine, don't they?"

"Mm," I said. "Delicious."

"It was nice of her to make them."

"Mmm," I said, stretching my smile wide across my face. "So nice."

Yes, our lovely assistant had made us sandwiches. She'd also packed our equipment bags, and though I'd carefully gone through everything again myself (when it comes to the art of staying alive, I trust nobody but me), I had to admit that she'd done an excellent job. But the best thing she'd done that day, as far as I was concerned, was stay at home. Tonight it was going to be the three of us. Like it always used to be.

A few people were walking in the square—residents, probably, judging from their expensive coats. They glanced at us as they passed, taking stock of our swords, our dark clothes and watchful stillness, and hurried on, heads down. It was a funny thing about being an agent, something Lockwood had once said: you were admired and loathed in equal measure. After dark, you represented order and all good things. They loved to see you then. In daylight, you were an unwelcome intrusion into everyday life, a symbol of the very chaos that you kept at bay.

"She's a great addition, isn't she?" Lockwood said.

"Holly? Mm. She's fine."

"Strong-willed, I think. Not afraid to lay into that old harpy, Wintergarden. Really spoke her mind." He had pulled back his coat and was checking the line of plastic canisters looped across his chest; at his belt, magnesium flares gleamed. "I know you had some concerns at first, Lucy. . . . It's been a couple of weeks. How are *you* getting on with Holly now?"

I blew out my cheeks, stared at his lowered head. What was there to say? "It's okay . . ." I began. "Not always so easy. I suppose I *do* find sometimes that she—"

Lockwood straightened suddenly. "Great," he said. "And look, here's George."

Here *was* George, his stocky figure scampering across the street. His shirt was untucked, his glasses fogged, his baggy trousers spattered with water. He had a shabby backpack slung over his shoulder, and his rapier swung behind him like a broken tail. He splashed breathlessly to a halt.

I looked at him. "You've got cobwebs in your hair."

"All part of the job. I found something."

George *always* finds something. It's one of his best qualities. "Murder?"

He had that glitter in his eye, a hard light, diamond-sharp, that told us his researches had borne exciting fruit. "Yep, so much for that old biddy claiming her daddy's house had never seen a spot of violence. It's bloody murder, pure and simple."

Lockwood grinned. "Excellent. I've got the key. Lucy's got your tools. Let's get out of this wind and hear the grisly details."

Whatever else she may have been, Miss Fiona Wintergarden was not a liar. Her house *was* splendid, every room a florid testament to her wealth and status. It was a tall building, slender in width, but extending back a good distance from the square. The rooms were high-ceilinged and rectangular, sumptuously decorated with ornate plaster and patterned wallpapers featuring oriental flowers and birds. Heavy curtains cocooned the windows; display cabinets were set against the walls. One room on the ground floor was lined with dozens of small, dark paintings, as neatly regimented as lines of waiting soldiers. We found a splendid library; elsewhere bedrooms, bathrooms, and corridors all maintained the opulent feel. Only at the attic level, where the walls were suddenly plain whitewash, and a half dozen tiny servants' rooms clustered beneath the eaves, did the luxurious skin peel back to reveal the bare bone and sinew of the house beneath.

Of all its features, it was the stairwell that most concerned us, and here again our client had told the truth. It *was* a remarkably elegant construction and the dark heart of the building. Approaching from the front door, you almost immediately came upon it: a great oval cavity cut right up through the house. The stairs hugged the right side of the oval, tight against the wall, curling steeply counter-clockwise to the level above. On the left side, a slim banister arced around, cordoning off the stairwell from the hall; beyond it, a flight of steps led down to the basement. Standing in the hall—or on each landing—you could look up to see the curl of the stairs repeated again and again until you reached a great oval skylight at the attic, or down to the black-and-white tile flooring of the kitchen basement below.

None of us liked those tiles, which looked very clean and scrubbed. It was there that the night-watch boy's body had been found.

Aside from the skylight high above, the landings and stairwell had no access to natural light. The effect was of an inward-looking space, heavy and silent and turned toward the past, with little con-nection to the outside world. Though it was only mid-afternoon, the electric lanterns, set in floral sconces at intervals along the walls, were already on. They emitted a cold and greasy glare.

The first thing we did, while it was still light, was give the house the once-over. We went through it systematically, in silence, listen-ing as our footsteps rang on the varnished floorboards. We made readings, noted temperatures, took turns using our psychic senses. It was too early to get anything spectacular, but it was worth checking just in case.

Then we focused our attention on the stairwell.

We started in the basement, at the entrance to the kitchen, and worked our way slowly up. From the outset it was clear that the stairs, and the landings close to the banister, were colder than the rest of the house—not by much, but consistently down by five or ten degrees. That was all we found. Lockwood didn't see anything. I listened, but heard nothing sinister whatsoever, unless you counted George's stomach rumbling.

On the staircase's final curl, where it rose from third floor to attic level beneath the pale eye of the skylight, Lockwood bent to the baseboard. He placed his finger on it, then put it to his lips. "Salt," he said. "They've cleaned up, but there's been salt spilled here."

"The night-watch girl?" George was making notes with a stubby pencil; he had a spare one tucked behind his ear. "Some kind of last defense?"

"So she must have been found here," I said. Yes, found crouched against the wall, mute and mindless. . . . I looked at the bland plaster, the nondescript emptiness of the space, searching out the horror that had happened here. Other than the salt, there was no trace of it. Perhaps that was the worst thing of all.

An hour had passed; the skylight had grown dim. On the attic landing, the last shaft of daylight shrank into shadow. Grayness swelled out around the curl of the staircase. We went back downstairs.

It was time for food, and George's story. None of us wanted to use the kitchen in the basement where the boy had died. We set up camp instead on the ground floor, in the room of paintings, dragging in a table and some chairs, and laying out our water bottles, biscuits, sandwiches, and reviving packets of chips. We lit the gas lanterns and set one at either end of the table. I found a socket, filled the electric kettle, and switched it on. George got out some papers from his investigations at the library. We made tea and settled ourselves down.

"One day we should do this somewhere nice," George said. "You know, have a picnic where nothing's going to want to kill us. It would be quite fun."

"What would we find to talk about, though?" Lockwood asked. He took a swig of tea. "Come to think of it, what did kids *do* with themselves in the days before the Problem? Most of them didn't even have to work, did they? What was it—school or something? Life must have been so *dull.*"

"And safe," I said. "Don't forget that."

"Not so safe if you lived in *this* house," George said darkly. "Not if you were a servant lad known as 'Little Tom.'" He consulted his notes for a moment, leaning forward like a short, roundish general assessing battle plans, then took a bite of biscuit. "It was the summer of 1883 when the killing took place. According to the *Pall Mall Gazette*, the house was owned by a fellow named Henry Cooke, an old soldier and merchant, who'd served out in India. It was his son, a certain Robert Cooke, who was arrested one hot July night for the murder of a servant, Thomas Webber, also known as 'Little Tom.' He was put on trial at once, and found guilty."

"How did he kill him?" I asked. "And why?"

"*Why*, I don't know. I don't have many details. *How*, yes. He stabbed him with one of his father's hunting knives. The article says that the argument began down in the kitchen, late one evening. Little Tom was first attacked there, and badly wounded. Then a terrible chase took place, under the horrified gaze of many witnesses—guests, servants, and other family members—before the final fatal blow was struck. There was blood everywhere. The *Gazette* calls it 'the house of horror.' *Another* one! London has *so* many. I should make a list sometime."

I was looking at the ceiling of the room. It was decorated with swirls and spirals formed of plaster molding, as tight and intricately fibrous as bone marrow. "That pretty much fits in with the bloody footprints," I said.

Lockwood nodded. "And with what the night-watch kid told Wintergarden. The chase begins down in the kitchen and spirals up through the house. Maybe poor Little Tom was cornered in the attic and killed there."

"What happened to the murderer?" I asked. "Hanged?"

"No. He was sent to Bethlem psychiatric hospital. They realized he was crazy, you see. Anyway, he died soon after. While walking on the grounds, he evaded his captors, ran out into the road, and threw himself beneath the wheels of an undertaker's carriage."

Lockwood made a face. "A cheery tale."

"Aren't they all?"

Outside, over the square, the sun was fast descending. Black clouds had piled around it, seeking to smother its dying light. A great flock of birds wheeled over the elm trees, spiraling and twirling like a living twist of smoke. We finished our tea.

"Good stuff, George. . . ." Lockwood had taken off his rapier and leaned it against his chair. He had his coat collar up, and his face was mostly in darkness. His long fingers tapped on the table, beating the rhythm of his thoughts. "Now," he said, after a pause, "we need to get to work. But we *don't* treat this as a normal case. I want you both to listen carefully. The haunting, as reported, is a complicated one. We've got the bloody footprints climbing the stairs from bottom to top. We've got these two mysterious shapes, locked into their chase. We've got feelings of extreme terror that affected the night-watch kids. And we've got the fact that *something*—either all or part of this—did something terrible to those children. One witness is dead, the other driven mad." He crumpled a chip bag and put it in his pocket. "It's confusing, and we can't leave anything to chance."

"It's definitely unusual to have *two* apparitions manifesting in the same haunting," George said. "That raises big questions. Are they *both* active spirits, or is one just a visual echo of the original event, conjured up by the other? I've seen that happen. There was that nasty case in Deptford with the sailor and the Burmese python, where—"

Lockwood held up his hand. "We all know that story, George. Stick to tonight."

I'd been shifting impatiently in my seat. "It's probably not as confusing as you make out. It's Cooke's wicked spirit driving this. We need to find the Source and destroy it."

"Sure," Lockwood said, "but not tonight. Tonight it's observation only. We don't engage. The ghosts have a specific trajectory. They appear at the bottom, shoot straight up the stairs, and vanish somewhere at the top. It all happens really fast. Here's what we do: we rig up three separate iron circles. George is in the basement, Lucy's on the second floor, I'm stationed at the top. We wait, we watch what happens. Afterward we compare notes. No, don't argue." (I'd opened my mouth in a querying sort of way.) "This is a two-night mission. Holly tells me it's standard practice at Rotwell's."

"Oh, that's got to be all right, then," I said.

There was a slight pause. "What about the footprints?" George asked.

"The footprints linger, and we can investigate them later. It's these nippy spirits we need to observe. Sounds to me as if they'll go straight past us, but if by chance they *do* approach, use your weapons without a second thought. Understand?"

George nodded.

"Lucy?"

"Yes, yes, of course. Fine."

"One other thing: none of us leaves our iron circles for any reason whatever. And Lucy, I don't want any attempt at psychic connection. I've been thinking about the way you spoke to that woman's ghost the other week. Yes, it got results, but I didn't like it. We don't know what we're dealing with here. We *do* know it killed a child."

"Of course I understand that," I said. "No problem."

"Right. You brought the skull along with you? Good. See if it'll give you any insights. Let *it* take the risks, not you. And now we'd better get moving. If *you* can't feel something coming, I *can*."

He stood abruptly, reached for his rapier. Our picnic was dissolved.

An hour later, with the sun's light firmly extinguished, we'd rigged ourselves up okay. I stood on the second floor landing, surrounded by my chains, facing the stairwell. My bag was inside; I had some salt-bombs out and ready. I was maybe five feet from the banister, where the ghosts were said to pass on their curving progress up the stairs.

I'd gone for a double circle, two chains winding over each other like coiling snakes. It would be tough for any spirit to overcome. Still, given that the night-watch girl had been driven mad with shock, I *did* wonder whether standing behind chains was going to be protection enough. After all, we'd presumably still *see* whatever it was she saw. From the taut expressions on the others' faces as we'd separated, I guessed they were wondering the same thing. But none of us mentioned it. You don't get far being an agent who overthinks. George thinks masses, and he kind of proves the point.

Just outside the chains, I'd plonked the ghost-jar unceremoniously on the floor. It was glowing with a sour green light, but I couldn't see the face. The ghost was there, though.

It let out a long, appreciative whistle. *"Nice pad,"* it whispered. *"I could get used to this. So, then . . . Lockwood. I heard him telling you off just now."*

"He wasn't telling me off." I looked over the banister into the stairwell. We'd turned off the wall lights but had set out snuff-lights on the stairs. Every third step had its own small candle. Some were tall, others short; all were lit and unprotected, vulnerable to whatever influence might pass them. Their warm spheres of light interlinked and overlapped in the darkness, like giant spiraling bubbles trapped in time. It was quite pretty, in a sinister sort of way.

"Are you going to listen to him?" the skull said. *"I wouldn't listen to him. If you want to make psychic contact with a killer ghost, why not? I say, Go, girl!"*

"You are *so* obvious. I wouldn't do anything that stupid." Far below me, in the basement, I could see the dim red glow of George's lantern. Like me, he'd fixed it so almost no light showed; by flipping a switch, you could open the shutters and gain full power in the blink of an eye. Lockwood, somewhere two floors above, would have a similar setup. I imagined him up there, standing alert and watchful in the dark. I felt a twist in my chest, pleasant and painful at the same time: probably indigestion from those stupid sandwiches.

"Now," I said, looking back at the jar, "I brought you here for a reason. What do you sense? Anything?"

"*I don't think he's listening to you anymore,*" the voice persisted. "*It's that Holly who's distracted him. . . . Oh, don't deny it! Just because I'm evil doesn't mean I can't see what's right in front of my nose.*"

"You don't *have* a nose." I stepped back over my chains. "Tell me about the stairs!"

"*Well . . . bad things happened here.*"

"Thanks. *I* could have told you that."

"*Could you? Can you see the blood all over it? Can you hear the screams?*"

"No."

"*More fool you. You're not as perceptive as you think. For instance, you're thinking too much about Lockwood to even notice there's something creeping up behind you . . . right now!*"

A creak on the floorboards. I squealed, spun around. Before I could react, a flashlight flicked on, and a familiar spectacled face loomed out of the darkness. "George!"

"All right, Luce."

"What are you doing leaving your circle? Get back!"

He shrugged. "Well, nothing's coming now, is it? Could be hours yet. Got any gum?"

"No! Go back to your place. If Lockwood saw . . ."

"Relax. We're safe for the moment. Did you say you had some gum?"

"No. Yes . . . Somewhere. Here, take it." I fished out a packet and passed it over. "You okay down there?"

"Bearing up." He fumbled with the wrapper, fingers shaking. "There's a pool of spreading cold on the tiles. Where that boy fell, you know. And I'm getting a funny taste in my mouth. . . . Miasma's starting." He shoved the pack of gum into my hand and shivered. "Here, you'd better keep it. I'll get back down."

"Lucy! George!" Lockwood's voice echoed down the stairwell. "Everything all right down there?"

"Yes!"

"Good. Stand tight! I think the atmosphere's starting to change."

George grimaced, gave a wave. A moment later he was a plump shadow fleeing down the stairs, setting the candles jerking. The bubbles of light stabilized, resumed their placid spiral. I sat cross-legged in the circle, watching the darkness, and waited for something to happen.

My head jerked up. I felt a cold and queasy prickling, as if invisible insects, small and numberless, were scurrying across my skin. My neck ached. I was acutely aware that considerable time had passed. My mind had been stretched out thin, my consciousness somewhere remote; now it snapped back to attention. What time *was* it? I checked my watch. Its luminous digits, solid and reassuring, showed nearly twelve fifteen. Midnight had passed!

I cleared my throat, stretched, looked around. The house was silent. The snuff-lights gleamed on the staircase much as before, but I thought their orbs had shrunk, as if under unseen pressure. I looked at the ghost-jar. It no longer glowed, but shone black and still as wine. And what was that shimmering on the surface of the glass?

Frost. I stretched my hand in front of me, out beyond the chains—and pulled it sharply back. It was like dipping my fingers into a bath of icy water.

I got stiffly to my feet. I had a foulness in my mouth, as if I'd swallowed something bad and couldn't shake the taste. I found gum, ripped off the wrapper, furiously began chewing. Furious was the word. Everything I did felt jagged, edgy. I could sense my psychic nerves being pulled steadily out of shape.

Nothing had actually *happened* yet, but it was the buildup that really got to you. It was the knowledge that you were being pulled back toward the replay of an evil event, something that had twisted the personality of the house out of true. Everything was moving backward, and the past had more power than the future—George called it Time Sickness. He reckoned that was why it felt so unnatural, so fundamentally *wrong*.

"*Watch the candles.*" It was the skull's voice in my ear. "*Watch their light.*"

And sure enough, the candles were twitching, responding to a minute agitation of the air. I could feel the hairs on my arms rise, my breathing tighten. My ears hurt, as if I were descending in an elevator, too far, too fast. I closed my eyes and listened. From some-where came a cry of mortal pain.

I opened my eyes. "George?"

An almighty bang. I jumped where I stood. The noise echoed up the staircase, was swallowed by the dark. I knew it had come from below, from the basement. The candle auras had stilled; they gleamed like the irises of sightless eyes.

"George?"

No answer. I cursed, drew my rapier, stepped out of the circle into the freezing dark. I crossed to the banister, and looked down.

Two flights below, something was coming up the stairs. I could see dark smears appearing on the steps. Whatever made them was invisible, but it moved slowly, spattering them as it went, extinguish-ing each candle as it passed.

Darkness in the basement; no red glow from George's lantern. I gripped the banister, craned my head out to see if I could—

The last candle on the basement stairs died. Gleams of wetness appeared on the floorboards of the hall. Was that a cloudy hand gripping the banister for support . . . ?

No—there were *two* hands, one some way behind the other. And now first one, and then the other, flowed suddenly forward, picking up speed, angling around to the flight that would bring them up to me.

"*Lucy* . . ." It was the voice from the jar. "*I'd step over here sharp-ish, if I were you.*"

Still I clutched at the rail. How *cold* it was, tearing at me through my gloves. It was so hard to think of moving. My limbs were far too heavy, my body somehow far away.

On the stairs, two racing, cloudy forms dragged darkness up behind them like a cloak. Fast as you could snap your fingers, the candlewicks they passed snuffed out.

"*Bet Holly would have the wit to get back to safety,*" the skull remarked.

Something needling jabbed inside me; indignation cut through ghost-lock. I shoved my body backward, threw myself across the landing. Tripping over the chains, I fell into the circle, on top of my bags, and sprawled there as two shapes erupted past me.

They moved in utter silence, pale other-light flowing off them in swirling ribbons. The first, so small and fragile, the cloudy imprint of a child. How thin the body was, how slight the shoulders! You couldn't see any details. It was only as solid as a candle flame, and the lower half tapered into nothing. The head was bowed; it thrust itself desperately forward, tiny hand trailing on the banister.

And now, pooling out of the darkness at its back—a second shape, luminous also, as if woven from the same substance as the first. But larger, much larger, a bulky adult form, and the other-light streamed around it more darkly. Again, no sense of the face or appearance, only of a great arm reaching out, a bull head swinging to and fro.

The child's form passed by, darting up the next flight with the pursuer closely following, and away they climbed toward the third floor. Out went the candles above me, quick as blinking. Cold followed in their slipstream and with it, sound: a thin sucking movement of dead air. They were gone. I waited, hunched forward on my knees, teeth clenched, lips bared. Still the cold deepened; and now, from high in the house, came a final dreadful screaming.

Something fell past me. I sensed its bulk, I heard the rush of air beyond the banister, and tensed, waiting. . . . But there was no sound of impact from below.

It was only then I saw the black, wet marks that defaced the boards beyond the chains. The straggling stains of bloody, running feet.

I was still there, crouching, staring at them, a minute or two later, as the temperature grew warm, the scent of smoke and candle wax trailed into the circle, and I heard the calm voice of Lockwood calling from above to say that the manifestation was over.

Chapter 11

The footprints lingered for one hour and seventeen minutes. George timed it on his watch. They were formed of a thin black ectoplasmic substance that radiated extreme cold. When Lockwood touched one with the point of his rapier, it steamed and spat fiercely, sending snakes of black vapor coiling up the silver blade. It was an interesting phenomenon. George mapped them; I made sketches of some of the clearer prints, the ones that weren't too faint, or too awash with blood.

"They're small feet," Lockwood said. "Not tiny, like a young child's, but pretty slim and slender. Must be Little Tom's, not Robert Cooke's."

"We should measure them, really," I said. "But I don't want to get too close."

"Good point, Luce." He wore gloves, and had pulled a dark blue scarf out of his bag, his only concession to the chill on the stairs. "I guess we could do a comparison. . . . Who's got the smallest feet among us?"

"Holly has," George said, without looking up. "No question."

I spoke through gritted teeth. "She's not even here."

Lockwood nodded. "You're right, George. They *are* petite, aren't they? I bet they're about that size. We should measure Holly's feet tomorrow."

"On it."

"Of rather more importance," I said tartly, "is where to look for the Source of all this. Where do we think Little Tom died?"

In the ordinary way, the best place to look for a Source is near where the death took place, but this manifestation presented problems in that regard. Even our surveillance hadn't helped much. The servant had first been stabbed in the basement, and the haunting had certainly *begun* there, with a sudden ferocious blast of energy that sent George flying in his circle and his lantern crashing against the wall. He hadn't seen the two figures, as I had. Lockwood, waiting at the top of the house, had glimpsed them briefly. As they reached the attic, the shapes—moving fast—had seemed to merge. Then there'd been the deafening scream—then nothing. But *I'd* heard something falling through the air.

"If Cooke pushed Tom off," George said, "as Lucy reckons, he would have died when he hit the basement floor."

"Unless he was already dead from his wounds," I said. "Poor little guy."

"So the Source could be at the top or the bottom," Lockwood said. "We'll look tomorrow. And let's have less of the 'poor little guy,' please, Lucy. Whatever he was in life, Tom's ghost is part of this dangerous haunting. Think of what happened to the night-watch kids."

"I *am* thinking of them," I said. "And what I'm also thinking of, Lockwood, is that horrible monster chasing the child. Cooke's ghost. That's the evil driving this. That's what we need to tackle."

Lockwood shook his head. "Actually, we don't really know one way or the other. We've got to be careful with all Visitors. I don't care if a ghost's friendly, or needy, or just wants a big cuddle. We keep it at a safe distance. All the big agencies follow that policy, Holly says."

I didn't intend to be angry. Basically I knew that Lockwood was right. But my emotions felt stretched right then; it had been a long night—and, back at Portland Row, a long few days. "This ghost is a lad being chased to his death!" I snapped. "I saw him as he passed; he was running for his life. Don't shrug at me like that! He was so desperate. We've got to feel sympathy for him."

That was a mistake—I knew it at once.

A light in Lockwood's eyes flicked out. His voice was cold. "Lucy, I don't have sympathy for *any* of them."

Which, let's face it, was a bit of a conversation killer. The argument stopped there. Because, like the closed door on our landing, the circumstances of our leader's past were both un-ignorable and impossible to tackle. His sister had died by ghost-touch. His *sister.* When that subject came up, there wasn't really anything more to say. So I dutifully shut my mouth and hung around with the others, until, at around one thirty-four in the morning (George timed it), the plasmic footprints grew faint, then softly luminous, then faded clean away. Those footprints had the right idea. We more or less did the same.

She may have made great sandwiches, and she may have had small feet, but at least I could console myself that Holly Munro was desk-bound. *She* didn't wear a rapier. She didn't do what *I* did, going out nightly and risking her life to save London. This knowledge enabled me to hold it together when I got home to discover she'd been in my bedroom and, in a spasm of brisk officiousness, tidied all my clothes.

I meant to mention it to her (calmly, politely, in that way we had) the following morning, but it slipped my mind. By the time I got up, there were a lot of other things going on.

When I came into the kitchen, Lockwood and George were clustered around the table like it was a pretty new assistant, reading a copy of the *Times*. Holly Munro, cheerfully immaculate in a cherry-red skirt and crisp white blouse, was doing something with the salt bin behind the kitchen door. She'd had it installed to replace the usual mess of bags and canisters we kept there. I eyed her skirt as I came in; she eyed my saggy old pajamas. George and Lockwood didn't look up or acknowledge I was there.

"Everything all right?" I said.

"There's been trouble in Chelsea overnight," Ms. Munro said. "An agent killed. Someone you know."

My heart jerked. "What? Who?"

Lockwood glanced up. "One of Kipps's team: Ned Shaw."

"Oh."

"Did you know him well?" Holly Munro asked.

Lockwood stared back down at the newspaper. We'd known Ned Shaw well enough to dislike him, with his close-set eyes and unkempt mane of curly hair. He'd had an aggressive, bullying nature. Our hostility had even brought us to blows, though Lockwood had fought alongside him in the 'Battle in the Graveyard' at Kensal Green Cemetery. "Not really," he said. "Still . . ."

"It's awful when that happens," Holly Munro said. "Happened to me at Rotwell, more than once. People I'd seen in the office every day."

"Yeah," I said. I shuffled around to the kettle. The kitchen was too small with Holly in it. It was hard to move about. "How did he die?"

Lockwood pushed the paper away. "Don't know. It's only mentioned at the end of the article. I think word had just come in. The rest of the news is no better. The Chelsea outbreak's getting worse, and there've been clashes, people protesting about being forced to leave their homes. Police on the streets are having to deal with the *living* now, not the dead. The whole thing's a complete dog's breakfast."

"At least our case is going smoothly," Holly Munro said. "I hear you did very well last night, Lucy. It sounds like a terrifying ghost that badly needs destroying. Would you like a whole-wheat waffle?"

"I'm all right with toast, thanks." *Our* case. I pulled back a chair, scraping it across the linoleum.

"Should try one," Lockwood said. "They're yummy. Okay. The plan for today: our aim is to all get back to Hanover Square after lunch and hunt for the Source before it gets dark. Our client is impatient. Believe it or not, Luce, Miss Wintergarden's already been on the phone, 'requesting,' in her own delightful style, that I personally update her about what we've discovered so far. I've got to nip over to the hotel where she's staying now and give her that briefing. Meanwhile you, George, are going to head back to the Newspaper Archives to get more details on the murder. You reckon there must be more info out there."

George had been scribbling with a felt-tip pen on our Thinking Cloth, writing out a list of names: *Mayfair Bugle, The Queens Magazine, The Cornhill Magazine, Contemporary Review* . . . "Yeah," he said, "there were loads of magazines in late Victorian times, and some of them carried sensational stuff, about true crimes and all that. I bet there's an account of the Little Tom murder there somewhere, though it might be tricky to find in the time available. It could give us a clearer sense of what happened and help us find the Source." He threw the pen down. "I'll get going shortly."

"We've got big deliveries of iron and salt this morning," Holly Munro said. "I'll monitor that, and get your bags ready by early afternoon. You'll want more candles."

"Great," Lockwood said. "You can help Holly, if you like, Lucy."

"Oh, I'm *sure* Lucy doesn't want to do that," Holly said. "She'll have something more important to do."

Lockwood chewed a piece of waffle. "I'm not sure she has."

The kettle boiled.

"Actually," I said brightly, "I do. I think it would be much more useful if I went down to the Archives—and helped George."

It wasn't often that George and I went out together during the day (in fact I'd almost forgotten what he looked like when not surrounded by shadows, ghosts, or artificial light), and you could count the times I'd volunteered to help him at the National Newspaper Archives on the fingers of no hands. If George was surprised by my decision, however, he gave no sign of it. A few minutes later, he was strolling placidly through London at my side.

We walked south through the streets of Marylebone in the general direction of Regent Street. Though the Chelsea containment zone was a mile or two distant, the effects of the outbreak could be felt even here. There was the smell of burning in the air, and the city was quieter than usual. The cafés and restaurants of Marylebone High Street, which like all other commercial establishments closed at four thirty, were only ever busy at lunch; today their interiors were mostly gray and empty, with forlorn waiters sitting idly at tables. Trash bags lay uncollected on the sidewalks; litter blew across the street. More than once we saw yellow-and-black DEPRAC tape blocking the entrances to buildings, and ghost-crosses daubed on windows: the signs of live hauntings, as yet undealt with by any of the agencies. They were busy elsewhere.

Outside a seedy Spiritualist Church on Wimpole Street, a scuffle was going on. Black-clothed followers of the Ghost Cult that worshipped inside were grappling with one of the local Neighborhood Protection leagues, who'd been trying to strew lavender on the church steps. Middle-aged men and women, gray-haired, outwardly respectable, shouted and screamed at one another, snatching at collars, twisting arms. As George and I drew near, they broke apart and stood in panting silence as we walked between them. When we'd passed, they closed up and began fighting again.

They were just adults. They were all equally clueless. When nightfall came, they'd all stop squabbling and scurry home in sync to bolt their doors.

"This city," George said, "is going to hell in a handcart. Don't you think so?"

For the first few blocks we hadn't talked at all; I wasn't in the mood for it. But air and exercise had partially roused me out of my gloom. I stamped my boot heels on the pavement. "I don't even know what that means."

"It means everyone's getting frantic, and no one's asking the right questions."

We zigzagged down to Oxford Street, where the flea market iron and silver stores, palm readers, and fortune-telling booths stretched for miles in both directions; crossed over at Oxford Circus; and started down Regent Street. The Archives were not far away.

"I know why you've come along," George said suddenly. "Don't think I don't."

I'd been having dark thoughts about waffles, and the unexpected statement made my stomach lurch. "Does there have to be a reason?"

"Well, I'm guessing it's not the thrill of my company that brings you here." He glanced at me. "Is it?"

"I love being with you, George. I can scarcely keep away."

"Exactly. No, you've made it pretty obvious," he said, "what's on your mind. You need to be careful, though. Lockwood isn't pleased."

We stepped in unison over one of the runnels of flowing water that protected the clothes stores on Regent Street. It was one of the safest areas of the city, and the streets were busier now. "Well, I'm sorry about that," I said, "but I don't think he's got any right to object. It's his fault. I didn't ask for this."

"Well, nor did Lockwood."

"Of course he did. He hired her, didn't he?"

George gazed at me, his eyes hidden behind his glasses. "I'm talking about your fascination with this ghost, this Little Tom. What were you talking about?"

"Oh, yes. Yes. The same. That's why I'm here with you. I want to know the story."

"Right . . ." We walked another few yards in silence. Up ahead was the Rotwell Building, a shimmering hulk of plastic and glass. Above the entrance, on a pole, the agency's red lion symbol stood rampant. "So how're you finding Holly?" George asked.

"I'm . . . adjusting," I said. "Slowly. You're obviously over the moon."

"Well, she's making us more efficient, which has to be good. Not that I'm sure about everything she does. I caught her trying to get rid of our Thinking Cloth the other day. Said its scribbles made the kitchen look like the inside of someone's head. Well, it—but that's the point."

"Yes," I said. "That's what I find hard. All her fussy rules and regulations. And then there's the way she looks. . . . There's a word for it."

"Yeah," George said, with feeling. "*Glossy*. Or were you thinking *lustrous?*"

"Um, no . . . that wasn't quite it. I meant, sort of more . . . *overmaintained.*"

He pushed his spectacles up his nose and glanced at me. "She knows what a comb *is*, I suppose."

"Are you looking at my hair? What are you saying?"

"Nothing! I'm not saying anything. Absolutely not. Oh . . ." George's wriggling awkwardness froze suddenly into something deeper, an expression of numb discomfort. "Heads down, Luce. . . . Don't look now."

Directly ahead of us, outside the Rotwell building, stood Quill Kipps. With him were his two close associates, Kate Godwin and Bobby Vernon.

In the daylight Kipps looked slighter than usual. As ever he was flamboyantly dressed, but his face was gray, and there was a haze of ginger stubble on his chin. He wore a black armband tight upon his sleeve, and carried a thick sheaf of documents under one arm. He'd already spotted us. This was a blow. If we'd had the chance, we'd have crossed the street or something.

We drew level with them. Vernon was remarkably small and scrawny; it was as if someone had shaved bits off normal-sized agents and created him from the scrapings. Godwin, a Listener like me, was as chilly as ground-frost, and probably about as hard underfoot. They nodded at us. We nodded at them. There was a pause, as if everyone were going through the usual round of hostilities and cheap comments, only silently, to save time.

"We're sorry to hear about Ned Shaw," I said finally.

Kipps stared at me. "Are you? You never liked him."

"No. Still, that doesn't mean we wanted him dead."

His narrow shoulders shrugged skyward beneath his trim silver jacket. "No? Maybe. I couldn't say." Kipps often seemed engulfed in bitterness when he spoke with us. Today his hostility seemed less automatic and less personal, yet more deeply felt. I didn't answer. George opened his mouth to speak and then thought better of it. Kate Godwin checked her watch, stared off down the street like she was waiting for someone.

"How did it happen?" I said finally.

"Typical DEPRAC foul-up," Bobby Vernon said.

Kipps rubbed the back of his neck with a pale hand. He sighed. "It was a building on Walpole Street. Open floor-plan office. We were working our way through it, taking psychic readings. Some of Tendy's group were up on the floor above. Bloody idiots disturbed a Specter, drove it down the central stairway to our level. Came straight through a wall where Shaw was and clasped him around the head before any of us could move."

Kate Godwin nodded. "He didn't have a chance."

"I'm so sorry," I said.

"Yeah, well. It'll happen again," Kipps said. "Not to us, maybe, but to someone." His eyes were always red-rimmed; I thought they seemed redder than normal. "We're out again tonight on a three-line whip. Barnes has us all performing like so many dancing bears. The Chelsea outbreak's crazy. There's no system to it—or if there is, *I* can't see it."

"Got to be a system," George said. "*Something's* stirring up the ghosts in that area. There'll be a pattern, if you know where to look."

Kipps grimaced. "You think so? The best minds in DEPRAC have failed to find it so far, Cubbins. I've just been at a meeting here, and no one's got a clue. The most they've come up with is to suggest holding a special agency parade to reassure the public that nothing's wrong. Can you believe it? We've got thousands of people evacuated, ghosts rampant, rioting in London—and they're planning a *carnival*. The world's gone mad." He scowled at us as if it had been *our* suggestion, and flourished the sheaf of papers. "Oh, and see this? Copy of all the case reports the different teams have filed in the last week. Apparitions, Glimmers, chill spots—you name it. Hundreds of incidents, and no pattern whatsoever. All team leaders are supposed to read it now, and come up with our own suggestions. As if I'll have time for that! I've got a funeral to go to." He slapped the papers disgustedly against his fist. "I might as well lob this in the trash."

We stood there awkwardly. I didn't know what to say.

"You can give it to me, if you like," George said. "I'd be interested."

"Give it to you?" Kipps's brief laugh had no humor in it. "Why should I do that? You hate me."

George snorted. "What, you want me to blow you a kiss? Who cares whether I *like* you or not? People are dying here. I might be able to *do* something with it, do us all a favor. If you want to read it yourself, fine. Otherwise give it here. Just don't put it in the stupid bin." He stamped his foot, red in the face and glaring.

Kipps and his companions blinked at him, slightly taken aback. I was a bit, too. Kipps looked at me; then, shrugging, tossed the papers across to George. "Like I say, *I* don't want them. I've got other things to do. We may see you at the carnival—*if* Lockwood and

Co.'s invited, which I strongly doubt." He gave a cursory wave, and with that, the three Fittes agents sloped off into the crowd.

If the National Newspaper Archives building were ever haunted, it would be a devil of a job to sort it. Spreading over six vast floors, each honeycombed with eight-foot-high shelves and book stacks, it's bigger than any factory and more complex and labyrinthine than the oldest Tudor house. Plus, you'd be constantly tripping over all the scholars crouched in gloomy recesses, staring at old documents, trying to understand the history of the Problem. History was what the Archives were about; you could smell it in the air, taste it on your breath. After half an hour of leafing through century-old magazines, you felt it fused to your fingertips, too.

George liked it; he knew his way around. He took me to the Periodicals section on the fourth level and showed me the Catalogue—a series of giant leather-bound books that summarized the contents of the floor. For events of recent decades, there was an Index, too, which cross-referenced stories contained in all the magazines. For old stuff, though, you had to locate the periodical you wanted, choose the relevant date, and sift through the endless yellowed pages yourself, looking for your story.

Armed with a list of magazines from George, I weighed in, finding copies of the *Cornhill Magazine* and *Mayfair News* from summer 1883, and taking them to the reading tables perched above the central atrium. I began to browse, looking for any mention of the horrors of Hanover Square.

Soon I had the smell of stale ink in my nostrils. My eyes ached from poring over minute print. Worse, my mind ached from all the half-glimpsed irrelevant details. Victorian controversies. Forgotten society ladies. Essays on faith and empire by hairy, self-confident men. This was stuff that would have been dull when it was published, let alone more than a century later. It was ancient history. How could George enjoy doing this?

Ancient history . . . That was exactly what Lockwood had once said about his sister, who'd died only six years ago. The more I thought about it, the more I realized how present she was, influencing his every action. I remembered his coldness the night before; his dismissal of my empathy for the little ghost. And of course Holly Munro had backed him up today: she wanted the thing destroyed, no questions asked. I'd only seen her for five minutes, but she'd been irritating that morning.

I continued reading, moving among the shelves, steadily working through George's list. My mind wandered. Whenever I passed the Catalogue and Index, I thought about the events, six years before, in Portland Row.

Once, when I returned to the tables, I discovered George there, surrounded by magazines, copying lines into his notebook. "Found out about our ghost?" I asked.

"Nope. Not a sausage on that yet. I'm taking a break, checking out something else." He yawned and stretched. "Don't know if you remember, but when Miss Wintergarden came to see us, she was wearing a little silver brooch."

"Oh, yes," I said. "I was meaning to ask you about that. Was it the same as—?"

"It *was*. An ancient Grecian harp or lyre. The precise same symbol we saw on Fairfax's goggles, and on that box that Penelope Fittes was holding, you know, when we spied on her in her library."

I nodded. Combe Carey Hall . . . the Black Library of Fittes House. . . . Months separated the two incidents, but as I'd almost died on both those nights, I didn't have any problem recalling them. The odd little harp symbol had puzzled us ever since, the few times we remembered it. It represented . . . what had Wintergarden called it? "Was it the Orpheus Club?" I said.

"Orpheus Society. I've just been looking it up." George adjusted his glasses as he tried to decipher his own spidery handwriting. "It's listed in Debrett's *Almanac of Registered British Groups, Clubs, and Other Organizations* as a 'theoretical society for prominent citizens to research the Problem and the nature of the Other Side.' They make it sound like a talking shop for posh bigwigs, but we know there's more to it than that. It's got a registered address in St. James's. Not a clue what it is, but we should check it out sometime." He eyed my latest pile of tomes. "How are you getting on?"

"Nothing so far. How recent does the Index go, by the way? Last few years?"

"They keep it up to date as far as they can, yes. Why?"

"No reason."

Some while later, with George elsewhere, I strolled over to the Index shelf.

I found the volume I wanted. The one for six years before. A list of subjects contained in the magazines and newspapers of that year: events, hauntings, features, names.

On impulse I flipped to the Ls.

There wouldn't *be* anything. I knew that. I wasn't doing any harm. But when my inky finger ran down the column, there it was:

Lockwood, J.

I felt as cold as when I'd entered the sister's room. The name, apparently, was mentioned in the *Marylebone Herald*, the monthly paper for our area of London. It gave the date, and the catalogue number for the bound edition.

It was the work of a moment to locate the relevant file. I went to a remote alcove and sat there with the folder on my knee.

The death of Miss Jessica Lockwood (15), daughter of late psychic researchers Celia and Donald Lockwood, has been reported by St. Pancras Coroners. In the latest tragic incident to hit the family, she was ghost-touched in an accident at her home in Marylebone, last Thursday night. Her younger brother was unable to stop the attack, and she was pronounced dead on arrival at the hospital. Funeral arrangements will be announced. The family requests that no flowers be sent.

That was it, just the scantiest mention, but it contained enough to keep me sitting there, unmoving. Many things to think about, and one most of all. The way I remembered it, when we'd talked about his sister, Lockwood had definitely implied that he hadn't been around when the accident took place.

This article implied that he had.

Chapter 12

The day got worse. Of course it did. By early afternoon, George and I had still found nothing (at least nothing, in my case, that we'd *officially* gone to find). It was time to get home to the office, but George wanted to do a final check on some obscure journals that were housed in another building, a few blocks from the main Archives. He said he'd follow later, so I tramped back alone to Portland Row. And when I entered the hall, the first thing I saw was Holly Munro, all outfitted in an agent's work belt and rapier. She had a cool leather coat on, and black leather fingerless gloves; also a wool sweater I'd never seen before.

She saw me staring. "This sweater? I know. It's not very flattering. It's one of Lockwood's old ones. He says it shrank in the wash. Still smells of him, though."

Lockwood peered out of the living room, carrying a workbag in either hand. "Holly's joining us tonight," he said. "Where's George?"

"He's still looking. But—"

"We can't wait for him. We'll only have an hour or two before dark, at this rate. He can meet us at the house. I've got your bag here, Lucy. We need to get going, so now's the time if you need to pee or anything." He disappeared.

Holly and I stood facing each other down the hall. She had that little smile on, the default one that might mean anything or nothing. I could hear Lockwood rummaging somewhere in the next room, whistling tunelessly between his teeth.

"I don't actually need to pee," I said.

"No." We stood there. Where had she gotten the gloves from? They looked suspiciously like the spare ones that I kept in my weapons locker. I recognized the sword for sure: it was one of the old blades we used for practice in the rapier room.

I took a breath. "So why—"

"Lockwood had—"

We'd both spoken at the same time. Now we both stopped—me the most decisively; after a pause, Holly resumed. "Lockwood had a difficult interview with Miss Wintergarden," she said. "She's demanding instant results. A most exacting lady. He says we need as many pairs of eyes as possible this afternoon, to try to find the Source before nightfall. I offered to come along, and he's found me a few things to make sure I'm protected and kept warm. I hope you don't mind this, Lucy."

"No, not at all," I said. Why should *I* mind? It was just like her to assume I had some problem with it. I gestured at her outfit. "Is this wise, though? What experience in fieldwork have you had?"

"I went out on plenty of assignments at Rotwell's," she said. "In fact, when I started out, I got my First and Second Grade certificates, and afterward did rapier training so that—"

"Yeah," I said. "But you should know that this visitation isn't a Type One or anything. It's much more formidable than that."

Holly Munro pushed a stray hair or two behind her ear. "Well, I've seen some things. I was there in the Holland Park Cellar case, when our party got blockaded underground by those seven spectral dogs. It was quite a tight spot. And after that—"

"I heard about Holland Park, Holly, and I can tell you the thing that makes the bloody footprints is ten times worse. I'm only saying. I don't want to frighten you. I just wouldn't want you to get hurt."

Her bland smile flickered. "I can only do my best."

"I just hope it'll be enough," I said.

Lockwood came out of the living room, stepped between us, and swung his overcoat down off the rack. "Everyone happy?" he said. "Great. I've left a note for George. Jake should be here with the taxi any minute, so let's get the equipment outside. Are those bags yours, Holly? Please—don't bother yourself. Let me."

Fifty-four Hanover Square was no more and no less welcoming than the day before. Dull shafts beamed down from the skylight high above, illuminating odd corners of the staircase, facets of wood, worn steps, random portions of the wall. I listened, as I always do when I enter such a house, but it was hard to hear with all Holly and Lockwood's twittering: he softly explaining the locations of our previous vigil, she asking endless questions and laughing at his remarks. I tried to block it out, and simultaneously stifle the annoyance that twisted deeper in my chest. Annoyance had to be avoided, along with other negative feelings. Bad things happened to agents who didn't keep their emotions under control.

I consoled myself with the thought that we'd soon be too busy trying to stay alive to worry about any of that. Plus, George would turn up, and the dynamics would change.

But George didn't show.

We got on with it anyway, hunting for possible Sources, first in the basement, then in the attic. The basement I disliked intensely: two people, to my certain knowledge, had fallen to their deaths there. The kitchen itself, separated by a kind of arch from the bottom of the stairwell, was modern and inoffensive enough, but the tiled area made my skin prickle and our thermometers drop. We probed the tiles with penknives and tested the risers of the stairs, but found no hidden cavity where a relic of the original tragedy might be found. I tested the walls for hollow spaces; Lockwood got down on his hands and knees and crawled inside the little closets that had been built beneath the staircase itself, exploring them minutely with his flashlight. We found nothing. Holly Munro discovered a nearby storeroom containing a lot of old black furniture, but on inspection we thought it early twentieth century rather than Victorian.

"It's possible that the tiles *themselves* are the Source," I said, "if that's where the final act of the tragedy played out. We could lay a chain net here and see if the haunting still takes place."

Lockwood rubbed dust off his trousers. "Good idea. But first, we'll search the attic."

In some ways the top of the stairs mirrored the bottom: the

actual area of interest was very small indeed. The servants' rooms lay beyond a paneled corridor and didn't have much to do with the tiny attic landing, which was little more than a set of polished floorboards, perhaps twelve feet square, bounded on one side by the final neat elm balustrade. Wan blue sky showed through the skylight. As I'd done the day before, I looked over the banister and saw the stairs' great flattened spiral corkscrewing smoothly down through the gray interior of the house, around and around, deeper and deeper, all the way to where shadows enfolded it in the basement four floors below.

It was a terrible drop. Poor Little Tom, to have fallen there.

If anything, the attic was even less fruitful than the basement had been. We found a cold spot, and a loose floorboard, which got Lockwood excited, but when we pried it up we found nothing but dust. A few spiders scuttled out, which might have meant something. There were no dried bloodstains, no dropped knives, no sinister fragments of clothing; and the rest of the landing was bare.

"Just a thought," Holly Munro said, "but might the staircase itself be the Source? If the boy bled all over it, if the terror he felt as he ran up it was still fused into the wood . . ."

". . . the whole thing could be the channel to the Other Side," Lockwood said. He whistled. "It's possible. Not sure how *that's* going to go down with our client, if we tell her she needs to rip her precious staircase out."

"I've never heard of a Source *that* big," I said.

Lockwood was staring up at the sky beyond the glass; it was like a slab of uncooked bacon now—gray and pink, laced with pale striations. "There *have* been cases. George would know. . . . I wish he'd hurry up. You said he only had a couple of journals to look through." He checked his watch, came to a snap decision. "All right, we need to get cracking. We'll lay out chain nets in the basement, like you suggested, and on the landing here. If that stops the haunting, all well and good; if not, we'll think again. I want us to observe as we did yesterday, and not engage. I'll take the basement this time, see if I spot anything different. Lucy, you can watch up here. Otherwise candles, defenses, everything as before."

"What can I do?" Holly Munro asked.

I smiled at her, leaned against the banister. "Tell you what," I said. "I'm *really* parched. Could you get the kettle on, do you think, Holly? And, if you can stretch to it, I'll have a couple of biscuits, too. Thanks *so* much."

Our assistant, after only the most minuscule hesitation, nodded. "Certainly, Lucy." Smiling her compliant smile, she pattered down the stairs.

"She's good," I said. "I'm glad you brought her."

Lockwood was watching me. "You need to be a bit more generous. She doesn't *have* to be here tonight."

"I'm just worried for her sake," I said. "You felt the energy of the apparitions last night. She's a novice at this. Look—she doesn't even know how to attach a rapier to her belt. She nearly tripped over it then." I allowed myself the smallest grin, saw Lockwood's gaze on me, and looked away.

"Well, you needn't worry too much," he said slowly, "because I'll keep an eye on her. She can stand beside me in my circle. That'll keep her safe. *You'll* be all right, I know. So get your chains set up now. I'll see you downstairs in a few minutes." And with that he was off, spiraling away down the stairs, his long coat drifting—and me watching him go, hot-eyed.

Nothing in the next few hours contributed much toward improving my mood. The house went dark, and our lines of snuff-lights bloomed into soft, pale life, marking the route for our ghosts. We ate, rested, checked our supplies. George didn't turn up. This was perplexing; we worried that events in the containment zone had somehow spilled over to delay him. Certainly, I missed his company, as Lockwood remained distinctly chilly toward me over sandwiches and biscuits. Holly's presence unsettled me. She was at once submissive and assertive, her inexperience overlapping with her smooth self-confidence. Both these aspects, in different ways, contrived to snare Lockwood's attention. It left me out on a limb, feeling awkward and exposed.

Lockwood had laid out a silver chain net on the basement tiles with, a little way off, a loop of iron chains. True to his word it was a capacious one, just right for two. As night set in, he and Holly retired to it, still chatting softly, while I had to trudge off to my lonely vigil at the other end of the stairs. Part of me knew I was being unreasonable. Nothing Lockwood was doing was essentially *wrong*. But the rightful pattern of events—of him and me working side by side—had been disrupted, and my disapproval chafed at my belly, as if I'd swallowed a bucketful of sharp stones.

Up on the attic landing, I sat inside my iron chains, between two shuttered lanterns, with my rapier set out in front of me like a dessert fork at a table. A chain net lay close by, in the center of the floor. I got out a book. I'd known I was in for a long wait, so this time I'd brought something to keep me occupied. It was a battered paperback thriller from Lockwood's shelves. Perhaps it had once belonged to Jessica, or to his parents, Celia and Donald Lockwood, the eminent psychic researchers, who had died in some tragic incident long ago. . . .

Anger surged through me. I shut the covers with a snap. In thirty seconds that single bald paragraph in the Archives had told me more than Lockwood had managed to in all the months I'd lived with him! The names of his parents! The circumstances of his sister's death! It would have been funny if it weren't so pathetic! What was he scared of? He seemed quite incapable of properly opening up, of giving me the trust that I deserved. Oh sure, he was *charming* enough, when he wanted to be. But it meant nothing. You could see it in his behavior now, the ease with which he mollycoddled his new assistant, while turning his back on me.

They were probably still chatting down in the darkness, side by side. Me, I had no one. I didn't have George. Heck, I didn't even have the *skull* (since Holly was unaware of my connection with it, we couldn't easily bring it along this time). There was nobody here to talk to. I was entirely alone. . . .

I shook the self-pity away. No, I was being stupid. Lockwood's behavior didn't mean anything. I turned the lantern up a notch and opened the book.

I didn't care.

Even so, black thoughts lingered over me as I began to read.

And so the night progressed, following its familiar pattern. Across long hours, the atmosphere of the house declined, insensibly,

like a noble family brought low, down the generations, to a state of
inbred madness and decay. The air grew cold and clammy, bringing
hints of foul sensations.

Everything was happening exactly as before.

I kept my head down, chewed gum, turned the pages of the book.

Midnight came. Doors opened between worlds. Presences
arrived.

I waited. Only when the crash in the basement told me
Lockwood's lantern had blown over did I pick up my sword and get
to my feet.

Silence rose through the building, pouring up over the stairwell, blanking everything out. I waited for what I knew was coming,
rushing toward me up the stairs.

Waited . . .

Out went the candles on the flights below me. Out, out, out,
out . . . one after the other, fast as you can blink. And up swept the
shapes, just as before, the frail lad stumbling, and the monstrous
hulk behind him, hand grasping for his flowing hair. This time I
heard them as they came: the wrenching rasps of the pursuer, the
despairing panting of the doomed boy. Up to the top; and here he
was, framed for an instant in my sight: a lad no older than Lockwood,
with a beautiful, bone-white face and lips drawn back in terror. I
felt—in that moment—as if his eyes met mine, as if he looked out
beyond the hideous replay of the chase and saw me. Then he was
gone. The brutish shape behind fell on him as they reached the banister; bright streams of other-light enveloped them in the moment
of their final struggle. A thrust, a scream that pierced my heart, and
the landing went pitch-black. From further down came crashes, the

splintering of wood as something hit an intervening level—then a sickening impact far below.

I took a handkerchief out of my pocket and wiped the sweat off my face. I was cold and shaking, sick with pity. I flicked the lanterns high—and stopped, looking at the floor.

There were bloodstained footprints all around my circle. Not over by the silver net, but close beside the chains. Thick and bloody, and overlapping, like someone was pacing there. Desperate to get in. Desperate for a connection. . . .

When I closed my eyes, I still saw that poor pale face.

"I think it's in the basement." Lockwood spoke quite matter-of-factly; he seemed as calm and unmoved as ever. "I saw the figure hit the ground—not where my net was, in the middle of the tiles, but over by the wall where the arch leads to the kitchens. I don't think we checked there. That's where the Source must be. I'll dig around."

We'd rendezvoused in the room of paintings, where Lockwood had made us all a reviving cup of tea. Holly Munro looked like she needed it. Her customary smile was gone; her face was strained. "It was horrible," she said. "From beginning to end. Quite horrible."

I leaned against the table with my cup. "You saw something, eh?"

"It wasn't what I *saw*; it's what I felt. The presence of the thing." She shuddered.

"Yeah, it gets you that way," I said, "the first few times. What do you want me to do, Lockwood?" I didn't look directly at him.

"Even if I don't find anything downstairs, I'll soak the area with salt solution, and lace it with iron. That should be enough, but I'd like you to salt-wash the attic landing too, please, Luce, just to be on the safe side. If I find the Source, all well and good. Otherwise we'll treat the whole staircase the same way. You can stay here, Holly. You look exhausted."

"I'll do my share," Holly said. Her voice was all weak and quavering. She made it sound like it was a big deal, like she had only one leg and we were making her dance a hornpipe up the stairs.

I rolled my eyes, drained my drink, and went off to get the job done.

On the attic landing I kicked my circle of chains to one side, got out my water bottle and a canister of salt, and began mixing some solution in a plastic bowl from one of my bags. Perhaps I stirred it harder than was strictly necessary. Some slopped over the sides and landed on one of the bloody marks, which fizzed and bubbled like soup on a hot stove. I found a cloth wipe, carried the bowl over to the head of the stairs. Then I got on my knees and, slapping the cloth around angrily, began wetting the floor.

Trouble was, this was Lockwood's solution to *every* haunting. Eradicate the ghost. Don't engage with it. Destroy it. Cooke's ghost was dangerous, yes. We had to stamp it out. But that meant Little Tom had to go as well, without a second thought. I could talk to the foul skull in the jar till I was blue in the face, because it was safely constrained, but Lockwood would never let me try the same techniques in the field. It was such a waste.

I understood *why* he was so hard-line about it. Or did I, quite? *Her younger brother was unable to stop the attack. . . .* Was it still grief that affected him? Or a deeper guilt?

I sat back on my heels and wiped my hair out of my eyes. It was then I noticed that the bloody footprints had vanished. All across the landing, at the head of the stairs, the boards were clean once more. I checked my watch. Yesterday it had taken more than fifty minutes longer for them to go. That was a clear shift in the pattern of the haunting. I listened, newly alert. And now, as I sat there, I felt a pricking in my fingers, and cold air gently brushing my face. And noises, too. Something breathing—

Or mimicking the *sound* of breathing. Remembering what it was like to be alive.

I leaned over, turning the lanterns low. I closed my eyes and counted slowly up to seven, listening to the light, shallow, frightened gasps. It sounded like a panting dog.

I stood up, opening my eyes. I'd given myself time to adjust to the dark. Even so, it took me a few seconds more to notice the outline of a person standing below me on the stairs.

The other-light that had spun about him earlier had shrunk down almost to nothing. Like a bonfire's ash the morning after, he glowed with the faintest, grayest haze. I saw nothing of the face. But the thin shoulders were clear enough, and the poor bent frame, and the slight tilt of the head as he looked at me.

"Tom?" I said.

I knew without turning around that my circle had broken when I'd kicked it; that it was just a tangled mess of chains. No worries. I could get to it if need be. And right now I *didn't* want to, because I knew that all the iron would stifle my senses, make it hard to hear.

"What do you want, Tom?" I said. "How can we help you?"

Was it my imagination, or had the glowing figure shifted? I thought it had.

"Where's the Source?" I asked. "What ties you here?"

Sounds tickled my ear: they were horribly faint and frail, but I was close to hearing them, I knew I was. I stepped a half pace closer to the stairs.

The shape moved in answer to me, drifting up a step.

"How can we help you?"

No words came, just a sad, soft cry, mournful and pathetic. It was like some wild animal, mute and terrified, hanging back from human contact. But the thing about animals was, you could tame them. You just had to prove they could trust you. I moved closer, holding out my hand.

"Tell me what I can do."

I *definitely* heard something then: it might have been words, but they slipped by too fast, making me bite my lip in frustration. A thought occurred to me: my rapier was of iron, just like the chains. Its aura would be working against me right now, muting the sounds, repelling the pathetic ghost, repelling its confidence. The answer came with sudden clarity. I cast the sword aside—and the moment I did so, I had my reward. The serving-boy's pale face swam suddenly into view, as if illuminated by a greasy shaft of light. It was just as pitiful as I remembered: big black eyes, glittering with sadness; tears running down the cheeks.

"Tell me," I said.

"*I'll tell . . .*"

A thrill ran through me. He'd answered! I was *doing* it! Just like I had with the old man in the chair. My theory was right. You *could* make contact with them, if only you were prepared to open yourself up, to take that risk.

A voice called my name from far away. It was Holly Munro, a

level or two below. The ghost wavered, its face growing dim, as if sucked back into shadow. I cursed. Even now, without meaning to, our assistant was managing to mess things up. . . .

"Don't go," I said. I took a couple more steps forward.

The boy shrank back; then, slowly, light returned to the face. It smiled.

"*I'll tell . . .*"

A slam of a distant door; the noise reverberated through the house. Again the ghost became faint. I grimaced with irritation. More voices—through the haze of my concentration I recognized George down in the hallway, and Lockwood answering him. Ignore it! The ghost was smiling at me. If I could just get it to speak again . . .

"My name is Lucy," I said. "Tell me what you need."

The smiling ghost floated nearer, flecks of blond hair quivering like a burning crown upon its brow. The body was indistinct, the arms trailing at its side.

"*I need . . .*"

"Where's Lucy?" That was George. I heard Holly's murmuring answer, then George's voice coming echoing up the stairs. "Luce!"

"*Ignore it . . .*" I was smiling too, trying to keep the connection. The cold was painful now; it hurt my skin. And how watery and hesitant my smile was beside the boy's grin. How expectant it was, how avid.

"*I need . . .*"

"Hey, Luce! We got it wrong! Robert Cooke isn't the big one! He's the *little* ghost!"

I looked at the shimmering figure, smiling at me four steps down.

"The kid stabbed the servant! Little Tom was just the guy's

nickname because he was such a big bloke! The kid was crazy! He stabbed Tom, who chased him through the house. They got upstairs, and Tom was weak from loss of blood. He grappled with the kid, who pushed him over the top. We *so* got it all the wrong way around!"

The ghost fluttered closer.

"*I need . . .*"

We so got it all the wrong way around.

Oh lovely. I took a slow step back.

The ghost opened its mouth.

"*I need YOU!*" it said.

It smiled. It lifted its arms. They ran with blood.

Then it flowed up the stairs toward me.

I fell back, shrieking, scrabbling at my belt.

The first thing I found, I threw, almost directly at my feet, beneath the bloody, reaching hands. It was nothing but salt. The capsule shattered. The ghost blinked out and at once, like an interrupted strip of film that had been cut, spliced, and then re-formed, was there again, behind me, blocking my path to the rapier, net, and chains. I darted away, reaching for a flare, tripped over my bowl of salt solution, and fell back hard against the banister. Footsteps, flashlights, voices from below. My legs were wet. So were the ghost's eyes, wet with tears; bloody footprints appeared behind it on the floor. I reached for the flare, but my fingers were numb with cold and panic; I couldn't pull the canister free. In came the ghost, still smiling, grappling at the air. With a cry I threw myself away from it, over the banister; I swung out and over the awful drop, grasping the wood, twisting around to hang there as the shape drew near. It stretched out and over me, long arms spread wide; eyes cavernous, lips parted in a hateful, imbecilic smile. Someone was rushing up the stairs. Blood fell from the curling fingers; drops fell on my jacket, fizzing and steaming. The ghost leaned closer. A vast weight pressed down on me, willing me to topple backward into space—

Quite how Lockwood managed to leap so far, I never understood. He'd been miles off on the stairs, coming up them three at a time. Now he vaulted up and over the final curling rise of banister, cutting off the corner entirely. His momentum carried him forward like an arrow, over the hideous gulf. He was practically horizontal as he passed me, rapier slashing, coat stretched out like wings. The blade of the sword sliced through the space between me and the stooping figure. The ghost snapped back out of sight. Lockwood followed it; I heard his gasp of pain as he landed; then scuffles, thuds . . . and sudden silence.

I dangled alone over the drop. "Lockwood . . ." I called.

No good. My fingers were too numb, the wood too smooth. I began to slip. . . .

Then my wrists were firmly caught, and there was Holly Munro bracing herself against the balustrade and calling out, and here was George flinging himself alongside her, grabbing at my arms and pulling; and together, not gently, like fishermen dragging in a catch, they scooped and gathered me in slow, ignominious stages up and over onto the landing.

Where I saw Lockwood lying facedown on the boards.

IV

Unrest

Chapter 13

We sat together, three of us, in the kitchen at Portland Row. A blue haze hung around the room; dawn's pre-light was here.

"He'll be all right," I said. "Won't he?"

George was staring at the remains of his hot chocolate, as if he could read the future in its frothy dregs. "Yes, of course he will. Fine."

"It's just a bang to the head, right? Knocked him out for a bit, made him woozy. . . . But he's okay now."

"Yes."

"Well"—Holly Munro smiled—"that's what we *hope*. If it's a concussion, we'll know in the next few days. Whether he's cracked his skull or not, or if there's bleeding on the brain." She mixed her fruit salad and cherry yogurt with a spoon.

A day before I'd have bristled at her prim and proper manner, at the clear way she fixed her eyes on me. But I didn't have the energy or the will to sustain that grievance now. Lockwood's condition was *my* fault. And Holly Munro had pulled me up when I was about to fall.

"He's awake, and he wants breakfast," George said. "That's a good sign."

She nodded. "I've replaced his bandages, and I think the bleeding's almost stopped. Sweet tea, food, and lots of bed rest, that's all we can do." She got up, put toast in.

"Fat chance of keeping him in bed," George said. "I've already caught him sneaking down to the phone, wanting to call Wintergarden."

Holly Munro smilingly flicked the kettle on. "You're about to do that, aren't you, George?"

"Absolutely. I'll wait until nine, then give her the good news. Everything's in hand. Right, Lucy?"

"Sure." I pushed my uneaten cereal away.

Everything, as far as the Case of the Bloody Footprints was concerned, *was* in hand—in spite of (or because of) me. Lockwood, in his frantic leap to save me, had sliced his sword clean through the essence of the ghost. Flexing, warping, it had faded back across the attic landing. George, arriving moments after Lockwood, had seen it drift through the arch that led to the servants' rooms, and fold itself down into the floorboards of the passage beyond. With me saved, he'd hurried over and stabbed his penknife into the exact place. The next half hour had been spent anxiously tending to Lockwood, unconscious following the impact of his fall. Only after he came around and we had his head wound stanched did George head for the passage alone, carrying a crowbar and a chain net. Hacking and cracking noises followed. When he returned, it was with a bundle tightly wrapped in silver: a battered tin box, filled with a Victorian woman's shawl.

Right now, that silver bundle was dumped on the kitchen table, between the mugs, the cereal boxes, and the breadboard. There was plenty of breakfast on offer. George had eaten well. Even Holly was decorously vacuuming up a range of healthy options. I hadn't had a thing.

"Lucy," George said, "you'd better eat."

I nodded. "Yeah. I will."

Holly was arranging plates and butter on a tray. "You mustn't be too downhearted, Lucy. If you hadn't exposed yourself to ghost-lock, the Visitor wouldn't have revealed the whereabouts of its Source. So really, our success is all due to you. . . ." She smiled over at me. "Looking at it one way."

A small hot cord knotted tightly in my stomach; it had been there since I'd stuttered out my first round of apologies and thanks several hours before. "Thank you," I said. "You're very kind."

George was gazing at me. "What exactly *did* you experience, Luce?" he said. "What made you put the rapier down?"

What indeed. Looking back on it, I found it hard to accept how easily I'd been manipulated by the ghost with the bloody hands. But I wasn't about to say anything in front of Holly. I wasn't even sure I wanted to talk to George.

"Were you in a trance?" Holly asked. "I knew two trainee agents once who were mesmerized by a Solitary on Lambeth Walk. They were only just rescued in time, like you. They said it was like being in a dream."

"I'm not a trainee," I said. "On the contrary, I was thinking very clearly."

"You *thought* you were," George said crisply. "Obviously, you weren't. There's a theory that some ghosts feed off psychic atmosphere. They pick up on emotions and play on it. Were you feeling particularly abandoned or needy up there?"

"No, of course not," I scowled. "Not at all." I didn't look at him.

"Just that it sounds as if a sense of neediness and abandonment was what drove Robert Cooke mad," George went on. "I got the full story in the end, in a penny dreadful pamphlet called *Mysteries of London*. I found it quite quickly in the other Archives building, but I was trapped there when DEPRAC cordoned off the street. That's why I was so late. There was a riot going on, and then someone saw a Limbless, or said they did, and it was hours before I could leave the building. But the penny dreadful account of the Horror of Hanover Square couldn't have been clearer. This Cooke—he was sixteen, by the way—had been more or less abandoned by his father, who was always abroad, but had a very close bond with his mother. She spoiled him rotten. Then she died, and he was looked after by an old nurse, who spoiled him even worse. Then *she* died, too, and was replaced by a manservant—this so-called Little Tom. He was a big man, a bit slow, and apparently more or less mute. The kid resented him, and began to maltreat him—working himself up into fits of rage when Little Tom forgot stuff, or didn't hop to quickly enough. Anyway, one night the kid goes berserk—the servant had lost his favorite boots or something. He goes down to the kitchen, begins laying into Tom, snatches up a knife, and stabs him. There's blood everywhere, and Tom's badly hurt, but he's strong and he's angry. He chases Robert Cooke up through the house to the attic landing, where they tussle again. Tom falls over the banister. Cooke's arrested, sitting there in a lather of gore." George stretched back in his chair, sniffing discreetly at an armpit as he did so. "That's how it happened, anyway. Boy, do I need a bath."

"That shawl you found," Holly Munro said. "His mother's?"

"I should think so. Something that was precious to him. Who knows what weird mix of neediness and resentment turned him mad?"

I shrugged. "Clearly one very confused individual."

"Yeah," George said. "There's a lot of it about." He looked at me.

"Well, now," Holly Munro said heartily, "Lockwood will be getting impatient. I'll take him his breakfast."

"I'll go if you want," George said. "You must be tired, Holly."

I stood abruptly. "No," I said. "I'll do it." Without waiting, I gathered up the tray.

Of all the rooms in a house, the bedroom is supposed to give the clearest insight into the personality of whoever inhabits it. That theory probably worked with my room (scattered clothes and sketch pads), and certainly worked with George's, providing you could wade deep enough in among the library books, manuscripts, crumpled clothes, and weapons to see. Lockwood's was trickier. There was a row of old Fittes Almanacs set out on a dresser; there was an armoire, with his suits and shirts all neatly put away. On the wall a few paintings of far-off lands—rivers winding through rain forest;

volcanoes rising above tree-lined hills—suggested the travels of his parents. I guessed it had once been their room. But there were no photographs of them, or of his sister, Jessica, and the striped wallpaper and gold-green curtains were, in their genteelly blank way, as uninformative about Lockwood as if it had been a whitewashed box. He might have slept there, but I always felt he didn't really *inhabit* the room in any tangible sense.

The curtains were drawn; a bedside light was on. Lockwood lay in bed, resting back against two striped pillows, thin hands folded on the counterpane. A neatly wound white bandage, tilted like a wonky turban, obscured the crown of his head; in one place a dark stain showed where his cut had bled; a spray of dark hair tufted out from under it on the other side. He was pale and thin—nothing new there—and his eyes were bright. He watched me as I set the tray down.

"I'm sorry," I said.

"Don't worry about it. You apologized before."

"I wasn't sure you'd remember."

"I don't remember everything. I remember waking with my head in someone's lap." He grinned. "Don't know if it was yours or Holly's."

"It was George's, actually."

"Oh, was it?" He cleared his throat and shuffled hurriedly up into a sitting position. "Right . . . Fine."

"I've been told to tell you to stay in bed. George is most insistent about it."

"He's deputy today, is he? I'm okay. Holly took care of my bump.

Look how neatly she did it. She has a certification in first aid, you know."

"Of course she has." I passed him the tray.

He did stuff with jam and toast. I stared off at the nearest picture. It showed a carved block of masonry, overgrown by jungle, almost lost in the shadow of the trees.

"A Mayan spirit gate, somewhere in the Yucatán peninsula." Lockwood said without looking up. "My parents went there, apparently. . . ." He crunched on his toast. "So," he said, "it's finally happened. I warned you it would, but you wouldn't listen. You forgot all your agent training, and you followed your little obsession. And you risked all our lives."

I took a deep breath. Now that the moment had come to try to explain, I found I didn't have the words. "I know it's bad. But I talked to it, Lockwood. And it talked back."

"And promptly tried to kill you. Big deal."

"So it was the wrong ghost, but . . ."

"Wrong ghost?" He laughed at me then, softly, but without mirth. "Lucy, there will never be a right ghost. Never! And you will not do anything like that ever again. Is that clear?"

Frustration flexed inside me. "I'm the only one who can *do* this, Lockwood. Doesn't that count for anything? I know the way it turned out was stupid, and yes, this is all my fault. But Lockwood, listen: you should've felt the connection—"

"Lucy," he interrupted, "you're not listening to *me*. I'll ask again: *Is that clear?*"

I rolled my eyes. "Ye-es."

"I hope so," Lockwood said, "or next time I'll leave you behind."

"And what? Bring Holly Munro along instead?"

He went all pale and silent then. "It's up to me who I take and don't take," he said slowly, "but I sure as hell won't bring anyone who jeopardizes the safety of other agents. If you want to spend the rest of the winter dealing with Cold Maidens and Stone Knockers on your own, just say the word." He stared down at his plate. "Holly's efficient, she's helpful, she keeps this place clean. Oh, and yes, she saved your life. What precisely do you have against her, anyway?"

I shrugged. "She's irritating. She just gets in the way."

Lockwood nodded. "I see. Yeah, Holly really got in your way with her frantic lifesaving leap last night. I didn't save you. George would have been too slow. But so what if she grabbed you? She's *irritating*." He threw the sheets aside. "Tell you what, I'll go down now and tell her to let you drop next time."

"Get back in bed!" The cord inside my stomach knotted tighter. My nerves jangled, my heart pounded. "I know full well what I owe her! I know how thoroughly perfect she is!"

Lockwood slapped his hand on the bedside cabinet. "So what's the problem?!"

"Nothing's the problem!"

"So . . ."

"So why did Rotwell's let her go?"

He waved his arms about his head. "What?"

"Holly! If she's so great, why did Rotwell's let her go? You told me, when she first arrived, that she'd been 'let go' by Rotwell's. I'm just interested. I'd like to know why."

"It was something to do with internal reorganization," Lockwood cried. "She suddenly found herself working for someone she didn't get along with, and she asked to move. They wouldn't do it, so she resigned. Nothing too mysterious, is it?"

"I guess not!"

"So that's fine, then!"

"Yes!" I said. "It's fine!"

"Good!" Lockwood's pajamaed legs subsided on the bed. He flopped back against the pillow. "Good," he said, "because my head hurts."

"Lockwood, I—"

"You'd better go and get some rest. You need it. We all do."

You know me. I'm obedient. I spent the next few hours up in my bedroom. I dozed a bit, but I was too wound up to rest and too tired to do anything else. I spent a lot of time staring at the ceiling. At one point I heard George whistling in the shower, but otherwise the house was silent. Lockwood and George were in their rooms; Holly, so I supposed, had gone home early.

I *was* grateful to her, of course I was. I was grateful to all of them. Oh, how good it felt to be *so, so* grateful. . . . I let out a long, sad sigh.

"Penny for your thoughts."

I craned my head and squinted at the windowsill. Since coming back from our first trip to the Wintergarden house, I'd not heard a peep from the skull in the jar. It had been sitting on my sill, next to my pile of laundry bags, deodorants, and assorted crumpled clothes. Now a faint mint-green glow hung around the glass, barely perceptible against the drab November sun. The plasm was as translucent as

I'd ever seen it, the worn brown skull mostly silhouetted, though the light caught some notches and wiggling sutures on its dome. There was no sign of the horrid face. It was just the horrid voice today.

"*I know what it's like,*" it remarked. "*Everyone hates me, too.*"

"I've got a question for you," I said, shuffling up on my elbows. "It's lunchtime, it's daylight, and you're a ghost. Ghosts don't come out in daylight. And yet still you're here, annoying me."

It gave a throaty chuckle. "*Maybe I'm different from the others. Just like you're so very different from those around you, Lucy.*" The voice grew cavern deep; it rang like a corpse-bell. "*Different, isolated—and ALO-O-ONE. . . . Ooh, that was spooky,*" it added. "*Almost frightened myself there.*"

I glared at it. "That's no answer, is it?"

"*To be honest, I've forgotten the question.*"

"You're able to manifest in daylight. How?"

"*Actually,*" the voice said, "*the main reason's probably the properties of my silver-glass prison. Just as it stops me from getting out, so it weakens the power of the light coming in. I'm in a perpetual twilight, in which I can function perfectly well.*" The glow dimmed; for a moment I thought it had gone. "*So thrill me,*" it said. "*Why are you so mournful? Maybe I can help.*"

I leaned my head back against the pillow. "It's nothing."

"*'Nothing' nothing. You've been staring at the ceiling for the last hour. That never does anybody any good. Next you'll be cutting your throat with that pink disposable razor there, or trying to flush your head down the john. I've seen girls do that,*" it added conversationally. "*Don't tell me. It's that new assistant.*"

"It's not. I'm fine with her now. She's okay."

"She's suddenly okay?"

"Yes. Yes, she is."

"*Wrong!*" The voice spoke with sudden passion. "*She's a cuckoo in your nest! She's an interloper in the nice little kingdom you've made your own. And she knows it. She loves the effect she's having on you. That kind always does.*"

"Yeah, well." I groaned and rolled into a sitting position on the side of the bed. "She saved my life last night."

It chuckled again. "*Big deal. We've all done that. Lockwood. Cubbins. There's me, of course; I've saved you loads of times.*"

"I was talking to a ghost. I got so obsessed with it, I threw away my defenses. Holly saved me. And that means," I went on doggedly, "that I'm okay with her now. Understand? You don't need to go on about her. It's not a problem anymore."

"*In fact, who hasn't saved your bacon? I expect even old Arif at the corner shop's done it once or twice, you're that hapless.*"

I threw a sock at the jar. "Shut up!"

"*Keep your hair on,*" the voice said. "*I'm on your side. Not that you appreciate me. A helpful comment here, a shrewd opinion there— that's what I offer, free of charge. The least I deserve is a quick thanks once in a while.*"

I got up from the bed. My legs felt weak. I hadn't eaten. I hadn't slept. I was talking to a skull. Was it any wonder I felt weird? "I'll thank you," I said, "when you tell me something useful. About death. About dying. About the Other Side. Think of all the things you *could* speak about! You've never even told me your name."

A whispered sigh. "*Ah, but it's not as simple as that. It's hard to bring life and death together, even in speech. When I'm here, I'm not there—it all becomes misty for me. You should understand what it's like—you of all people, Lucy—to be in two worlds at once. It's not easy."*

I went to the window and looked at the skull, at its battered landscape of nicks and marks, at the sutures winding like zigzag rivers through a wasteland of bone. It was the nearest I'd ever been to it without its repulsive ectoplasmic face popping into view. Two worlds . . . Yes. The thing is, that *was* what it seemed like, in those brief moments when I made a psychic connection. On the attic landing, I'd experienced two realities at once, and one undercut the other. Throwing my rapier away had been crazy, suicidal . . . yet, in the context of communicating with a ghost, it made perfect sense. Perfect sense, providing you found the right ghost. I thought of the bloodstained boy.

"Why do you think you threw away your sword?" the voice said. *"Why do you think you became so confused? None of your friends have a hope of understanding. It's complex, and confusing, to do what others can't. Trust me, I know."*

"Why *are* you different?" I said. "There are so many Visitors . . ."

"Ah." The voice was a trifle smug. *"But I want to come back. That's the difference."*

The doorbell rang, far off in the house.

"I'd better go," I said, "or Lockwood will try to answer it. . . ." When I got to the door, I looked back at the jar. "Thank you," I said. I went downstairs.

George and I converged on the landing just as the bell rang again. Lockwood's turbaned head was already poking around his door. "Who is it? A client?"

"Not your concern!" George called. "You're staying in bed!"

"It might be an interesting client!"

"None of your business if it is! I'll deal with it, understand? I'm your deputy! Do not get out of bed!"

"All right. . . ."

"Promise?"

"I promise."

Lockwood disappeared. Shaking our heads, George and I went to the door. Standing on the step was Inspector Montagu Barnes, looking more hangdog and weatherworn than ever. In the drab light of afternoon, it was hard to know where the folds of his face ended and his saggy trench coat began. "Cubbins," he said, "Miss Carlyle. Mind if I come in?"

If we *did* mind, we couldn't have done anything about it. We ushered him into the living room, where Barnes came to a halt, bowler hat in hand.

"You've tidied up a bit," he said. "Didn't know you had a carpet."

"Just getting on top of things, Inspector." George pushed his glasses up his nose and spoke authoritatively. "What can we do for you?"

Barnes looked about as relaxed and at ease as a man wearing fiberglass underpants. He gave a heavy sigh. "I've just had Miss Fiona Wintergarden on the phone. A very . . . influential lady. It's slightly hard for me to believe, but she's seemingly delighted with you after a job you did last night, and she's *requested*"—he emphasized the word, glaring around as if daring us to contradict—"that I employ your services for the Chelsea outbreak. I've come over to officially ask Mr. Lockwood if your company might join the investigation."

The inspector's mouth snapped shut. With his unpleasant duty over, he visibly relaxed. "Where *is* Lockwood, in fact?"

"Ah," I said. "He's ill."

"He was injured at the Wintergarden house," George said. "Bump on the head."

I nodded. "Might be a concussion. Very serious. I'm afraid he's unavailable."

"But it's all right," George said. "I'm his deputy. You can talk to me." He waved the inspector to a seat and lowered himself into Lockwood's chair.

"Afternoon, Barnes." Lockwood strode briskly into the room. He wore his long dressing gown, pajamas, and Persian slippers, and his turban looked bigger, bloodier, and more lopsided than ever. Barnes stared at him as one in a trance. "Something wrong?" Lockwood asked.

"Not at all . . ." The inspector collected himself. "I like it. Head wounds clearly suit you."

"Thanks. Right. Hop out of that chair, George. So . . . did I hear right? You're finally asking for our help?"

Barnes rolled his eyes, puckered his lips, and made some important adjustment to the brim of his hat. "Yes," he said, "in a manner of speaking. The outbreak is raging, and we could frankly do with any assistance you might provide. There were riots last night too; and the affected area of London is . . . Well, you'll have to come and see."

"Bad, is it?"

Barnes rubbed his eyes with stubby fingers. He had short, ragged nails, bitten to the quick. "Mr. Lockwood," he said slowly, "it's like the end of the world."

Chapter 14

The next evening, we saw it for ourselves.

DEPRAC had set up temporary headquarters in Sloane Square at the eastern margin of the containment zone. The square had been cordoned off from the public; giant warning posters hung from billboards, and unsmiling officers stood at entry points. Lockwood, George, and I showed our passes and were waved through.

The surrounding streets had been silent, dark and empty, though we'd seen broken windows, overturned cars, and other scattered evidence of recent protests. The square, however, was bright and filled with feverish activity. Spotlights on trucks had been drawn up in the center, illuminating everything in stark and pitiless detail. The grass was bleached out, the faces of hurrying agents and officers seared white as bone. Black rubber cables coiled across the shining asphalt like monstrous veins, supplying power to temporary ghost-lamps on the roofs and to outdoor heaters near the catering vans.

Everywhere we looked, people thronged. Bands of agents, trotting after their supervisors, patting their belt pouches, testing their swords; long-haired Sensitives, lining up drippily at the tea urns like rows of weeping willow trees; night-watch kids, be-scarfed and watch-capped, clustering as close to the heaters as they dared; suited adult DEPRAC workers rushing back and forth like they actually did something for a living beyond letting children enter a psychically ravaged area of London on their behalf. A hair salon on one corner had been commandeered; here representatives of Mullet and Sons, the rapier dealers, had created an outpost where swords could be replaced, repaired, or just scraped free of ectoplasm, once each team returned from its nightly expedition into the haunted wastes of Chelsea.

At the western end of the square, imposing iron barriers, ten feet high and fixed into concrete bases, had been dragged across to block the entrance to the street beyond. This street was the King's Road, which ran from Sloane Square for more than a mile southwest to the lavender factories of Fulham Broadway. In more ordinary times, it was the spine of a popular shopping district, with residential streets radiating from it like the barbs of a feather. The past six weeks had changed all that. Now a single gate in the barrier, locked and guarded, provided the only access, with a squat watchtower of scaffolding and wooden boards rising beside it.

As arranged with Barnes, we made straight for the tower.

The inspector's deputy, Officer Ernest Dobbs, met us at the foot of the gantry. He was a stolid young man, a typical DEPRAC officer from the tip of his cauliflower ears to the spit-and-polish predictability of his studded boots. He regarded us skeptically, eyes lingering on the wad of gauze now taped to Lockwood's forehead above his left eye. Then he led us up the steps. At the top he stood aside and waved a negligent hand.

"Here you go," he said. "Welcome to Chelsea."

The ghost-lamps of the King's Road were still on. They stretched away into the wintry dark, two strings of flickering white orbs, carrying with them the dark fronts of the buildings on either side. Dark, but not *entirely* dark: at certain windows, faint spectral glows could be seen, dim blues and greens that pulsed and wavered, and here and there went suddenly out. Far off, at the junction with a side street, a pale figure flitted away into the night. I heard snatches of screaming carried on the wind—fragments of noise that neither started nor stopped, but just repeated on a mindless loop.

A small group of agents clustered below a lamp not far from the barrier. Their supervisor, a woman, gave an order; they crossed into a house and were gone.

Near them, one of the shops had its window smashed and gaping. Glass lay strewn across the sidewalk, mixed with iron and salt. On the opposite side, a great black stain was smeared across a shop front and the sidewalk had been blistered by a magnesium blast. Leaves and twigs from recent storms lay on the road and on the cars parked at its curbs. Twists of newspaper fluttered in doorways. Many of the buildings had ghost-marks daubed on the windows. The entrance to a side street was thickly strewn with iron.

No one lived or worked here. You could feel the atmosphere, despite the barrier and the damping effect of all that iron. The air crackled with wrongness. It was a dead zone.

"See that delicatessen on the left?" Dobbs said. "We had a

Lurker there, just behind the cold meats counter. Victorian gent in a stovepipe hat. Then there were Glimmers in the pub opposite, and also the Specter of a one-armed mail carrier, don't ask me why. Night before that, Wraiths chased Grimble agents down the alley by the bookies there. The Wraiths were destroyed by flares when they reached the main road, but it was close. That's just this bit. Chelsea goes on for miles. Shows you what we're up against."

Somewhere in the mists, a faint *tac-tac-tac* sound started, soft, steady, and rhythmic.

"Digging up a body somewhere," Dobbs added. "We're finding Sources, but none of them's the heart of the cluster." He turned away.

I looked beyond him at the spotlit oasis of Sloane Square. "So all this activity isn't making much difference?"

"It's not making any difference at all."

We found Inspector Barnes in his command center, a solemn brick building on one corner of the square, which in more ordinary times functioned as the Chelsea Working Men's Club. We showed our IDs, passed through a busy corridor lined with salt-bags, went up some stairs and into the main lounge. It was a room that, even when filled with desks, filing cabinets, and shirtsleeved DEPRAC personnel, still carried an odor of pork rinds and beer. At its far end Barnes was signing papers for an underling on a table laced with half-drunk cups of coffee. Behind his back, a large-scale street map of Chelsea had been peppered with dozens of multicolored pins.

Lockwood and I found chairs; we sat, waiting for Barnes. George got out a folded piece of paper and began poring over it, occasionally gazing at the map on the wall. I passed around pieces of chocolate, watching Lockwood out of the corner of my eye. With his pale skin, open collar, and ruffled, unkempt hair, he looked more like a consumptive poet than an agent. His gauze bandage, which had been taped at a piratical angle over his eyebrow, was Holly Munro's work. She had insisted on fixing it before allowing him out, and had almost succeeded in coming, too, "to keep an eye on things." Lockwood had declined her offer, but my satisfaction hadn't lasted long. He had remained quiet and withdrawn throughout the journey. In fact, he'd scarcely spoken to me all day.

He sat now, gingerly fingering his forehead, as Barnes finished with the papers, answered someone's query, shouted at someone else, took a swig of cold coffee, and turned to us for the first time. "So, this is what you wanted," he said. "You're at the nerve center of the Chelsea outbreak. What do you want me to tell you?"

"We've had a peek over the wall," Lockwood said. "Looks fairly grim."

"If you want to go in, you can be my guest." Barnes rubbed wearily at his mustache. "But you can see what we're up against right here." He jerked a thumb at the map behind him. "That's the sum total of spectral encounters in Chelsea these last few weeks. It's a super-cluster, complete chaos. The worst I've seen in thirty years. Questions?"

George squinted at the pins. "What's the color-coding?"

Barnes sniffed. "Greens are Type Ones, yellows Type Twos. Reds indicate an encounter where someone has been attacked. Blacks"—he scratched at his mustache and looked at his knuckles before setting his hands softly on the desk—"blacks mark a death. There've been twenty-three so far, including agents. So you can see that, roughly speaking, an area of half a square mile has experienced this extreme upsurge. Yet up until four weeks ago, Chelsea was no worse than anywhere else."

"Any pattern in terms of sub-types?" Lockwood asked. "Any kind of ghost that's more frequent than the rest?"

"It's random. Mostly Shades and Lurkers, of course; but plenty of Specters and Phantasms. Wraiths, too, and rarer kinds; we had a couple of Limbless and a Screaming Spirit. In many cases we've found their Sources—but the overall picture's not changed."

"How much of the district's been evacuated now?"

"Most of the King's Road and surrounding streets. Not the western end—the attacks taper off sharply there. But most of the shopping district is closed, and we've got hundreds of people camping out in churches and sports centers. As you must have heard, they blame DEPRAC. Some of the ghost-cults are getting lively. There's been violence, protests. Unrest is spreading."

"I hear Fittes and Rotwell are going to put on a nice show to make everyone feel better," I said.

Barnes tapped the tips of his fingers together with deliberate care. "Yes, the carnival. It's Steve Rotwell's idea—a great big party, all about 'reclaiming the night.' There's going to be a grand procession from the Fittes tomb to the Rotwell one. Floats, balloons, free food and drink. The lot. And when that's all been swept up, we'll still have this little mess to sort out."

There was a silence. "You need to find the heart of the supercluster," George said.

"Think we don't know that?" Barnes's pouchy eyes, small and shrunken with exhaustion, glittered balefully at him. "We're not stupid. And it so happens we know precisely where the heart is. You can see it for yourself." He took a cane from his table, leaned back, and prodded at the map. "We're here, on the eastern side. And here's the King's Road running down, straight into the area with the thickest density of hauntings. Now, if you analyze the position of the pins, Cubbins, you'll find that the exact geographical center is *here*, where the King's Road meets Sydney Street."

"And what's at that corner?" I asked.

"Barry McGill's Tip Top Fish and Chip Shoppe," Barnes said. "That's its name. I don't eat there myself. And it's clean. Well, when I say *clean*, I mean supernaturally so. Its problem is grease, not ectoplasm. Anyway, we've taken it apart and found nothing. The shops and houses around it are innocent too. We've checked back, and the history of that area is quiet. No obvious plagues or atrocities—which are what we *always* expect to find at the heart of a cluster. So that's your precious center, Cubbins." He tossed the cane onto the table. "What do you say to that?"

"It's obviously *not* the center," George said.

Barnes uttered an oath. "And you know where is, I suppose?"

"No. Not yet."

"Well, feel free to find it for me. Right, I'll get you passes to the containment zone, Lockwood, as Miss Wintergarden requested. Try not to get yourself killed, and—more importantly"—Barnes picked up papers and sat back in his chair; he was already moving on to something else—"do your best to keep out of my sight."

"I'm going in," Lockwood said, when we were back out in the square a while later, holding passes with the ink still wet. "I want to walk around a bit, get a feel for the place. Don't worry, I won't engage with anything. What about you, George?"

George had his faraway look, the one that made him look like a constipated owl. "At the moment," he said, "it would be a waste of time for me to go in there. I'd rather do a quick errand. Come with me, if you want, Luce. You could be useful."

I hesitated, looked over at Lockwood. "Depends if Lockwood needs me."

"Oh, no thanks. I'll be all right." His smile was automatic, unengaged. "You go with George. I'll see you both back home." A wave, a swish of the coat; he walked away toward the barrier. After a few steps he was lost behind agents, Sensitives, technicians.

I felt a jab in the center of my chest—pain, and anger, too. I spun on my heel, rubbed my hands together in a show of enthusiasm I didn't altogether feel. "So where are we going, George? Some midnight library?"

"Not quite. I'll show you."

He led the way out of the square, south past DEPRAC cordons, down another street strewn with evidence of the protests: discarded placards, bottles, litter of many kinds.

"This is terrible," I said, stepping among the debris. "People are going mad."

George stepped over a broken AGENTS KEEP OUT sign. "Are they? I don't know. They're scared. They need to let their tension out. Never good to bottle things up—is it, Lucy?"

"I suppose."

We crossed an empty street. Away to the right I could see another one of the iron barricades—we were following Chelsea's perimeter toward the Thames.

"So you think Barnes is wrong somehow?" I said. "The center of the super-cluster's not *at* the center? How does that work?"

"Well," George said, "Barnes is making a *lot* of assumptions. He's treating this like an ordinary haunting event, when it so plainly isn't. At this scale, how can it be?"

I didn't reply. It didn't matter; after a moment George continued as if I had.

"Let's think about it," he said. "On the most basic level, what's a Source? No one really knows, but let's call it a weak point, where the barrier between this world and the next has grown thin. We saw that in Kensal Green, didn't we, with the bone glass. That was a window, somehow. A ghost is tied to the Source. Trauma or violence or injustice of some kind stops a spirit from moving on, and, like a dog tethered to a post, it circles that object or place until someone severs the connection. Okay. So what's a cluster? There are two kinds. One is when a single terrible event has created a whole lot of ghosts in one fell swoop. Blitz bombs did that, and plague, and there was that hotel in Hampton Wick that had been destroyed in a fire, remember? We found more than twenty crispy-fried Visitors in the abandoned wing. The *other* kind is when there's a powerful original haunting that gradually spreads its influence over the area. Its ghosts kill others and so, over many years, a troupe of spirits, from different times and places, is assembled. Combe Carey Hall was a great example of that, and Lavender Lodge. It's this second type of cluster that DEPRAC's assuming is going on here."

"Well, it must be," I said. "There's no connection between all the Visitors Dobbs was going on about. They're all from different times and places."

George shook his head. "Yeah, but what's triggering them? Barnes is looking for some key ghost that's igniting all the other hauntings in this area. But I think he's missing a trick. These ghosts haven't been building up *slowly*; they've all become super-active almost overnight. Two months ago the Problem wasn't any worse here than anywhere else in London. Now we've got whole streets being evacuated." He crossed the street beside me, shoelaces flapping, hands weaving as if physically molding his idea. "What if it isn't some terrible *ancient* event that's igniting all these spirits, but something terrible that's happening *now*?"

I looked at him. "Such as what?"

"I haven't the faintest notion."

"You mean like lots of people dying?"

"I don't know. Maybe."

"People aren't going missing. There's no evidence of any disaster going on. Call me picky, George," I said, "but that doesn't make any sense at all."

He stopped and grinned at me. "Nor does Barnes's theory. That's what's so exciting. Anyway, next up," he went on, "we need a bit of expert advice."

"One of your powdery old pals from the Archives?"

"On the contrary. We're going to see Flo Bones."

I stopped and stared at him. *That*, I hadn't expected. Florence Bonnard, aka Flo Bones, was a relic-girl of our acquaintance. She dug for psychic jetsam on the Thames shoreline and sold it on the black market. She had decent psychic abilities, it was true, and had given us invaluable help from time to time; it was also true that she wore garbage bags, slept in a box under London Bridge, and could be smelled two clear blocks away. Tramps had been known to cross the street to get upwind of her. Which would have been acceptable if she'd been sweet and gentle-natured. Sadly, talking to her was like striding naked through a thornbush: not impossible, but there was a definite element of risk.

"Why?" I demanded. "Why are we going to see her?" You can tell I put a bit of emphasis into it.

George took his map out of his pocket. "Because Flo is the unwashed queen of the river, and the river marks the southwestern boundary of the outbreak zone. Look here: the outbreak forms a sort of funnel shape with the Thames along one side. There must have been alterations in activity that Flo will have noticed. I want her perspective on it before we go any further. Will Barnes or Dobbs or anyone have thought to chat with her? I don't think so."

"They won't have chatted to the carrion crows, either, or the foxes on the rubbish dumps," I said. "Doesn't necessarily make it worth doing."

Even so, I went with him.

For an occupation that was officially classified as criminal, the relic-men had a pretty well trodden set of haunts: certain pubs and cafés along the riverbank where they met and bartered their nightly hauls. George and I did the rounds and, a couple of hours later, discovered Flo.

She was outside an eatery in Battersea, picking at her evening breakfast of scrambled eggs and bacon in a grubby Styrofoam tray.

As usual she wore the odious blue puffer jacket that thoroughly masked any human shape, as well as carrying the knives and rods and mud picks of her trade. Her straw hat was pushed back, exposing her blond hair, her pale face, and the shrewd lines at the corners of her eyes. I wondered, as I often did, what she would have looked like if she'd had a bath and all-around fumigation. She wasn't that much older than me.

She glanced at us, nodded, and continued making fast work with the plastic fork. We drew as close as was comfortable, watching her shovel the yellow globules into her mouth. "Cubbins," she said, "Carlyle."

"Flo."

"Where's Locky?" The fork paused. "Off with his new girl, is he?"

I blinked. "No . . ." I said. "She doesn't come out on cases. She's not even an agent, really. More of a secretary and housecleaner than anything." I scowled at Flo. "How d'you even know about her?"

She scraped unconcernedly at the corner of the tray. "Didn't."

"I don't understand."

"It's been eighteen months since he hired you. That's about standard. I figured he'd have prob'ly moved on to the next one."

"Actually," George said, stepping between us and nudging my hand away from my rapier hilt, "Lockwood's busy working on the outbreak. He's sent us to ask you something."

"A question or a favor? Either way, what's in it for me?" Bright teeth gleamed.

"Aha." George ferreted in a dark corner of his coat. "I have licorice! Lovely tasty licorice . . . Or maybe I don't . . . 'S'funny, I must've eaten it." He gave a shrug. "I'll have to owe you."

Flo rolled her eyes. "Classy. Lockwood does this sort of thing so much better than you. So what do you want? News from the underworld?" She chewed ruminatively. "It's the usual round of backstabbings and unexplained disappearances. The Winkman family's in business again, they say. With old Julius in jail, it's been left to his wife, Adelaide, to get the black market side up and running. Though it's young Leopold who everyone *really* fears. Worse than his old man, they say."

I was still scowling at Flo. I remembered Winkman Junior as a smaller, squatter version of his father, gazing at us when we gave evidence in the dock. "Come off it," I said. "He's only about twelve."

"Doesn't stop *you* from gadding about like you own London, does it? Better keep your wits about you, Carlyle. The Winkmans are lying low, but it was *you* who put Julius away. They'll want hideous, grisly revenge. . . . So"—she tossed the tray aside and clapped her hands together briskly—"I make that one bag of licorice you owe me, Cubbins."

"No problem," George said. "I've made a note. Only that's not strictly what we're after this time, Flo. It's the Chelsea outbreak. You work the shores along there. A couple of blocks inland, all hell's breaking loose. But what's it like by the river? Are you seeing more activity?"

Flo got up off the post where she was perched, stretched carelessly, lifted up the mud-crusted base of her coat, and set about scratching something in the recesses within. "Oh, yeah—there's been a definite upsurge. 'Ticularly on the southwest side. The streets are thick with them there. I've stood at Chelsea Wharf, seen three Shades and a Gray Haze with one sweep of the eyes. 'Course, you never get 'em within fifty yards of Old Mother Thames. Just too much running water, ain't it?"

George nodded automatically, then with more enthusiasm. He was staring at his map. "Yes . . . yes, that's true. Thanks, Flo, you've been enormously helpful already. Listen, can you keep an eye on the river edge for me? Particularly that southwest side. I'd like to know if it continues to have the most Visitors. Any patterns you see, let me know. There'll be licorice by the ton in return, obviously."

"Okay." Flo finished scratching, adjusted herself, and picked up her burlap sack. With one quick motion, she slung it over her shoulder. "Well, got to fly. Tide's low tonight. There's a rotted hulk off Wandle Keys that needs pilfering. I'll see you." In a few steps she'd vanished in the river mist. "Hey, Carlyle," her voice drifted back. "Don't worry about Locky. He must like you really. It's been eighteen months, and you're still alive."

I stared after her. "What does that even mean?"

But Flo had gone. George and I were alone.

"I wouldn't pay any attention," he said. "She just likes to annoy you."

"I guess."

"Likes to play with your emotions, like a cat batting at a helpless mouse."

"Oh, thanks. That makes me feel just dandy." I looked across at him. "How come she doesn't ever give *you* a hard time?"

George scratched the tip of his nose. "Doesn't she? I've never thought about it."

Chapter 15

L ockwood returned from his Chelsea excursion early the following morning, having spent the hours of darkness walking its streets silently and alone. He seemed both energized and baffled by the experience, which had served to back up what we'd seen from the viewing platform and heard from Inspector Barnes.

"The whole area's awash with psychic activity," he said. "Not just Visitors, though there *are* plenty of those. It's the whole atmosphere of the place, like everything's been disturbed. All the usual sensations we look for are there, drifting like invisible clouds along the streets. Chill, miasma, malaise, and creeping fear—you can feel them rolling at you down the alleys, or stealing out of the houses as you pass. They engulf you—it's all you can do to draw your rapier. You stand in the road, heart pounding, wheeling around, waiting for the attack—and then they're gone. I'm not surprised there have been so many casualties among the agents trying to make sense of this. It's enough to drive anyone mad."

He had seen a number of spirits at a distance—in upstairs windows, in gardens, and the backyards of shops. The streets were mostly clear, peppered instead with jumpy groups of agents, who seemed randomly dispersed. Halfway down the King's Road he had helped steer an Atkins and Armstrong team out of a Gibbering Mist; later, a conversation with a Tendy supervisor leading four shivering operatives across a little park had led him to Sydney Street, the supposed center of the disturbance. It had seemed neither better nor worse than anywhere else.

"They're digging up all the graveyards," he said, "and sowing salt on the ground. Rotwell teams are bringing out equipment I've never seen before: guns firing salt-and-lavender sprays. It's not doing a bit of good. Frankly, I don't see us making a difference unless we come up with something new."

"That's up to me," George said. "And I've got a theory. But I'm going to need some time."

He was given it. From then on George undertook no new cases, but instead slipped seamlessly into research mode. Over the next few days we scarcely saw him. I glimpsed him once or twice slipping away from Portland Row at dawn, backpack bulging with papers, the documents he'd gotten from Kipps clamped under his arm. He haunted the Archives and the libraries of southwest London, returning only as night fell. He went back to speak to Flo Bones. In the evenings he sat alone in the kitchen, scribbling obscure notes on the margins of the Thinking Cloth. He said little about what he was doing, but he had that old spark back in his eye, glittering behind his glasses like a firefly buzzing in a jar. That showed me he was on to something.

While he labored, the rest of us drew back from Chelsea. Lockwood visited it once or twice more, but achieved little, and soon returned to ordinary cases. This was what I was doing too. We didn't, however, work on anything together. With her usual cool efficiency, Holly Munro divided things equally between us, juggling our clients and our time.

Holly had been hired to give us respite and enable us to work more easily as a team. It was a strange thing, but we now seemed busier—and more isolated from each other—than ever before. Somehow Lockwood and I never went in the same direction, or even went out at the same moment. We got up at different hours. When we met at home, our smiling assistant was generally there too. Since the Bloody Footprints debacle, he and I had rarely been alone. And Lockwood seemed happy enough for it to continue that way.

I didn't think he was still angry. I'd somehow have preferred it if he *had* been. He just appeared to have removed himself from me, cloaked himself in the old detachment that had never really gone away. He was always scrupulously polite; he answered my questions, made bland inquiries into how I was getting on. Otherwise he ignored me. His head wound healed; only the faintest scar showed on his forehead, just below the hairline. Like everything else about him, he wore it well; but I knew it to be a sign of my incompetence and failure, and the sight of it pierced my heart.

I couldn't help feeling annoyance, too. Yes, I had brought him— and the others—into danger; I'd messed up, I couldn't deny it. That didn't excuse the way he'd locked himself away, as if behind iron barricades, and utterly shut me out.

This was how it had always been with Lockwood, of course. Silence was his default response. He'd probably been like this ever since Jessica died.

Her younger brother was unable to stop the attack . . .

A case in point: his sister. He'd told us *something* about her, but hardly enough. I still didn't understand what had actually happened in that room. Without his testimony it was impossible to know.

Actually—*not* impossible. It *could* be done. I had Talents that could find things out. As I walked across that landing in my anger and frustration, I often glanced at that door.

A week passed. George worked; Holly organized; the skull made regular rude comments. Lockwood and I kept going our separate ways. Now large posters were appearing near every Tube station advertising the coming carnival: elegant Fittes ones, with silver hue and sober font, inviting us to "Reclaim the Night"; garishly bright ones for the Rotwell Agency, complete with a grinning cartoon lion trampling a ghost and holding a huge hot dog in its paw. Meanwhile, each day saw further demonstrations in the streets around Chelsea, clashes between protesters and police: people injured, water cannons used. The night of the grand festivity approached in a tense and nervous atmosphere.

Lockwood had originally been reluctant to attend the carnival, as he was annoyed that we hadn't been asked to contribute to the agency procession. To our surprise, however, we received a special invitation. Miss Wintergarden—now luxuriating in the freedom of her ghost-free town house—was one of the VIPs accompanying the procession. She invited us to join her as her guests. The prospect of such a central position was one Lockwood could not resist. On the afternoon of the great day, the four of us made our way across London to the Fittes mausoleum, which was where the carnival would begin.

Yes, that's right. The four of us. Holly Munro came too.

The mausoleum stood at the eastern end of the Strand, at the point where it became Fleet Street. It occupied an island in the center of the road. A church had stood there once, but it had been bombed in the war, and the stark, gray building that housed Marissa Fittes's remains was its replacement. It was oval-shaped, with a concrete dome. On the western side two majestic pillars framed the entrance, which faced back in the direction of Fittes House. A triangular pediment atop the pillars was carved with the Fittes emblem: a noble unicorn. Monumental bronze doors led into the interior, which on special days was open so that the public could see the pioneer's simple granite tomb.

Darkness was falling now, but the carnival was a display of organized defiance, and there were many reassurances on show. Ghost-lamps hung suspended on cables above the roads. Lavender fires burned on corners. Lamplit smoke swirled above the crowds that washed between the buildings like a restless tide.

Higher still, a giant inflatable rapier, silvered, shiny, and the length of a London bus, bobbed and buffeted against the soft, black night. The entrances to Waterloo Bridge and the Aldwych were choked with booths and sideshows. "Shoot the ghost" stalls rubbed up against "Poltergeist rides," in which vast mechanized arms whirled shrieking men and women into the air. Merry-go-rounds featured cartoon phantoms, stalls sold cobweb cotton candy; sweets in the form of skulls, bones, and ectoplasm were everywhere on display. As with the midsummer fairs that normally featured such entertainment, it was the adults who were the most eager customers. Tonight they were protected; tonight the central streets were lined with lavender and salt, turning this artery of London into a fairyland of color that could be exploited safely. They hurried past us, men and women, old and younger, faces flushed with excitement at the transgression and the danger of it. An air of forced hilarity hung over them. I could feel their desperate need to turn their night fears into something childlike and unthreatening.

We stood silently at a corner, hands on our sword hilts, watching the world skip by.

"The grown-ups seem happy," Lockwood said. "Don't you feel old, sometimes?"

"Yeah," George said. "All the same . . ."

Lockwood nodded. "Yes, I could do with some ice cream, too."

"I'll get them," I said. There was a stand opposite. "Holly? What do you want? A lentil and hummus wedge, or something?"

Her hair was pulled back beneath a fur-lined hat, showing her face to good advantage. She had on that coat that was ever-so-slightly like Lockwood's, and, to my annoyance, wore a rapier, too. "Actually, I think a soft-serve twist. It's a special occasion."

"Oh, I thought you only did healthy." I went to the stand and got in line for cones.

Beyond the mausoleum I could see the carnival procession waiting—a row of ornate floats, constructed on the open tops of

Sunrise Corporation trucks, and decorated with agency colors. On some, giant logos had been erected. The looped chains of Tendy & Sons wobbled on the end of a white mast; behind them I spotted the Grimble fox and the all-seeing owl of Dullop and Tweed. Each had been fashioned from papier-mâché, steel, and wood, then gaudily painted. They were vast effigies twenty feet high. Around them stood willing young agents, ready to lob candy and pamphlets into the crowds. There were one or two show floats, too, housing troupes of actors who were to recreate famous scenes from agency history. Shivering corpses in white makeup prepared for battle with gallant agents dressed in historic costumes. They would perform throughout the parade.

At the head of the line stood the largest vehicle, decked out in red and silver, the colors of the two great agencies. Above it, bobbing gently against the darkened sky, hung two vast helium balloons, firmly cabled—a unicorn and a rampant lion, the symbols of Fittes and Rotwell respectively. You could just see the chairs where Penelope Fittes and Steve Rotwell would sit.

"Miss Carlyle? Lucy Carlyle?"

"Yes?" The voice had barely carried above the noise of the crowd, and I didn't recognize it. Nor did I at first make much of the very short and stocky person, swathed in a fur overcoat, with a broad-brimmed bowler hat concealing his bent head, who stepped suddenly toward my line. His trousers were of soft velvet; beneath them, expensive patent leather boots shone in the white lamplight. I caught a glimpse of an ivory cane held between heavily jeweled fingers; then, with a swift flick of his wrist, he tipped the hat back so that his face was revealed. It was a boy with a broad smooth countenance, a wide mouth and cheeks that subsided into his soft thick neck like folds of uncooked dough. Strands of oiled black hair were visible at the temples. Small eyes glared at me, sharp and blue as crystal shards.

I knew him immediately. There was only one person with a face like that. Or rather, there were two, but the elder one was swarthier, hairier, and in prison. That other individual was the notorious Julius Winkman, the black marketeer. This youth was his son, Leopold, a chip off the old block.

"What can I do for *you*, Master Winkman?" That's what I *should* have said, in a cool, collected voice. As it was, I was too surprised; I made a goggling sound and just stared at him with my mouth open.

George, suddenly at my side, spoke for me. "Can we help you?"

"I have a message," the boy said. "My father sends his compliments, and says he'll be seeing you all very soon."

"Doubt it," I said. "Your daddy got twenty years, didn't he?"

Leopold Winkman smiled. "Oh, we have ways and means, as you'll soon see. And here's something in the meantime, Miss Carlyle, by way of being on account."

With that, swift as a portly snake, he stuck out his hand and prodded me sharply in the solar plexus with the head of his cane. The air was driven out of me; I gasped and doubled over. Leopold Winkman flipped his hat rakishly low across his eyes, spun on his shiny heel, and began to saunter away. His picture of serene progress was interrupted by George, who, whipping his rapier from his belt, stuck it diagonally between Leopold's legs so that he tripped, lost his balance, and tumbled forward into the crowd, bumping into three burly workmen and spilling their drinks on their wives and girlfriends. An altercation ensued, as Leopold unsuccessfully tried to escape, lashing out at all comers with his little cane. As his cries were swallowed by the angry throng, George helped me upright and led me back across the street.

"I'm all right," I said, rubbing my stomach. "Thanks, George. But you don't have to bother about me."

"Oh, okay."

"Rats—I never got the ice cream cones."

But it didn't matter. When we got back, Lockwood was looking at his watch. "We'd better get to our seats," he said. "Time's flying. Wintergarden won't want us late."

He led the way among the stalls and under the shadow of the Mausoleum where a row of armed officials studied a guest list and waved us in among the floats. Giant balloons moved above us; streamers gusted, engines revved. We walked through gas fumes.

Miss Wintergarden had said she was important, a friend of high society. As with other matters, she hadn't lied. It turned out that she was on the first and biggest float, the VIP one. Up a gangway we went and out onto a wooden platform fixed to the top of the truck. It was very broad, extending out on both sides. Flags flew from poles above, and plastic lions and unicorns stood at intervals along the sides like sentries on castle battlements. Rows of chairs were already filled with the broad backsides of the great and good, men in dark, expensive overcoats, women heavily be-furred. Young members of the Fittes and Rotwell agencies moved along them, pouring out mulled wine and offering sweetmeats. From a far-off seat, Miss

Wintergarden saw us, fluttered her fingers condescendingly, then paid us no further attention.

Lockwood, George, and I hung back, uncertain where to sit, but Holly Munro seemed galvanized. She smoothed down her coat, adjusted her hat, and sashayed between the seats, nodding to people that she passed, exchanging little waves with others. She seemed miraculously at ease. At the front of the platform she looked back and beckoned. By the time we reached her, she was already talking to several of the most important people on the float, among them the leaders of the two great agencies, Penelope Fittes and Steve Rotwell.

We knew Ms. Fittes already, and were on good, if distant, terms. A striking woman of indeterminate age, the twin auras of beauty and of power were intertwined about her and could not be easily separated. She wore a long white coat that dropped almost to her ankles; the collar and cuffs were made of brilliant white fur. Her long dark hair had been lifted and ornately styled; it was fixed in position by a curling silver band. She greeted us warmly, which is more than could be said of the man beside her—Steve Rotwell, chairman of the Rotwell agency.

It was the first time I'd seen him properly in the flesh. He was a big man, solid beneath his heavy coat, and handsome in a ponderous sort of way. He was thick-jawed and clean-shaven, with unusual green eyes. His fair hair was turning gray behind his ears. He nodded at us distantly, his gaze wandering elsewhere.

"A wonderful evening," Lockwood said.

"Yes. A remarkable attempt to entertain the people." Penelope Fittes pulled her coat more tightly around her neck. "It was Steve's idea."

Mr. Rotwell grunted. "Cakes and carnivals," he said. "Keeps everyone happy." He turned away from us, looking at his watch.

Ms. Fittes smiled at his back. You could possibly surmise her impatience with the whole proceeding, but she was too well bred to reveal it. "And how is Lockwood and Company faring?"

"Oh, trying to make our mark," Lockwood said.

"I heard about your job for Fiona Wintergarden. Well done."

"I'm busy researching," George put in. "Wanting to achieve big things. I'm hoping to join the Orpheus Society one day. Have you heard of it?" He looked at her.

Penelope Fittes hesitated, then her smile broadened. "Most certainly."

"Not sure I have," Lockwood admitted. "What is it?"

"It's a loose association," Ms. Fittes said. "Industrialists who are trying to understand the mechanics of the Problem. I encourage their work. Who knows what we might uncover if we use our ingenuity? We would be pleased to welcome you one day, Mr. Cubbins."

"Thanks. Though I'm not sure I really have the brains."

She laughed prettily. "Now, Mr. Lockwood, you must meet one of my companions. This is Sir Rupert Gale."

The person beyond her had been leaning on the rail around the platform. He turned: a young man with blond hair, cut short at the back and sides, but tightly curled above his forehead. He had a neatly manicured mustache, full lips, and very bright blue eyes. His cheeks were pink with cold. Like most of the others on the float, he was smartly dressed; unlike them, he leaned idly on a polished cane. He transferred this to his left glove, so that he could shake Lockwood's hand.

"Sir Rupert." Lockwood didn't betray, in the causal way he spoke, the fact that we had encountered the man before. Last time we saw him, he'd chased us up a drainpipe onto a factory roof, expertly wielding a sword-stick hidden in his cane. He was a collector of forbidden artifacts, and we'd stolen a very important one from under his nose after Winkman's black market auction. True, we'd been wearing ski masks at the time and had jumped into the river to escape him, but we were under no illusions. Our role had since become common knowledge. He knew us, too.

"Charmed." The gloved grip held Lockwood fast. "Haven't we met?"

"I don't think so," Lockwood said. "I'd surely remember."

"Thing is," Sir Rupert Gale said, "I remember faces. I never forget 'em. Even parts of faces. Even chins."

"Oh, there are dozens of people with ugly mugs like mine," Lockwood said. He kept his hand locked in the other's; he coolly held the young man's gaze.

"Sir Rupert is a good friend of the Fittes Agency," Penelope Fittes said. "His father helped my grandmother, long ago. He helps train young agents in swordfighting and other martial skills."

"I'd love to give you a demonstration." Sir Rupert let go of Lockwood's hand. "We must have a chat one day—about your business, and mine."

Lockwood smiled faintly. "Any time you like."

A horn sounded. Penelope Fittes made her way to the front of the platform; we retreated along the float. Someone pressed hot drinks into our hands. Firecrackers burst above the streets, bathing us in silver and red; the truck gave a jerk and began to move.

"Bit forward of you to ask about the Orpheus Society, George," I whispered.

George frowned. "No . . . she was totally chilled about it, wasn't she? Kind of surprised me. I thought it might be more hush-hush, somehow."

He took a chair; Holly Munro stood chatting with members of the Rotwell contingent. Lockwood and I remained standing, staring out over the crowds.

Along the Strand the convoy went, carving its way slowly down the center of the road through wreaths of lavender smoke. Tinned music blared from speakers at the corners of the platform: dramatic, patriotic songs. Ms. Fittes and Mr. Rotwell waved. Behind us came the first show float, with actors in old-fashioned costumes hunting ghosts through Styrofoam ruins to the accompaniment of drums. Agents threw candies and other freebies down; the crowd cheered. People leaped and surged to catch them.

Cakes and carnivals, Steve Rotwell had said. *Keeps everyone happy.*

But did it? It seemed to me that ripples of electric energy were running through the crowd. Not quite the random chaos you'd expect. Subtle waves of movement like wind blowing through the wheat fields close to my childhood home. Behind the cheers rose other noises—hisses and murmurings that lapped against the rumble of the wheels. Pale faces stared up at us beyond the smoke.

Lockwood had sensed it too. "There's trouble brewing," he whispered. "Everything's wrong. The fair I sort of understand, but this parade thing's weird. I don't know who it's going to convince. I feel awkward and exposed up here."

"It's dire," I agreed. "Look at those idiots capering on the float behind. And the worst of it is—we're going so slowly. The whole thing's going to take *hours*."

But it didn't. Our journey was very short.

We were halfway down the Strand, not far from Charing Cross Station and Fittes House, when members of the crowd broke through the cordons and surged across the road. The float stopped, its engine idling. One of the agents took a tub of candies and tossed them from the float: I watched them fall, glittering like rain. Then something else shot through the air—large and dully shining. It landed in the float not far from me, striking the middle of the platform with a crack of broken glass. At first I thought it was one of the ghost-lamps strung above us, and that its cable had somehow broken. Then I felt the wave of cold and sudden psychic fear and realized the truth—but I was still standing rooted to the spot when the first Visitor appeared in the air before me.

Chapter 16

It was a pale, bent thing, stooped and thin. Yellowed, diaphanous rags coiled around it. Though its outline held firm, its substance bubbled up and over like soup in a pot. Glimpses of a rib cage, of a folding, twisting spine, of flesh and sinew welled up, stretched, and were sucked back in again. The head was lowered, the white arms crossed over the face as if it feared to see us, fingers splayed above like splintered horns.

Those of us young enough—those of us who *saw*—had our rapiers out before the second ghost-bomb landed. That would be Lockwood, George, and me; Holly Munro, observing us, struggled to pull her rapier free. Some of the younger Fittes agents, the ones not throwing candy, dropped their trays of drinks and reached for their belts. But the adults were blind—even the ones right by the ghost looked straight through it, merely adjusting their coat collars as if they felt a sudden chill.

Another crack of glass; another Visitor unfolding, up by the front of the float. Other ghost-bombs landed in the crowd. Almost at once we heard the screams begin.

Lockwood and I started forward; George, too. Sir Rupert Gale had also reacted. He pulled at his cane, drawing out a silver blade. Above us, Penelope Fittes and Steve Rotwell turned, responding to the outcry of the crowd. A few startled dignitaries began to rise.

The first ghost moved. Its head rotated impossibly; it flowed backward, through the nearest seat, straight through its occupant, a short, fat tweedy woman. Threads of plasm lingered on her contours as it pulled around her and away. Her eyes rolled upward, her arms jerked in rhythmic spasms; she slid soundlessly onto the floor.

"Medics needed!" Lockwood roared. A wave of fear had engulfed the company; people were throwing chairs back, milling back and forth, too stupid to wait and listen to their senses. Old as they were, faint sensations might have alerted them to the ghosts, and so kept them alive.

The Visitor moved with random darts and scurries, hiding its head as if in pain. Two men toppled as it touched them, collapsing against others, redoubling the panic. I was almost on it. I raised my sword.

A Rotwell operative stepped out in front of me, a magnesium flare in his hand.

"No! Not here!" I shouted. "You'll—"

Too late. He threw it. The flare shot past the ghost, bounced off the back of the nearest seat, and exploded against the side of the platform. Fragments of wood blasted into space; Greek Fire rained down upon the crowds. The platform gave way. A whole section crumbled like a sea cliff, propelling three people, including a screaming Miss Wintergarden, out onto the street below. Sir Rupert Gale, caught by the explosion, was spun to the very edge, left clinging to the broken boards. George escaped unharmed; he reached the ghost and carved the air around it with his rapier, seeking to prevent it from touching the people on either side.

The Visitor had been peppered with burning iron, and the ghost-lamps hanging above the street weren't doing it much good, either. Plasm steamed from it. As it cringed back from George's blade, it removed its arms from its face. It had no features, no eyes or nose; nothing but a sagging triangular mouth. At the front of the platform neither Penelope Fittes nor Steve Rotwell had lost their heads. From beneath his coat, Rotwell had drawn a sword—longer, thicker than a normal rapier. Ms. Fittes had taken her hair band off, shaken her dark hair free. The band was a crescent moon—sharp, made of silver. She held it like a knife.

Rotwell jumped down among the seats, swatting a chair aside. He strode toward the second Visitor—a Phantasm—which several of his agents had pinned back. Holly Munro had been shepherding people to the far corner of the platform. She reached the fallen woman, and knelt down at her side.

Lockwood clutched my arm. "Forget the ghosts!" he cried. "The bombs! Where'd the bombs come from?"

A squawking lady in furs and silver collided with me; I cursed, shoved her away. I jumped onto a seat, spun around, looking down into the street. There were Visitors here, too, fracturing swiftly in the glare of the ghost-lamps. Around them the crowd bent and crumpled, then tore itself to tatters as it fled in all directions.

"I can't see anything," I said. "It's carnage."

Lockwood was beside me. "The bombs weren't thrown from the crowd. Above us. . . . Check the windows."

I stared at the buildings all around. Rows of windows, black, blank, identical. I couldn't make out the details of what was inside. High above us, the Fittes and Rotwell balloons dinked and swayed.

"Nothing. . . ."

"Take it from me, Luce. Whoever did it is somewhere up—"

There. Two windows changed shape; two patches of darkness grew and gathered form. Two figures leaped from the first floor windows directly overhead, hurtling down to land upon the platform. Twin thuds of booted feet.

Only Lockwood and I saw them; everyone else was fixated on the ghosts. For a split second I had a clear view of the man nearest to me. He wore black sneakers, faded jeans, a black zip-up top. His face was hidden behind a black ski mask, but through the mouthhole poked an overhang of bright white teeth. In one hand he had a rapier; in the other a snub-nosed gun. Strapped across his spindly chest—his top was half unzipped—a leather belt held odd devices. They looked like short batons, the kind relay runners use, with clear glass bulbs at one end. Pale light swirled in them. I knew what they contained.

An instant's glimpse; then he was away, he and the other man, flitting across the platform. They went toward the front of the float where Penelope Fittes stood in her bright white coat, a crescent dagger in her hand.

Lockwood and I ran, too; but we were too far away to intercept them.

As they drew close, the nearest raised his gun.

Lockwood threw his rapier, hard and horizontal, like a javelin; it nicked the assailant's arm, knocking the gun away.

Then I was on him, striking left and right. He parried my blows with quick defensive moves. It told me he was agent-trained.

The other man ignored us. He walked quickly toward Penelope Fittes, reaching in the pocket of his jacket. Now his hand too held something small, snub-nosed, and black.

Ms. Fittes saw it. Her eyes widened. She fell back against the rails.

The edges of the float were decorated with plastic lions and unicorns. Lockwood grasped a unicorn by its horn and snapped it off its pole.

The assailant aimed his gun—

Lockwood dived forward, swinging the unicorn in front of him.

Two blasts; two thuds, so close in time they became one thing, a start-stop noise. The unicorn spun out of Lockwood's grasp, a pair of neat round holes halfway up its neck.

Now the man I was fighting brought his greater strength to bear; his swordplay became faster. His blows jarred my rapier in my hand.

All at once he stopped, looked down in some surprise. I was surprised too. He had a sword point poking through his chest.

The man swayed, then toppled sideways. Behind him Mr. Rotwell pulled his blade clear.

The remaining assailant had turned toward Lockwood. But now from the other side Sir Rupert Gale strode forward, rapier raised and moving fast. The man paused, fired at Sir Rupert, and missed. With a spring, he bounded away along the platform.

Lockwood was scooping up his rapier. "We can catch him yet, Luce," he cried. "Come on!"

We ran along the platform, almost empty now. Past George, busily subduing the Visitor with salt and iron; past Holly, tending to the fallen. The second ghost had vanished, destroyed by Rotwell's agents. Mr. Rotwell and Ms. Fittes themselves were left behind.

The man in black reached the end of the truck, gave a mighty spring, and landed on the cab of the following vehicle. Lockwood leaped after him, coattails flapping; a moment later I did the same.

Over the cab roof, boots clattering. Onto the show float, racing under gothic arches, cutting through a confusion of screaming performers. The assailant swung his sword, fired his gun in the air. Men in ghost-sheets and women in long bloody dresses took running jumps over the edge in clouds of talc, landing in the crowds like phantoms from on high. Tidal waves of terrified yells rolled out around us. The man in black turned, aimed the gun at us; it didn't fire. He tossed it away, kicked at a foam arch, sent it tumbling down. Lockwood dived one way, I the other. It crashed between us, squashing a small actor.

Running jumps to the next float, decorated with the mustard hues of Dullop and Tweed. Above us loomed their papier-mâché symbol, a giant all-seeing owl. The assailant threw a flare; it burst against the owl, tearing a hole and sending a rain of burning matter onto our heads.

Lockwood and I didn't break our stride. We ducked, brushed hot embers from our hair, ran on.

It was the official Rotwell float, the next one, and again it was close enough for the fugitive to leap to. Here were scattered piles of plush lions, Rotwell soft drinks, and other gifts to be given to the crowds. The agents who'd been in charge of them were gone. The man in black slipped and skidded on the toys and bottles; with a curse he turned, hurled down a ghost-bomb. A willowy figure rose up—and was instantly sliced to ribbons by simultaneous slashes of our swords.

We were almost upon him, so close I could hear his ragged breath. He reached the back of the float. Beyond was a gap, impossible to jump: the next float was many yards away.

"Got him," Lockwood said.

But there, at the end of the truck: the Rotwell lion, a giant helium balloon straining at the end of a tethering cable. The man in black slashed the rope free, caught it as it whipped away. He was carried up and out over the Strand. He tossed his sword clear; now he dangled from two hands.

Lockwood and I slammed into the side of the truck. Lockwood exhaled. "Drat. Not sure I can quite match that."

"It's blowing him toward the river."

"You're right, it is. Come on."

Down onto the street, amid the deserted stalls and sideshows. A moment before, a mass of people had stood here. Now it was a field of hats and lavender, of scattered charms and abandoned shoes. The Poltergeist rides had stopped mid-session; trapped customers called to us from atop the extended arms. Down the road, off the Strand, and up the gentle rise to Waterloo Bridge, Lockwood and I kept running, side by side.

I glanced across at him—his eyes were bright, his face set, his long legs swinging beside mine. We were in step together, perfectly in sync. And in that moment the world around us dimmed and blurred. Tensions and disagreements fell away. Everything was simple. It was just us, together, chasing a giant helium lion down a central London street. Everything was as it should be—back in its proper place.

Perhaps Lockwood had had similar thoughts. He grinned at me; I grinned at him. A swell of joy rose in me, displacing the ache of my muscles, my burning lungs. It was like the previous few weeks just hadn't happened. I wanted it to last and last—

"Hope I'm not disturbing anything."

Drawing abreast of us, sword-stick moving easily: Sir Rupert Gale, punctiliously polite as ever. If he'd had a hat, I bet he would have raised it as he ran.

"Hello." I didn't strictly *want* to answer, but his courtesy was catching. "This fellow's a trier, isn't he?" Sir Rupert nodded at the precariously dangling form ahead of us; the river's breeze had caught the lion, which was now being buffeted dangerously. The man was being dragged, bumping against a wall. "I swear I almost want him to get away."

"Getting away from you is a tough art," Lockwood said. "I bet only the very best can do it."

"Ha, ha! Yes!" Sir Rupert Gale smiled as he ran. "He's going to go out above the river. If I had my Purdey twelve-gauge shotgun with me, I'd take a potshot now and chance it. He's not so high the fall would kill him."

He had no gun, and we could not run fast enough. Even if we had, the balloon was still too high to catch. It floated out above the bridge. For a moment the Rotwell lion was beautifully illuminated by the lanterns on the parapet, sparkling like a Christmas bauble on a child's tree. We saw the man clinging desperately below it, still masked, his jacket and shirt pulled up so that his pale back and stomach were exposed. Strong winds took him; the lion was whirled around. I thought it might be looping back toward us. Then it was pulled out to the center of the river, and that was when the figure lost his grip and fell, thirty, forty feet, into the black Thames. He hit it hard. The waters closed over him. We ran to the balustrade, the three of us, and craned our necks, but saw nothing.

Minutes passed. The lion balloon was already almost lost to sight, a glittering point of red carried by river winds east toward Blackfriars Bridge, the Tower, and, ultimately, the sea.

"Dead and drowned, I suppose," Lockwood said.

Sir Rupert nodded. "You'd think. Then again, we all know better than that." He tapped gloved fingers on the balustrade.

I stepped away. "Who were they?" I said.

"Enemies of Fittes and Rotwell, presumably," Lockwood said. "Anyway, he's gone."

"Yes." Once again Sir Rupert Gale tapped his fingers on the stone. He turned away from the edge and, in the same deftly casual movement, his rapier flicked up and jabbed straight out at Lockwood's side. The action was so quick I didn't fully comprehend it; nor the way Lockwood's arm shot down to block the sword tip with his rapier guard. For a second, the blade was caught in it, trapped in the twisted fronds of metal; I could sense Sir Rupert's exertion, Lockwood's, too. It gave me a chance to see how close the sword had been to slicing cleanly beneath the ribs. It would have traveled into his lungs and pierced his heart. Then the young man sprang back, wresting the tip free. His eyes were bright, he balanced lightly on the tips of his toes.

"Fast," he said. "Well done."

"You, too." Lockwood turned to face him, bending his wrist as if it pained him. "Of course, *I* never attack from behind."

"Oh, hardly behind, Mr. Lockwood. You had a fair chance, as you've just proved most admirably." Sir Rupert ran a hand through his hair. "Well, our mutual enemies have gone, as you say, but here we are—you and I alone together. Isn't this a wonderful opportunity to settle our dispute?"

"Hey," I said. "In just what sense is he alone? I'm here too."

"Don't worry, Luce," Lockwood said. He flicked back the edge of his coat and lifted his rapier. "Well then, Sir Rupert? Come on."

"You can't do this!" I cried. "There'll be witnesses! The others will be here in five minutes—"

"Miss Carlyle," Sir Rupert Gale said, "a few seconds is all I need."

Lockwood's grin was flinty. "That was what *I* was going to say."

Shouts and beams of swirling flashlight. Up along the crest of the bridge came George, followed by a host of Fittes and Rotwell agents. Lockwood and Sir Rupert Gale stood looking at them. Then Sir Rupert laughed and returned his rapier cleanly to his belt.

"And now we're heroes together," he said. "What an experience. What an excellent evening."

He smiled at us; we smiled at him. Three crocodiles on a muddy shore could not have smiled at each other more eloquently or with such gleaming teeth. We stood waiting, the three of us, and a moment later were engulfed by shrill inquiries and breathless congratulations.

Chapter 17

In the aftermath of the carnival attack, certain things swiftly became clear. Other things did not.

Remarkably, only one person had incontrovertibly lost his life—the assailant killed at Mr. Rotwell's hand. The body of the other, despite police (and relic-men) combing the Thames shoreline the next day, was never found. Unlikely as it seemed, it was possible he had escaped.

Within minutes of the attack, the Strand and surrounding streets were sealed off, and the grand parade abandoned. Twelve people, eight from the crowd and four from the Fittes and Rotwell float, had suffered ghost-touch. All were treated on site by medics traveling with the parade. Speed of response ensured that all of them pulled through—even the tweedy lady first enveloped by the Visitor. She had been kept alive by an adrenaline injection administered on the spot by Holly Munro.

George had single-handedly subdued the original ghost. After surrounding it with iron, he had hunted across the platform till he found the splinters of broken glass that marked where the missile had struck. There too he found a piece of jawbone, complete with two brown teeth. When this was wrapped in silver, the Visitor had vanished. Further exploration by other agents located five other Sources scattered among the debris of the floats and street.

Penelope Fittes was uninjured. Steve Rotwell had sprained a wrist while helping his operatives subdue the second Visitor. Both leaders appeared in a photograph on the front cover of the *Times* the following day, Rotwell's arm displayed prominently in a monogrammed sling.

Curiously enough, despite ending in complete disaster, the carnival—from the point of view of the authorities, at any rate— was a notable success. The shock of the attack seemed to bring the people of London to their senses. Perhaps it was the very human nature of the assassination attempt. Perhaps it was outrage at the real physical danger Ms. Fittes and Mr. Rotwell had been in. Present difficulties notwithstanding, they were icons, representatives of the noble firms that had done so much to keep the population safe for over fifty years. Whatever the answer, after that night the Chelsea protests more or less evaporated. DEPRAC and the agencies were left to go about their business undisturbed.

One other immediate result of the events was a new celebrity status for Lockwood & Co. A photograph of Lockwood during the chase appeared on page three of the *Times*, and in several other papers. He was caught mid-jump between two floats, his coat flying out behind him, his hair blowing back, his sword held so loosely in his hand it seemed he scarcely touched it. He was a thing of light and shadow, fragile and dynamic like an airborne bird.

"That's one I'm definitely putting in the album," George said.

We sat in our living room, bottles of lemonade on the table, glasses in our hands. The fire was on; we had the curtains shut against the dying day. Piles of crumpled newspapers lay between us, scrutinized and cast aside; it almost seemed like our old habits of mess and squalor were back again. Holly Munro had been too busy to worry about it. She'd been fielding calls all day. She was with us now, our casebook open on her knee. Up on the cabinet, the skull in the ghost-jar, quiet and unnoticed, overlooked the happy scene.

"Oh, I shouldn't bother really, George," Lockwood said. He took a sip from his glass. "Though if you do, the one in the *Guardian's* got the nicest resolution. They don't crop the coat like the *Times* does, either. Plus, you get a bit of Lucy's knee as well."

I snorted good-naturedly. My knee aside, I wasn't in any of the published photos, but for once the papers *had* mentioned me by name. In fact, all of us got in. My action against the assailants; George's struggles with the ghost; Holly's life-saving efforts with the syringe: all this had been noted and praised. But Lockwood, who had protected Ms. Penelope Fittes at the crucial moment, was the one singled out for the highest commendation. Certain rich industrialists who had been on the beleaguered float were quoted as mentioning awards.

"We've had so much interest since last night," Holly Munro said. "Requests for interviews, and many possible cases. All of them thanks to you."

"Thanks to all of us," George said.

"You know, it shouldn't be just me in the picture," Lockwood said reflectively. "It should be the whole team. Though I guess the shot wouldn't be quite so dynamic. We all did so well."

"*Yeeuch. . . .*" That was the skull, its voice echoing faintly in my ears. "*How utterly nauseating. Pardon me while I quietly vomit over here.*"

I glared at it over the heads of the others. As far as Holly Munro was concerned, the skull was a trapped ghost like any other. I couldn't talk back to it, or even make rude gestures. Silent glaring was my limit. But it's hard to glare successfully at a skull.

"*What's with all the lovey-dovey stuff, Lucy?*" it whispered. "*You should be vaulting the coffee table and pouring your drink down Munro's blouse. Look at her, little Miss Prim and Perfect, taking center stage. You're not standing for this. Go on, punch her! Kick her shins! Snatch off her shoes and throw them in the fire!*"

"Will you just—" Everyone looked at me; I cleared my throat. "Will you all just raise a glass," I said, "to our success? To Lockwood and Co.! To the team!"

Everyone drank. Lockwood smiled at me. "Thanks, Luce. Nice one."

It wasn't quite the way he'd looked at me that moment during the chase, but it echoed it; warmth rushed through me. "So who was behind the attack?" I said, ignoring extravagant gagging noises coming from the jar. "The papers don't seem to have a clue."

"Could be ghost-cults," Lockwood suggested. "Some of the crankier ones actively resent all agents. They think we're blocking messages from the beyond. But their usual tack is angry leafleting, or making speeches at Hyde Park Corner on a Sunday. It's quite a step up for them to try to assassinate Fittes and Rotwell."

"Well, Fittes, anyway," George said. "No one fired at Rotwell."

"That's because he'd already jumped down to tackle the ghosts, hadn't he?" Lockwood said. "To be fair to Rotwell, he reacted quickly, much better than the other adults—except our friend Sir Rupert, of course. The way Rotwell killed the terrorist was . . . Well, you clearly don't mess with him."

"Right," I said. In the whirl of events I'd hardly registered it at the time, but Rotwell's brutally efficient dispatching of the assassin had somehow stuck with me. I shuddered at the memory. "Just another thought," I said. "Could it have been Winkman? When George and I met him just before, he threatened some kind of attack."

"Against *us*," George said, "not everybody. No, this was way too upscale for Leopold. For starters, whoever it was had the capability of creating those 'ghost-bombs.' The dead man had one of the unexploded bulbs on him, Barnes was telling me. They're quite sophisticated. Someone had to constrain those ghosts, fix their Sources in the glass. It's not amateur work."

"Might have been bought," I insisted. "Black market stuff."

"Yeah, but staging the attack. Think of the organization required."

"We just don't know," Lockwood said. "That's the long and short of it. No one's been able to identify the body yet. When that happens, we may get an idea. The good thing is that Penelope Fittes's life was saved, and few people were seriously hurt. True, Miss Wintergarden broke her leg in her fall, but she hardly counts,

I feel. And we've flushed *one* of our mysteries out into the open: we know a bit more about Sir Rupert Gale than we did before."

Holly Munro had been making neat little notes in the casebook, no doubt planning every last upcoming detail of our lives. "He comes from a very rich and powerful family. If what you say about him is true—"

"It *is* true," I said.

"Then he's not to be taken lightly."

"Maybe not," Lockwood said, "but if he'd wanted to act against us underhandedly, he'd have done it long before now. He's someone who waits for the sporting chance. We'll settle accounts one day. Now—" He sat up, took his glass in hand. "I'd just like to make a final toast. We've all done well. But there's one person who I feel should be thanked for their very special contribution."

His eyes met mine; I felt happiness run through me like syrup; even the tips of my toes felt warm and prickly. I was back in that moment during the chase. I *hadn't* been mistaken.

"Holly," Lockwood went on, "if it wasn't for you making the initial contact with Miss Wintergarden, we would not have been there at all last night. You gave us the opportunity to be in the right place at the right time. Thank you, on behalf of all of us, for what you're bringing to Lockwood and Co. You've done wonders in the office. I think one day you'll do wonders in the field." He raised his glass; the lemonade glinted in the firelight. Holly Munro looked charmingly embarrassed. George clapped her on the back just as she was about to take a sip, making her cough and gulp, also very charmingly. If it had been me, of course, I'd have spurted my drink like a fizzy comet across the room. But it wasn't me.

On the cabinet opposite the skull in the jar grinned as I played slowly with the glass in my hand.

"Oh, I didn't do anything," Holly said, when she had recovered. "You're the agents. I'm just the backroom player. . . . But, as I say, we *have* had some interesting requests this morning, if you want to see?"

And, what do you know, George and Lockwood did. Glasses in hand, they made immediate synchronized buttock shuffles across the sofa. Somewhere in my mind a gate slammed, a portcullis crashed down. I rose slowly. "I'm going upstairs for a bit," I said. "Just need a rest."

Lockwood raised his hand. "Don't blame you, Luce. You're a star. See you later."

"Yeah. See you."

I left the room, shutting the door softly behind me. The hall was cool and full of bluish shade. It seemed soft and flat, echoing the blankness I felt, my detachment inside. The voices of the others were muffled as I climbed the stairs.

The funny thing was, I still acknowledged the connection that Lockwood and I had made, the previous night, as we ran together side by side, and the rest of the world molded itself around us. It had been real, I didn't doubt it. But what I *did* doubt was Lockwood's ability to sustain that connection in any meaningful way. When the excitement was over, he just snapped back to his usual cool remove, keeping me at a distance. Well, that wasn't good enough anymore. We were closer than he admitted, and I deserved . . .

What did I deserve?

Information, at the very least.

And if he wouldn't share it with me, I'd take it for myself.

On the landing, I didn't hesitate. I went to the door, grasped the handle—so often seen, yet utterly unfamiliar in my hand—turned it, and walked right through. I closed the door (first rule: never linger on a threshold) and leaned back against the iron bands that sealed the psychic resonance inside. My eyes were closed. I felt the thrum of the death-glow on my skin; it ruffled through the roots of my hair.

How *strong* it was. You could feel her proximity.

Lockwood had said she'd never come back. But she was close. Close . . . The echo of the event that had occurred here still raged like cold fire.

What *had* occurred here?

I opened my eyes. Near dark. And in my haste and anger I hadn't brought a flashlight.

I couldn't put the light on (if it even worked), just in case someone saw it showing under the door. But it wasn't quite dusk yet, and of course there was that pale, pale blaze hanging above the mattress. I shuffled across the room, steering well clear of the bed, and pulled the curtains back.

Dust and dried lavender. It made me want to cough.

Balloons on the wallpaper, animals on the bulletin board: sad aspects of the departed girl. Curious decorations for a girl of fifteen, as if she'd clung to childhood. They'd been relics of the past even before she'd gone. Blue-gray shadows lay over the furniture and boxes, the piles of crates and lavender bouquets. So many boxes. It was only now that I realized how much of the room was filled with them. This was where he kept it all, still near at hand, but out of sight and almost out of mind: the remnants of his family.

I didn't want much. Just something. Something about the sister or the parents that would help me understand him.

He'd said, that time he'd brought us here, he'd said there were pictures in the dresser. I stepped around boxes, inched my way across; silent, silent as I could. They were below me, somewhere downstairs.

The first drawer stuck, and I didn't want to force it. The second was filled to the brim with tiny cardboard boxes of many shapes and colors. I opened one: a golden necklace, with a dark green stone, lay on a sheet of cotton batting. His sister's? No. His mother's? I put it back, slid the drawer shut. The next was packed with clothes. This I shut too—more hurriedly this time.

When I bent to the last, one of my knees clicked painfully—I'd jarred it jumping between trucks. The drawer was stiff, and very heavy; I stuck with it, easing it slowly out. . . .

It was filled with photographs.

There was no rhyme or reason, no albums, no order. They were lying loose, packed in madly one on top of the other, as if they'd been forced. Some were torn and crumpled where they'd gotten caught in the edge of the drawer, some creased, some upside down. The mess was so tightly jammed they'd become almost a single solid thing, and in the atrocious light, it was hard to make out anything at all. Many seemed to be of foreign landscapes like the painting in Lockwood's bedroom: towns and villages, wooded hills. Many, but not all.

The photo I picked up couldn't have been that old, but all the colors had faded, leaving it a sort of yellowish-green. It had two people in it. The older was a girl with dark hair in a kind of long bob. She wore a knee-length skirt and a white shirt with a frilly collar of the kind I remembered my sisters wearing when I was very young. Her face wasn't as slim as Lockwood's, and the nose was different . . . but she had his eyes. She was gazing out of the picture with that calm, direct, black-eyed look I knew so well. It made my stomach turn over to see it. And she was about my age, heading toward mid-teens. Her expression was serious and expectant, like she had something she wanted to say to the person holding the camera but was waiting until he or she had finished the shot. I wondered what it was that was on her mind. Looking at her, I felt pretty sure she was the type to have gotten her point across.

Sitting on her lap was a small boy, much younger. She had her arm firmly around his waist. His legs were sloping to the side, with him leaning sideways, as if he was itching to be off and away. In fact he was already moving, for the head was slightly blurred. Still, you could see the familiar dark hair and eyes. You knew who he was.

I replaced the picture and leafed my fingers gently down among the photographs, delving into Lockwood's past. And as I did so, his voice sounded suddenly on the landing, loud, vibrant, directly outside the door. A thrill shot through me, the terror of revealed transgression. I sprang upright, stepped back, and immediately stumbled over one of the low cardboard boxes on the floor behind me. Even as I fell I knew I mustn't make a noise; I twisted around, threw out a hand to stop myself—

My fingers closed on the wooden board at the foot of the bed.

I tensed my muscles, came to an abrupt and jerking standstill, almost horizontal, boots twisted behind the box, arm bent, face almost on the footboard. I stretched out my other hand and pressed it palm down on the rough, tired fibers of the carpet, softly taking my weight.

And now there was George's voice, replying to Lockwood. They were at their bedroom doors. Going to get some rest; copying me.

"Yeah, but we need to keep an eye on her," George said. "Out in the field, I mean."

"She's stronger than you think. Don't underestimate her."

Holly, always Holly. The two doors closed. I allowed my body to sag across the box. When I was sure everything was silent, I did a half roll sideways, off the box, onto my knees, and grabbed the bedpost to pull myself up.

How cold the wood was; I was much nearer the death-glow than felt comfortable. I thought of the black scorch mark hidden beneath the covers. I thought of the face of the black-eyed girl. Then, like electricity arcing through a wire, sound crackled upward through my fingers, out of the past, through my eyes and teeth. And everything went—

Dark. There was a child's voice calling in it, high and shrill.

"Jessica? Where are you? I'm sorry. I'll come now."

Silence in the dark. No answer. But something heard: a cold malignant presence, waiting in the room. I felt its anticipation. Lacking life, it was drawn to its warmth with powerful hunger. Very recently, released from its prison, it had tasted life—and drained it clean away.

"I'm here now, Jess. I'll come and help."

The presence swelled in eagerness. Chill spread out from it, rippling against the walls.

"You needn't sulk," the child said. Footsteps on the landing. The sound of an opening door.

And then? A scream (the child); the cold presence welling up and outward (I sensed its triumph); a sudden twang of metal scraping; and then a sharper and more bitter cold—the cold of iron. And then: confusion. A frenzy. A stabbing, slashing mess of shrieks and curses; a carving and a cutting, an evisceration; a spectral power torn asunder, swallowed up by grief and rage.

And then—

Almost nothing. The presence, in all its hunger and its chill malevolence, was gone.

Just a boy's voice calling in the dark. Sobbing out his sister's name.

"Jessica . . . I'm sorry . . . sorry. . . ."

The voice dwindled away; the refrain (never varying, never ending) grew fainter. It shrank into the past and could not be heard. And then, when I raised my head, I realized that I could once again see the pale light burning above the empty mattress, and my hand was still clamped on the wooden board. I pried my fingers open. It was dark outside the window. I was crouching by the bed, and my knee hurt horribly.

Even then, in the desolation and emptiness that came afterward, it took me an age to gather the courage to get up, open the door, and slip out onto the landing. What if he'd heard? What if he came out, right then, with the sounds of his sister's death still tingling on my fingers and his child's voice echoing in my ears? What would I do? What would I honestly say to him?

But the door did not creak, and my footsteps made no noise, and I crossed the silent landing safely. I allowed myself a big sigh of relief as I began to climb the attic stairs.

At which there was a violent bang behind me, and a voice shouting my name.

Screaming Spirits and sudden visitations of the Limbless have frightened me less. I spun around, face contorting, body sagging against the wall.

"George! I was thirsty! I just went down to get a drink of water!"

"Yeah?" His fist was filled with papers; he had a pen behind his ear. "Listen, Lucy. I know what's going on!"

"A drink of water is all it was, I swear! I ate too many salty chips at tea, and— Oh, you're talking about the Chelsea outbreak, aren't you?"

Behind the spectacles I saw it blazing, that old familiar fire. "Yes," George said. "The outbreak. I've cracked it, Luce. I've figured it out. I know where it began."

V

Dark Hearts

Chapter 18

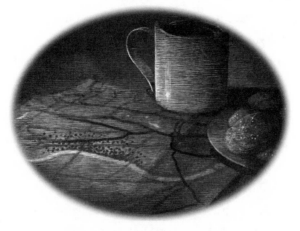

"It's amazing what you can come up with," George said the following morning, "when you lie awake in bed. It's such good thinking time. I've been working with the maps, and the documents Kipps gave me—you know, the ones that list all the Visitor encounters in Chelsea over the last few weeks. And I've been doing a *lot* of ferreting in the Archives. But it's only when you lie there and let the information settle in your mind that you start to see the pattern."

"And you have?" Lockwood asked.

"Oh yes, I see a pattern now."

Breakfast time, and we were at the kitchen table. But the bowls and jam jars and sticky fragments of toast had been cleared away. We were suited and booted and ready for business; there wasn't a bathrobe or rumpled T-shirt to be seen. Holly Munro, coming up from her early morning vacuuming of the office, had caught the expectant atmosphere. She produced newly baked honey biscuits from a tin and set them in the center of the Thinking Cloth. We had mugs, tea, and, in George's case, a manila folder stuffed with documents. Everything was set for him.

It was fortunate, from my point of view, that his moment of inspiration had come now. It allowed me to relegate my experience of the night before to the back of my mind. Or try to. For whenever I looked at Lockwood, so coolly contained and self-assured, the memory of that desperate little voice came rushing back, and set me squirming in my seat. Nor could I forget the echo of that little boy's violent grief, the fury that had instantly avenged his sister and—years later, in his every action—*continued* to avenge her.

Well, I'd wanted to understand him better, and now I did. Eavesdropping on his past had been effective. But as I should have expected, it didn't exactly make me feel too good.

At least there were other things to distract me now.

George opened his folder and selected the topmost paper. This he unfolded and pushed along the table to us. "Here," he said. "What do you think of this?"

It was a map of the Chelsea district, very similar to the one behind Barnes's desk, only festooned with George's indecipherable pencil scrawls. There was the Thames, there was the King's Road, and there were all the hauntings that had taken place over the last few weeks. Unlike the DEPRAC map, George hadn't color-coded them. Each was marked with a neat red circle, dozens and dozens of them. In some areas the streets were almost completely obscured by overlapping dots, which merged together like spreading stains.

We stared at it. "Well . . ." I said at last, "it's spotty."

"I looked a bit like that once," Lockwood remarked, "when I had hives one time. George, I'm sorry. I can't make out anything there."

George adjusted his spectacles and grinned. "Of *course* you can't. Which is just one of the reasons why poor old Barnes has got things so wrong. So—this is a summary of every supernatural incident that's been recorded in Chelsea up until a couple of nights ago. Impossible to see a pattern, I agree. The only thing you can hope to do is pinpoint the geographical center—that's Sydney Street—and hunt there. But we know that's been a red herring."

He paused to take one of Holly's biscuits. Our fragrant assistant was listening to George with rapt attention. We all were. Despite his untucked state, his slouching posture, despite the apparently leisurely manner with which he dunked the biscuit in his tea, excitement crackled around him like forked lightning. The charge had built up in him over weeks of solitary work; now it sprang into all of us unbidden. He pointed at the map with a stubby finger. We leaned helplessly forward.

"One thing you might notice," George said, "is the shape of the spotty super-cluster. It's kind of like a squashed rectangle: narrow to the west and wider in the east, like a shoebox that's been stepped on. And the reason for *that* is the first clue to what's going on here. First off, here's the Thames: the largest mass of running water in London. We know that no ghosts can cross it—so that's the southern border of the cluster."

"I think even Barnes knows that," I said.

"Sure, but look to the north. See here, along the Fulham Road? What's along here?"

"I know that!" Holly Munro exclaimed. "Iron foundries for the

Sunrise Corporation! When I worked for Rotwell, senior management often attended meetings there. I sometimes went with them. There's a number of small ironworks there."

"*Exactly*," George said. "And not just Sunrise. I think Fairfax Iron's got some factories in Fulham, too. So the smoke that discharges from all those chimneys settles over that part of London, taking with it tiny particles of iron. And that's why spectral activity is blocked here. The super-cluster stops at this northern boundary."

Lockwood whistled. "I see where this is going. . . . So here in the west, down at the squashed end of the rectangle, there's got to be something else, too, something plugging the gap, stopping the contamination from spreading. . . ."

And then I had it. "The Brompton lavender works!" I said.

We all knew the site. It was the biggest in the city, where they shipped in fresh stuff from the north of England and worked it into perfumes and ointments, or dried it nicely for cushions, displays, and other home defenses. "But it's down here at Sand's End, isn't it?" I went on. I pointed at a great bend, where the river turned south. "There's a gap between it and the Fulham ironworks. Why can't the outbreak get through?"

"Because the wind blows off the river and spreads the lavender scent inland," George said. He chuckled. "It closes off the gap perfectly. So you've got the Thames to the south, the iron district to the north, and the lavender factory in the west: three strong geographical influences that stop the haunting from spreading. They act as a kind of funnel that distorts the shape of the cluster. And if the cluster's distorted, there's no point in looking for a conventional center to it, is there? Which brings me to this. . . ."

He got out another map and spread it on the table. Lockwood pushed our cups out of the way to make room; Holly put the plate of biscuits on the floor.

It was similar to the first, except that the dots were colored orange, and there were far fewer of them, particularly to the north and east.

"This is the situation one month ago," George said. "It was already bad, but not nearly as crazy as now. I got most of this from that report Kipps gave me. See how there's already plenty going on in the middle of the King's Road? But also in the west, too. And if we go even farther back . . ." He produced yet another map, this one with only the smallest smattering of green dots. "This is *six* weeks ago, when it all officially began. See where the center of activity is now?"

"Looks like it's shifted farther west," I said, "back along the King's Road. There's not so much going on, though."

"No, it was only just getting started. But here's the clincher."

A fourth map. It had the fewest dots of all—just seven, in fact. They were all dark blue, like spots of ice, and all were set in a little bow-shaped arc around the western tip of the King's Road. "This is two months ago," George said, "before the whole thing blew up. Nothing special—just a Shade in a launderette, a couple of Tom O'Shadows, a patch or two of Gray Haze. . . . Incredibly minor stuff, scarcely made the local papers at the time—I had to really grub about to find reports of 'em—and they aren't included in DEPRAC's tally. Barnes probably wouldn't consider them to be part of the outbreak at all." He looked around at us. "But *I* do. If you start here, and then look at the others in sequence, you'll see the pattern I'm talking about."

"It's a wave," I said.

"Right. A ripple of supernatural activity spreading from a single focus, flowing out along the only channel available to it, through the heart of Chelsea."

"And that focus—" Lockwood prompted.

"Is just about *here*." George stabbed his finger at a blank portion of the map, around which the seven blue dots circled like an arc of orbiting moons. It was a block on the south side of the King's Road, right at its western tip, not far from the river and the lavender works. It seemed to be a single large building.

There was a respectful silence. Lockwood exhaled slowly. "You're a genius, George. I've said it before."

George selected a giant biscuit from Holly's plate. "You can say it again if you like."

"Why DEPRAC hasn't figured this out," I said, "is beyond me. What idiots they are."

"I actually might not have noticed the pattern myself," George admitted, "without Flo Bones's help. She's been patroling Chelsea's river edge for days. She confirms that the strongest supernatural activity she's noticed is all down in that corner. She's seen masses of spirits swirling about, displaying signs of agitation. That's where the psychic wave breaks most heavily on the shore." He prodded the map in the same place again. "No question about it. The power's emanating from there."

"So what *is* this place," I asked, "at the end of the King's Road, and why haven't we heard of it? And why, if it's the focus"—I gestured at the maps—"aren't there any dots on it at all?"

"Good questions." Taking his time, in the manner of a plump

magician producing a rabbit from a hat, George reached into his folder once more. He pulled out a picture, a black-and-white copy of a photograph taken from a newspaper clipping.

It showed the front of an imposing building, twice the height of the shops around it; a brooding, square construction in a heavy, classical style. Flags flew from the parapet. Squared columns were inset into the walls. It had a lot of windows, tall, rectangular, reflecting the blank sky. The ground-floor windows were shaded beneath awnings; people in old-fashioned clothes walked the sidewalks there, past indistinct but intricate displays. In the center, a darkly uniformed figure could be seen standing outside a rank of broad glass doors.

"That, my friends," George said, "is Aickmere Brothers department store, once world famous, still celebrated, and now—in my opinion—the probable focus of the Chelsea hauntings."

"Never heard of it," I said.

"I have." Lockwood twisted the photograph to face him. "I went there once as a little kid, I think. It used to have a great toy department."

At his side, Holly Munro was nodding. "Me too. My mother took me to Aickmere Brothers to look at the silver jewelry. I remember it being very ornate and splendid, but also a bit shabby."

"That would be right," George said. "It's the largest department store outside central London, and one of the oldest and grandest anywhere. It was originally built in 1872, and expanded greatly between 1910 and 1912. When its Arabian Hall, known as the 'Hall of Wonders,' was unveiled a hundred years or so ago, it supposedly featured fire-eaters, belly dancers, and a live tiger in a cage. Those glory days, I think, are long gone. But people still go there—to this very day, in fact—because that side of Chelsea hasn't been evacuated. It's a couple of blocks from one of the DEPRAC cordons. And there have been no reported hauntings in the store at all."

"If your theory's correct," Lockwood said, "that's more than a little odd."

"Isn't it? All the more so when you uncover its past history. I've been looking back for historical mentions of this part of Chelsea, to see if there's been any ghostly activity. When I became interested in Aickmere's, I honed in on that specific site." George took a bite of biscuit. "Well . . . I found things."

I looked at him. "Bad?"

"You remember Combe Carey Hall?"

Lockwood and I exchanged looks. "The most haunted house in England? Yes."

"It's not as bad as that."

"Thank God."

"Thing is, I can't imagine why." George patted the plump manila folder. "Turns out, you see, this end of the King's Road is an historic black spot. Half the worst possible things you can think of took place just about there."

I took a punt. "Plague?"

"Yup. The Black Death swept through in the 1340s. See how the road swerves just beside Aickmere's? That's because there was a plague pit there, where they piled the bodies and dosed them with quicklime. Used to be a little mound on the spot, and a circle of stones, but the Victorians leveled it when they were widening the thoroughfare."

"There are plenty of other plague pits in London," Lockwood objected. "Sure, they've had cluster hauntings associated with them, but nothing on the scale of this."

"I know," George said, "and I can't begin to explain *why* this has stirred things up so much. I'm just giving you the facts. So we've got plague. What else d'you reckon?"

"War," I said. "Battle or skirmish."

"Another point to Lucy. She's good at playing Atrocities. Yes, it's a Blitz bombing. In 1944, Aickmere Brothers was closed for six months after a doodlebug landed on the building next to it, pulling down the side wall and part of the roof. Ten people were killed, including air raid wardens stationed on that roof. Twelve years ago, store management called in agents after those wardens were seen reenacting their shrieking death-falls through several floors: they fell straight through Haberdashery and Home Furnishings and landed in Cosmetics."

"Was the Source found?" Holly Munro asked.

"I believe bone fragments were discovered and store defenses were improved."

Lockwood pulled doubtfully at his collar. "I don't know, George. . . . None of this strikes me as anything particularly special. And if those Visitors were dealt with—"

"I'm just getting warmed up. There's a big one you haven't thought of yet."

"Executions!" I said. "Murders, hangings, garrottings! Um, torture in general! Um . . ."

"All right, all right, hold on. Yes to all of that, but you need to be more exact."

"Suspected occult activities!"

"No. Go back to the last bunch. Where, historically, would you find all those nasty things taking place?"

"Prison," Holly Munro said. She flicked an imaginary piece of fluff off the hem of her dress.

"Bingo." George looked around at us. "Prison. The King's Prison, to be exact, a notorious hellhole first constructed in 1213 by order of King John. It's said they put it well outside the city, so that no one could overhear the awful sounds from inside."

I pointed to the map, at the blank rectangle that marked Aickmere's department store. "You're saying it was right here?"

"No one knows the exact site. It was pulled down in Tudor times. But it was supposed to be at the western end of the King's Road somewhere, and we do know the plague pit was dug outside it. So . . ."

"So now we're definitely on to something!" There was a light in Lockwood's eyes; he rubbed his hands. "Okay, now I *am* interested. If Aickmere's is on roughly the same spot as an old medieval prison . . ."

"It wasn't even a *nice* medieval prison," George put in. "Other medieval prisons looked down on it, it was so foul. It was a place where anyone who'd displeased the sovereign was put away, and there weren't too many rules about what happened to them after that. It had an unlucky history. It was burned down twice, and sacked during the Peasants' Revolt, when a troop of soldiers was ambushed and put to the sword. In those days the whole region was marshy, an unhealthy tract of mud and tributaries of the Thames, and a fearsome breeding ground for disease. Lots of inmates died and their bodies were just chucked in the river. It was famous for its appalling overcrowding, too. By the end it was more of a hospital than a prison—most of the inmates were lepers and other outcasts with terrible diseases. The Tudor authorities drove them out and knocked the whole place down, and I don't think anyone was too upset to see the last of the King's Prison."

We contemplated this. "So, not a good place to choose for a holiday break," I said. "We get the message."

"But a *very* good place," Lockwood said, "to generate Visitors, though the question must remain why the store itself isn't having any current trouble. That's brilliant, George—well done. Well, we'll have to go and check it out." He smiled around at us. "And we're going to need backup. If it's even half the place George thinks it is, three of us certainly won't be enough."

I looked at him. "You're saying you want Holly to come too, I suppose?"

"Be glad to," Holly Munro said.

Lockwood hesitated. "Well, if you want to, Holly—why not? That's a great idea, Luce. But actually I was thinking of a much bigger unit, so we can separate into smaller teams, cover ground more quickly. It'll mean asking DEPRAC to loan us some agents—ten or twenty, maybe—but that won't be a problem." He pushed his chair back. "Holly, if you can stay and get our supplies ready, we'll get cracking and see Barnes now."

"You think he'll play ball?" George asked.

"Barnes may be grumpy," Lockwood said, "but when I show him your findings, he'll act soon enough. He knows how good we are." He winked at us. "Don't worry. I know we have our differences, but there's a lot of mutual respect there. If he hesitates, I'll sweet-talk him. He won't let us down."

"That total and utter idiot," Lockwood growled. "That mustachioed imbecile. That benighted, blinkered jobsworth. He's a clown! A fraud! An oaf! I hate him."

"How's the mutual respect thing going?" George said.

We were in Sloane Square, outside the Chelsea Working Men's Club, in the heart of DEPRAC operations. Lockwood had gone inside to talk to Barnes; George and I were settled at a plastic table near the catering vans, and we were just tucking in to our first round of tea and hot dogs when Lockwood returned. Jaw clenched, cheeks flushed, he threw himself into a chair.

"He's not interested," he said. "He doesn't want to know."

George stared at him. "So what's his take on Aickmere Brothers? What's he think of my presentation?"

"Nothing. He didn't even look at it."

"He didn't look at my lovely dotted maps?" George set his hot dog down. "How can he have a valid counterargument, then?"

"He doesn't. Didn't even look me in the eye. Basically he cut me off as soon as I told him the address. He said there's another big push going on in central Chelsea tonight, and he can't spare anyone to 'fool around' in the outlying areas. That's a direct quote."

"I'm surprised," I said. "We know he's a twit, but he's normally a conscientious one."

Lockwood drove his hands into his trouser pockets and stared balefully at the DEPRAC agents hurrying all around. "I'd have thought he would at least have heard me out. It's not like I even mentioned George's name, or did anything else stupid to annoy him. I don't get it. This whole outbreak's a disaster. He should be dying for any new idea we could come up with. As it is, we're stymied. I just don't see that we can go to Aickmere's on our—" He gave a start, and shrank down in his chair. "Oh no . . . Don't look now. It's Kipps. I saw him skulking nearby when I was speaking to Barnes. He must have heard the whole thing."

Sure enough, here was Quill Kipps, jeweled rapier glinting, mincing across the square in our direction. George and I glared at him as he drew near. Lockwood looked away.

Kipps halted. He did disdainful things with his eyebrows. "Well, that's charming," he said. "I've had warmer welcomes in newly opened tombs. Now, Tony . . . I happened to overhear what went on in there between you and Barnes—"

A muscle moved in Lockwood's cheek. "Did you?"

"I heard him giving you the brush-off yet again."

Lockwood moved a paper cup from one part of the table to the other.

"If you're wondering *why*," Kipps went on, "it's because right now Barnes isn't his own man. He's got high-up people from Fittes and Rotwell who are advising him, and *they* keep telling him the center of the cluster's in the heart of Chelsea. He's got to do what he's told. There's no mystery about it. That's how DEPRAC works."

I frowned at him. "DEPRAC monitors the agencies. Not the other way around."

Kipps's thin face quivered with amusement. "Do you think so? You're so adorable, Carlyle."

"And so you've come to crow about it," Lockwood said.

"Well, yes—but also to see whether you wanted any extra personnel for your investigation."

There was a pause in which the three of us sat frowningly, trying to decipher the insult hidden in this statement. We couldn't find one, which made us frown all the more. Lockwood picked up the cup and moved it back to its original position. "You're offering to help us?"

Kipps winced as if he'd just found something disagreeable stuck to the bottom of his shoe. "Not quite. I'm offering to take part. It would be me, Kate Godwin, and Bobby Vernon. You know my team."

Lockwood stared. "I thought you were working for Barnes."

"Not any longer. I've applied to transfer to other duties."

"Because—"

"May I?" Kipps took a chair, folded himself in to it. He glanced back at the King's Road barriers. "No matter what Barnes says, no one has a clue what's going on in there. It's a free-for-all, chaos every night, and it's already cost me the life of one agent. It's not going to cost me another. Nor do I want to sit quietly back, doing nothing. If you've got a worthwhile lead, I'll work on it with you. That's all."

George, Lockwood, and I sat silent. It isn't often we're all lost for words, but it happened now. I kept alternating between staring at a pool of spilled coffee on the tabletop and glancing at Kipps. Ordinarily the coffee would have interested me more. Now I couldn't help returning to our rival: to his oiled-back hair, his too-tight trousers and flawless jacket, the look-at-me jeweled pommel of his sword. Clearly his proposal was absurd. Of *course* it was. And yet . . .

"Well, it's good of you," Lockwood said, "but I'm sorry. It wouldn't work. Teams have to work seamlessly, with absolute trust between agents. You can't have endless bickering, and— Yes, George?"

George had raised a hand. "Surely a *bit* of bickering's all right, now and again."

"Hardly."

"We do it."

"No, actually we don't. At least not very often. Or not at the key moments . . . Look, will you just shut up? I've forgotten what I was saying." Lockwood ruffled his hair distractedly. "The point really is that bad things happen to disjointed teams. It's dangerous out there."

"Bad things can happen to any team," Kipps said, after a silence. "As for the dangers, I can assure you I'm well aware of them."

Lockwood held his gaze a moment. "Yes, of course you are," he said. "I'm sorry. Look, it's a kind offer, and I appreciate it, but I don't think it would work."

"I somehow didn't think you would," Kipps said. He stood. "Good day to you."

He began to stalk away.

"Lockwood—" George began.

"Wait!" And that was me, pushing my chair back, standing up and glaring down at Lockwood. Why did I do it? On any other occasion I'd just have sat there, quietly going along with him. Not now. Not, somehow, after the previous night. A tension rose up inside me, needing to find expression, needing to get out. In part I just wanted to *do* something—to throw myself into a job that wasn't merely the usual grind. I knew Holly had a host of new cases ready; I knew we'd be splitting up to deal with them. This was different: bigger, odder, perhaps more dangerous, and I didn't want Lockwood's pride preventing us from giving it a go.

And that was the other thing: his pride. It was a fundamental part of him, just like his ability to close off from me, from others, from common sense. I couldn't challenge him about his sister or his past, but I *could* challenge him on this.

"I think we should take Kipps up on his offer," I said. "There are people dying out there, Lockwood, and we can't stand back from it. We need to act. We need to engage, even if that does mean making compromises. That department store is massive: even if we're just doing a reconnaissance, we need a proper team. And Kipps's team is good—we know that. If we have faith in George," I said, "in all the work he's done, we should do this. We owe it to him. More than that, we owe it to ourselves."

Lockwood gazed at me. I suddenly felt very hot and red in the face. "I just don't think we have any choice," I said. I sat down hurriedly. George was doing the thing with the pool of coffee, alternating between staring at it and me. Kipps, displaying a sensitivity I wouldn't have associated with him, stood a short way off, seemingly engrossed in the attempts of two tiny Bunce agents to carry a massive sack of iron filings out of a nearby tent store. All around us rushed the DEPRAC staff and agents on their busy, busy errands; the noise of the square cocooned us. Lockwood just gazed at me. I waited to hear what he would say.

Chapter 19

Aickmere Brothers department store, reached by a lengthy taxi ride that looped around the edges of the Chelsea containment zone, was easily the most impressive building on the western reaches of the King's Road. A hulking yet austere presence, occupying an entire block, it rose four clear stories to its parapeted roof. Grooved pilasters—decorative columns embedded into the stonework—ran like ribs along the walls. Windows glittered; high above us colored pennants snapped and ruffled in the wintry breeze. A brightly uniformed doorman stood sentinel outside the entrance. From a distance—when you were standing on the little knoll of green grass opposite, where the road kinked south—it looked every bit the equal of the mighty stores of Oxford Street. As you crossed the street, however, you began to notice the smog stains on the peeling stone facade, the tired paintwork on the door frames, even the flakes of dandruff scattered on the shoulders of the doorman's patched coat. Not everything was quite as glamorous as it seemed.

Which included the pretty patch of grass opposite, surrounded by chichi fashion shops and coffee bars. George, nudging me as we crossed, pointed at it. "Plague pit."

"And the prison?"

"Most likely under Aickmere's."

Fifty yards farther up the street, a line of DEPRAC barricades, identical to the ones in Sloane Square, prevented access to the heart of Chelsea. Aickmere Brothers was certainly fortunate not to have been caught up in the evacuation; then again, it had not reported any ghosts.

"Curfew at five. Closing's at four." The doorman, a boggle-eyed, red-faced man with a mustache like that of a bearded walrus, looked askance at us as we filed through the revolving doors: Lockwood, George, Holly Munro, and me. Each of us scarcely squeezed our workbags through, particularly me: my backpack bore a heavy, jar-shaped load. Our rapiers jangled against the panels of curving wood.

Once, the mighty entrance hall would have proclaimed the store's glories with a fanfare. Spiraling plaster columns, decorated with gold leaf, held up a blue-painted ceiling, studded with stars, planets, and plumply capering cupids. On the walls, murals show-cased fauns, nymphs, and a host of exotic wildlife. Straight ahead of us, twin escalators, on either side of a central stair, led up to the next level. You could imagine the live music, the jugglers and fire-eaters of long ago. . . . Now the murals were faded, pasted-over with DEPRAC warnings and announcements of forthcoming sales; and the gold leaf on the columns had peeled away. Shoppers idled among cases of uninspiring lavender goods and a few shabby mannequins. Schmaltzy music piped distantly through a crackly speaker system.

The only remotely impressive thing in the hall was a vast fake tree in front of one set of escalators, constructed of metal and slabs of bark, with tissue leaves of red, orange, and gold. It looked intricate and fragile. We set our bags down before it. Lockwood went over to reception.

"It's gone downhill since I was last here," Holly Munro said. "Or maybe I was too young to notice."

She unbuttoned her coat and took off her gloves. As usual, she'd made herself up like we were heading out to a society garden party—instead of what we *were* doing: ghost-hunting on the grim side of London. Maybe it was wrong, but I *so* hoped she'd fall into an open coffin or catacomb or something before the night was out. It didn't have to be a very *bad* fall. Just a dusty one. Involving bones.

George was surveying the room. "Yeah, don't think much of the displays," he said. "Some of these mannequins are hideous. . . . Oh—it's you, Quill. I thought you were an exhibit."

Quill Kipps, Kate Godwin, and Bobby Vernon stepped forward out of the shadows of the tree. They too carried heavy bags; Bobby Vernon had an enormous salt-gun strapped to his shoulder.

"This," Kate Godwin said, "is precisely why I was against coming here. We'll have comments like this all night. He's worse than the ghosts."

George held up his hand. "Sorry, I'll be good now. This is Holly, everyone."

General introductions followed. Kipps was all smarm and oil; I swear Bobby Vernon let out a giggle as he shook Holly's hand. Kate Godwin was just as stiff as I had been when first meeting Holly; our assistant seemed to affect girls that way.

Lockwood returned, coat swinging behind him. He grinned at us. "Hello, team."

Kipps gave a sniff. "You're late."

"I'm team leader," Lockwood said. "Meetings don't start till I arrive. By definition, therefore, *you* were early. Right, I've asked to see the manager. Once we've got the go-ahead, we'll start looking around, talk to the staff while they're still here. We can do that singly or in groups, it doesn't matter—but after dark, we're not taking any chances. *Then* we'll go around in pairs."

Bobby Vernon was so small that when he stood beside us he looked like he was in the next room. He lifted a stick-like arm. "How's that going to work?"

Lockwood frowned. "Bobby?"

"I count seven of us. That's three pairs and one poor sap left over."

"Ah, well, yes. . . . Didn't I tell you? We've got someone else coming. Actually I'd hoped they'd be here by now."

"Who?" I said. None of us had heard this before. It seemed to me Lockwood had a vaguely evasive air.

Kipps sensed it too. "I trust it's a proper agent, and not some weirdo friend of yours, Tony, brought in to make up the numbers."

"Well—"

"Here I am, Locky." We turned and looked back across the hall: there, just emerging from the revolving doors, with the rips in her long blue puffer jacket catching on the handle and her Wellington boots leaving a delicate trail of greenish mud on the marble floor, was Flo Bones. Through the window glass behind her, the doorman's face could just be seen—bog-eyes popping, jaw lolling—staring after her in horror and bafflement. To be honest, Kipps's team looked much the same, and even Holly Munro's smooth calm was momentarily ruffled. Flo had her damp, stained burlap bag over her shoulder; as she approached she slung it off onto a pile of lavender pillows, unzipped her jacket, and bent her arms up in a languorous stretch. We got the unwashed shirt, the holed sweater, the frayed rope belt holding up her jeans; oh, yes, and the tidal smell. It was the full works.

"Ooh, that's better," Flo said. "Me corns are killing me today. So, Locky, aren't you going to introduce me to these nancies? Actually, don't bother—I can guess 'em well enough from your descriptions. All right, then, are you Kipps? Heard a lot about you and those nice plastic jewels you've got pasted on your rapier hilt. I can get you more like that. They wash up sometimes on Woolwich beach, just below the crematorium."

Kipps looked like he had been slapped between the eyes with a dead fish; as, in an olfactory sort of way, he had. "Er . . . no. No, thank you. And you are?"

"Florence Bonnard. Accent on the *second* syllable, if you don't mind. You must be Kate Godwin—bit thinner than I expected, but there's no escaping that chin. And you"—Flo grinned enigmatically at Bobby Vernon—"I'm very pleased to see *you*, Bobby. Ask me what my bag's for."

Vernon had edged slightly away. "Er . . . What *is* your bag for?"

"That," Flo said, "is my relic-bag. To put *things* in." She leaned close to Bobby. "Things I find in the soft, moist darkness of the river mud. . . . Want to look inside? I could pop you right in, you're that small."

Vernon gave a squeak and vanished behind Kate Godwin; now Flo turned to Holly Munro. I must admit I was looking forward to this bit, but our assistant preempted Flo's advances. She strode forward, hand outstretched. "Holly Munro, Anthony Lockwood's new assistant. Very pleased to meet you."

I waited for the verbal assault; or, better yet, a quick over-the-head toss into the lavender cushions. But Flo seemed taken aback. Her eyelashes fluttered; beneath her grime, I swear she flushed. "Charmed, I'm sure."

They just shook hands. Somehow, this annoyed me too.

"Right," Lockwood said. "Good. Everyone knows each other. So let's get started. The manager's waiting."

"I'm not sure we should bother. . . ." Kate Godwin was still eyeing Flo. "Surely it's a safe bet all the ghosts will have scarpered now."

The current chairman of Aickmere Brothers, Samuel Aickmere, represented the fourth generation of the family to run the store. He was a fussy, nondescript man (middle-aged, bland-featured, with hair that had started, rather timorously, to recede) who had tried to make himself less so by way of his clothes. He wore a dark wide-shouldered suit with a strong purple pinstripe. A purple handkerchief, crisply folded, jutted like a potted plant from his breast pocket. The cuffs of his shirtsleeves seemed slightly longer than necessary; you could scarcely see his fingers. His tie was shockingly pink; I sensed Lockwood flinching as he shook his hand.

Mr. Aickmere cast his eyes over our rapiers and workbags without pleasure. As we explained our purpose, his lips pressed tightly together.

"Quite impossible, I'm afraid," he said, once Lockwood finished. "This is a reputable commercial establishment. Can't have your sort in here."

We looked at him. Aickmere's office wasn't particularly large. Sure, it had room for a marble-topped desk, chair, garbage can, filing cabinet, and dark green yucca plant. One or two submissive employees standing in front of the desk, caps in hand, might just have squeezed in too. But eight hard-bitten agents, bristling with rapiers, flares, and grim-faced purpose? We must have been quite an unnerving sight, standing there—and that was *before* you assessed us individually. George was just finishing a tuna sandwich, holding his hand underneath to catch the falling flakes. Bobby Vernon sported his enormous salt-gun. Kipps was Kipps. Flo was Flo. I kind of understood the guy's point.

"Mr. Aickmere," Lockwood said, "there is a major spectral incident going on all around you, a stone's throw from your door. You understand that we are empowered to investigate its cause, wherever that might be?"

"It is ridiculous to look here! We have no dangerous Visitors in Aickmere's!"

"In Chelsea? Really? That's a remarkable claim."

"There was some little trouble, a dozen or so years ago. It was swiftly dealt with."

"That would have been the air-raid wardens?" George said.

"I don't remember the details." The man waved one sleeve at

us airily. "But after the event, the building was reconstructed with supernatural safety in mind. We have iron laced into the foundations and into many walls. Our staff wear silver brooches and are trained in all necessary Visitor defenses. There are lavender sticks and Rotwell salt-sprays in every room. Why? Because our customers expect and demand a safe shopping experience. And they get it— of course they do. We have a whole silversmithing department, for heaven's sake! No, there is no need for you to linger here."

"We'll be very discreet," Lockwood said.

The manager smiled at us; the smile was a tight, hard thing, a line of defense scratched across rock. "I know what DEPRAC's like. Closing honest shops down. Bolder's in Putney. Farnsworth's in Croydon. That won't happen here."

"No one's trying to get you closed down," Lockwood said. "And if there *is* anything to be found, it's in your interests to have it cleared."

"Agents leave devastation in their wake! They disrupt smooth service and endanger innocent lives!"

"George, how many of our clients have we managed to kill now?"

"Hardly any. A very small percentage."

"There. I hope that reassures you, Mr. Aickmere. We will conduct quiet investigations and be on our way."

"No. It's my final word."

Lockwood sighed; he rummaged in his pocket. "Very well, I have here a DEPRAC warrant card, signed by Inspector Montagu Barnes, which—"

"Allow me." Kipps stepped forward. "Mr. Aickmere, my name is Kipps. I'm a team leader for the Fittes Agency, and one of my areas is Public Safety Noncompliance. We take refusal to adhere to operative statutes very seriously and have the power to authorize a detainment team to exercise immediate penal restraint in such circumstances." He put his thin, pale hands together and cracked his knuckles like a rifle volley. "I do hope that this won't be necessary in your case?"

Aickmere blinked at him. "I can't say. I haven't a clue what any of that means."

"It means," Kipps said, "let us do our job, or we'll lock you up. That's basically the size of it."

The manager sat back in his chair. He removed the purple handkerchief from his pocket and dabbed at his forehead. "Ghosts after dark, children running amok . . . What an age we live in! Very well, do what you must. You won't find anything."

Lockwood had been staring at Kipps. "Thank you, sir. We appreciate it."

"It's a bit late for courtesy now. . . . Well, I have one stipulation! I *insist* you don't disturb any of our displays, particularly our Seasonal Creations."

"Seasonal Creations? Oh, you mean like the tree thing in the foyer?"

"That 'tree thing' is 'Autumn Ramble,' hand-created by noted installation artist Gustav Kramp. Did you know that every piece of dry driftwood and tissue leaf has been personally glued by hand? It took an *age* to piece together, and it's very, very expensive. I simply *won't* have you ruining it."

"We'll certainly try to be careful," Lockwood said, after a short pause.

"We run a tight ship here at Aickmere Brothers," Mr. Aickmere said. "Everything in its proper place." As if to prove it, he adjusted two pens beside the blotter in the center of his desk. "And my staff cannot be distracted from their duties."

"Certainly not. We'll be sure to treat everything in your store with appropriate respect—right, everyone?"

We nodded. George leaned in close to me. "Remind me to blow my nose on 'Autumn Ramble' when we get downstairs."

"One thing," Lockwood said, as we were filing out. "You say you have no dangerous Visitors here, yet you give your people silver brooches. Does that mean—?"

"Oh yes, the place is haunted. 'Course it is. Where *isn't*, these days?" The folded handkerchief at Mr. Aickmere's breast lolled forward as if waving us toward the door. "But my staff are quite safe. If you wear your silver, keep your eyes open, and lock up during daylight, there's nothing to trouble you here."

But the chairman's view was not entirely backed up elsewhere in the building.

"Mornings are all right," the attendant in Men's Wear said. "And late afternoons, funnily enough, when you get the sunlight streaming through the windows. It's noon *I* don't like, when the streets outside are bright, and in here it's full of shadow. The air goes thick. Not hot, exactly. Just stuffy. You smell all the cardboard and plastic wraps piled in the basement, the ones we've taken off the new clothes."

"Is it a bad smell?" Lockwood asked.

"No . . . Gets a bit much, that's all."

"I don't mind it when it's busy," the young woman in Cosmetics said. "When there's people coming through the doors. Quiet times, I have to pop out. Talk to the doorman, get a breath of air."

"Why?" I asked her. "What makes you go outside?"

"The air's so still. Oppressive. I think the air conditioning units aren't up to snuff."

Four other staff members, working on separate floors, also had comments to make about the general atmosphere and the apparent deficiencies of the air conditioning. But in Handbags, Belts, and Leather Goods, Miss Deidre Perkins, 55, a tall, thin-lipped person dressed in somber black, was more concerned with something else.

"If there *is* a Visitor," she said at once, "you'll find it on the third floor."

I looked up from my notebook. Holly Munro, interviewing staff nearby, also drew near. "Really? Why?"

"Karen Dobson saw it there. She came down from Lingerie with a face like all horrors. Just before closing one afternoon in September, it was. Said she saw it at the far end of the passage." Miss Perkins sniffed disapprovingly. "She may have been lying. Karen *did* have a tendency to exaggerate. *I* never saw anything."

"I see. So this was an actual apparition? And before dark?"

"It was a Visitor, yes." Miss Perkins was one of those people who avoided using ghostly terminology if at all possible. "Night hadn't fallen, but it was a stormy day. Already very dark outside. We had the lamps on."

"Perhaps I could speak to Karen. Which department does she work in?"

"She doesn't, anymore. She died."

"Died?"

"Sudden-like, at home." Miss Perkins spoke with gloomy satisfaction. "She smoked. Expect it was her heart." She adjusted a rack of hanging belts, smoothing them between her hands. "I suppose *she'll* be a Visitor now, and all."

"It doesn't work that way," I said.

"How do you *know*?" Miss Perkins's facade cracked; all at once there was anger in her voice. "How do any of you *know* how or why our friends or family choose to come back? Do you *ask* the Returned their motivation?"

"No, ma'am, we don't," Holly Munro said. "It's not considered wise."

Holly glanced at me, then, as I knew she would. In the Wintergarden house, I'd done precisely that. And much good it had done me. I pressed my lips together.

"And this figure that Karen Dobson saw?" I prompted. "Did she describe it?"

Miss Perkins had moved on to a tray of purses and wallets. "Thin thing on all fours. Crawling down the corridor toward her."

"Nothing more about its appearance?"

Her bony fingers moved across the tray, adjusting, adjusting, adjusting. "Little girl, I don't think she hung around long enough to find out."

A couple of hours we took, wandering around that store. I spent a good deal of it on my own. I interviewed the staff, but I also took stock of the building itself, tried to make a connection, suss out its personality. I found it surprisingly hard to do.

The layout was clear enough. It was a typical old-style department store, with each floor divided into formal sections. We had Bargains in the Basement; and Cosmetics and Visitor Defenses on the Ground floor. Visitor Defenses—consisting of more cut-price iron than you could shake a nightstick at—occupied, rather forlornly, the old Arabian Hall, looking almost comically insignificant beneath the golden pillars and winged griffins. Ladies' Fashions, Kitchenware, and Children's were on One; Men's Wear was on Two, together with Habadashery and Home Furnishings. Three was mostly taken up with Furniture, while Four was Office Supplies and a few meeting rooms. To my eyes, the quality of goods seemed a little tired, though Holly Munro claimed that some of the ladies' fashions were okay. There were four elevators—two centrally placed ones for customers (on the Ground floor, these were accessed behind the escalators) and two for staff at the north and south ends of the building—and also three staircases. Most people used the central staircase, which was next to the escalators and was impressively fashioned from coffee-colored marble, but there were narrow flights of stairs at the north and south ends too, extending the height of the building.

At the back of Aickmere's, each floor had a long, echoing store-room, accessible only by staff, where goods were piled in rows of cardboard boxes before being made ready for display. George spent his time prowling around these rooms, particularly the one at basement level, but I couldn't feel any real psychic difference in them. In fact, the sensations I got from the whole place were fairly muted—perhaps odd, given our theory that it was the focus for the whole Chelsea thing.

That's not to say there was nothing. Underlying it all, fading in and out as you passed Visitor Defenses or the wall racks of lavender beside each interconnecting door, was a faint yet palpable unease. It was like a tingle on the skin, a prickling in the stomach; familiar to me, but not the usual malaise, chill, or creeping fear. As the afternoon drew on and the flow of customers ebbed away, the sensation grew stronger. Around me, silent staff members, pale and preoccupied, locked up registers, and tidied up displays. I went to a quiet corner, opened my backpack, and twisted the tap at the top of the ghost-jar.

"Ah," it said at once, "*stand aside! Let me use my enormous talent to solve your difficulties! Ooh, yes . . . I feel that disturbance too. Yes, that's very odd. That's* interesting. . . ."

"What do you reckon it is?"

"*How do I know? What am I, a miracle worker? Give me a chance here. I need to think.*"

Outside the windows, the sky was almost black. A buzzer sounded; down in the foyer, the staff gathered, muffled in their coats, eager to be gone. They filed out silently through the revolving doors. We watched from the fringes of the foyer: Lockwood and George beneath the artificial tree; Holly and Flo at the entrance to Cosmetics; Kipps and his crew up on the first-floor balcony, just across from me.

Mr. Aickmere was the last to leave. He spoke a few terse words to Lockwood, pressed buttons on the wall. The escalators stopped dead; the speakers gave a sudden crackle, a final, dying whine. Silence. Now the lights across the departments were one after the other shut off, leaving only a dim yellow nightlight humming in the foyer. Aickmere drew back, retreated through the door. We heard the key turn in the lock, his footsteps hurrying off along the King's Road.

"And now we're alone," Lockwood said. "Good! The investigation can properly begin!"

None of us took issue with him as we gathered silently beneath the tree. It would have been easy enough to do so, but there wasn't any point. We all knew the score.

Yes, all the *living* inhabitants of the store had left. But that didn't mean we were alone.

Of course not. After dark, we never are.

Chapter 20

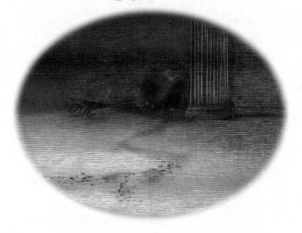

There's nothing like the onset of night to bring out the best in an agent, and for some of us the darker it is, the better. I'm talking visually here. Suddenly every embarrassing pimple is cloaked in shadow; jaws become firmer, waistlines sleeker. Unwashed faces become pale and interesting; the lankest hair acquires a glamorous sheen. The rougher points of personalities recede too; thoughts turn to survival and to the job at hand. So it was with the ragtag band that Lockwood had assembled that evening. For once, as we stood beneath Aickmere's tissue tree, our similarities outweighed our differences. Kipps and Lockwood, Kate Godwin and I—we were all made of the same stuff. We had our rapiers and other weapons; we shared a cool seriousness of purpose. Even Flo looked businesslike, her straw hat casting a ring of shadow across her face, her coat pulled back to reveal her great curved gutting knife and the sinister array of implements she normally used to winkle objects from the river mire.

George handed around some chocolate; we compared notes on what we'd learned.

"Mostly just seems to be worries about the air quality," Lockwood said. "Something unpleasant but hard to fathom." He leaned casually against a counter, face lit by a flickering gas lantern. "Then there's that story of the girl who saw a crawling figure. That stands out a mile, because it's so definite and strange."

"What kind of ghost might it be?" Holly Munro asked.

No one knew.

"A couple of people say they heard a voice calling out their name," Bobby Vernon said. "It was always at dusk; always when they were leaving. It sounded like someone they knew was far off in the building, calling them back inside."

"Did they ever follow the sound?" I asked.

"Er, no, Carlyle, they didn't," Kate Godwin said. "Because they weren't completely stupid. Who would ever obey a disembodied voice?"

"Oh, you never know. *Some* people might be tempted." Holly Munro used her sweetest, most eyelash-batting tones—as she always did when she was referring to me.

Flo Bones shuffled her feet impatiently. "I don't know about all this, Locky. . . . There's not much to go on here. Are you *sure* this place is the focus?"

"It's pretty thin pickings so far," Lockwood admitted. "Aickmere could tell as much from my manner when I spoke to him just now.

Exactly what he expected, he said. We're going to have a *very* dull evening. He still maintains there's nothing significant here."

"No, he's wrong," I said slowly. "There *is* something. I can sense it."

I still detected that oddly prickling feeling, so familiar, yet so hard to read. The skull appeared to be having similar problems analyzing it; it hadn't yet reported in.

"*I* don't hear anything," Kate Godwin said. She was a Listener too, and that made her suspicious of my insights. "What do you think it is?"

"I don't really know," I said. "It's like background buzz, a kind of radiation. It's strong, but also muffled—like it's mostly blocked but managing to seep in anyway."

"You need to get your ears syringed," Godwin said.

Lockwood shook his head. "If Lucy says there's something, we need to take notice. Where's it strongest, Luce? The basement?"

"No. I get it everywhere."

"Even so," George said, "I'd like us to play close attention to the basement. It surely overlaps where the old prison was, so you'd think any phenomena might start there. . . . What else did Aickmere say to you, Lockwood? Any hints or friendly warnings?"

"Nothing. Oh, apart from telling us again to keep the place tidy and—above all—not to touch that tree."

"Like we'd mess it up," Kipps growled. "What does he think we're going to get up to tonight? Have a wild party in Men's Wear? We've got a job to do."

Lockwood grinned. "True, and we'd better get on with it. Right, I'm going to put us into pairs for the first stage of the night."

And he did. He divided us into teams of two. He himself would go with Kipps. Kate Godwin and Bobby Vernon formed a second natural pair. Next, George (who remained remarkably calm at the news) was lumbered with Flo Bones.

Guess who was left for me?

I felt like the kid in the playground who's always chosen last. I began checking through my equipment with ostentatious care.

Holly didn't seem overjoyed either. "So . . . Lucy. We're doing the second floor?"

"That's right. . . ." I was synchronizing watches with Lockwood and the others. The initial stint was two hours only; then we'd rendezvous by the first-floor stairs to make sure all was well. I snapped my notebook onto its belt-clip, ran my fingers across the familiar pouches. The weight was right; everything in position. I gave my partner a token smile. "So, Holly—shall we go?"

Two by two we stole away: George and Flo were covering the basement and ground floor, Godwin and Vernon the highest levels. Lockwood and Kipps climbed the central stairs with Holly and me, flashlights flowing over the gleaming marble. On the first floor they vanished into Ladies' Fashions, while we continued up the stairs.

The Men's Wear department filled three interconnecting halls. It was pretty dark, because we were a fair way above the level of the street lamps. Silver-faced mannequins, gleaming dimly in the half-light, sat or stood on pale white pedestals between the dangling racks of clothes. Suits, trousers, row upon row of neatly pressed shirts. . . . There was a smell of mothballs, fabric-conditioner, and wool. I felt it was colder than when we'd passed through earlier.

Holly carried bags to the far end, where we would start. I hung back a moment.

"Well?" I said.

"*I've done my thinking,*" the voice from my bag announced. "*And I've had an idea.*"

"Great." What *was* that odd sensation, so deep down and far away? It had really been bugging me. I wanted the skull's insight. "Let's hear it, then."

"*Here's my tip: lure her down to Kitchenware and brain her with a skillet.*"

"What?"

"*Holly. It's a golden opportunity. There are lots of pointy things there too, if you prefer. But basically a simple smack with a rolling pin would do fine.*"

I gave a snort of fury. "I'm not interested in killing Holly! I'm concerned about the weird vibes I'm getting in this place! Is mindless violence your solution to everything?"

The ghost considered. "*Pretty much, yeah.*"

"You disgust me. The consequences—"

"*Oh, you wouldn't get* caught. *That's the whole point. Just do it quietly like, and blame it on the supernatural forces that are infesting the place. Who's to know?*"

I contemplated getting into a heated debate with the skull about the moral implications of murder but decided it was futile. Also I had no time: my partner was pattering back toward me down the aisle.

"Okay," I said loudly as she drew near, "we'd better get on with it, Holly. You *do* know how to record psychic data, don't you?"

She was nervous—breathing fast. I saw her jacket moving rapidly up and down. "Yes," she said, "I do know that."

"Using the Fittes-Rotwell grid method?"

"Yes."

"Fine. Then let's begin. I'll take the readings and you record them." Ignoring the whispers of the skull, which kept suggesting different unlikely kitchen utensils that could be used for murder, I sketched out a map of the room. Holly and I went to the first point on the grid, a corner filled with neatly piled sweaters. Above us, a mannequin wearing a plaid shirt, woolen cardigan, and slacks pointed jauntily into the dark. "So the temperature here," I said, "is . . . fifty degrees. I see nothing and . . . I hear nothing. So there's no prime indicator, no malaise or chill or anything. That means you can put little zeros in the boxes there. . . . Okay? Got that?"

"I told you, I know how to do it. And, by the way," Holly said, "I can take readings too. I *do* have some Talent. I trained as a field agent when I was little."

I was already pacing out the strides to the next point. "Yeah? So what happened? Did you find it too dangerous? Not to your liking, I mean?"

"I found it scary, yes. You'd be stupid not to."

"Yeah, I guess. Temp here's fifty too."

She noted it down. "But that wasn't why I stopped," she said. "They put me in a desk job after the Cotton Street killings. Maybe you heard of that, even in that little place up north you came from?"

"It *wasn't* a little place, as it happens," I said. "It was a very substantial northern town, which—" I stared past her, suddenly alert. "Did you hear that?"

"What? No."

"I thought . . . a voice. . . ."

"What did it say? Where did it come from? You want me to note it down?"

"I want you to stop gabbing." I stared up the aisle into the dark. I couldn't hear anything now besides Holly hyperventilating. If there had been a distant voice, calling my name, it wasn't there now.

Holly was watching me closely. "Lucy, you're not going to go wandering off, following the voice, are you?"

I stared at her. "No, Holly. Obviously I'm not."

"Fine. Because at the Wintergarden house you lost control and—"

"It's not going to happen! It's gone, anyway. Shall we just get on with the survey?"

"Yes," she said primly, "all right."

We got on with the survey.

"*I heard all that,*" the skull hissed in my ear. "*I've got one word for you:* egg whisk."

I shook my head, spoke under my breath. "That's stupid. I couldn't kill her with that. Anyway, *egg whisk* is two words."

"*No, it isn't.*"

"It is so. And I don't think she meant any harm, then. She was just—"

"*If I was out of this jar,*" the skull said, "*I'd throttle her for you. I'd do it as a favor. Think how nice it would be just to follow your urges for once. You could do it right here. Use a coat hanger as a garrote.*"

I ignored it; there were other things to think about. The temperature was dropping, and now thin wires of white-green ghost-fog showed too, winding around the bases of the clothes racks, lapping at the pedestals of the mannequins. Holly and I continued taking readings up and down the shadowy hall, past T-shirts and sock racks, shelves of slippers and old men's vests. Our scribbled notes showed a gradual increase in secondary phenomena, particularly chill and miasma, but we also noticed something else:

Apparitions.

They began as faint gray forms, seen always at the far end of an aisle. In the half- light they were uncomfortably similar in size and shape to the costumed mannequins, and it was only when one suddenly drifted sideways that I realized, with a shock, that they were there at all. They did not seek to approach us; they made no sound. Neither Holly nor I could detect any aggressive intent; still, they unnerved us by their watchful presence and by their number, which seemed to grow steadily as we proceeded along the hall. When we got to stairwells, and looked down, we could see them clustering far below, looking up at us with blank black eyes in soft gray faces. When I gazed back through Men's Wear, I could see them hovering in the shadows, silent and discreet.

Or not entirely silent.

"*Lucy . . .*"

That voice again. Far off, a patch of darkness welled toward me.

"Skull?" I risked a whisper to my backpack. Holly was a few paces ahead of me, and I didn't think she'd notice. "Did you hear that? Spare me your usual nonsense. I haven't got time."

"*The voice? Yes, I heard it.*"

"What is it? How does it know who I am?"

"*A presence is building. Something pulls itself toward you.*"

"Toward me?" I went all cold. "Why not Holly? Or Kate Godwin—she hears stuff too."

"*Because you're unique. You shine like a beacon, attracting the attention of all dark things.*" It chuckled. "*Why d'you think I'm chatting with you?*"

"But there's no reason—"

"*Listen,*" the skull said, "*if you want to avoid all this, you're in the wrong job. Go be a baker's girl or something. Better hours, nice floury apron . . .*"

"Why the hell would I want a floury apron?" I took a deep breath. "These things watching us—tell me what they are."

"*There are many spirits wandering in this place. Most seem lost; I sense no willpower in them. But there are other, stronger, powers here that* do *have will. One of them is hunting you.*"

I swallowed, gazed out into the dark.

"*Oh, and here's more good news,*" the skull added. "*I've finally got an answer for you about that odd sensation you're feeling. I know where you've felt it before: it's like the bone glass. Remember? That's what the feeling's like.*"

The *bone glass*. . . . I knew at once that it was right. That queasy, prickling background sensation I'd experienced since arriving at Aickmere's? It *was* familiar. I *had* known it before.

At Kensal Green Cemetery, six months earlier, Lockwood, George, and I had discovered a curious object, a mirror or "bone glass," that had certain odd capabilities. Most startlingly, we guessed it gave its owner the ability to look across to the Other Side. Since anyone who looked into it invariably died—and since the glass was smashed at the end of the case—it was hard to be certain about this.

But just being close to the thing had made me feel ill; and I now realized that my sensations here were very similar indeed.

"*It's* not *the bone glass, of course,*" the skull went on. "*It's different—bigger and farther away. But it's the same sort of feeling. A disruption in the fabric of things. Take it from me, Lucy. Strange stuff's going on around here. . . .*"

With that the skull's presence suddenly receded. Holly Munro was at my side. I hadn't noticed her come close.

"Why are you talking to yourself, Lucy?"

"I wasn't. Er, I was just thinking aloud."

It was an excuse that wouldn't have convinced a three-year old, and it was touch-and-go with Holly. She frowned and opened her mouth to speak—but at that moment a familiar voice called both our names. And there was Lockwood, coat swishing, lantern swinging from one long pale hand, advancing swiftly through the dark.

I hadn't realized until I saw him how tense and strung out I was; also how desperately I missed him at my side. I felt both worse and better as he drew near.

"Lucy, Holly—are you all right?" He was smiling, but I could see anxiety in his eyes. "People are getting jumpy. I'm checking up on everyone."

"We're okay," I said. "There's just an awful lot of ghosts around."

"Yes, though they're holding off for now." He flashed his grin at us. "The worst thing that's happened so far is George knocking a leaf off that stupid tree in the foyer. We'll stick it back on later. Hopefully Aickmere won't notice."

"Lucy's been hearing voices again," Holly Munro said.

I glared at her. I'd been *about* to tell him—probably—and I didn't like it slipping out like it was some kind of guilty secret, or the way Lockwood looked at me so sharply.

"Lucy?" he said. "Is this true?"

"Yes," I said huffily. "Something's called my name twice. It's fine, though—I'm not going to do anything stupid. And besides, I've got Holly here to look after me."

He was silent for a long moment; I could see him wrestling with his doubts. At last he said quietly, "We're meeting up in half an hour. Think you'll be okay till then?"

"Yes, of course." The way I said it probably sounded abrupt, like I was cross with him for asking. I wasn't at all—just like I wasn't *entirely* sure I'd be okay. The skull's words had spooked me. My spirits felt oppressed. I kept wanting to turn around, just in case something was sneaking up behind . . . but I certainly wasn't going to admit any of that in front of Holly.

"Well . . . see you both soon, then," Lockwood said.

Soundless as ever, he faded into the shadows.

Holly Munro and I stood in the hall for a moment, watching him go, darkness swirling around us. Then we resumed our psychic survey. Never overly talkative when we were alone, we now fell entirely silent, other than whispering new readings to each other. We were unsettled. I looked over my shoulder more often than was necessary.

At last the silence between us became oppressive. I cleared my throat.

"So," I said—I wasn't particularly interested; I just wanted to relieve the tension—"this Cotton Street killing you mentioned earlier. What *was* it? Big deal for you?"

Holly nodded briefly. "You could say that. I was the sole survivor of a four-strong team that got attacked by a Poltergeist in a Cotton Street studio. I got out of an attic window, rolled down the tiles, and fell against the chimney. Lay there all night, more dead than alive. My supervisor and two other colleagues weren't so lucky."

It was a rough story, but even as she spoke I was distracted. I had that sudden unpleasant feeling of something close and creeping near. I looked behind me—and saw nothing. . . . When I looked back, I found Holly still watching me, waiting for my reaction.

I took a moment, tried to focus on what she'd said. "Yeah. Sounds bad."

"That's all you're going to say?"

What, did she want me to hold her hand? The precise same thing had happened to me, too. "I'm sorry," I said. "But if you were an agent . . . stuff happens."

There was a pause. Holly gazed at me. After a while she said, "They took me off the front line. It was meant to be temporary, but I was good at desk work and found I didn't want to go back. But don't think I haven't got the ability to do this, Lucy. I'm rusty at it, but I'm still capable."

I shrugged. I scarcely heard her. I was concentrating on the atmosphere of the hall. A faint, dusky radiance from the streetlights below filtered through the windows and gave everything grainy definition. It wasn't so strong that our Talents would be impaired, but neither did we need to switch on our flashlights to find our way. Holly drifted away from me. She crossed to the nearest racks and walked between them, brushing her fingers along the soft lines of shirts.

I stood looking down the room.

My feelings of anxiety had deepened all the time we'd been on this floor; now, all at once, without warning, they intensified into dread. I found my gaze was fixed on the dark space at the end of the hall, beyond Checkout and the final racks of clothes, where a tall, squared archway opened on to the cross-passage that led to the elevators and stairs. The details of the passage could not be seen: it had no windows, and the streetlights did not penetrate there. It was a blank emptiness, small, but of infinite depth.

"Lucy . . ."

Sweat ran down the side of my face; I couldn't look away.

I could hear the rustlings of Holly's fingers as they ran along the shirts. Down in the street, a dog barked, perhaps a stray. But that was the last thing I heard, for now cold silence engulfed me—suddenly, violently, as if it had come rushing up the hall from the passage at the end. It hit me like a fist. Something pressed hard on my temples; I grimaced, opened my mouth, but I could not call out. My limbs were marble; my hands locked at my side. I was as fixed and frozen as one of the mannequins.

And I watched that notch of darkness.

I watched as something moved into it.

It came from the right-hand side beyond the arch, a human figure crawling on all fours. Scarcely blacker than the blackness all around, it dragged itself along on knees and elbows with a series of slow, slow, jerking movements. Now and again it advanced in swift scuttles, as a hunting spider might, but the overall impression was of obnoxious weakness and of pain. Thin legs dragged behind it; the head hung low between the rolling shoulder blades and could not be clearly seen.

Across the space at the end of the hall the crawling figure went; it reached the other side of the arch and disappeared along the passage in the direction of the elevators. A moment passed, and then a flowing thread of darkness streamed across the gap after it. It looked like a thick black rope, shimmering, quivering at its edges. At first I couldn't make out what it was; then pieces of it broke away, and I recognized them. It was a great host of spiders, silent, intent, moving like a single living thing. They too passed out of view in the direction the awful jerking figure had taken, and with that the dread that held me in its grip relaxed, and I could move again.

The pall of silence lifted about me; once more I heard Holly's fingers as they brushed through cloth and, outside in the street, another bark from the poor stray dog.

There was pain in my mouth, and my lips were wet. When I touched them, my fingers ran with blood. In my numbness and terror, I'd driven my teeth into my tongue.

Chapter 21

I shook my head to clear the icy dullness from my brain. *"Holly!"* I hissed.

Give the girl her due; she was at my side at once, fancy sneakers soundless on the polished floor. Her voice seemed oddly loud. "What?"

"Did you see *that?*"

"What are you talking about? I didn't see anything."

"Or even feel it? It was down beyond the arch there—something moved across it."

"I didn't sense anything. . . . Are you all right, Lucy? You're shaking."

"I'm not shaking. I'm fine. You don't need to put your hands on me."

"There's a chair here. Why don't you sit down?"

"I don't *want* to sit down. What are you, my nursemaid?"

"Well, let's go find the others. It's time we met them anyway."

Lockwood and Kipps were already waiting near the first-floor stairs. We stumbled down the steps to them. "Poor Lucy's seen something," Holly Munro said as we drew close. "She's terrified."

"I am *not* terrified." Where the spectral chill had been, hot rage was now pulsing through my veins; I struggled to keep my voice steady. To be honest, it wasn't strictly clear that she'd intended to have a dig at me, but I didn't care right then. "I'm fine, thank you. It was something very strong, that's all."

"Tell us, Luce," Lockwood said.

I told them as best I could.

"Did it look at you?" he asked. "Were you attacked in any way?"

"It didn't stop or look at me. It just went past—but I've never experienced such ghost-lock. . . . And such chill, too—I still feel cold now. . . ." I shivered; I sat down on a step. "The *spiders*, Lockwood— have *you* ever seen that before?"

"I've not. There've been cases, though, haven't there, Kipps?"

"Red Lodge, famously," Kipps said. "And at Chislehurst Caverns back in '88. Others, maybe. One or two. Not many."

"What the hell was it *doing*? The way it was crawling along the floor . . . God . . ."

"I think she should leave," Holly Munro said abruptly. "She's in no state to go on."

"Like *you* could know that!" I cried. "Like *you* could sense anything! You were standing right next to me, and you didn't pick up any of the chill or the creeping fear! You weren't ghost-locked at all!"

"You make it sound as if that's a bad thing," Holly said.

"Oh, give me a *break*."

"What was that?" It was Lockwood who'd spoken, but we'd all spun around. One of the clothes racks on the far side of the room had tumbled over with a crash. A shadow came lurching toward us: Kate Godwin, rapier out, blond hair disarranged. Her usual cool self-possession was gone.

She halted by us, white-faced, breathing hard. "Have you seen Bobby?"

We stared at her. "How can you have lost him?" Kipps said. "I only looked in on you five minutes ago."

"Five minutes? More like hours. I've been searching all over . . . I can't find him."

"What time *is* it?" Holly said. "I can't tell how long we've been here either."

I looked at my watch and felt a new stab of fear. "The hands have stopped."

Kipps cursed. "Mine have gone backward."

"Everyone calm down," Lockwood said. "Forget the time. The entities here are playing tricks on us. Kate, tell us what happened."

Kate Godwin pushed her bangs back. Her blue eyes, bright, angry, and distressed, flickered between us; she couldn't keep them still. "We got to the top floor, furniture department, all the sofas and things. We started looking around. I heard a voice again—it distracted me. It sounded like—well, it doesn't matter *what* it sounded like. I followed it a short way. Then Bobby shouted that he'd seen something. He sounded . . . odd. I looked around—he was running off into the dark. I went after him . . . but he'd gone. *Gone,* Quill." She looked as if she were about to cry.

"For heaven's sake," Kipps said. "I thought we told you to stay together."

Her face twisted. "We *were* staying together! But then he—"

"It's all right," Lockwood said. "We'll find him. What was this voice you heard?"

She hesitated, glanced over at Kipps. "It doesn't matter."

"Not good enough," I snapped. "You're part of a bigger team now. You need to tell us everything."

Kate Godwin swore. "Don't order me about, Carlyle. If you must know, I thought I heard Ned Shaw."

Kipps gave a start. "Kate, Ned died miles from here. And we . . . we followed proper procedures, with iron and everything. He can't have . . . he can't have come back."

"How clearly did you hear his voice?" Lockwood asked.

Kate Godwin shook her head disgustedly. "Quite obviously I can't have. I must be going mad. It's the kind of nonsense Carlyle pulls. But Bobby . . ."

"Yes, we need to find him fast. But before that we should— George!"

Out of the dark, two *more* hurrying figures: George's low-slung form followed by the taller, even more shapeless outline of Flo Bones in her whopping coat. They looked like two melting marshmallows, both flushed and breathing hard.

"There's weird things going on, Lockwood," George began. "Flo's just seen something in the basement—not one of these ordinary Shades, but something with the semblance of— Who was it, Flo?"

Unlike Kate Godwin, unlike Kipps, unlike—it has to be admitted—*me* (my heart was still beating fast; I still saw the vision of that horrid, dragging thing), Flo Bones seemed her usual calm and caustic self. "The name wouldn't mean anything to you," she said crisply. "But I can tell you the essential point." She lifted her straw hat and scratched at a clump of hair. "It was someone dear to me and also dead. I felt a strong desire to follow the apparition . . . but Cubbins, here, threw a salt-bomb and pulled me back."

"Great work, George. . . ." Lockwood spoke slowly; he looked around at us all. "Taken alongside Kate's experience, I'm beginning to wonder if we might be dealing with—"

"With a Fetch," George said. "A ghost that makes a psychic bond with the onlooker, and takes on the guise of someone closely connected to them. Might be someone living, might be someone dead. Either way, it's really disorienting. It feeds off something that's uppermost in the mind, so if you're fixated on something, or grieving, then you're particularly vulnerable."

"Doesn't explain what *I* saw," I said.

"Maybe not, but Kate heard Ned Shaw," Holly said. "And we think that Vernon may have seen something that made him act oddly too. He's gone off: we don't know where."

"And we need to *find* him," Godwin snapped. She gave a sudden cry. "What are we doing hanging around, yabbering like this? I don't care if it's a Fetch or a tiny Glimmer! We've got to get on with it!" She made a sudden movement toward the stairs.

Holly put out an arm. "Wait. Not on your own."

"Get your hands off me."

A ringing sound interrupted us. Lockwood was rapping his rapier on the glass top of a display case. "Listen to you! You're arguing over nothing. We're forgetting the first rule of entering a haunted location: *Remain calm*. Whatever we're dealing with, we're risking its feeding on our emotions." He fixed his rapier to his belt. "Sorry as I am to say it, we're out of our depth here. The Source is well hidden, and far too powerful. We need to find Vernon and get out."

"That means splitting up again," Kipps said. "If we're searching."

"I know, and I don't like it, but I don't see how it can be helped."

"Agreed. But Kate comes with us."

"Fine. George and Flo, Lucy and Holly, you stick to your pairs. Whoever finds Bobby lets off a flare, and the rest of us will join you right away. Then we hit the exit. No one lets anyone else stray off alone, or get distracted by any sound or shape. That's an order. Act at all times as if you're joined at the hip. Questions?"

Holly and I looked at one another, but said nothing.

The groups dispersed. Lockwood hung back, waiting for me.

"You're very pale, Lucy," he said. "This thing you saw—"

I held up my hand. "I'm not going to back out. We need to find Vernon. It's a race against time."

"I knew you'd say that. I know how strong you are. Okay, then— but be careful."

"It's not a problem," I said. "Only—do you *really* want me to go with Holly again?"

He grinned at me. "Of course. You complement each other."

"We so don't. We *never* say nice things about each other."

He rolled his eyes. "*Complement*, not compliment! With an *E*, Lucy. Yes, obviously I know *you* never say nice things about *her*— that would be too easy. The other way around? You'd be surprised.

But you make a good team anyhow, whether you like it or not." He turned aside. "Now, shut up and get going."

Well, it was a good-bye of sorts. We went our separate ways.

Hunting for a fellow agent in a haunted building is never much fun. It complicates matters. Not only were we still keeping psychic watch (we *had* to: the drifting Shades that thronged the halls kept pace with us, never drawing too close, but never dispersing, either; and we knew other presences prowled the echoing halls), we had to exert all our ordinary senses for sight or sound of Bobby Vernon, too. The two activities were not really compatible: when we concentrated on one, we neglected the other, which consistently increased our underlying anxiety and alarm.

I particularly disliked the open halls and the blank, dark spaces at the ends of aisles. I kept expecting to see the crawling figure, far off and coming after me.

The strain of being doubly alert soon told. Holly and I lapsed into sullen silence, communicating mainly by gestures. We hurried through Cosmetics and Visitor Defenses on the ground floor, then climbed the backstairs at the north end of the building right up to the top floor. Office Supplies was empty both of Visitors and Bobby Vernon, and so were the Aickmere meeting rooms. By unspoken agreement we then descended to the third floor, which was where he'd disappeared, and tight arrangements of sofas, chairs, and tables spread out in jumbled parodies of real homes. Sometimes we called out for him, softly, instinctively unhappy at disturbing the silence; mostly we just listened. We looked in closets, chests, and storerooms. Sometimes we saw the others at a distance, or heard them calling; but all sounds and all shapes were suspect now, and we kept away from them. Bobby Vernon was nowhere to be seen.

We arrived at the elevator lobby, and the main stairs. "No good," Holly Munro said. "We'll try the next floor down."

The skull in my backpack had been quiet for some time, since before I'd seen the apparition and its train of spiders. Now I felt its presence stirring at my back.

"If you leave him now," it said, *"he'll die."*

"But he's not up here." I ignored Holly Munro's baffled look; to her it sounded like I was talking to the empty air. "We've tried everywhere."

"Have you?"

I looked around the lobby. Stairs, walls . . . creamy marble and mahogany. Behind us the two brass elevator doors gleamed. The power was off. There was no point looking there; Vernon would have been unable to take the elevators, or even open the doors.

Even so . . . I stepped close to the doors, put my ear to them. It seemed I heard a moan, a muffled cry.

"Bobby?" I said. "Can you hear me?"

"He *can't* be in there." Holly Munro stepped close. "The electricity—"

"Quiet. I think he answered. I heard a voice."

I stabbed at the buttons on the wall. They were dead and unresponsive, but I had an alternative in my bag.

"A crowbar?" Holly hung back. "Do you think that Mr. Aickmere—"

"Stuff Aickmere! He said this place had no ghosts! Shut up and help me shove."

I slammed the bar in between the metal doors and strained to pry them apart. Grim-faced, not looking at me, Holly grasped the metal too. We exerted our strength. At first we made not the slightest impression; then something internal made a reluctant extended cracking sound. The doors slid open—a small distance, perhaps a quarter of their width. But it was enough.

Inside: blackness. And a feeble moaning, coming from below.

My penlight showed the hollow interior of the shaft: oil-stained bricks and loops of black cables, but not the elevator itself. When we craned our heads out over the drop, we saw the roof of the car about six feet below. And on it, curled in a forlorn ball, with his knees drawn up and his arms tightly wound about his spindly knees, was Bobby Vernon. He looked in bad shape.

"What the hell happened to him?" I said. "Think he's ghost-touched?"

"No. But see the bruise on his face?"

Vernon's eyes rolled upward, winking and twitching in the beam of the penlight. He coughed raggedly. "I hurt my head; think my leg's busted."

"Oh, great . . ." Something made my skin crawl. I looked back into the darkness of the Furniture Hall. The blackness there seemed to swirl. "How are we going to get him out?"

"One of us could slip in there," Holly said. "It should probably be me."

"Why? Why? You were looking at the width of my hips then, weren't you?"

"Of course not. You hold the doors open. You're much stronger and burlier than me." Holly shimmied through the doors, turned to face me, bent to grip the edge, and with surprising agility jumped down into the dark.

I jammed the crowbar into the aperture, fixing the doors open, and flourished the penlight through the hole. She was crouching beside Vernon, touching his leg.

"What happened to you, Bobby?" she asked.

"Ned. I saw Ned. . . ."

"Ned Shaw?" I looked down at Holly. "That's their dead friend."

"I saw him . . . he was standing in the dark, smiling at me. . . ." Vernon coughed his ragged cough again; his voice was weak. "I felt I had to go to him. . . . I don't know. He didn't turn away, but he sort of receded, flowed away from me, past all the tables and chairs. I followed. . . . He went into the elevator—it was all lit up, I swear. Doors open, lights on. He stood there waiting for me, smiling. I walked in. . . . Then the lights just went out and the elevator wasn't there. I fell. Hit my head. My leg hurts. . . ."

"It's all right," Holly said. She squeezed his hand. "You'll be fine."

Annoyance flared in me. "Bobby, you're an idiot. Holly—can you help him stand? I could pull him up, maybe, if I grab him."

"I can try." She did so; plenty of groans and whimpers ensued.

"*Better hurry, Lucy.* . . ." The skull's whisper was casualness itself. "*Something's coming.*"

"I know. I feel it. Bobby—hold out your hands. I can reach you, pull you up."

He was vertical now, draped on Holly, one leg raised, hobbling and squinting like a poor imitation of a pirate. "I can't . . . I'm too weak."

"You're not too weak to lift your arms." I was on my hands and knees now, reaching between the doors. "Come *on* . . . hurry it up."

He lifted a frail hand; a ninety-four-year-old dowager summoning a servant to refill her cup of tea would have raised her arm more vigorously. I swiped at it and missed.

"We might need to get Lockwood," Holly Munro said.

"There's no time. . . ." I looked back into the dark. "*Do* it, Vernon."

My second swipe struck home. I grabbed his wrist. Launching myself backward, I hoisted him up, ignoring his cries of pain. A moment later Vernon's face, bruised and groggy-looking, appeared in the aperture. I heaved—out came his spindly shoulders, his pigeon-chest . . .

"Oh, hell," I said. "He's stuck."

Holly gave a squeak from below. "How *can* he be stuck? He's thinner than me."

"I don't know. . . ." My eyes swiveled. Away among the darkened furniture, amid those blank and meaningless arrangements of armchairs and settees, a voice came calling. "*Lucy* . . ."

"Help me!" I shouted. "Push his backside! Get him out of there."

"I'm *not* pushing his backside!"

"There's a Visitor coming, Holly. *Why* is he wedged?"

"I don't know! Oh, I do! He's got his work belt caught."

"Well, can you free it?"

"I don't know. I don't know. . . . I'm trying to reach. . . ."

I still had one hand clasped on Vernon's wrist. With my other, I got my rapier out. Away in the hall I heard a rhythmic scraping. . . . Something approaching on bony hands and knees.

"Holly . . ."

"I've never taken off someone else's belt before! You have *no* idea how uncomfortable this makes me!"

I stared beyond the arch. Was that a rustling of a thousand tiny legs?

"Holly . . ."

"There! I've done it! Quick! Pull! Pull!"

I heaved once more. This time Bobby Vernon came free like a knobbly-kneed knife through butter. He popped out so fast, I fell over on my back.

A moment more, and I was scrabbling for Holly, helping her up too. Her clothes were oily, her sleeve torn.

Vernon was lolling on the floor. He was in a bad way, eyes tight shut, and moaning. I grasped him under the arms. "Holly—stairs. We need to *go*."

Through the arch the scraping sound and its soft, attendant rustling were growing very loud. I knew that at any moment something hateful would emerge into the light.

She grasped Vernon's ankles, and together we picked him up. He didn't weigh too much, but it was difficult enough. It was a good thing it was him, and not George.

A few spiders skittered through the arch, out into the lobby. Then we were around the corner and starting down the stairs.

In Men's Wear, on the floor below, we stopped, shoulders aching, desperately out of breath. We put Vernon on the floor in the center of an aisle, midway between clothes racks and a checkout counter. The air was brittle, cold; the fog high enough to wind around our calves. Vernon lay in it as in a milk bath. I took a small lantern from my pack; we lit it, looking at the oily pallor of his face. It was quiet. There were Shades clustering far off among the aisles, but they kept their distance as before. Both Holly and I stood rigid, staring, letting the panic wash over us; the adrenaline ebbed quickly, leaving us weary and irritable.

"He's bleeding," Holly said. "I have a first-aid kit. Shall I—?"

"Oh, you might as well, yeah. You're the expert."

She did swift, efficient things with bandages. I stood with my jaw clamped, guarding them both, watching the way the shadows moved inward, pressing in against the lantern.

Holly was deft, careful, and knew what she was doing. It gave me a sour feeling to watch her. Lockwood had said we complemented each other. Yet another way in which he was just so wrong.

Vernon coughed again, said something unintelligible.

Holly stood up, put her bandages away. "Do you see that thing?"

"No."

"Do you hear it?"

"No! I'll tell you if I do." I shook my head. "God. Can't you use your own senses for a change? What are you even doing here?"

"Lockwood asked me to come, didn't he? It's not my fault my Talent's not as sharp as yours."

"Well, you could always have said no to Lockwood."

"Like you do?" She gave her trilling laugh.

"What?" I stared at her. "What does *that* mean?"

"Like you ever do that." She waved her hand as if it would magically dissolve the words she'd just said. "Nothing. It doesn't matter. We should get going."

It was the little gesture that did it, the wave of the hand. All at once, the rage I'd been chewing on for so long was too big for my mouth; it was all I could do to spit it out. "Don't talk to me about Lockwood in that airy-fairy way," I said. "You know nothing about him. You know nothing about me. How about from now on you keep your patronizing comments to yourself?" The verbal onrush felt so good, I was giddy with it.

Her eyes were hot and wet then. I didn't care. It was good to see. "Oh, that's rich," she said. "That's rich. You've been patronizing me ever since I arrived!"

I blinked at her, genuinely taken aback. "Sorry? *Me* patronizing *you?*"

"There you are. You're doing it again!"

"What? That's not patronizing you. That's just me doing a verbal backflip because you've said something so astronomically wrong and dumb. There's a difference, you know, Miss Munro."

She gave a hoot of rage. "See? You can't open your mouth without doing it! Patronize, patronize, patronize. What's wrong with you? You've been hostile to me from the word *go!*"

"Me? I've been a model of self-restraint!"

"Oh, sure. All your snorting and tutting! All your eye-rolling whenever I tried to contribute."

"Guys, guys . . ." It was Bobby Vernon, clutching at us from below. "I'm only half-awake and probably a bit delirious, and was just in the middle of a dream about a goldfish, but even *I* know this isn't a good idea."

"*On the contrary.*" This was the skull. "*You've waited long enough for this, Lucy. Don't forget the coat hanger garrote. It's an option.*"

I listened to neither of them. I was too busy laughing in her face. "See, Holly?" I said. "This is a classic example of what you do! You stay all sweet and perfect, and twist things around magically so *I'm* the one to blame! You're the one who patronizes me! I can't blow my nose without you telling me I'm doing it wrong."

"Oh, I wouldn't *dare* do that!" she said. "What, and risk getting my head bitten off?"

"I can't stand the way you criticize everything," I cried, "without actually *saying* so! You're like a prim, uptight little schoolteacher, looking down on everything I do!"

She stamped her foot. "Well, you—you're like a . . . a stupid little dog, always yapping and growling. You made it plain from the first you didn't want me there. Every time I said something, you'd start sneering and rolling your eyes, and spitting out the sarcasm. So many days I could hardly bear to come in. I almost quit a couple of times."

There it was again! This is what she was so good at doing. Twisting it, giving you the guilt. But it didn't work this time. My discomfort fueled my fury. "Rubbish! I always tried to be friendly and welcoming, even when you started going into my room and doing those weird things with my clothes!"

"It's called folding!" Holly shouted. "You should try it sometime! You lived in a hellhole before I came! It was disgusting!"

"I was *happy* with that hellhole! I was happy with the way it was!"

Someone tugged my arm. "This isn't good," Bobby Vernon croaked. "Can't you give each other girly smiles until we get out of this place?"

I shoved his hand away. "Shut up, you."

"Yes," Holly Munro snapped. "It's *your* fault we're still here."

"Hey, see? You agree about *that*," Vernon said. "Come on. It's not so hard. . . ."

"You think I'm just a dumb assistant! You can't cope with the fact I saved your life!"

"Oh, you're wrong there, buddy. I can cope with that. What I can't cope with is your endless sniping, your chipping away at me continuously while staring at me with that super—super silly—with that bloody thing you do with your eyebrows!"

She gazed at me blankly. "Super silly?"

Bobby Vernon lifted a hand. "Supercilious."

"Thanks." I put on a stupid voice. "'No, Lucy, not like that. *Rotwell does it this way. Rotwell does it that way.*' If you like Rotwell so much, go back to that agency!"

"I *didn't* like working for Rotwell! He was disgusting. He's violent and ambitious and he doesn't treat his employees well. But don't pretend you're so caring, Lucy Carlyle! I told you about what happened to me at Cotton Street, and you couldn't have cared less!"

"That's not true! How dare you say that?"

"Then why didn't you show it, Lucy?"

"Because . . . because the same bloody thing happened to me! I lost my team as well! They all died too! All right? It upset me!"

"Well, I didn't know that!"

"Well, I didn't *ask* you to know about it, did I? It's my business!"

"Like Lockwood's past is your business too?" She glared at me in triumph. "I know you went into that room. I heard you from downstairs."

"What?" I took a deep breath then, chest painful with rage. And as I did so, there was a small, drawn-out scraping sound from the checkout counter down the aisle. We all looked over: me, Holly, Bobby Vernon on the floor. At first we couldn't see what had made the sound. Then we noticed that one of the tape dispensers, small, but heavy, made of shiny stone, was moving slowly along the surface of the counter. It went of its own volition, scratching, trembling, scraping across the glass.

It reached the side of the cash register, bumped into it, once, twice, and then again, as if seeking a way past. Then, as we watched, it began to rise up the cash register, pressing hard against it, shuddering and screeching. When it got to the top, it flipped slowly onto its side, paused, and then, with sudden violence, shot along and over the edge, to fall back down onto the glass counter with a violent crack.

We stood there, staring. Suddenly, in the silence, I could feel immense pressure stabbing at my ears. It was like a great wave suddenly hung over us, quivering, only momentarily frozen; we were in its shadow.

"*Oops.*" That was the skull.

"Now you've done it," Bobby Vernon said.

Holly Munro and I looked at one another. Just looked. We didn't bother trying girly smiles or anything. It was too late for that.

Chapter 22

Too late for anything, but we gave it a go.

No sooner had the tape dispenser hit the glass than Holly and I dived behind the nearest available shelter. It was a low display case, like a kind of open-topped table, stuffed with a hundred varieties of golf socks. Holly and I crouched there, bent close, our faces nearly touching. Bobby Vernon was crumpled between us, half-conscious, breathing heavily.

It was very quiet in the room now. True, the psychic echo of our argument rebounded between the walls, on and on and on. Invisible lines of power thrummed in the room, taut as piano wire, heavy with built-up charge. But the only actual *sound* was a soft, rhythmic rustling. I peeped up from behind the case and looked over at the desk, at the counter with its jagged crack and the tape dispenser sticking up from the fractured glass like the bow of a sinking ship.

A little stack of papers—brochures, maybe—lay on the glass. One corner of the stack was riffling in a nonexistent wind.

The pages would ripple upward, then fall still, then ripple up again.

I ducked back down.

"Can you see anything?" Holly asked. The terror was plain in her eyes. Her voice shook with the effort of trying to rebuild her shattered emotional calm. I nodded.

She stared at me. A twist of hair had fallen in front of her face; she was chewing the end, eyes wide in the half-dark. "So . . . so the *Fittes Manual* says the first thing we have to do is establish Type," she said.

I knew quite well what the *Fittes Manual* said. But damp fear had replaced the remains of anger in my belly. I just nodded again. "Yes."

"We know it's kinetic," she breathed. "It moves things around. But is there any kind of apparition?"

I peeped up above the socks again. I could smell the lanolin in the wool, and the cleanness of the plastic packaging. The thought crossed my mind that Lockwood and George both needed socks, and that it would be Christmas soon; my next thought (less pleasantly) was that it was highly unlikely I'd survive the night to get to Christmas. I looked across the hall. It was now empty of all the dark shapes that had clustered there earlier. Either they'd been driven back, or absorbed into the mass of cold, pulsating energy that hung vibrating around us—energy our argument had summoned into being. I ducked my head down once more. "No."

"No apparition? Oh, so it's a . . . so it might just be a . . ."

"It's a Poltergeist, Holly. Yes, it is."

She swallowed. "Okay. . . ."

I dropped Vernon's leg and reached out to grip her arm. "But it's *not* going to be like Cotton Street," I whispered. "This time it's going to be fine. You understand that? We're going to get out of this, Holly. Come on. We can do it. We just need to get down two floors and across to the entrance. That's not too far, is it? We do it quietly, and we do it carefully, and we don't attract its attention."

Over on the distant desk, the papers rippled, on-off, on-off, their hum soft and rhythmic like the purring of a giant cat.

"But Poltergeists . . ."

"Poltergeists are blind, Holly. They respond to emotion, noise, and stress. So listen to me. We make for the back stairs—they're the closest. We go down to the ground floor and we find the others. We do it all step by step, stage by stage, very quietly and very calmly, and we never, *ever* panic. If we keep everything nice and neutral, it's likely it won't even notice us again."

I gazed at her steadily in what I hoped was a calm, reassuring manner. On balance it was probably more a wild-eyed lunatic stare.

"Good luck with that. . . ." Bobby Vernon said.

He was only half-conscious, but he knew. Poltergeists, you see . . . Here's the thing: they're bad. Hard to deal with, hard to pin down. Impossible to control. Where other Type Two Visitors always give you something to aim at, Poltergeists have no physical manifestation at all. No apparition, no substance, no shadow. This, for agents, is a major disadvantage. It doesn't matter how faint a Phantasm, say, might be; once you've locked on to its shimmering translucent form, you can lay salt, strew iron, or lob flares to your heart's content. A Raw-bones may make your bowels twist tight in abject terror, but at least you're never in any doubt about where it is. That's simply not the case with a Poltergeist. It's everywhere and nowhere, and all around you, and more than any other ghost it feeds off every drop of emotion you give out. It feeds off it and uses it to *move* things. Just a small amount of rage or sadness can fuel its power.

Just a small amount . . .

Oh, God. What had we done?

What had *I* done, more to the point? I felt sick; I closed my eyes.

"Lucy?" Holly's hand brushed my knee. She was giving me a wobbly grin. "It'll be all right, you said? So . . . what do we do?"

I felt a flush of gratitude to her. My answering grin was probably equally wonky, and watery as hell. I jerked my head along the aisle toward the back staircase at the far end of the floor. "We get up— very slowly. . . . We retreat a few yards at a time, along toward those doors. We just walk, we don't hurry. We keep our heart rates down."

"I can't. . . . It's impossible."

"Holly, we just have to do our best."

Standing up was the hardest part. Standing up in plain view. Like I said, Poltergeists respond to sound and emotion, so technically it made no difference whether we were hiding behind a cabinet or wearing top hats and sequins and high-kicking like a pair of excited go-go dancers—provided we did it *silently*. But it didn't *feel* that way. Just the thought of being suddenly exposed to the thing beside the counter made cramps race across my stomach on skittering spider legs. Still, we had no choice.

Whispering to Bobby Vernon to be silent, we both grabbed appropriate parts of him and, on a mouthed count of three, stood up. We stared over at the desk, at the purring pile of papers. Up and down went the pages . . . up and down in the cold, cold air. . . . So far, so good. The rhythm hadn't altered. Still, the dark crackled with psychic charge: it seemed that the tiniest movements we made would send shockwaves across the hall.

I nodded my head. Holly was nearest the staircase; that meant she would have to walk backward, arms looped under Vernon's shoulders, with me gripping his legs, following behind. Vernon himself, eyes half open, seemed scarcely aware of what was going on. He worried me. I feared that he might suddenly call out and attract unwelcome attention.

Holly shuffled backward; I shuffled after. Out of the corner of my eye I watched the papers on the desk fluttering, fluttering. . . .

Down along the aisle we went, between the hanging coats, pressing each foot down with tender, soundless care. Steadily we drew closer to the stairwell doors.

"Say," a voice said in my ear, "*this is exciting. I almost think you might make it.*"

The skull! I rolled my eyes in dismay, biting the corner of my lip. Would his presence disturb the Poltergeist? I looked over at the desk, at the gently ruffling papers.

"*Unless Holly trips and drops little Bobby and his head knocks on the floor with a whopping great thud,*" the ghost continued amiably, "*like a tufty coconut cracking on a rock. I honestly think this might happen. Look at the way her little hands are slipping. . . .*"

It was true. Holly had stopped, and altered her grip under Vernon's armpits. Her face was as pale as I'd ever seen it. But we weren't far from the doors.

"*I call this a nice refreshing change,*" the skull said. "*You can't talk back! Or reach around to turn my tap off. Means I can tell you what I think of you, without you giving me any lip.*"

We shuffled on. I squinted frantically across the room.

It was okay. On the desk, nothing had changed.

"*Don't worry,*" the skull said. "*It's not interested in me. We entities, by and large, keep ourselves to ourselves. It won't pay any attention to what I do.*"

I breathed out with relief. And just then Holly nudged a coat with her elbow, making its hanger scrape gently on the rail.

"That, *on the other hand . . .*"

My eyes flipped around; I looked at the pile of papers.

They were suddenly very still.

Holly and I exchanged glances. We waited. I counted to thirty in my head, forcing my breathing to remain calm. The room was dark and silent. Nothing happened. The papers didn't move.

I expelled air very, very slowly. We tiptoed on.

"*Hey, maybe you're okay now!*" the skull said. "*Maybe it's gone.*"

An empty coat hanger on a rack on the other side of the room spun up and over in a whizzing 360-degree turn, then rocked back and forth with ever smaller movements until it was once again quite still.

"*It hasn't, you know. I was just kidding.*"

We froze, watched the space. Again everything was still. I

nodded to Holly. Grimly, grappling Vernon tighter, moving slightly faster, we inched along the aisle.

Away across the room, a *ting* of metal. One of the lights in the ceiling swung softly in the darkness. Holly started to slow, but I shook my head and we redoubled our pace toward the stairs.

We needed to hurry now. We needed to get out.

"Don't make the mistake of thinking it's over there," the skull said in my ear. *"Or by the coats . . ."*

I gritted my teeth. I knew what it was going to say.

"Truth is, it's everywhere. It's right on top of us. It coils around us like a snake. We're all inside it. It has already swallowed us whole."

All at once a squealing screech of feedback came from the speakers in the ceiling, followed by a low-level, crackling hum. Holly and I both jumped. Behind Holly's head a pair of blue pajamas on a rail jerked too, as if someone was in them, legs bending, arms jabbing outward in a brief, appalling spasm.

Almost as fast as it had started, the energy went out of it. The pajamas hung limp, without animation.

A moment later we slammed through the swinging doors into the pitch darkness of the back stairs.

I dropped Vernon's leg, flipped a penlight from my belt, and shoved it between my teeth. The light showed Holly, sagging against the wall, easing Vernon to the ground.

"Oh, God . . ." she said. "Oh, God . . ."

"We can't stop here, Hol," I hissed. "We've got to move. Pick him up! Come on!"

"But, Lucy—"

"Just do it!"

Onward, stumbling, down the stairs, contained within our bobbing sphere of light. We weren't trying for quiet anymore, and we weren't attempting to suppress the fear that, choking, rose within us. Holly was sobbing as she went; Bobby Vernon's head bounced side to side as we careered against the walls.

We reached the turn. Behind us, the doors at the top burst open, smashing back against the wall. Their panels of glass shattered; fragments cascaded down the steps, rained past us into the dark. A squall of air buffeted against us as we collapsed onto the landing below.

"In there!" I'd been planning to keep going down, all the way to the ground floor, but I didn't want to be stuck in the stairwell now. I nodded toward the door leading back into the store. Holly shouldered her way through—we entered the silence and darkness of Kitchenware at the far end of the first floor.

"Holly," I whispered, "you're tired. Swap with me. Let me go in front now."

"I'll be all right."

"Side by side, then." The aisle was wide enough for us to go abreast. It wasn't too far. Through Kitchenware, then Ladies' Fashions, then down the main stairs to the ground floor—that's all we had to do.

Far off I heard voices calling us. Living voices—Lockwood, George . . .

"Don't answer them," I said. "Keep silent."

We went as fast as we could. I kept expecting the door behind us to crash open, as if the ghost were chasing us. But Poltergeists don't work that way.

When we were beside a stack of colanders, something slapped me in the face.

I cried out, dropping my flashlight, letting go of Vernon's legs. He moaned, thrashed in Holly's grip.

Another slap, stinging across my cheek. Cursing, I drew my sword, swung it around me in a wild sweep. Nothing.

In the next aisle, something smashed against saucepans.

Holly gave a yelp; a red mark bloomed like a flower on her cheekbone.

There's only one good thing about Poltergeists: no ectoplasm, so you can't get ghost-touch, even when you're slapped around by them. It almost makes up for the higher than average chance of being brained by a sofa or skewered by a banister rail. We snatched Vernon up, staggered on.

Somewhere behind, a clattering; dozens of utensils cascading to the floor. And now came a horrendous din, a tumbling of tortured metal, peppered with grunts and snarls, as if a great beast was thrashing and writhing in their midst.

But the beast was ahead of us too. Farther along our aisle: a rack of knives of every size and shape. They quivered and trembled on their hooks.

Uh-oh.

I pulled us out of the aisle and down along a parallel one, just as the weapons burst free. Down behind a rack of chinaware we fell, rolling over in a heap as dozens of carving knives screamed through the air, embedding themselves in the floor around us, splintering plates, bouncing off copper pots.

Bobby Vernon opened an eye. "Ow! Careful. I'm in pain here, you realize."

"You'll be a darn sight worse off shortly," I snarled, "if you don't shut up. Come on, Holly! Get up! We're doing so well."

"What would doing badly look like?"

Feedback welled up through the sound system, vibrating jaggedly through the nerves of our teeth. We heard bangs and screams from elsewhere in the building. Somewhere ahead, at the entrance to Ladies' Fashions, came an almighty tearing, a wrenching sound that told of something heavy and substantial being uprooted from the floor.

For a moment I hung back, unsure whether to go on.

"Skull," I said. "I don't know . . ."

"You have to, else you'll die."

"All right." Practically using Vernon as a rope to pull Holly upright, I got us going again. We stumbled forward. In the next aisle, two display cases swung sideways and slammed into another.

"Mr. Aickmere's going to be pleased," the skull said.

"Yeah. He'll be delighted."

Holly was staring at me. "Who were you talking to just then?"

"No one! You!"

"I don't believe you."

Five Pyrex bowls flashed past my head and shattered against the wall. The wind whipped at my boots, threatening to snatch my legs out from under me. "Look, does it really matter right now?"

"If we're going to be working together, Lucy. . . ."

"Oh, hell! All right! I'll tell you! It's an evil haunted skull that lives in my backpack! Happy, now?"

"Well, yes. It explains a lot." Several aprons, flapping like bats through the air, thrashed at Holly's face. She batted them away. "See, that wasn't so bad, was it? You only had to say it."

We ducked through the archway into Ladies' Fashions, just before an entire solid display case, whistling behind us, cracked against the arch and lodged there.

"What's going on?" the skull growled. "You're telling everyone about us now? I thought we had something special going."

"We do! Shut up! We'll discuss this later."

"You know, Lucy"—Holly Munro gasped—"I used to think you were just plain weird. Now I see how thoroughly wrong I was."

Ladies' Fashions was quiet, at least compared to Kitchenware. Cold air cut against our ankles, keeping pace with us. At the far end I could see the elevator lobbies and the marble that enclosed the grand stairs and escalators down to the ground floor.

"Nothing sharp in here," I said. "That's one blessing."

To the left of us—I could see it, but Holly, with her back to it, could not—the head of a mannequin turned slowly around, fixing us with its blind, bland smile.

And now the room erupted. An entire clothes rack reared up, slowly at first; then, with a kick like a bucking horse, it flung itself in a somersault through the air. Holly screamed; we launched ourselves back as it smashed into the pillar opposite and toppled down to block the aisle like a fallen tree.

Other racks were caught up, tossed high, sent smashing through windows and crumpling against walls. All around us coats were torn free of their pegs. They swirled up above us, hoods empty, sleeves billowing as if filled with invisible limbs. They hung in the air like witches on their sticks; the howling wind blew them around and around. Down they came now, thumping against our heads, whipping us with their trailing belts, slashing our skin with their zippers and buttons.

Bending low, pulling Bobby Vernon between us, we raced toward the escalators, dodging falling debris, dancing aside as floor tiles popped loose between our feet and went spinning off to crack in shards against pillars and walls. Clothing battered against us; a pair of pastel nylon trousers wrapped itself around my face, pressing close, clinging so tight, I felt my breath being stifled. I tore it away, looked over my shoulder at the whirling chaos at our back.

Far off, beyond the racing clothes and tumbling furniture, in a dark, still space, I saw a shadow crawling after me on hands and knees. It raised a stick-thin arm.

"*Lucy* . . ."

Then Holly and I had vaulted the marble wall and jumped down onto the smooth metal strip that sloped between the escalators. Vernon landed awkwardly; he shouted out in pain. Holly slipped, skidded on her backside down the slope. Vernon tumbled after her. I kept my footing, slid after them; and so, because I remained upright, saw what was happening in the grand foyer of Aickmere's department store.

Light greeted us from below: oddly swirling light. It came from four agency lanterns, spinning in midair.

It had occurred to me more than once to wonder where the others were. Where, in particular, Lockwood and George might be. I'd heard their voices far away, but they hadn't come for us—and I couldn't fathom why.

Now I understood.

The Poltergeist, and its energies, had not been confined to the halls through which Holly and I had been running. Far from it. It had been active in the foyer, too. Display cases lay scattered, racks embedded in the plaster pillars of the room. The murals on the walls were ruined, embedded with shards of glass torn from the entrance doors. The great artificial tree, Autumn Ramble, of which Mr. Aickmere was so proud, was at that moment spinning upward from its mount at the bottom of the escalators, its thousand lovingly handcrafted tissue leaves being torn off by whirling centrifugal force. And in the center of the room, the very floorboards were being ripped asunder too, wrenched up and outward, nails snapping, before being whipped out to break against the ruined walls. Loose earth from below floated upward into space and joined the lanterns spiraling around and around.

In all that room a single area remained untouched—a roughly semicircular space just in front of the revolving doors. It was surrounded by a set of iron chains, of triple thickness, wound around each other for extra security. Within this boundary, the floor was thick with strewn defenses—salt and iron filings, lavender sprigs, other pieces of random chain, tossed down for desperate protection. The spectral hurricane that blew around us beat against the edges of this sanctuary, making the border quiver; inside, however, everything was still.

And here stood my companions, swords out, shouting, beckoning to us.

There at the back, jamming the revolving door open with a plank of wood: Kate Godwin and Flo Bones. In the center of the space, Quill Kipps, slicing through lavender cushions with his rapier so that the stuffing spilled out onto the floor. And at the front, right on the lip of the chains, gesticulating, calling, urging us on: Lockwood and George.

My heart swelled to see them. I skidded down the bottom of the slope, jumped over Holly and Bobby Vernon, who were sprawled on the ground, and helped them to their feet. It was all I could do to stand upright, the wind blew so hard. A bent clothes rack, twisted as easily as a paper clip, crashed onto the escalators from above, twitched once, then lay there like a dead thing.

"Lucy!" That was George. "Please, come on! The place is tearing itself apart!"

George always was a master at telling you things you already knew. We started forward. Vernon looked green; Holly's face was bloodied, either from her fall or from the buffeting we'd had upstairs.

In front of us the hole in the floor was widening. The floor burst open. Earth spat against our faces; a piece of wood struck my arm.

Lockwood threw his rapier away; he stepped out of the circle. I saw him stagger as the wind caught him; his coat billowed up and outward. With an effort he kept his feet, leaped across the edge of the hole. Then he was beside us, grinning that old grin.

He took Bobby Vernon from us, supporting him under the arms. "Well done," he shouted. "I've got him. Get to the door, quick as you can."

But this was easier said than done. The floor was being ripped away, and a cavity opening beneath it. It spread wider, like a mouth gaping, extending around the edge of the iron chains. And even *under* them. Boards fell way—a portion of the chains now hung down into the hole.

Lockwood grabbed Vernon's arm, spun him bodily across. Beyond the chains, Kipps and George snatched at him, pulled him to safety. Next came Holly; she could barely stand. Again Lockwood swung her across. She fumbled at the other side, almost fell back into the hole. George grasped her; beyond, Kipps bundled Vernon toward the door.

Now Lockwood turned to me. The fury of the air redoubled. Wood, earth, tissue leaves, pieces of fabric—we were lost together in a storm of whirling debris. "Just you, Luce," he shouted. His eyes sparkled; he held out his hand. . . .

The floor ruptured. Boards burst upward, as if an invisible fist had slammed down. I lost my balance, stepped back, and the floor tipped away beneath me. Air caught me, lifted me up and away— No, not far. I immediately jerked back, caught fast. My backpack had snagged on a broken spar of floorboard. For an instant I hung there, outstretched like a flag tethered to a windblown mast.

Lockwood gave a cry. He reached for me. I saw his pale face. His hand found mine.

Then he was picked up and whipped away from me. I saw him spin off without a sound. I screamed, but my words were gone. Something behind me ripped and tore; then the backpack straps broke, and I was blown free too, whirled out and up across the room like a cast-off doll. I collided with something hard; lights burst before my eyes. Voices called my name; they pulled me away from life, away from all loved things. Then I was plummeting into darkness, and both my mind and body were lost.

VI

A Face in the Dark

Chapter 23

You know it's bad when you can't tell if your eyes are open or not. When it's so pitch-black, you might be dead or dreaming. Oh, and when you can't seem to move any part of your body, so that it feels like you're floating as a ghost might float. Yeah, that's bad too.

Utter silence doesn't help much either.

I lay there. Nothing happened for a time. Inwardly I was playing catch-up, still running through a screaming storm of broken glass and wood and whirling clothes. . . . Then, like a switch had been touched, my sense of smell suddenly flicked on. I got mold and dirt and the bitter tang of blood, as if someone had shoved it all violently up my nose. It made me sneeze, and with that sneeze came shooting darts of pain that acted like signposts in the dark. All at once I could tell where my body was, twisted out awkwardly, lying on rough ground. I was bent on my side, one of my arms pressed beneath me, arms pressed beneath me, the other flung out like I was one of those discus throwers you get on old Greek pots. It seemed to me that my head was lower than my body, and pressed against soft cold mud. When I breathed, I could feel my hair shifting against my face.

Rather to my surprise, when I tried to move, my limbs responded without too much searing agony. Everything was sore—I was one big bruise—but nothing seemed broken. I half rolled, half slid my body sideways, wincing as it collided with unknown objects. At last it lay on the horizontal. I curled my legs in close, pushed myself up, and sat there in the dark.

I put tentative fingers to my brow; one whole region of my hair was matted and sticky, presumably with blood. I'd suffered a bad blow to the head. How long I'd been unconscious was impossible to say.

Next I felt at my side. Rapier: gone. Backpack: gone. The skull, with all its unnecessary and inappropriate comments: gone. Stupidly, I kind of missed it. There was an empty space in my head where I felt its voice should be.

Part of me wanted to curl up again and just go back to sleep. I felt woozy, uncoordinated, and oddly disconnected from my predicament. But my agent training kicked in. Slowly, carefully, I put my hands to my belt.

It was still there, the pockets packed and full. So I wasn't helpless yet. I crossed my legs stiffly. Then I ran my fingers among the canisters and straps until I came to the little waterproof pouch close beside the rapier loop. The matches pouch. *Always carry matches.* As rules go, it's up there with the best. It's probably somewhere around rule seven. I wouldn't put it as high as the biscuit rule, but it's definitely in the top ten.

Rule 7-B, obviously, is to keep your match box well stocked. In the past I'd sometimes let that slide, but Holly, with her attention to detail, had always made sure it was stuffed full. I could feel how crammed it was as I got it out, and felt a flush of gratitude, which immediately morphed into guilt.

Holly . . .

I thought of our argument, the way I'd laid straight into her, how my fury and stupidity had stirred the Poltergeist to life. It gave me a dull, sick feeling. I thought of her leaping over the gap, and then of Lockwood reaching out for me—and the sick sensation in my belly deepened like an ocean trench.

The Poltergeist had caught him up and flung him away.

Was he all right? Was he even alive?

I gave a sob of self-pity, and at once swallowed it back down. I didn't like the hollow echo. I also didn't like the way my skin prickled at the sound. No more displays of emotion! Wherever it was I'd ended up, I could already tell I wasn't alone.

Presences watched me. The same presences I'd detected up in Aickmere's—but closer now—closer and stronger. And also— somewhere very near, I thought—that queasy, buzzing sensation, the one that had reminded the skull and me of the hateful bone glass we'd dug up in Kensal Green. . . .

I rubbed my eyes. It was so hard to be sure of anything. My head spun.

I struck the first match. A teardrop of light swelled upward in the dark, illuminating the dirt-stained contours of my hand. Out of the matches pouch I took out two tiny candles, both short white nubs. I put one down carefully on the ground, and lit the other, holding it at an angle till the flame took, and light waxed around me and I could see.

I sat on dark packed earth strewn with pieces of stone. At my side and back, where I'd been lying, lay a mound of rock and earth, and here and there pieces of jutting timber. There were also scattered tissue leaves from the display tree, glinting red like blood, and burst lavender cushions, and forlorn scraps of clothing—shirts, dresses, even twists of underwear—that had been sucked down with me into the hole.

Up above was a jagged snag of blackness. Whether it zigzagged up through a continuous tear in the earth and eventually reached the store above, or whether its sides had now fallen in, burying me alive, I couldn't tell. The light of the candle didn't extend into it.

What it *did* illuminate were walls of carved gray stone. I felt rather than saw them stretch out ahead of me and arch brokenly over my head. I was in a man-made chamber, old and of unknown extent. And at once I knew where I must be.

The prison. The notorious King's Prison. George had been right, as usual: part of it still existed underground, and the Poltergeist, in its fury, had torn a way through to it.

In a way, it had done me a favor. This was where the focus was for the Chelsea outbreak: this was the Source—for Poltergeist, crawling figure, and all.

Speaking of which, not three feet from where I sat, bony arms outstretched, skull scarcely protruding from beneath the pile of earth, lay a skeleton. For an instant I thought that I must have killed it in my landing, then I realized how ridiculous the idea was.

I looked at it. "Hello," I said. "Sorry."

The skeleton said nothing.

It couldn't help its bad manners. I got to my feet, rather shakily, and took a few paces forward, nose twitching in the candle smoke.

Stonework all around me, rough-hewn and dank with glistening white mold. The walls drew inward; I felt as if I were being funneled toward something, drawing closer, step by step, to an inevitable fate. It was not a pleasant sensation, particularly since everything still spun before my eyes. I took a breather, leaning against a wall.

I rested my head against the pitted stone. At once, sensations looped out of the past. Voices calling, crying, shouting for help. The passage was filled with bodies, pushing past me, pushing through me, shoving, cursing. All around me, a stink of desperation and fear—I was buffeted, pinched, sent spinning into the center of the passage—

Where I stood alone in the silence, the candle burning low in my hand. My sensitivity was getting stronger all the time. I couldn't even take a rest.

I stared at the wall. From floor to ceiling it was covered with faint scratches: letters, initials, Roman numerals. The marks of prisoners, who had lived and died here. . . .

"*Lucy* . . ."

Out of the darkness, somewhere straight ahead—that voice!

I cursed under my breath. It figured. Well, I might as well finish everything at once. "All right," I said. "Keep your hair on. I'm coming."

Shuffling like an invalid, holding the candle first high, then low, so that I could judge the uneven ground, I proceeded down the passage. I took care not to touch the walls again. White roots protruded between stones, and the walls glistened with moisture. Puddles appeared underfoot; for a few steps I was splashing through pools of shallow water, then the floor rose, and I walked once more on solid rock.

I was at a cross-junction; two other passages extended out from my corridor, to left and right. The one to my left was immediately blocked by a set of metal bars, rusted, twisted, blackened by age. To the right, my candlelight reflected on steps that disappeared into a solid expanse of foul-smelling, jet-black water. I ignored both side passages and continued straight on, and almost immediately stepped out over a pile of shattered wood into a larger space.

Somebody was whispering up ahead. When I lifted the candle, the whispers went still.

"Don't be shy," I said. "Speak up."

I laughed. They *were* shy. They were very quiet. The ground was tilting in front of me again. My head hurt, and for a moment my vision blurred; then things cleared and I could see well enough who'd been doing the whispering. They were right there in front of me, lying in piles around the side of the room. Maybe after all my splashing around in that passage I had water on the brain, but it seemed to me that they looked like the driftwood that piles up on riverbanks after a season of floods and storms. Trees stripped bare: all spindly white twigs and branches, lying on their sides, broken and intertwined.

Only they weren't trees, of course, but skeletons.

Some of them had bits of cloth still on them, but most were nothing but whorls and spars of bone. They were a mess of bony apostrophes, commas, and exclamation marks brushed off some giant's notebook into a tangled, ungrammatical heap. I could see skulls, and mandibles with glinting teeth, and ragged remnants of feet and hands, with most of the little bones lost or dangling. Ribs rose in spikes like clumps of shore grass, or broken racks for bicycles outside an abandoned station. In places the heap was thigh-high. It was a big, rectangular room, and the bones nested against all the walls, save at the far side, where a slab of gray blankness indicated another exit.

I walked slowly to the center of the chamber, shielding the candle's brightness with a cupped hand. I did it out of courtesy as much as anything. So many bones . . .

And the proprietors of those bones were all right there.

Hovering above the bony driftwood hung a multitude of white shapes, almost like candle flames themselves. Very still and very faint, like teardrops falling upward and glowing with their own peculiar light, they had no definition except for dark round notches where the eyes should be. They floated there and stared at me. And as I stood in the center of their room, I felt the full force of their inspection, and with it their centuries-old misery and hate.

"It's all right," I said to them. "I understand."

What had George said about the history of the prison? How it ended up being more of a hospital than a jail. The final inhabitants were lepers and people with other terrible illnesses. No one went there, everyone despised it. In the end the Tudor kings had driven them out and razed the place to the ground.

Driven them out . . .

I looked at the ring of broken skeletons.

Only they hadn't actually bothered, had they? They hadn't

driven them out at all. They'd just trapped them underground and sealed them in, and pulled the prison walls down on top of them. Left them in the dark to die.

Simpler. Tidier. Solved a couple of problems at once. They were criminals and they were infected. Who was going to care?

Was it any wonder that this little room was the source of so much energy and rage?

"I understand," I said again.

The shapes flickered, their dark eye-notches fixed on me, unblinking. I projected my sympathy outward as best I could. Whether they would comprehend the emotion; whether—if they did—they would readily *accept* it, after so long lying buried and forgotten, was impossible to say. So many hundreds of years, with no one any the wiser as to their existence. . . .

Well, I wouldn't blame them either way. I looked down past the dying candle and caught sight of something on the floor. I squatted down, not without a stumble (if only the floor would stop spinning!), and glared at it. It took me a moment to realize what it was—and that the skeletons were not themselves the deepest mystery of the room.

The flagstones where I crouched, unlike the corridor I'd come up, did not have dust on them, though dust was piled up thickly in and around the bones on either side. On the surface of one stone, not far from my left boot, something was lying, a cylindrical fragment, both white and brown. At first I thought it was a piece of bone, but as I lowered my candle close, I realized the truth: it was a cigarette end.

A butt from a modern cigarette. . . .

I stared at it, frowning, head throbbing, trying to make sense of it.

Around me, movement. When I looked up, the ring of pale white shapes had moved inward toward me. I held up an impatient hand.

"All right, all right," I said. "Give me a minute. I've just got something here."

I stood up. Now that I thought about it, I could see that the whole center of the room was remarkably clear—of bones, of dust, of debris of any kind. It was like it had all been swept out to the sides. Someone was very keen on housekeeping. You'd think Holly Munro had been at work.

The thought made me giggle, and the giggle instantly woke me up. I frowned at the incoming ring of shapes. "You need to give me some space here," I said. "You're putting me off. Stand back a little, please."

I went into the middle of the room, and after a moment to steady myself—everything was swaying in front of my eyes—bent down to scowl at the flagstones. I saw scratch marks in the stone, and here and there what I thought were splashes of candle-wax. I put a finger out to touch one of them, and almost fell over.

"You are seriously annoying me now," I said. The glowing shapes had drifted closer and were no longer hovering above the mess of bones. Now they formed a circle around the edges of the cleared area. I could feel the force of their attention, the anger directed at me. "I'm not supposed to talk to you," I said. "And I certainly won't do it if you don't step back. Go on!" The shapes retreated. "That's better. What have you been doing here," I said, "with all this wax and stuff? What are these circular scrapes? And this black burn mark here, right in the center? Have you been naughty? Have you been setting fire to something?"

The shapes said nothing, but echoes of the atrocity that had occurred here rose up black behind them; I could feel it welling above us, seething and dreadful, like a sandstorm about to snuff out a desert town.

"I'll get you all a decent burial," I said. "Proper coffins, proper rites. None of that furnace stuff. Don't worry—I'll talk Lockwood into it. He's a little cranky when it comes to your kind, but I can fix it. Don't worry. Lockwood will sort you out. . . ."

At least he would if he was actually alive and well.

Out of nowhere, the thought came suddenly that he wasn't. More than a thought—a conviction. What was I *doing*? What was I doing, talking to ghosts when Lockwood had been pulled away into the storm? Pain lashed through me. My head pounded; I almost sank down to my knees.

Was he back there, under the rubble? Maybe he was! He would have come for me ages ago, otherwise. My fear lapped out against the edges of the room in great almighty swells. All at once I could hear the figures whispering together again.

"You'll have to speak up," I said sharply. "Like I told the old guy in the armchair, this is your big chance! People like me don't come along that often. Speak up and speak *clearly*. . . ."

It was then that I saw that my candle was burning low.

That was okay. I had another in my pouch. . . . Only, actually, I didn't. Somewhere, back at the fall of rubble, maybe, I'd dropped it. No—I remembered setting it carefully down on the floor. I rolled my eyes at my own stupidity.

It was okay. I'd have to go back and get it.

When I turned around, the shapes were blocking the way.

"Now," I said, "you need to just let me— Ow!" Hot wax had burned my fingers. The candle was so low, the molten stuff was sloshing out. I set it on the floor between my feet and reached for the match box. Striking another match, I looked around for something else to light. Maybe the ghosts had candles. They'd clearly been using some recently.

"Do you want to move back, guys? I can't see where you keep your— Hey!" One of the shapes had swept forward, more decisively than before. I got a glimpse of pale ribs within the shining body and outstretched arms; the eyes were flickering black flames—then I pulled a tin from my belt, ripped off the lid, and scattered salt in a blazing emerald arc to keep the form at bay. I'd done it so fast I hadn't even thought about it; it was the old agency training kicking in.

"I'm sorry!" I said. "I'm on your side. You just need to keep back, that's all."

A ripple of disquiet ran through the shapes; their glow darkened, their outlines seemed to grow, become more angular and jagged. I cursed, threw my match down and, with shaking fingers, lit another. The candle at my feet was almost out. Light was dimming in the chamber. I held the match low, and over its bulb of radiance glared around at the encircling ghosts.

"What is it with you?" I snarled. "I want to help, and you always just end up trying to kill me. . . ."

Another splash of salt, a ring of bright green fire; again the shapes drew back, whispering sadly to themselves. I could feel my panic rising; it was no good. I couldn't control them. Individually they were weak, and I could bend them to my will; collectively, no: their anger was too strong.

What did I have? A bit of salt, hardly any iron—all used up in Aickmere's. Just one magnesium flare. I scrabbled at my belt and, in doing so, dropped the match. By the last light of the candle, I reached for the match box, but my fingers shook too much; the matches spewed out of the box, spilled uselessly on the floor. I gave a cry, bent down to retrieve them—and saw the ghosts come sweeping in toward me.

That was the moment the nub of candle chose to finally go out.

Chapter 24

I would have thrown the flare then, just chucked it out at random and blown a few of the shapes to smithereens—the act would have given me a spark of satisfaction, even as the others fell upon me and bore me down. But I did not throw the flare. Because though the candle's light had gone, another now replaced it—a pale encroaching light that stole out of the passage I had not yet entered, spreading across the slimy stone. It was not a light of the living, but a corpse-light, cold and faint, that gave no nourishment to what it touched. Still, it made me pause, and the effect it had on the ring of ghosts was no less definite. They at once stopped their advance, hesitating, looking back toward the oncoming glow. Their outlines grew tremulous and disturbed.

The light spread out into the chamber, pouring like milk through the heaps of tangled bones. Blood pulsed in my ears. The quality of the air had changed. The ghosts began to shrink back toward the walls.

The passage seemed to distort; the walls flexed and fluttered. A cold breeze blew toward me, carrying that same soft dry voice I'd heard in Aickmere's.

It called my name.

The ghosts sank away, flowed down into their heaps of tangled bones, and vanished.

I waited, clutching my flare.

From the darkness, of the darkness, untouched by the other-light through which it passed, a shape was crawling toward me down the corridor.

Up in the store, I'd run from it, but there was nowhere for me to run now.

The flare was slippery in my palm. I held it without hope or expectation. More even than the fearsome energies of the Poltergeist; far more than the twittering prison ghosts tied to the skeletons, I knew this apparition emanated from the very center of the Chelsea outbreak. Powerful as a flare might be, this thing was more potent still.

The cold breeze died away. I stood at the center of a bulb of silence. The shape came out into the chamber, and there was nothing between it and me.

As when I'd seen it near the elevators, it crawled awkwardly, in rolling leaps and jerks, as if its joints were misshapen or put on back to front. Its head was bowed; long hair—at least, I *thought* it must be hair, despite the way it waved and coiled so oddly—fell down across its face, so that it was hidden. But I could see enough to know how painfully thin it was, the skin black and shrunken on the bones, like those mummies they used to have in museums before DEPRAC closed them all down. It was tight and dry and desiccated-looking; you could hear the fingernails clacking on the flagstones, see the skin on the arms shearing tight with every swing, the wrinkles creasing so deep, you'd think they'd split in two.

Ahead of it, an advance guard of spiders: shiny black and scurrying.

The figure drew close and, with a single mysterious fluid movement, raised itself; now it shuffled forward on its back legs, arms twisting and jerking as if still pushing it along the ground. I couldn't see the face, but teeth glinted beneath the lankly swirling hair. The outline was hazy, almost fibrous, like the rough edges of an unfinished mat or carpet. As I watched, these fibers sank away; the shape grew solid, its edges more defined. And as it swelled and altered, I felt a corresponding opposite sensation. It was like the inward suction of a bellows, or a hatch opening beneath me—I felt my strength drain out. It poured away.

My head spun; everything went black. I closed my eyes.

"Lucy."

And opened them.

I was still on my feet in that same forgotten place. The otherlight had faded, and a different shape stood before me in the dark. I stared at it, frowning.

"Lucy."

And all at once my legs buckled with joy. Because I knew it! I knew the voice. It was the one I wanted to hear more than any other.

I felt I would dissolve with relief. My heart leaped within me. I had the flare still in my hand. I lowered it and stumbled forward.

"Lockwood—thank goodness!"

How could I have been so stupid as not to have recognized him instantly? The shape at first had seemed so dark and oddly insubstantial. Yet now I saw the slim, high shoulders; the curve of the neck, that familiar buoyant flick of hair. . . .

"How did you find me?" I cried. "I knew it! I *knew* that you would come—"

"Ah, Lucy . . . *Nothing could stop me from doing that.*"

I could tell from the outline of the face that he was smiling, but the voice was so sad that it brought me up short.

I peered at him, trying to pierce the darkness. "Lockwood? What is it? What's the matter?"

"*Nothing could keep me from you. Nothing in life or death. . . .*"

A cold shaft opened inside me. It was a well, bottomless and black.

"What—?" I said. "What are you talking about? What does *that* mean?"

"*Do not be scared. I cannot harm you.*"

"Now you're *really* frightening me. Shut up." I didn't understand; even so, I felt my bones turn to water. I could barely speak. My tongue felt tied to the roof of my mouth. "Shut *up*. . . ."

The figure stood there in the shadows. Now it said nothing.

"Come closer," I said. "Come into the light."

"*It's best I don't, Lucy.*"

It was then that I saw how frail and wispy his substance was.

How—though solid seeming at the head and torso—the legs were faint as gauze, and tailed off into nothing. He hovered above the flagstone floor.

My own legs gave way. I sank to my knees. The flare cracked against the stone.

"Oh, no," I whispered. "Lockwood—no. . . ."

The voice spoke softly, calmly. *"You must not be sorry."*

I slapped my hands against my face. I kept them there, blocking out the sight.

"It is not your fault," the voice said.

But it was. I knew it was. I curled my fingers, raking the nails into my skin. I heard a strange and awful cry, like some desperate, wounded animal, and realized it was me.

Coherent thoughts did not come. Images only. I remembered him throwing the chain net across the attic between the grasping ectoplasmic coils; leaping between me and the black-dressed woman at the window. I remembered him running along the tops of the carnival floats, dodging the bullets of the enemy; and at the Wintergarden house, launching himself across the stairwell to strike the murderous ghost and save my life.

Save my life *again*. . . .

I also remembered the photograph from his sister's room—that impatient, blurry child.

I rocked back and forth, tears pooling against my palms. I was a huddling, crumpled thing. This wasn't right. It *couldn't* be right. None of this was happening.

"Lucy." I lowered my hands. I could not see the shape; my

eyes were awash. But I could hear, and he was speaking, clear and calmly, that way he always had. *"I did not come to give you pain. I came to say good-bye."*

I shook my head, my face wet. "No! Tell me what happened."

"I fell. I died. Is that not enough?"

"Oh, God. . . . Trying to save me. . . ."

"It was always going to be this way," the shape said. *"You knew it in your heart. My luck couldn't go on forever. But I'm glad I did it, Lucy. You've nothing to be guilty about, and I'm glad you're safe. Safe. . . ."* the voice added drily, *"with barely a scratch on you."*

I gave a wail at that. "Please—I'd have done anything for it to be the other way—"

"I know you would," Again I could tell that somewhere in the dark he was smiling a sad, sad smile. *"I know. Now . . ."* The form seemed to shrink back. *"I have been here too long."*

"No! I need to see you. . . ." I said. "Please. Not in the dark. Not like this."

"I cannot. It would distress you."

"Please—show me."

"Very well." Bright blue fire erupted around the shape; flames as delicate as liquid glass pooled up against the ceiling. And I saw him.

I saw a great and bloody wound, open in the center of his chest. His shirt had been ripped open by the force of whatever had driven through it. Tattered remnants of his coat hung on either side, fading, at its base, with the rest of the apparition.

I saw his thin, pale face, twisted and terrible, his eyes dull and despairing. Yet, even so, he smiled at me, and the tenderness and grief contained within that smile made the image horrible beyond imagining.

Blackness flared at the edge of my vision; I felt as if I would pass out. Instead I lurched to my feet and staggered toward him, hands outstretched. And as I did so the bloodied head turned suddenly to look back along the passage, and I saw that it was not a solid head at all but an empty mask, and that its hollow contours were filled with wisps of shadow.

The face turned back to me. *"Lucy—I must go now. Remember me."*

From the front, it was perfect: I could see the pores in the skin, that little mole I always noticed on the side of his neck. The hair, the jaw, the crumpled details of the shirt and coat—everything was right. But from the side and back . . . it seemed to me that not just the head but the body itself had been utterly scooped out, hollow as a fibrous papier-mâché shell.

"Wait, Lockwood . . . I don't understand. Your head . . ."

"I must go." Once more, the figure looked behind it, as if something had disturbed its concentration. And I wasn't wrong. It was an empty thing. Thick black fibers dangled at the margins, like the edges of an unfinished rug. Beyond was a net of grainy wisps, intricate yet chaotically woven, like a great gray spiderweb that had been molded into a contoured membrane. I saw the inverse of Lockwood's face, the curve of the cheekbones, the indentation of the nose.

There were blank holes where the mouth and eyes should be.

Now it faced me once more. The mouth smiled sadly; the eyes shone with wisdom and remote knowledge. *"Lucy . . ."*

Those fibers . . . I thought of the jerking, crawling thing.

My head cleared. I staggered back, filled with revulsion and relief.

"I know what you are!" I cried. "You're not him!"

"*I am what is to come.*"

"You're a Fetch! An imposter! Feeding on my thoughts!" The flare! Where was it? I couldn't see it in the dark.

"*I show you the future. This is your doing.*"

"No! No, I don't believe you."

"*Not everything you see is what has passed. Sometimes it is what is yet to be.*"

A pale smile shone in the pale, pale face. It looked at me with kindness and with love.

Then a sword point cut straight through it.

Down from the scalp, through the hair, right through the center of the nose and across the mouth and chin; down into the substance of the chest. It all happened in an instant; the body showed no more resistance to the blade than a bag of air.

Lockwood's head and body peeled away on either side, split in two by the shimmering silver point. The black wisps from the voids behind the contours of the hollow face drifted free, like twists of black juice tumbling in water. The body fell away, dissolved to threads of plasm that coiled themselves to vapor and then to nothing.

Behind it, in the exact same spot, hair tousled, face bloodied, coat torn, one hand held outstretched behind him to counteract the driven blow, was Lockwood.

He had no gaping wound in his chest. His shirt, white, but a little grubby with dust and mud, was still done up neatly to the second button. He grinned at me. "Hey, Lucy."

I didn't answer. I was too busy screaming.

A little later on we were sitting together on a block of stone at one corner of the chamber. Lockwood had kicked a few skulls away to make a clear space near us. He'd scattered a bit of iron and salt over the piles of bones to discourage further nuisance, and two candles from his belt pouch were burning brightly in the middle of the floor. Somehow he'd even found some chewing gum. It was all quite cozy, really.

"So, you're all right?" he said for the tenth time.

"I think so. I don't know." I stared at my knees. Lockwood gave my arm a friendly squeeze. He had a scrape down the side of his face, and a corner of his lip was puffy. Still, he looked an awful lot better than the white-skinned thing that had stood and talked to me before. "You know," he said, "we need to find a way to get back up top; George will be having kittens up there."

"George! Is he okay? The others . . ."

"Fine. George is fine."

"And . . . and Holly?"

"Good. Good. . . . A little bashed up. We all are. They all went to find medics for Bobby Vernon. Kipps was going to try to contact Barnes. I left George in charge of it all when I climbed down the hole after you."

"You shouldn't have done it," I said. "You shouldn't have risked yourself."

"Come off it," Lockwood said. "You know I'd die for you." He chuckled. "Heaven knows, I've come near it often enough. Scrambling down a crack in the ground is nothing. . . . Hey, look at you now, you're shaking. Put my coat on. Come on, I insist."

I didn't argue. I'd had enough of that. And the coat *was* warm. "I don't remember any of it," I said dully. "You know, how I got down here. I know I must've banged my head when I fell—I haven't been thinking quite straight since." I thought of the skeletons, and our one-way conversations. Then I thought of the hollow boy.

Lockwood nodded. "I'm not surprised. It was all a little hectic. Well, after you were sucked down the hole, the Poltergeist blew itself out. It was like you were the focus of it, Luce. All that raging air just stopped, like it was frozen in time. You could hear things thumping to the floor all around the building. I was quite lucky—I was in midair, quite high up when it happened, but I was over the escalators, so I didn't fall too far. I landed on that central part, and just slid gently down. I lay there, upside down, watching all those tissue leaves wafting slowly down across the foyer. It was like falling snow. Apart from their being red, of course. It was quite pretty. I wish Mr. Aickmere had been there to see it. Got to admit the place doesn't look quite so attractive now."

I rubbed my eyes. "That poor department store . . ."

"Oh, think of all that free publicity we're going to give it," Lockwood said. "It'll do really well." He scratched the bridge of his nose. "Either that or go out of business. Anyway, who cares? One thing's for sure, they'll have to do something about the hole in the floor. It goes pretty deep, and the earth is very unstable. I had quite a job getting down in one piece. When I got to the bottom, I hacked through this layer of broken stone and dropped down into the old prison chamber. I found one of your candles on the floor and knew you were alive. I set off up the passages, but got lost—at least, I ended up in one that was half-filled with water. I don't think you went *that* way."

"No."

"But in the end it paid off for me because, before I found you, I came across the entrance to a long straight tunnel, part waterlogged and stinking of the river. I swear I could hear the lap of the Thames at the far end—it wouldn't surprise me if that was another way out. We could try it, maybe—save us trying to climb back up the hole."

I looked at the floor, so carefully swept clean. "I think it *will* be a way out," I said softly. "Lockwood, the ghost you saw with me—"

"Yes, what *was* that thing? I heard you talking to it, but to me it seemed just a horrible tangle of black wisps. I could hardly make out a shape at all, even when I crept close with my rapier."

"So you didn't see its face?"

"Should I have?"

"Oh, no—it doesn't matter."

There was a silence, then. In truth, I found I couldn't easily speak of the Fetch to him. To forestall immediate questions, I pointed out the signs of previous activity in the room: the swept floor, the cigarette end, the burn mark in the center, and wax stains here and there. Lockwood was at once alert; he paced the chamber, studying it with a frown.

"You're quite right," he said. "This is a mystery. Someone has been here, and very recently. Look at the marks here: it's Chinese wax they've been using"—he scraped it with his finger and held it to his nose—"scented with jojoba oil. You get that at Mullet's.

Top quality stuff. And as for that cigarette . . . Its brand might tell us something. . . ." He picked it up and scrutinized it, rolling it between his fingers, scanning it against the candle light, narrow-eyed. "Hmm . . . aha. Yes. . . ."

"So what brand *is* it?"

"Haven't a clue. It just looks white and tobacco-y to me. But I bet we could find someone to tell us more." He gazed around at the skeletons. "So what on earth were they doing? You know, Luce, George *said* that something funny might be going on to stir so many ghosts up so quickly these last few weeks. And he was right. I want him to see this. He's got just the right kind of slightly fussy, obsessive mind that might notice something. We need to do it fast, too, before Barnes shows up. As soon as he does, you can bet DEPRAC will boot us out and take over."

I nodded. That *was* usually how it went. "The Chelsea outbreak . . . do you think we've stopped it?"

Lockwood was all energy again; he held out his hand to pull me up. "We'll find out soon enough." He looked over at the skeletons, peppered with salt and iron. "But if this room *doesn't* turn out to be the Source, with all this lot, *and* with an unknown someone doing something weird, I'm a Bunchurch agent. Look at the bones! If these guys were all entombed alive here, that's enough psychic charge to light up a city district." He patted my arm. "And *you* found it, Luce. You did so well."

That wasn't how I was feeling. "Lockwood," I said slowly, "about the Poltergeist . . . you were right, earlier. I *was* the focus. When we were upstairs, I . . . I argued with Holly. I picked a fight with her. We stirred the Poltergeist up. I'm really sorry, Lockwood. It's all my fault. I couldn't control myself. I'm a liability. I could have killed us all."

"You and Holly saved Bobby Vernon, don't forget," Lockwood said, but he didn't actually contradict what I'd said.

"She probably told you, did she?" I said. "Maybe she didn't have time."

"No, she didn't say anything. She seemed worried about you, Lucy. We all were."

He produced a penlight and led me out of the room of bones, down a narrow passage. We went in silence for a while.

"Lockwood," I said, "I need to apologize. About recently. I've not been myself."

It was a tight corridor; we walked almost side by side, following the beam of light. His voice was calm and quiet in the dark. "Well, neither have I," he said. "After what happened at the Wintergarden house, I'm afraid I haven't treated you very well. I know I might have seemed standoffish. It's just"—he took a deep breath—"I didn't trust myself to be with you. I was too anxious about what might happen."

I stepped carefully over a fallen stone. Water was pooling around our feet. "Um, what might happen in exactly what sense?"

"In an operative situation, when our lives were again in danger. Your Talent is just so extraordinary, Luce—yes, we go left here; I know it *looks* like sewage, but it's algae, mostly—I mean, I heard you talking to that thing just now. It's getting easier for you, isn't it? It's not just the skull anymore. It's unique, your Talent, but it makes you so vulnerable. And I have to look after you."

Something knotted tightly in my chest. In the dark of my mind I saw again the palely smiling face. "No, Lockwood, you really don't. You mustn't. It's not your responsibility to—"

"But it *is*, Luce. Look, I know I don't talk about it, but it's happened to me before. Losing someone dear to me. I can't let it happen again."

I stopped. Water was up to our knees; the meager flashlight beam showed a break in the wall, and beyond it, over tumbled blocks, an earthen passage. Lockwood gestured with the flashlight to indicate we should go through, but I didn't move. I couldn't go any farther without—

"Lockwood," I said, "I've got to admit to something. I'm going to tell you, and then you can switch the flashlight off and just leave me here if you want. Block the tunnel in. I don't care, and I'll deserve it."

There was a pause; water sucked and flowed through the gap in the wall.

"Blimey," Lockwood said, "it isn't you who's been pinching my stash of Choco Leibniz biscuits from my desk drawer, is it? I always thought it was George."

"No. That wasn't me."

"Then it *is* George . . . that little devil. Or I suppose it might have been Holly . . ."

"Lockwood."

"Yes."

I took a deep breath. "I went into your sister's room. I looked at one of the photos—of you and your sister. I'm so sorry. I had no right to do it. And that's not the worst of it, Lockwood. When I was going out, I fell and touched the bed and I heard . . . I didn't mean to, I swear it, but I heard echoes, Lockwood, echoes of what happened, and I know it's unforgivable, and you can do what you want to me, I'll completely deserve it, but it's been killing me ever since, and that's it," I finished. "I haven't got anything more to say, and I'll shut up now."

More water, doing its sucking and flowing thing.

"Take another breath now," Lockwood said. "I'd advise it."

"Okay."

"I should be angry with you," he said. "I should be furious. . . ." He turned the flashlight downward, directing it against the wall beside us, so that we were both picked out in discreet shadows, neither violently spotlit, nor given that creepy under-lighting that makes even the best-looking person look like a shambling Type Two. Not quite seeing each other's faces helped right then, at least for me. Maybe Lockwood felt the same.

"It's not that I don't want to share that stuff, Lucy," he said at last. "It's just . . . too painful for me."

"Oh, I know! Of *course* I know that. I—"

"Will you shut up for a minute? My sister was like you, you know, in a lot of ways. Hotheaded sometimes, stubborn, but faithful to a fault. She looked after me, and I adored her. But I was a kid, Lucy, and I was lazy and willful and all the rest of it. I just wanted to do my own thing, so I didn't listen to her half as often as I should. On the night it happened, she was going through one of the boxes that our parents had left. You never knew what might be in them. She asked if I wanted to help. No, I wouldn't. I was too busy outside climbing the apple tree, and messing about in the playroom, which is where the office is now. I was down there as it happens, by the garden door, when I heard her scream. I ran up—but it was too late. . . ."

What happened after that, I can scarcely recall. Maybe *you've* got a better idea than me."

That was the only time his carefully neutral tone wavered; and I was gladder than ever that I couldn't meet his eyes.

"I destroyed the ghost that did it," he said, "but what good was that? It was too late. And I felt . . ." I could sense him groping for the words. "Under the anger and the sorrow, Lucy, I was just left feeling hollow. Because I should have been in the room. I should have been there for her. And it's not going to happen to me again. Whatever the cost, as long as you're in my company, be sure I'll always be there for you." He moved the flashlight around to face the gap in the wall. "But I swear, if you go in that room again without my permission, or steal my Choco Leibniz, for that matter, I'll never forgive you. And now perhaps you can hop through that gap first. It may or may not be algae this time, and I'd like it to be you who finds out."

It was mostly water, as it happened; we proceeded slowly up the tunnel.

"Thank you," I said, after a silence. "Thank you for telling me all that."

"That's okay. So now you know a little about how it began for me. After that, what option did I have but to become an agent? I got a job with a man called Sykes."

I whistled. "Yeah, 'Gravedigger' Sykes . . . That's a really cool name."

"Mm . . . His first name was Nigel."

There was a pause. "Why tell me that? It takes the shine off, somehow."

"He was still a cool customer. The bane of Fittes and Rotwell while he was alive. He'd heard about what I did to . . . to the ghost. That's why he gave me the job. So now you know."

"Yes, only . . ."

"My parents? Oh, they're another story entirely. A *very* long time back."

I nodded. "Maybe you hardly remember them," I said. "You were so small."

"Oh, I remember them, all right." Lockwood smiled at me. "They were my first ghosts. And look, I think I see the exit from the tunnel now."

He pointed: far ahead a pale blue coin hung above the water, shimmering, as we waded slowly nearer, with the first light of the dawn.

Chapter 25

So night bled into morning, and Lockwood & Co. emerged blinking from the darkness with its future changed.

The tunnel terminated beneath an abandoned wharf on the north shore of the Thames, a couple of blocks from the department store. There was evidence that the entrance had been carefully concealed: a large number of rotten posts had been propped against the muddy bank; some, sawn through and ingeniously attached to a kind of rough panel, had clearly been set across the hole to hide it from view. The way the panel had been cast aside suggested that someone had made a hasty exit, and boot prints in the mire supported this. Even as Lockwood and I watched, however, the incoming tide was pooling in the prints, and soon they were lost to view.

At Aickmere Brothers, or what remained of it, much was going on. A DEPRAC ambulance had recently removed Bobby Vernon. The prognosis had been favorable, a sprained ankle and suspected concussion being the worst of it. Kate Godwin had gone with him to the hospital. The others were sitting outside the shattered glass entrance doors, shivering in the half-light and talking in muted voices to other agents, who were arriving in dribs and drabs from across Chelsea. Periodically, people would go up to the doors and peer in wonder at the ruined foyer. From a distance it looked like a doll's house that had been picked up and briskly shaken by an angry toddler. There was almost nothing standing; everything lay formless and in heaps. In the center of the floor, startling in its vastness, a chasm opened to the buried rooms below. George and Kipps were grim-facedly fixing a rappeling line to one of the columns, prior to climbing down in search of Lockwood and me.

Our arrival changed the mood at once. Everyone crowded around, bombarding us with questions. I was patted on the back, grinned at, given high-calorie energy drinks, congratulated, scolded, urged to keep moving, and told to sit down, all at the same time. George offered me doughnuts, Flo Bones nodded at me with some-thing approximating good-natured contempt. Even Kipps seemed relieved at my reappearance, though he immediately got into an argument with Lockwood about what to do next. He wanted to wait for Barnes and lead DEPRAC down in triumph to the underground chambers of the prison. Lockwood had other plans.

While they discussed the matter, I hung back on the fringes of the crowd, and so saw Holly.

She was definitely not her normal radiant self. By her standards, she was bedraggled. Actually, though, compared to me, her clothes were fashionably ripped, her face delicately bruised; she came within a whisker of making beaten-up look stylish.

Our eyes met. "Hey," I said.

"Hello."

"How are you?"

"Fine. . . . You?"

"Bashed about a bit, but good. . . . I'm glad you're okay."

She nodded. "So you made your way back in the end. I'm pleased."

"Yeah."

"I found something," she said, "caught on a spike in there. I wonder if it might be yours. . . ." It was my backpack that she had in her hand, battered, covered with brick dust. You could just see the top of the ghost-jar peeping out from under the top flap. There wasn't any indication that she'd looked at it. Might have. Couldn't tell.

I took it from her. "Thanks," I said.

"No problem."

Let's face it, it wasn't the most thrilling conversation you'll ever hear; not exactly one to be carved on your tombstone or strung up in lights over your front door. But it was good enough for me. Because, for once, there wasn't a subtext to it. No hidden agenda. It was weary, wary, and cautiously forgiving. It was what it was, basically, and that was a start.

Lockwood won the argument with Kipps. He at once sent George back to the wharf to locate the hidden entrance, and then to find and survey the secret room of bones. George lost no time. Flo Bones, perhaps because she felt that anything associated with the riverbank was more her business than anyone else's, went with him.

Not long after that, Inspector Barnes arrived.

He came in a squad car, with four DEPRAC vans accompanying

him. The agents who filed out from the first three—a motley crew of gray-faced kids from the Grimble, Tamworth, and Atkins and Armstrong agencies, who'd been up all night fighting Visitors in Chelsea—weren't much good for anything. They'd have had trouble dealing with a Lurker or a Tom O'Shadows between them. But the fancy-suited, stony-faced men and women who issued from the fourth van were a different matter. They didn't wear DEPRAC uniforms, or any visible symbol of an agency. They looked both narrow-eyed and watchful. I wondered if these were the advisors Kipps had mentioned; the ones who'd been telling Barnes what to do.

Certainly Barnes's mustache looked ragged in the early morning light; he had a beleaguered, feral air, as of one who hasn't slept, or washed, for quite some time. With his suited associates standing in the background, he rounded on us instantly, accusing us of a host of misdemeanors—wasting police time, misleadingly claiming to be on official DEPRAC business, and wanton destruction of public property.

He mentioned this last one before he'd had a chance to look inside the building. The glass sprinkling the sidewalk was all he'd seen. When he at last drew breath, Kipps jerked his thumb toward the foyer. "You don't know the half of it yet. Take a look in there."

Barnes did so; his jaw sagged. He clutched at the revolving door for support. Part of it promptly fell off and landed on his toe.

"What have you *done?*" he gasped. "I buy my socks from here!"

"You'll see we found the focus of the Chelsea hauntings," Lockwood said cheerily. "It *would* have been easier if you'd given us a few more personnel to help us, Mr. Barnes, but I have to say that Quill Kipps and his team have done a first-class job. It was very good of you to let them join us." Here Lockwood glanced fleetingly toward the watching men and women in their dark suits. "The short account of it is that we fought off the strongest Poltergeist I've ever encountered, and in so doing discovered the remains of the long-lost King's Prison hidden underground. Lucy Carlyle went in and discovered a *lot* of unburied skeletons—I think you'll find this is the original Source of the Chelsea outbreak. Anyway, George Cubbins has the details of how it spread. He can show you presently."

An unprepossessing scene followed, in which Barnes attempted to save face by backtracking a bit on his earlier criticisms, pretending that he *had* in fact had something to do with our expedition, while at the same time questioning us aggressively about what had actually happened. You could see the panic and distrust flaring in his pouchy eyes.

At last one of the women spoke. "These skeletons. How do we get to them?"

"It's not easy, I'm afraid." Lockwood pointed at the crack in the foyer floor. "It takes quite a bit of squeezing down. You might want to come back later with a properly equipped team."

"I'll be the judge of that," the woman said.

"I'm sure you will." Lockwood gave her his most gleaming smile. "Who actually *are* you? You're not the cleaning staff, I hope? If so, you're going to need a hefty broom."

Judging by her reaction, the woman wasn't the cleaning staff. In the course of the loud words that followed, none of us chose to mention the existence of the tunnel under the wharf. The aim was to give George and Flo more time.

In the middle of all this, a chauffeured car pulled up. It was none other than Mr. Aickmere himself, freshly Brylcreemed and shiny-new, coming to inspect his store and check that none of his precious displays had been disturbed by our nocturnal activities. Noticing the broken glass beside the entrance, he at once accosted Barnes with shrill, indignant cries. The inspector, taken by surprise, could not prevent him from approaching the foyer, and so glimpsing the devastation within. Mr. Aickmere's response was emphatic, not to say violent, and soon the men and women in gray suits were rushing to Barnes's aid. Lockwood, Kipps, Holly, and I exchanged quick looks; we judged this to be a good time to slip away.

Gradually, throughout the rest of the day, things fell into place. For most of us, at least.

Lockwood and Kipps went off together to speak to the newspapers; Holly and I went back to Portland Row. We did the usual cleaning-selves-up, showery-type things that you do after a job, and I went so far as to lend her one of George's towels. We were sitting in the kitchen with the kettle on when George himself entered, whistling. I hadn't had a chance to look at him properly that morning, but he seemed even more disheveled and weatherworn than earlier. He dropped into the seat opposite with a weary but jaunty air.

"What happened?" I said. "I don't remember that black eye."

He dumped his bag down on the floor. "Only just been given it, as it happens," he said. "Flo and I found your room of skeletons, Luce—and *boy*, is it fascinating. I've been taking all sorts of measurements and notes down there. I'd still be doing it, in fact, but I hadn't been at it more than an hour when a gang of Rotwell agents showed up along the tunnel and started cordoning everything off.

They told me to get lost. Of course, *I* told them to get knotted. We shared some stirring words, during which I made a few telling points about their behavior, not to mention their clothes sense, facial asymmetry, and parentage." He chuckled. "I was quite eloquent, actually, so much so that one of them tried to brain me with a femur he'd picked up off the pile of bones. So I lobbed a lumbar vertebra at him, and then Flo got going with the muck prong she keeps under her petticoats, and after that things got quite exciting for a while before we were finally escorted off the premises. But it doesn't matter. I had time to draw a little diagram of the room before I went. I'll show you later. Right now, I need a bath to cleanse my sweaty bits." He peered over the top of his glasses. "Speaking of which, isn't that my towel, Holly, you're wearing 'round your hair . . . ?"

It turned out later that the Rotwell operatives, working officially under DEPRAC command, had introduced a team of crack agents with the latest salt-guns, the ones connected to canisters of compressed spray strapped onto their backs. They spent three days cleansing the vaults of the King's Prison and clearing out the mass of skeletons. I'd hoped the remains could be treated with respect and given a proper burial, but that wasn't how DEPRAC worked. The bones were taken to the Clerkenwell furnaces and burned without further ceremony.

Careful observations were made in Aickmere Brothers for several weeks afterward, but no Visitors were seen there again.

As for the wider effects on the district of Chelsea, Lockwood's claim that we had scotched the outbreak was put to the test the very next night. As darkness fell, agency teams tentatively entered the Containment Zone as usual, with Penelope Fittes, Steve Rotwell, and a group of top DEPRAC psychics observing from the watch-tower on Sloane Square. A light drizzle hung in the air. The agents walked along the King's Road and dispersed into the surrounding streets. Time passed while the dignitaries drank tea beneath their umbrellas and looked at copies of George's maps, which Lockwood, who was present, had given them. In due course the agents returned and made their report. Ghostly activity had not ceased, but it seemed markedly less frenzied than on previous nights. Several Visitors that had previously been observed were no longer there; others seemed pale shadows of their former selves, slower and less formidable, and far easier to corral with iron and salt-bombs. In short, it was the first noticeable improvement in Chelsea for several months, and the agents were hopeful that it was the start of the turning of the tide.

Lockwood hung around long enough to receive congratulations from Ms. Fittes, give Mr. Rotwell a cordial bow, and wink at Inspector Barnes. Then he departed. Before he was out of earshot, he could hear Barnes once again becoming the focus of incessant questions.

One way and another, in fact, things were looking good for Lockwood & Co. And I would certainly have shared the general happy exhaustion—would have been more than satisfied with the endless phone calls, and the flurry of reporters now knocking on our doors—if I hadn't still been haunted. Not by an *actual* ghost, but by the memory of one. Its face remained before me. Its words echoed in my ears. When I sat with the others, and still more when I lay on my own in the quiet of my room, I could not escape the vision of the other Lockwood. I could not rid myself of the hollow boy.

Chapter 26

CHELSEA OUTBREAK ENDS!

MASS TOMB DISCOVERED UNDER FAMED DEPARTMENT STORE

TRIUMPH FOR COMBINED AGENCY TEAM

FIRST INTERVIEW WITH A. J. LOCKWOOD AND Q. F. KIPPS INSIDE

People across London can sleep more easily in their beds tonight following the discovery of a previously unknown mass grave beneath Aickmere Brothers, the noted department store on the King's Road. The sealing, removal, and destruction of this unprecedented Cluster Source signals at last the end of the so-called Chelsea outbreak, which conventional DEPRAC teams have long been unable to suppress. Effects have been immediate: in the past few nights, recorded disturbances in the district have fallen by 46%, with further significant decreases expected.

Today's *Times of London* reveals the full story of how, following three months of terror for the hard-pressed population, a special joint task force, comprising operatives from the Fittes and Lockwood agencies, discovered the ruins of the medieval King's Prison buried below the Aickmere Brothers building. In a special interview, team leader Anthony Lockwood, Esq., and his close associate, Quill Kipps of the Fittes Agency, discuss how they masterminded their exploration of the necropolis, and the methods used for combating the ferocious Poltergeist that guarded the entrance to the subterranean world.

"We knew it would be dangerous," Mr. Kipps says, "but with precise preparation and dedicated teamwork, we got there in the end." For his part, Mr. Lockwood explains that the Poltergeist was not the only Visitor encountered in the tunnels below Chelsea. "More than thirty skeletons were discovered in the central chamber," he says, "and at times dozens of spirits surrounded us. But were we daunted? No! We've shown that, with courage and determination, even the most terrifying Visitor can be faced and overcome."

Praise for the team has come from the highest quarters. In a rare statement, Fittes Agency chairman, Ms. Penelope Fittes, said: "I'm so proud of my employees. Too often in the past, rivalry between agencies has hampered investigations. I hope this operation is a symbol of the future. When extraordinary companies cooperate, extraordinary results can be achieved."

Full Lockwood/Kipps Interview: see pages 2–3

King's Prison "Room of Skeletons" foldable 3-D paper model: see pages 38–39

Aickmere Brothers Fire Sale: Free £10 Voucher Inside! See page 40

And after it all ended, did we return to our old ways of doing things? Were we ever quite the same? Did we go back to going on missions together, just Lockwood, George, and I—simple missions, like dodging ectoplasmic tentacles in attics—before heading home for tea?

There was a feast arranged at Portland Row one afternoon, a few days after events in Chelsea had come to their conclusion. Holly had done most of the organizing, so bowls of olives, salads, wholewheat ciabatta bread, and plates of interestingly limp cold cuts were very much in evidence. Fortunately, at the last minute George made an emergency run to the shops, returning with a supply of cheap sausage rolls, fizzy drinks, and smoky bacon-flavored chips; also a chocolate fudge cake of surpassing size, which he hoisted proudly into the center of the kitchen table.

Holly and George had had a running argument about that table, Holly insisting that our Thinking Cloth, with its mural of scribbles, notes, and grotesque cartoons, looked like the wall of a public lavatory, and would put her off her hummus dips. She wanted it discarded for the occasion and replaced with a crisp white alternative. George refused. Ever since breakfast, he had been working on a diagram on one corner of the cloth, and he didn't want it moved. In the end, through sheer bespectacled stubbornness, he got his way.

By midafternoon, the kitchen was ready. Every surface groaned with delicacies; the kettle was on; Holly had thrown all the wrappers away. The skull in the jar, which had been making atrocious pop-eyed faces at Holly whenever she turned toward it, causing her to spill two bowls of cashew nuts and one of taramasalata, had been removed upstairs in disgrace. Now in came Lockwood, fresh from numerous phone calls in the office, and we all sat down to dine.

He was in good form that day, Lockwood, vibrant with positive energies. I remember him sitting at the head of the table, creating a towering sandwich stuffed with sausage rolls and smoky bacon chips (much to Holly's horror—to appease her, he balanced a minuscule leaf of parsley on the top) as he spoke about the potential new clients the agency now had. Like the rest of us, his recent injuries were still in evidence—the cut on his forehead, his grazed cheek, his bruises, the weariness stamped beneath his eyes—yet somehow all they did was serve to highlight his vigor and vitality.

George was happy too, making last-minute tweaks to the complicated diagram on the cloth before him, while at the same time demolishing plateloads of miniature Scotch eggs. He made a spirited early play to sample the chocolate fudge cake, too, but Lockwood decreed that this should be left to the end.

As for Holly, she was back in her smooth and flawless groove once more, smiling benignly at the goings-on while remaining slightly detached from it all. At George's behest, she unbent enough to try a single small Scotch egg; mainly, though, she stuck to sparkling spring water and a walnut, raisin, and goat cheese salad. In a funny sort of way I was pleased she kept her standards up. It was somehow reassuring.

Me? Yes, I was there. I ate and drank and joined in with the others, though inwardly I was far away. After a while we looked (again) at the day's newspapers, which Holly had left folded beside Lockwood's plate.

"Every time I see this coverage," Lockwood said, "I can't believe our luck. When you combine this with what happened on the Strand, we've dominated the papers for more than a week."

Holly nodded. "The phone's been ringing nonstop," she said. "Everyone wants Lockwood and Co. You're going to have to make some decisions about expanding."

"I need some advice about that." Lockwood took a spear of cucumber and stuck it thoughtfully in the dip. "Actually, I'm seeing Penelope Fittes next week. She wants me to come in for an informal breakfast meeting. More of a thanks for the carnival thing than anything, I suppose, but still . . . I could ask her." He grinned. "Did you read the bit where she called us a 'top agency'?"

"And what about Inspector Barnes's quote?" George added. "What was it again? 'A group of talented young agents that I'm proud to oversee.' Can you believe his nerve?"

Lockwood crunched the cucumber. "As always, Barnes follows his own agenda."

"He's not the only one." George gave the paper a prod. "I'm not sure I approve of Kipps getting equal billing with you here."

"Oh, that's just to keep him sweet. To be honest, we *do* owe him for supporting us, and it's paid off for him now. Did you hear he's been promoted? Section leader or something, wasn't it, Luce? You're the one who told me."

"Yeah, Fittes Division Leader," I said.

"That's it. Awarded by Penelope Fittes herself. Still, that didn't prevent Kipps from having a massive fight with me about the way we handled the Room of Bones at the end. He was furious that the Rotwell team got there before anyone from his agency."

"Well, *you* didn't tell them to go in, did you?" George said.

"No. I don't know who did, actually. I suppose it must have

been Barnes. . . ." All at once, Lockwood fixed me with his dark eyes. "Are you all right, Lucy?" he asked.

"Yes! Yes. . . ." He'd startled me; I'd been drifting. Just for a moment the living Lockwood, sitting at the table, cutting himself a piece of Holly's trendy delicatessen cheese, had been lost, hidden beneath the gory, white-faced apparition of the underground room. . . .

I blinked the mirage away. It was fake! I *knew* it was. I *knew* it was a lie. I'd seen Lockwood himself slice the Fetch in two just as cleanly as he did that cheese.

But try as I might, I couldn't shake my mind clear.

I show you the future. This is your doing.

"Have a piece of Parma ham, Lucy," Holly said. "Lockwood likes it. It'll really put the blood back in your cheeks."

"Er, yeah, sure—thanks."

Holly and me? We'd adopted a mutual policy of careful toleration. Over the last few days, for want of anything better, we'd kind of muddled by. Don't get me wrong—we still riled each other. Her new habit of sweeping up crumbs around my plate *while I was eating*, for example—that got my goat. Meanwhile, she was less than thrilled by my (justifiable) habit of rolling my eyes and gasping aloud whenever she did something especially finicky, precious, or controlling. But things didn't threaten to ignite the way they once had. Perhaps it was because we'd already said everything there was to say, that awful night at Aickmere's. Or perhaps it was simply because we no longer had the energy to be furious anymore.

"Speaking of the Room of Bones," George said, as he moved his plate of ciabatta crusts to one side, "I'd like to show you something, courtesy of the noble Thinking Cloth." In front of him was his diagram, multicolored and carefully inscribed. Imagine a square with a circle inside it, and inside that circle nine precisely arranged dots. Right in the middle of *that*, another small circle, crosshatched in black, with several thin, spidery pencil lines radiating from opposite sides of it like broken bicycle spokes. On one side of the circle stretched a long red stain.

George smoothed out the cloth. "This is my plan of the room," he said, "taken from the measurements Flo and I noted down the other day. Lucy and Lockwood were absolutely right. Someone else *was* here, and they were doing something very specific. Look how the skeletons were pushed back to form a kind of perfect circle around the edges. I know they weren't originally like that, because I found bone fragments in the center of the room. Someone carefully arranged them that way. They then rigged up nine candles in a ring: the wax marks show how these were positioned. After that, *something* happened in the middle of the room, right here." He pointed to the crosshatched circle. "It's an ectoplasm burn. I studied it particularly closely. The stones there were still very cold. The burn reminds me of others we've seen, where something otherworldly came through."

He didn't mention it, none of us did: but there was an example of a burn like that in our very house, on the mattress in the abandoned room upstairs.

"Interesting," Lockwood breathed. "And what's this sinister red stain?"

"That's some jam from breakfast this morning." George pushed his glasses up his nose. "But check these out." He pointed to the pencil marks radiating from the center. "The lines mark the position of a number of odd scrapes and scuff marks on the floor. They're *very* odd."

"Maybe where the bones were being dragged?" Lockwood suggested.

"It's possible. But to me they look more like they were made by metal." He chuckled. "Like that time I pulled those chains across the office floor, Lockwood, and left scratches on the wood?"

Lockwood frowned. "Yes . . . you still haven't revarnished that."

"You know what it reminds *me* of?" I said slowly. I felt sluggish; a weight pressed down on me. It was all I could do to speak. "The diagram as a whole, I mean?"

"I think I know what you're going to say," George said. "And yes, I agree."

"The bone glass from Kensal Green. Obviously it was much smaller, but it had a bony perimeter too, arranged in a kind of circle. There's no mirror or lens or anything here, I know, but . . ."

"Unless someone brought one in," Lockwood said.

"When I was up in the department store," I went on, "I could feel a kind of . . . psychic buzzing—a disturbance, if you like, which reminded me of the bone glass. Only it was gone when I actually got down to the room of bones."

"I wonder . . ." George said. "Maybe they were still at work down there when we first turned up. Maybe, Luce, you only just missed them."

"That's quite a creepy thought," Lockwood said, and oddly, since it involved meeting the living, not the dead, I found he was quite right. "Seems your earlier theory was correct, anyway, George," he said. "The spirits of the prison were stirred up by this weird activity, and that caused a ripple effect out across Chelsea. Flo swears the tunnel entrance wasn't there a few months ago, so it's very recent. I wonder what they were doing, and what they got out of it. . . . And who they were."

"We've got that cigarette butt you found," George said. "I took it to a tobacconist friend of mine. He says it's a Persian Light, quite an exclusive brand. But where that leaves us, I don't know. I didn't have time to find any other clues. It's just a shame those Rotwell agents took everything apart so fast."

Lockwood nodded. "Yes, isn't it? What do you think, Holly?"

"I still think that cloth is an eyesore," Holly said. "I don't know why you don't use pieces of paper, which I could then file away nicely. Look at the way you've got jam all over your drawing, George." She picked up a plate. "Right, who wants more hummus sandwiches?"

"Only a couple more for me," George said. "I'm saving myself for that whopping chocolate cake at the end."

Lockwood took a sandwich. "Penny for your thoughts, Lucy. You've been really quiet today."

It was true; over the last few days a new understanding had settled over me, slowly, softly, like a blanket or feather eiderdown. Its force was gentle, yet I buckled under the implications. Words weren't so easy to come by, then.

"I was just wondering," I said, in a small voice. "Do you think any ghost can show the future? I mean, obviously they show the *past*, mostly. That's what they're made of. But if Fetches—or other kinds of Visitor—can burrow into people's minds and sift their thoughts, which they seem to, could they possibly do other stuff? Like make predictions about what's to come?"

They gazed at me. "Blimey," George said. "You do realize that the profoundest thing *I've* been wondering this afternoon is how many chips I can possibly stuff in."

"No," Lockwood said firmly. "That's your answer, Lucy. Now—"

"Oh, well, there are plenty of *theories* about ghosts and time," George interrupted. "Some people think they're not bound by its rules at all—that's what allows them to keep coming back. They're fixed in a particular *place*, but able to roam back and forward across the years. If you follow that argument, why *couldn't* they make predictions? Why shouldn't they see things we don't?"

Lockwood shook his head. "I don't believe a word of that. Now, Luce, this Fetch you faced: did it have the shape of Ned Shaw, like the others said? You haven't told us much about it."

Not everything you see is what has passed. Sometimes it is what is yet to be. . . .

I pulled myself back, looked at him—the real Lockwood. The current, living one. "Oh—no. No, it was dark. I don't think I recognized who it was. Listen," I said, pushing back my chair, "I'm just nipping upstairs for a minute. Put the kettle on. I'll be back soon."

On the way up to my attic, I passed the sister's room. The pang I got from it wasn't quite the one of old. It wasn't the throb of curiosity; more of simple regret—regret at what I'd done there, and what those actions had revealed.

I understood now why Lockwood kept that room the way he did, empty and unused. It echoed the effect his sister's loss had had on him in the intervening years. He too had an emptiness—a ruined space—inside, a hollowness that no amount of activity could fill. He'd admitted this when I spoke to him (the real him) in the prison tunnels. It would keep driving him on. He would never stop; he would keep taking risks, tackling the hated enemy, protecting the people he worked with, the ones he cared for.

And if *I* were one of those . . .

I reached the attic bathroom, went in, and locked the door. It was only when I stood there with the taps running and the hot water splashing over my hands and banging away along the pipes below my sink, that I raised my pale and blotchy face, looked into the mirror through the stream, and knew I'd made my decision.

I show you the future. This is your doing.

It wouldn't be if I could help it.

I washed my face, went into my room. I stood by the window, staring out at the darkening sky and winter rain.

"Is this a private sulk or can anyone join in?"

"Oh, I forgot you were up here." I'd used the ghost-jar as a doorstop after taking him out of the kitchen. The phantom face was barely perceptible, just a few sketched lines superimposed on the glinting skull. But the sockets gleamed like dark stars.

"How's the party going? Holly Munro grooving away?"

"She's eating her walnut salad with reckless abandon, yes."

"Typical. So let me get this straight: she's still here?"

"I'd have thought you'd be used to that fact by now."

"Oh, I am. But it's like waking in the morning and finding you've still got a massive wart on your nose. Sure, you're used to it, but it doesn't exactly make you skip around the room."

I smiled bleakly. "I know. Still, don't forget she did you a favor. She pulled you from the rubble at Aickmere's."

"*I'm supposed to be grateful? That means more tedious time with you!*" The face in the jar shook disgustedly side to side. "*It's all going to pot around here. Take your boyfriend, Lockwood. He's getting far too much praise. His head's being turned. You watch—he'll be cuddling up to the Fittes Agency more and more now. Ha, look at you! I'm right. I can see it.*"

"He's meeting the director for breakfast, as it happens, but that doesn't mean . . . And by the way—"

"*Breakfast? That's how it starts. Coy smiles exchanged over omelets and orange juice. Won't be long before you're one of their departments, in all but name.*"

"Absolute rubbish. He's stronger than that."

"*Oh, sure. Lockwood's noted for his lack of vanity and ego. You know that tousled bed-head thing he's got going on? Takes him hours at the mirror to get that fixed just right.*"

"No, it doesn't. Does it? How do you know that? You're making it up."

"*Am I? What's your company called? Remind me. The Portland Row Agency, maybe? Marylebone Ghost-hunters . . . ? No! It's* Lockwood *and Co. Jeez. How modest. I'm surprised your official logo isn't a photo of his grinning face, maybe with a cheesy sparkle glinting on his teeth.*"

"Are you finished?"

"*Yeah. I am now, yes.*"

"Right. Good. I've got to get downstairs."

As usual, when you removed the sarcasm and filtered out the

malice, the skull made a surprising amount of sense, but it was hard to be grateful. He was a ghost. I was talking to him. He was a symbol of my problem too.

In the kitchen the tea had been brewed and fresh cups newly poured. On the table the giant chocolate cake now solely occupied center stage. George was hovering close by, flourishing a knife. He beckoned me in with it. "You returned at just the right time, Luce. I've been saving this cake all day, ready for our final celebratory toast. So far I've been thwarted by Lockwood's boasting, Holly's unkind remarks about the Thinking Cloth, and your disappearing act. But now—"

"*And* by your endless theorizing," Lockwood pointed out. "That part was the worst of the lot."

"True. Anyway, now you're here, Lucy, there's nothing to stop us giving this beauty the attention it deserves." With a flex of the fingers, George angled the knife toward the icing.

"Wait a minute," I said. "I've got something to say first."

The knife halted; George, poised, looked at me with a plaintive expression. The others put down their cups, alerted perhaps by the tremor in my tone. I didn't retake my place but stood behind my chair with my hands clasping the back.

"It's an announcement, I suppose. I've been doing a bit of thinking recently. It seems to me some things haven't been working out so well."

Lockwood stared at me. "I'm surprised to hear that. I thought you and Holly—"

Holly half stood up. "Perhaps I should go outside . . . ?"

"It has nothing to do with Holly," I said. I did my best to smile at them. "It really doesn't. Please, Holly, sit down. Thanks. . . . No, it has all to do with me. You all know what really happened at Aickmere's—it's not quite the same as the story we sold to the newspapers. The Poltergeist that wrecked everything—it got its strength from me."

"And me," Holly said. "There were two of us in that argument, you know."

"I *do* know that," I said. "But I started it, and it was my anger that mostly fueled its power. No, sorry, George"—he'd tried to interrupt—"I am *quite* sure about this. It's my Talent that did it. It's getting stronger, and it's getting harder to deal with, too. When it stirred up the Poltergeist it was working completely negatively, but even when I'm more in control—when I'm talking to ghosts, or listening to *them* talk—I'm sort of *not* in control anymore. And this is growing dangerous now. You all know what happened in Miss Wintergarden's house. And the other day, in the prison, underground, when I spoke with Visitors, *they* kind of called the shots, not me. I know none of you were present then, but I can't be sure that this loss of control won't happen again. In fact, I'm sure it *will*. And that's not acceptable for any psychic investigation agent, is it?"

"You mustn't put too much emphasis on this," George said. "Things happen to all of us. I'm sure we can all support you going forward, and—"

"I know you would," I said. "Of course. But it isn't fair. To you."

Holly was frowning, looking down at her lap; George was doing something with his glasses. I pressed my fingers hard against the wood of the chair, feeling its smoothness and its grain.

"Is that it?" Lockwood asked quietly. "Is that really what this is all about?"

I looked at him, sitting there beside me.

"It's enough," I said. "I put all your lives at risk, not once but several times. One way or another, I'm becoming a liability to the company, and I care too much about you all to let that happen again." It was super-hard to smile then, and it wasn't going to get any easier. So I just got on with it. "And that's why I've made up my mind the way I have," I said, "and why I'm resigning at once from Lockwood and Co."

There was silence in the room.

"So much for me enjoying this bloody cake," George said.

Glossary

* indicates a Type One ghost
** indicates a Type Two ghost

Agency, Psychic Investigation—A business specializing in the containment and destruction of **ghosts**. There are more than a dozen agencies in London alone. The largest two (the Fittes Agency and the Rotwell Agency) have hundreds of employees; the smallest (Lockwood & Co.) has three. Most agencies are run by adult supervisors, but all rely heavily on children with strong psychic **Talent**.

Apparition—The shape formed by a **ghost** during a **manifestation**. Apparitions usually mimic the shape of a dead person, but animals and objects are also seen. Some can be quite unusual. The **Specter** in the recent Limehouse Docks case manifested as a greenly glowing king cobra, while the infamous Bell Street Horror took the guise of a patchwork doll. Powerful or weak, most ghosts do not (or cannot) alter their appearance. **Changers** and **Fetches** are exceptions to this rule.

Aura—The radiance surrounding many **apparitions**. Most auras are fairly faint, and are seen best out of the corner of the eye. Strong, bright auras are known as **other-light**. A few ghosts radiate black auras that are darker than the night around them.

Chain net—A net made of finely spun **silver** chains; a versatile variety of **Seal**.

Changer**—A rare and dangerous **Type Two ghost**, powerful enough to alter its appearance during a **manifestation**.

Chill—The sharp drop in temperature that occurs when a ghost is near. One of the four usual indicators of an imminent **manifestation**, the others being **malaise**, **miasma**, and **creeping fear**. Chill may extend over a wide area, or be concentrated in specific cold spots.

Cluster—A group of **ghosts** occupying a small area.

Cold Maiden*—A gray, misty female form, often wearing old-fashioned dress, seen indistinctly at a distance. Cold Maidens radiate powerful feelings of melancholy and **malaise**. As a rule, they rarely draw close to the living, but exceptions *have* been known.

Corpse-bell—A deep-toned bell rung in churches to announce funerals.

Corpse-light—A pale and sickly supernatural radiance; another name for **other-light**.

Creeping fear—A sense of inexplicable dread often experienced in the build-up to a **manifestation**. Often accompanied by **chill**, **miasma**, and **malaise**.

Curfew—In response to the **Problem**, the British government enforces nightly curfews in many inhabited areas. During curfew, which begins shortly after dusk and finishes at dawn, ordinary people are encouraged to remain indoors, safe behind their home **defenses**.

Death-glow—An energy trace left at the exact spot where a death took place. The more violent the death, the brighter the glow. Strong glows may persist for many years.

Defenses against ghosts—The three principal defenses, in order of effectiveness, are **silver**, **iron**, and **salt**. **Lavender** also affords some protection, as do bright light and running **water**.

DEPRAC—The Department of Psychic Research and Control. A government organization devoted to tackling the **Problem**. DEPRAC investigates the nature of **ghosts**, seeks to destroy the most dangerous ones, and monitors the activities of the many competing **agencies**.

Ectoplasm—A strange, variable substance from which **ghosts** are formed. In its concentrated state, ectoplasm is very harmful to the living.

Fetch**—A rare and unnerving class of **ghost** that appears in the shape of another person, usually someone known to the onlooker. Fetches are seldom aggressive, but the fear and disorientation they evoke is so strong that most experts classify them as **Type Two** spirits, to be treated with extreme caution.

Fittes Manual—A famous book of instruction for ghost-hunters written by Marissa Fittes, the founder of Britain's first psychic investigation **agency**.

Ghost—The spirit of a dead person. Ghosts have existed throughout history, but—for unclear reasons—are now increasingly common. There are many varieties; broadly speaking, however, they can be organized into three main groups (*See* **Type One, Type Two, Type Three**). Ghosts always linger near a **Source**, which is often the place of their death. They are at their strongest after dark, and most particularly, between the hours of midnight and two a.m. Most are unaware or uninterested in the living. A few are actively hostile.

Ghost-bomb—A weapon consisting of a **ghost** trapped in a **silver-glass** prison. When the glass breaks, the spirit emerges to spread fear and **ghost-touch** among the living.

Ghost-cult—A group of people who, for a variety of reasons, share an unhealthy interest in the returning dead.

Ghost-fog—A thin, greenish-white mist, occasionally produced during a **manifestation**. Possibly formed of **ectoplasm**, it is cold and unpleasant, but not itself dangerous to the touch.

Ghost-jar—A **silver-glass** receptacle used to constrain an active **Source**.

Ghost-lamp—An electrically powered streetlight that sends out strong white beams to discourage **ghosts**. Most ghost-lamps have shutters fixed over their glass lenses; these snap on and off at intervals throughout the night.

Ghost-lock—A dangerous power displayed by **Type Two ghosts**, possibly an extension of **malaise**. Victims are sapped of their willpower, and overcome by a feeling of terrible despair. Their muscles seem as heavy as lead, and they can no longer think or move freely. In most cases, they end up transfixed, waiting helplessly as the hungry ghost glides closer and closer. . . .

Ghost-mark—A cross painted on the door of a haunted building to keep passers-by away.

Ghost-touch—The effect of bodily contact with an **apparition**, and the most deadly power of an aggressive **ghost**. Beginning with a sensation of sharp, overwhelming cold, ghost-touch swiftly spreads an icy numbness through the body. One after another, vital organs fail; soon the body burns bluish and starts to swell. Without swift medical intervention, often in the form of adrenaline injections to stimulate the heart, ghost-touch is usually fatal.

Gibbering Mist*—A weak, insubstantial **Type One**, notable for its deranged and repetitive chuckling, which always sounds as if it's coming from behind you.

Glimmer*—The faintest perceptible **Type One** ghost. Glimmers manifest only as flecks of **other-light** flitting through the air. They can be touched or walked through without harm.

Gray Haze*—An ineffectual, rather tedious **ghost**, a common **Type One** variety. Gray Hazes seem to lack the power to form coherent **apparations** and manifest as shapeless patches of faintly glinting mist. Probably because their **ectoplasm** is so diffuse, Gray Hazes do not cause **ghost-touch**, even if a person walks through them. Their main effects are to spread chill, miasma, and unease.

Greek Fire—Another name for **magnesium flares**. Early weapons of this kind were apparently used against **ghosts** during the days of the Byzantine (or Greek) Empire, a thousand years ago.

Haunting—*See* **Manifestation**

Iron—An ancient and important protection against **ghosts** of all kinds. Ordinary people fortify their homes with iron decorations, and carry it on their persons in the form of **wards**. Agents carry iron **rapiers** and chains, and so rely on it for both attack and defense.

Lavender—The strong sweet smell of this plant is thought to discourage evil spirits. As a result, many people wear dried sprigs of lavender, or burn it to release the pungent smoke. Agents sometimes carry vials of lavender water to use against weak **Type Ones**.

Limbless**—A swollen, misshapen variety of **Type Two ghost**, with a generally human head and torso, but lacking recognizable arms and legs.

With **Wraiths** and **Raw-bones**, one of the least pleasing **apparitions**. Often accompanied by strong sensations of **miasma** and **creeping fear**.

Listening—One of the three main categories of psychic **Talent**. **Sensitives** with this ability are able to hear the voices of the dead, echoes of past events, and other unnatural sounds associated with **manifestations**.

Lurker*—A variety of **Type One ghost** that hangs back in the shadows, rarely moving, never approaching the living, but spreading strong feelings of anxiety and **creeping fear**.

Magnesium flare—A metal canister with a breakable glass seal, containing magnesium, iron, salt, gunpowder, and an igniting device. An important agency weapon against aggressive **ghosts**.

Malaise—A feeling of despondent lethargy often experienced when a **ghost** is approaching. In extreme cases this can deepen into dangerous **ghost-lock**.

Manifestation—A ghostly occurrence. May involve all kinds of supernatural phenomena, including sounds, smells, odd sensations, moving objects, drops in temperature, and the glimpse of **apparitions**.

Miasma—An unpleasant atmosphere, often including disagreeable tastes and smells, experienced in the run-up to a **manifestation**. Regularly accompanied by **creeping fear**, **malaise**, and **chill**.

Night watch—Groups of children, usually working for large companies and local government councils, who guard factories, offices, and public areas after dark. Though not allowed to use **rapiers**, night-watch children have long **iron**-tipped spears to keep **apparitions** at bay.

Operative—Another name for a psychic investigation agent.

Other-light—An eerie, unnatural light radiating from some **apparitions**.

Phantasm**—Any **Type Two ghost** that maintains an airy, delicate, and see-through form. A Phantasm may be almost invisible, aside from its faint outline and a few wispy details of its face and features. Despite its insubstantial appearance, it is no less aggressive than the more solid-seeming **Specter**, and all the more dangerous for being harder to see.

Phantom—Another general name for a **ghost**.

Plasm—*See* **Ectoplasm**

Poltergeist**—A powerful and destructive class of **Type Two ghost**. Poltergeists release strong bursts of supernatural energy that can lift even heavy objects into the air. They do not form **apparitions**.

Problem, the—The epidemic of hauntings currently affecting Britain.

Rapier—The official weapon of all psychic investigation agents. The tips of the **iron** blades are sometimes coated with **silver**.

Raw-bones**—A rare and unpleasant kind of **ghost**, which manifests as a bloody, skinless corpse with goggling eyes and grinning teeth. Not popular with agents. Many authorities regard it as a variety of **Wraith**.

Relic-man/relic-woman—Someone who locates **Sources** and other psychic artifacts and sells them on the black market.

Salt—A commonly used defense against **Type One ghosts**. Less effective than **iron** and **silver**, salt is cheaper than both, and used in many household deterrents.

Salt-bomb—A small plastic throwing-globe filled with **salt**. Shatters on impact, spreading salt in all directions. Used by agents to drive back weaker **ghosts**. Less effective against stronger entities.

Salt-gun—A device that projects a fine spray of salty water across a wide area. A useful weapon against **Type One ghosts**. Increasingly employed by larger **agencies**.

Seal—An object, usually **silver** or **iron**, designed to enclose or cover a **Source**, and prevent escape of its **ghost**.

Sensitive, a—Someone born with unusually good psychic **Talent**. Most sensitives join **agencies** or the **night watch**; others provide psychic services without actually confronting **Visitors**.

Shade*—The standard **Type One ghost**, and possibly the most common kind of **Visitor**. Shades may appear quite solid, in the manner of **Specters**, or be insubstantial and wispy, like **Phantasms**; however, they entirely lack the dangerous intelligence of either. Shades seem unaware of the presence of the living, and are usually bound into a fixed pattern of behavior. They project feelings of grief and loss, but seldom display anger or any stronger emotion. They almost always appear in human form.

Sight—The psychic ability to see **apparitions** and other ghostly phenomena, such as **death-glows**. One of the three main varieties of psychic **Talent**.

Silver—An important and potent **defense** against **ghosts**. Worn by many people as **wards** in the form of jewelry. Agents use it to coat their **rapiers**, and as a crucial component of their **seals**.

Silver-glass—A special "ghost-proof" glass used to encase **Sources**.

Snuff-light—A type of small candle used by psychic investigation **agencies** to indicate a supernatural presence. They flicker, tremble and finally snuff out if a **ghost** draws near.

Solitary**—An unusual **Type Two ghost**, often encountered in remote and perilous places, generally outdoors. Visually it often wears the guise of a slender child, seen at a distance across a ravine or lake. It never draws close to the living, but radiates an extreme form of **ghost-lock** that may overwhelm anyone nearby. Victims of Solitaries often hurl themselves over cliffs or into deep water in an effort to end it all.

Source—The object or place through which a **ghost** enters the world.

Specter**—The most commonly encountered **Type Two ghost**. A Specter always forms a clear, detailed **apparition**, which may in some cases seem almost solid. It is usually an accurate visual echo of the deceased as they were when alive or newly dead. Specters are less nebulous than **Phantasms** and less hideous than **Wraiths**, but equally varied in behavior. Many are neutral or benign in their dealings with the living—perhaps returning to reveal a secret, or make right an ancient wrong. Some, however, are actively hostile, and hungry for human contact. These ghosts should be avoided at all costs.

Stalker*—A **Type One ghost** that seems drawn to living people, following them at a distance, but never venturing close. Agents who are skilled at **Listening** often detect the slow shuffling of its bony feet, and its desolate sighs and groans.

Stone Knocker*—A desperately uninteresting **Type One ghost**, which does precious little apart from tap.

Talent—The ability to see, hear, or otherwise detect **ghosts**. Many children, though not all, are born with a degree of psychic Talent. This skill tends to fade toward adulthood, though it still lingers in some grown-ups. Children with better-than-average Talent join the **night watch**. Exceptionally gifted children usually join the **agencies**. The three main categories of Talent are **Sight**, **Listening**, and **Touch**.

Tom O'Shadows*—A London term for a **Lurker** or **Shade** that lingers in doorways, arches, or alleyways. An everyday urban **ghost**.

Touch—The ability to detect psychic echoes from objects that have been closely associated with death or a supernatural **manifestation**. Such echoes take the form of visual images, sounds, and other sense impressions. One of the three main varieties of **Talent**.

Type One—The weakest, most common, and least dangerous grade of **ghost**. Type Ones are scarcely aware of their surroundings, and often locked into a single, repetitive pattern of behavior. Commonly encountered examples include: **Shades**, **Gray Hazes**, **Lurkers**, and **Stalkers**. *See also* **Cold Maiden**, **Gibbering Mist**, **Glimmer**, **Stone Knocker**, **Tom O'Shadows**, and **Wisp**.

Type Two—The most dangerous commonly occurring grade of **ghost**. Type Twos are stronger than **Type Ones**, and possess some kind of residual intelligence. They are aware of the living, and may attempt to do them harm. The most common Type Twos, in order, are: **Specters**, **Phantasms**, and **Wraiths**. *See also* **Changer**, **Fetch**, **Limbless**, **Poltergeist**, **Raw-bones**, **Screaming Spirit**, and **Solitary**.

Type Three—A very rare grade of **ghost**, first reported by Marissa Fittes, and the subject of much controversy ever since. Allegedly able to communicate fully with the living.

Visitor—A ghost.

Ward—An object, usually of **iron** or **silver**, used to keep **ghosts** away. Small wards may be worn as jewelry on the person; larger ones, hung up around the house, are often equally decorative.

Water, running—It was observed in ancient times that **ghosts** dislike crossing running water. In modern Britain this knowledge is sometimes used against them. In central London a net of artificial channels, or runnels, protects the main shopping district. On a smaller scale, some homeowners build open channels outside their front doors and divert the rainwater along them.

Wisp*—Weak and generally unthreatening, a Wisp is a **Type One ghost** that manifests as a pale and flickering flame. Some scholars speculate that all ghosts, given time, degenerate into Wisps, then **Glimmers,** before finally vanishing altogether.

Wraith**—A dangerous **Type Two ghost**. Wraiths are similar to **Specters** in strength and patterns of behavior, but are far more horrible to look at. Their **apparitions** show the deceased in his or her dead state: gaunt and shrunken, horribly thin, sometimes rotten and wormy. Wraiths often appear as skeletons. They radiate a powerful **ghost-lock**. *See also* **Raw-bones.**

The Screaming Staircase

"Stroud (the Bartimaeus series) shows his customary flair for blending deadpan humor with thrilling action, and the fiery interplay among the three agents of Lockwood & Co. invigorates the story (along with no shortage of creepy moments). Stroud plays with ghost story conventions along the way, while laying intriguing groundwork that suggests that the Problem isn't the only problem these young agents will face in books to come—the living can be dangerous, too."

—*Publishers Weekly*

"Authentically spooky events occur in an engagingly crafted, believable world, populated by distinct, colorful personalities. The genuinely likable members of Lockwood & Co. persevere through the evil machinations of the living and the dead and manage to come out with their skins, and their senses of humor, intact. This smart, fast-paced ghostly adventure promises future chills."

—*School Library Journal*

"Three young ghost trappers take on deadly wraiths and solve an old murder case in the bargain to kick off Stroud's new post-Bartimaeus series . . . A heartily satisfying string of entertaining near-catastrophes, replete with narrow squeaks and spectral howls."

—*Kirkus Reviews*

"Stroud brings the seemingly disparate plot points together with his usual combination of thrilling adventure and snarky humor. . . . all members of this spirit-smashing trio get in their fair share of zingers, providing a comedic balance to the many narrow escapes, false leads, and shape-shifting specters that otherwise occupy Lockwood & Co."
—*Bulletin of the Center for Children's Books*

A 2013 *Los Angeles Times* Book Prize Finalist
for Young Adult Literature

2013 Cybil Award for Speculative Fiction

CCBC Choices List

2014 Edgar Award Nominee

A Junior Library Guild Selection

The Whispering Skull

★"In fine form, Stroud sends Lockwood & Co. on a trail that leads from an upper-crust social event to the mucky margins of the Thames and into dust-ups with thugs, rival agents and carloads of ectoplasmic horrors that can kill with just a touch. For all their internecine squabbling, the three protagonists make a redoubtable team—and their supporting cast, led by the sneering titular skull in a jar, adds color and complications aplenty. Rousing adventures for young tomb robbers and delvers into realms better left to the dead."

—*Kirkus Reviews* (starred review)

★ "Stroud writes with a fine ear for dialog, a wry sense of humor, and a knack for describing haunted places. Creating tension that ebbs and flows, he slowly builds the dramatic narrative to a resounding crescendo, and he makes the quieter scenes that follow just as compelling. The second entry in the Lockwood & Company series, this imaginative adventure features one of the most hair-raising chase scenes in children's fiction. At the book's end, when the enigmatic Anthony Lockwood reveals a chilling secret, readers can only hope that more sequels are in the offing."

—*Booklist* (starred review)

★ "Lucy's growing abilities to communicate with the dead, especially the nasty spirit attached to a skull in Lockwood's home, add an additional layer of menace to an already creepy tale; Lockwood's secrets add intrigue and suspicion. The plot gallops along at a breakneck pace, giving little respite from the horrors within. For fans of scary fare, this page-turner is a dream (or nightmare) come true."

—*School Library Journal* (starred review)

★"[T]he best yet . . . a stunning ending to
a justly acclaimed trilogy."
—*The Horn Book*

THE RING OF SOLOMON

★"A riveting adventure for Bartimaeus fans, old and new."
—*Booklist*

★"So rarely do humor and plot come together in such equally
strong measures that we can only hope for more adventures."
—*The Horn Book*

★". . . this is a superior fantasy that should have fans
racing back to those [Bartimaeus] books."
—*Publishers Weekly*

★"Definitely a must-purchase."
—*School Library Journal*